The Asian American Experience

Series Editor
Roger Daniels, University of Cincinnati

Books in the Series

The Hood River Issei: An Oral History of Japanese Settlers
in Oregon's Hood River Valley
Linda Tamura

Americanization, Acculturation, and Ethnic Identity:
The Nisei Generation in Hawaii
Eileen H. Tamura

Sui Sin Far/Edith Maude Eaton:
A Literary Biography
Annette White-Parks

Mrs. Spring Fragrance and Other Writings
Sui Sin Far
Edited by Amy Ling and Annette White-Parks

Mrs. Spring Fragrance and Other Writings

Mrs. Spring Fragrance
and Other Writings

Sui Sin Far

Edited by Amy Ling and Annette White-Parks

University of Illinois Press
Urbana and Chicago

First paperback edition, 1995
© 1995 by the Board of Trustees of the University of Illinois
Manufactured in the United States of America

1 2 3 4 5 C P 10 9 8

⊚ This book is printed on acid-free paper.

Library of Congress Cataloging-in-Publication Data
Sui Sin Far, 1865–1914.
[Works. 1995]
Mrs. Spring Fragrance and Other Writings / edited by Amy Ling and Annette White-Parks.
p. cm. — (Asian American experience)
ISBN 0-252-02133-9 (alk. paper). — ISBN 0-252-06419-4 (pbk.: alk. paper)
I. Ling, Amy. II. White-Parks, Annette. III. Title.
IV. Series.
PR9199.2.S931995   94-14202
813'.52—dc20   CIP
13 digit ISBN 978-0-252-06419-7 (pbk.: alk. paper)

To L. Charles Laferrière, of Montreal,
whose zeal in recovering his great-aunt's accomplishments
and whose generous sharing
have helped make this book possible

Contents

Part 1: Short Fiction from Mrs. Spring Fragrance

From "Mrs. Spring Fragrance"

Acknowledgments

In addition to L. Charles Laferrière, to whom this book is dedicated, and to all the scholars mentioned in the introduction, we wish to acknowledge everyone who has researched this writer, read her works, and taught her in the classroom as having shared in this volume by contributing to a momentum of interest that has led to this reprint of Sui Sin Far's works. Special thanks go to Elizabeth Ammons for her enthusiastic support for this project. We are grateful to Marie Baboyant, reference librarian at the Bibliothèque de la Ville de Montréal, for retrieving and duplicating copies of Sui Sin Far's pieces in the Montreal newspapers. For deciphering poor copies and typing clean ones, we thank Linda Jorgenson of the English Department at the University of Wisconsin–La Crosse and Miseong Woo, a graduate student in theater and program assistant in the Asian American Studies Program at the University of Wisconsin–Madison.

Introduction

Amy Ling and Annette White-Parks

For the past two decades Asian American literature has been coming into fuller and fuller bloom. Its earliest shoot in the scholarly world may be traced to the 1972 publication of *Asian American Authors,* edited by Kai-yu Hsu and Helen Palubinskas, after which, since "a habitation and a name" had been established, both the contemporary production of Asian American texts and the scholarly retrieval of an Asian North American historical tradition have increased dramatically.[1] With Elaine Kim's landmark 1982 literary history, *Asian American Literature: An Introduction to the Writings and Their Social Context,* and King-Kok Cheung and Stan Yogi's 1988 *Asian American Literature: An Annotated Bibliography,* the tree has revealed itself to be deeply rooted, many-branched, and worthy of serious study.[2]

Among its most recent blooms are the texts of Maxine Hong Kingston, the novels of Amy Tan and Jessica Hagedorn, the poems of Garrett Hongo, and the plays of David Henry Hwang, which have attracted both critical and popular attention. Its earliest roots, however, date back a century to the work of three writers.[3] The first publication in English by an Asian American, *When I Was a Boy in China,* appeared in 1887, written by Yan Phou Lee (1861–1938?), a Chinese student who graduated from Yale in 1897.[4] Asian North American fiction, however, has its origins in the work of two Eurasian Canadian sisters: Edith Maude Eaton (or Sui Sin Far), 1865–1914; and Winifred Lillie Eaton (or Onoto Watanna), 1875–1954. Sui Sin Far began publishing essays, short fiction, and journalistic articles in the 1880s. Her first short story on Chinese North American subjects, "The Gamblers," appeared in the February 1896 issue of a journal called *Fly Leaf,* edited by Walter Blackburn Harte.[5] The first Asian American novel, *Miss Nume of Japan* by Onoto Watanna, was published by Rand McNally

in 1899. Lee's purportedly autobiographical but largely anthropo-
logical 1887 text, *When I Was A Boy in China,* and Watanna's
romance, *Miss Nume of Japan,* though peopled with North American
characters, are, however, both set in Asia. Sui Sin Far's work is thus
the first expression of the Chinese experience in the United States
and Canada and the first fiction in English by any Asian North
American.[6]

To get a sense of Sui Sin Far and the world of her stories, some
biographical and historical background is essential.[7] Sui Sin Far was
born in Macclesfield, a silk center in England, in 1865, shortly after a
series of wars and resulting treaties had forced China to open its doors
to merchants and missionaries from the West, furthering European and
North American efforts to colonize China's resources, including its
people. Having a Chinese mother and an English father gave Sui Sin
Far insights into both sides of this struggle—really global in scope—
and affected the writer and her siblings in the most intimate details of
their daily lives. The mother, Grace Trefusis Eaton, is said to have been
taken from China to England, where she received schooling, and later
returned to China. The father, Edward Eaton, a Macclesfield merchant,
made frequent voyages to Shanghai, where the couple met and married.
Since interracial marriage was a taboo in both cultures, theirs was an
unusual union.

Until she was seven, Sui Sin Far's primary home was in Macclesfield.
Then in 1872 the family migrated to North America, first to New
York and then to Montreal, Quebec, where they would permanently
settle. Various incidents in England had taught Sui Sin Far that she
was, in her words, "something different and apart from other children";
it was a lesson that her experience in North America reinforced. The
exclusion and abuse she suffered because of race ranged from children's
taunts ("I wouldn't speak to Sui if I were you. Her mamma is Chinese.")
to physical violence ("They pull my hair, they tear my clothes, they
scratch my face and all but lame my brother"). She experienced
prejudice from both sides of her heritage: "My mother's people are as
prejudiced as my father's." As the eldest daughter, who assumed the
duties of a second mother to thirteen siblings and financial responsibil-
ity for them as well as for her parents, and as a woman in a Victorian
society who chose not to marry, Sui Sin Far also knew the oppression
of gender. As a member of a family moving economically downward,
from merchant to impoverished working class, Sui Sin Far was removed

from school at age ten "to help earn my living," thus initiating her life's
struggle for money to live and time to write.[8]

In the late 1880s and 1890s, a period of rampant sinophobia, Sui Sin
Far began her career as a stenographer, a journalist, and a writer of
short fiction. In 1897 she moved to Jamaica for a year and then spent
from 1898 to 1912 on the West Coast and the East Coast in the United
States—supporting herself as a journalist and stenographer, squeezing
in writing time, and managing to find publishing outlets for her stories
in the major journals of her day. Described by her sister Winifred as a
"semi-invalid" most of her life, Sui Sin Far suffered bouts of rheuma-
toid arthritis, malaria, and the rheumatic fever that weakened her heart
and was a factor in her death at age forty-nine. Despite these obstacles,
Sui Sin Far never saw herself as a victim: "I was small, but my feelings
were big, and great was my vanity." Nothing extinguished her "ambition
to write a book" or distracted her from her goal of fighting the battles
of the Chinese in the papers.

After years of neglect, Sui Sin Far and her writings have gradually
begun to attract the attention of scholars and publishers, and some of
her work has become available to the general reader over the past two
decades. Although one of the early anthologies of Asian American
literature, *Aiiieeeee!,* mentioned Sui Sin Far as "one of the first to speak
for Asian American sensibility that was neither Asian nor white
American," this anthology included no samples of Sui Sin Far's work.[9]
Six years later Dexter Fisher's *The Third Woman* devoted half a page to
Sui Sin Far, calling her "one of the first women to write about the
Chinese American experience" and quoting a paragraph from her
autobiographical essay "Leaves from the Mental Portfolio of an
Eurasian."[10] Larger portions of "Leaves" were published in conjunc-
tion with an essay about the author by S. E. Solberg in *Turning
Shadows into Light: Art and Culture of the Northwest's Early Asian American Pacific Community.*[11] The complete text of "Leaves" and a short
story, "In the Land of the Free," were reprinted in the *Heath Anthology
of American Literature* in 1990, where they attracted considerable
attention.[12] In 1991 "The Wisdom of the New" was reprinted by
Legacy: A Journal of Nineteenth-Century Women's Literature, with an
introduction by Annette White-Parks, and "The Heart's Desire" appeared
in *Women's Friendships: A Collection of Short Stories.*[13] Other anthologies reprinting Sui Sin Far's stories included two volumes edited by
Wesley Brown and Amy Ling, *Imagining America: Stories from the*

Promised Land and *Visions of America: Personal Narratives from the Promised Land; American Women Regionalists, 1850–1910: A Norton Anthology,* edited by Judith Fetterley and Marjorie Pryse; and *American Women Writers: Diverse Voices in Prose since 1845,* edited by Eileen Barrett and Mary Cullinan.[14] The present volume is the first to reprint the major portion of *Mrs. Spring Fragrance* and a representative sampling of Sui Sin Far's uncollected essays, journalistic articles, and short stories.

Sui Sin Far's name is increasingly showing up at national conferences, and the number of scholarly works has multiplied.[15] Annette White-Parks recently published the first book-length literary biography of Sui Sin Far, entitled *Sui Sin Far/Edith Maude Eaton: A Literary Biography.* The scholarly works will be discussed at greater length in the introduction to the stories from *Mrs. Spring Fragrance.* Of further excitement is the extension of Sui Sin Far's reputation beyond scholarly circles. The Chinese Canadian community of Montreal, city of the author's longest residence, writing apprenticeship, and eventual interment, seems to have been inspired by the discovery of Sui Sin Far as a nineteenth-century heroine.[16] This group, mostly young Chinese Canadians, held a fundraising concert in September 1992 to honor "Edith Eaton," and they are making plans for a more tangible memorial.[17] Proposals include changing the name of the Chinatown metro station from "Place D'Armes" to "Sui Sin Far" and naming a ballroom in her honor at the Chinatown Holiday Inn. The publishing world is discovering her also, as illustrated by a Montreal publishing company's hiring a writer to work on a children's book about the Eaton family. In her novel *Bone,* the Chinese American writer Fae Myenne Ng created an "Edith Eaton School" in San Francisco's Chinatown for the three sisters in her book to attend.[18]

We see this burgeoning interest in Sui Sin Far, as a personality and a writer, as part of a broader movement to recover "lost" texts for contemporary readers and to make them, in the words of Jane Tompkins, part of "the picture American literature draws of itself."[19] In the last fifteen years, the works of Maxine Hong Kingston and Amy Tan have created great interest in stories by and about Chinese American women and Asian American authors in general. According to Bill Moyers, Hong Kingston's *Woman Warrior* and *China Men* were "the most widely taught books by a living American author on college campuses" during the 1980s.[20] Amy Tan's *Joy Luck Club* was nine months on the *New York Times* bestseller list and is now a major Hollywood film. The recognition of the multicultural quality of American life has led to an expansion of the body of prose and poetry we recognize as representing "American literature" and to a diversity and richness of literature in today's college curricula that was unknown before the civil rights and women's liberation movements of the 1960s and 1970s. Today we draw upon such writers as Sui Sin Far for our roots, ancestors, and foundations; in fact, Elizabeth Ammons calls Maxine Hong Kingston the "spiritual granddaughter of Sui Sin Far."[21] As interest in the works of African American literature has led to the exciting discoveries of Harriet Wilson's *Our Nig* and Linda Brent's *Incidents in the Life of a Slave Girl,* so, too, our search for comparable pioneer authors has led us to the writing of Sui Sin Far. Just as Wilson and Brent have provided insights into early African American life, this collection of Sui Sin Far's journalism, essays, and short fiction reveals the roots of Chinese immigrant and Chinese North American culture at the turn of the last century and brings to light the continuity and tradition of writers of Asian North American literature.

Mrs. Spring Fragrance, Sui Sin Far's only published volume, had a modest initial run of twenty-five hundred copies in 1912 and to our knowledge was not reprinted. Nevertheless, *Mrs. Spring Fragrance* is a seminal work, a foundation piece not only for Asian North American literature but also for a multicultural understanding of Canada and the United States. The original edition was divided between "Mrs. Spring Fragrance" and "Tales of Chinese Children"; almost two-thirds of the stories reprinted in this volume are from the first section. Some present-day readers may consider the somewhat flowery style of these stories dated. Others may take issue with a certain "orientalism" in the author's tone and with the feeling that she is as much outsider as insider to the Chinese North American community. In "Leaves," for example, the statement "the white blood in our veins fights valiantly for the Chinese half of us" may be interpreted to confer greater valor to and passion for her "white blood," as Lorraine Dong and Marlon K. Hom have pointed out.[22] We must remember, however, that being half English, educated entirely in English and English Canadian schools, and growing to maturity among English and French Canadians, Sui Sin Far—as Edith Eaton—could not help but imbibe some of the orientalist notions and terms of her place and time. What is significant is not that she occasionally lapsed (from our vantage point of hindsight) into the stereotypes of her day but that she was clear-sighted enough to recognize current national policies and social valuations as prejudicial and unjust and was courageous enough to speak out against them. Furthermore, she turned around the very thing that has been held against her — an English training — to give voice to a people who had no voice. We must also remember that Sui Sin Far was a writer of multilayered visions, all frequently operating at once. Nothing she writes should be interpreted in the absence of context or taken only at its surface, literal level.[23]

Sui Sin Far's stories are significant in many respects. First, they present portraits of turn-of-the-century North American Chinatowns, not in the mode of the "yellow peril" or zealous missionary literature of her era but with well-intentioned and sincere empathy. Second, the stories give voice and protagonist roles to Chinese and Chinese North American women and children, thus breaking the stereotypes of silence, invisibility, and "bachelor societies" that have ignored small but present female populations. Finally, in a period when miscegenation was illegal in nearly half the United States, Sui Sin Far's stories are the first to introduce the plight of the child of Asian and white parents. In making public her ambiguous position between worlds, Sui Sin Far initiated a dialogue between Chinese and European North Americans and their multicultural, multiracial descendants. In giving her "right hand to the Occidentals" and her "left to the Orientals," she not only speaks for Eurasians but also articulates the position of generations of bicultural Asian Americans and Asian Canadians and anticipates that of Asian adoptees into Caucasian families. Many themes that Sui Sin Far's writings introduced a hundred years ago continue to be relevant today: the need for interracial understanding and self-affirmation; the balancing of individual and community needs; the clash between tradition and change in recent immigrant experience; and the between-worlds plight of the racially or culturally mixed person.

Notes

1. Kai-yu Hsu and Helen Palubinskas, eds., *Asian American Authors* (Boston: Houghton Mifflin, 1972).

2. Elaine Kim, *Asian American Literature: An Introduction to the Writings and Their Social Context* (Philadelphia: Temple University Press, 1982); King-Kok Cheung and Stan Yogi, *Asian American Literature: An Annotated Bibliography* (New York: MLA, 1988).

3. For a fuller discussion, see Amy Ling, "Reading Her/stories against

His/stories in Early Chinese American Literature," in *American Realism and the Canon,* ed. Tom Quirk and Gary Scharnhorst (Newark: University of Delaware Press, 1994), 69–86.

4. Yan Phou Lee, *When I Was a Boy in China* (Boston: D. Lothrop, 1887).

5. Sui Seen Far, "The Gambler," *Flyleaf* 1 (February 1896): 14–18. Walter Blackburn Harte was married to the second Eaton daughter, Grace. James Doyle of Wilfred Laurier University is working on a biography of Harte.

6. For coverage of the women writers of Chinese ancestry, see Amy Ling, *Between Worlds: Women Writers of Chinese Ancestry* (New York: Pergamon, 1990).

7. For Sui Sin Far's context and biography, see Annette White-Parks, *Sui Sin Far/Edith Maude Eaton: A Literary Biography* (Urbana: University of Illinois Press, 1995).

8. The quotes in this and the following paragraph are from Sui Sin Far's autobiographical essay, "Leaves from the Mental Portfolio of an Eurasian," *Independent* 66 (21 January 1909): 125–32. See the entire text in this volume.

9. Frank Chin, Jeffrey Paul Chan, Lawson Fusao Inada, and Shawn Wong, eds., *Aiiieeeee! An Anthology of Asian American Literature* (Washington, D.C.: Howard University Press, 1974), xxi.

10. Dexter Fisher, *The Third Woman* (Boston: Houghton Mifflin, 1980), 435–36.

11. S. E. Solberg, "Sui, the Storyteller: Sui Sin Far (Edith Eaton), 1867–1914," in *Turning Shadows into Light: Art and Culture of the Northwest's Early Asian American Pacific Community,* ed. Mayumi Tsutakawa and Alan Chong Lau (Seattle: Young Pine Press, 1981), 85–90.

12. Paul Lauter, general ed., Juan Bruce-Novoa, Jackson Bryer, Elaine Hedges, Amy Ling, Daniel Littlefield, Wendy Martin, Charles Molesworth, Carla Mulford, Raymund Paredes, Hortense Spillers, Linda Wagner-Martin, Andrew Wiget, and Richard Yarborough, eds., *Heath Anthology of American Literature* (Lexington, Mass.: D. C. Heath, 1990), 885–95 and 895–901, respectively.

13. Sui Sin Far, "The Wisdom of the New," with an introduction by Annette White-Parks, *Legacy: A Journal of Nineteenth-Century Women's Literature* 6 (Spring 1991): 34–49; Sui Sin Far, "The Heart's Desire," with an introduction by Amy Ling, in *Women's Friendships: A Collection of Short Stories,* ed. Susan Koppelman (Norman: University of Oklahoma Press, 1991), 107–11.

14. Wesley Brown and Amy Ling, eds., *Imagining America: Stories from the Promised Land* (New York: Persea Books, 1991); Wesley Brown and Amy Ling, eds., *Visions of America: Personal Narratives from the Promised Land* (New York: Persea Books, 1992); Judith Fetterley and Marjorie Pryse, eds., *American Women Regionalists, 1850–1910: A Norton Anthology* (New York: W. W. Norton, 1991); Eileen Barrett and Mary Cullinan, eds., *American*

Women Writers: Diverse Voices in Prose since 1845 (New York: St. Martin's Press, 1992).

15. See S. E. Solberg, "Sui Sin Far/Edith Eaton: First Chinese-American Fictionist," *MELUS* 8 (Spring 1981): 27–39; Amy Ling, "Edith Eaton: Pioneer Chinamerican Writer and Feminist," *American Literary Realism* 16 (Autumn 1983): 287–98; Amy Ling, "Writers with a Cause: Sui Sin Far and Han Suyin," *Women's Studies International Forum* 9, no. 4 (1986): 411–19; Linda Popp DiBiase, "A Chinese Lily in Seattle," *Seattle Weekly,* 10 September 1986; Lorraine Dong and Marlon K. Hom, "Defiance or Perpetuation: An Analysis of Characters in *Mrs. Spring Fragrance,*" in *Chinese America: History and Perspectives,* ed. Him Mark Lai, Ruthanne Lum McCunn, and Judy Yung (San Francisco: Chinese Historical Society of America, 1987), 139–68; Amy Ling, "Pioneers and Paradigms: The Eaton Sisters," in *Between Worlds: Women Writers of Chinese Ancestry* (New York: Pergamon, 1990), 21–55; Xiao-Huang Yin, "Between the East and West: Sui Sin Far—The First Chinese American Woman Writer, *Arizona Quarterly* 7 (Winter 1991): 49–84; Annette White-Parks, "Sui Sin Far: Writer on the Chinese-Anglo Borders of North America" (Ph.D. dissertation, Washington State University, 1991); Elizabeth Ammons, "Audacious Words: Sui Sin Far's *Mrs. Spring Fragrance,*" in *Conflicting Stories: American Women Writers at the Turn into the Twentieth Century* (New York: Oxford University Press, 1992), 105–20; and White-Parks, *Sui Sin Far/Edith Maude Eaton.*

16. Reported in *Montreal Gazette,* 5 September 1992.

17. Sui Sin Far's grand-nephew L. Charles Laferrière was a guest at this concert and has been interviewed several times about his illustrious great-aunt in the Montreal papers.

18. Fae Myenne Ng, *Bone* (New York: Hyperion, 1993).

19. Jane Tompkins, *Sensational Designs: The Cultural Work of American Fiction, 1790–1860* (New York: Oxford University Press, 1985), 84.

20. Bill Moyers, *A World of Ideas,* vol. 2 (New York: Doubleday, 1990), 11.

21. Ammons, *Conflicting Stories,* 106.

22. Dong and Hom, "Defiance or Perpetuation," 139–68.

23. See Annette White-Parks, "A Reversal of American Concepts of 'Otherness' in Fiction by Sui Sin Far," *MELUS* (Spring 1995).

Part 1

Short Fiction from
Mrs. Spring Fragrance

Introduction

Amy Ling

The original 1912 edition of *Mrs. Spring Fragrance* was divided into two sections: Mrs. Spring Fragrance, which had seventeen stories and a total of 241 large-print pages, and Tales of Chinese Children, which was made up of twenty pieces, many of them brief sketches, totaling 102 pages.[1] This present volume includes fifteen of the seventeen stories from the first section and nine of the twenty from the second section, approximately three-fourths of the original edition. We selected for inclusion the stories we felt to be thematically the most significant and structurally the best developed.

As the first Asian American fictionist, Sui Sin Far attracted notice from the earliest years of the recovery of Asian American literature, and she has been the subject of both scholarly and popular articles. In 1976 S. E. Solberg offered a working foundation to scholars in "Eaton Sisters: Sui Sin Far and Onoto Watanna," a paper delivered at the Pacific Northwest Asian American Writer's Conference in Seattle, Washington. In 1981 his essay "Sui Sin Far/Edith Eaton: First Chinese-American Fictionalist" appeared. In 1982 William Wu in the *Yellow Peril: Chinese Americans in American Fiction, 1850–1940* acknowledged the insider perspective of Sui Sin Far's sympathetic stories about Chinese Americans. On the East Coast, I had been independently researching Sui Sin Far and recognized in her a rebellious and subversive stance, which I wrote about in "Edith Eaton: Pioneer Chinamerican Writer and Feminist." In 1986, in "Writers with a Cause: Sui Sin Far and Han Suyin," I presented Sui Sin Far as a spiritual foremother of a well-known contemporary Eurasian author; that same year, Linda Popp DiBiase brought Sui Sin Far to the attention of the general reader in her newspaper article "A Chinese Lily in Seattle," published in the *Seattle Weekly*. In 1987 Lorraine Dong and Marlon K. Hom published in "Defiance or Perpetuation: An Analysis of Characters in *Mrs. Spring Fragrance.*" In 1990, in a chapter of *Between Worlds: Women Writers of Chinese Ancestry,* I differentiated between Edith Eaton's confrontational stance and Winifred Eaton's accommodation and camouflage but saw both as alternate responses to racism. In 1991 Sui Sin Far was the subject of Annette White-Parks's doctoral dissertation, "Sui Sin Far: Writer on the Chinese-Anglo Borders of North America," which was latter revised and published as *Sui Sin Far/Edith Maude Eaton: A Literary Biography.* On the East Coast, a portion of Xiao-Huang Yin's dissertation at Harvard was on Sui Sin Far and was published as an essay entitled "Between the East and West: Sui Sin Far—The First Chinese American Woman Writer." In 1992 Elizabeth Ammons devoted a chapter of her book *Conflicting Stories: American Women Writers at the Turn into the Twentieth Century* to a sympathetic and sophisticated reading of Sui Sin Far's writings.[2]

Of all these scholarly scrutinies, only Dong and Hom were negative in their assessment of Sui Sin Far's work. Holding her late nineteenth-century characters and style up to late twentieth-century values of explicit and vociferous rejection of assimilation and stereotyping, they read Sui Sin Far's stories in a very literal fashion, missing the irony, the subtle nuances, and the humor and exaggerating the author's faults. They believe, for example, that Mrs. Spring Fragrance in her letter from San Francisco to her husband deliberately "chose to ignore the apparent discriminatory treatment of the Chinese in America,"[3] even though Sui Sin Far's tone was clearly ironic, and the very act of bringing up these discriminatory practices demonstrates that neither the character nor the author was ignorant of them.

To give Dong and Hom their due, however, Sui Sin Far is occasionally guilty of exoticizing and orientalizing in ways that may cause discomfort to the contemporary Asian North American reader. One example is her frequent use of the adjective *quaint,* as in the following examples: "He was a quaint, serious little fellow" (the son of Pau Lin and Wou Sankwei in "The Wisdom of the New"); "He was a picturesque little fellow with a quaint manner of speech" (in " 'Its Wavering Image' "). These descriptions would seem to be the judgment of an outsider to whom the other is unfamiliar rather than the insider describing people and scenes of the everyday. We must remember, however, that Sui Sin Far was indeed an outsider to Chinatown and unfamiliar with the Chinese language.[4] (Though her mother was biologically Chinese, she was "English bred with English ways and manner of dress," and, since she was married in Shanghai, could very well not have known any Cantonese, the language of most North American Chinatowns.) One can clearly see the contrast between the straightforward language of "The Story of One White Woman Who Married a Chinese" and "Her Chinese Husband," which both assume a white woman's perspective, and the flowery, honorific language of the stories that attempt to render for an English reader the flavor of translated Chinese.

All of this, however, should not distract us from the equally obvious and more significant fact of Sui Sin Far's momentous accomplishment. If we set Sui Sin Far into the context of her time and place, in late nineteenth-century sinophobic and imperialistic Euro-American nations, then we must admit that for her, a Eurasian woman who could pass as white, to choose to champion the Chinese and working-class women and to identify herself as such, publicly and in print, was an act of great determination and courage. Addressing a predominantly white readership, she had the audacity (to borrow Ammons's word)[5] to tell them, in such stories as "In the Land of the Free" and " 'Its Wavering Image,' " that they were racially prejudiced and abused the Chinese and, in such stories as "The Wisdom of the New" and "Pat and Pan," that, though well-meaning, their interference sometimes had tragic consequences.

But most of the stories in *Mrs. Spring Fragrance* sought to counter the prevailing notions that the Chinese were heathen, unassimilable, hatchet-waving rat eaters and pipe-smoking opium addicts who had no right to live in the United States or Canada. In the title story of the collection, she shows that Chinese have a sense of humor and a liveliness of spirit, that they can play baseball, sing "Drink to Me Only with Thine Eyes," and learn English well enough to dare, as in the story "The Inferior Woman," to write a book about white Americans—a mirror image of what Sui Sin Far herself was doing. She even dared to express the opinion that the Chinese custom of arranged marriages can be a good thing. In such stories as "The God of Restoration" and "Lin John," she demonstrates that the Chinese are capable of incredible patience and hard work. In "The Wisdom of the New," "The Smuggling of Tie Co," and "The Chinese Lily" she writes about Chinese women who make the ultimate sacrifice, which, as Jane Tompkins points out, is the "supreme act of heroism" in the Christian faith and the most powerful act available to the poor and powerless.[6] In defiance of the antimiscegenation laws then common in many states, Sui Sin Far's "Story of One White Woman Who Married a Chinese" and "Her Chinese Husband" lead the reader through the experience of an interracial romance, emphasizing spiritual values and respect for human dignity over insignificant racial differences. "Her Chinese Husband" makes a plea for the social acceptance of Eurasians and stresses the critical importance of their maintaining pride in both halves of their ancestry. The story also shows that the Chinese, too, can be narrow-minded and "hate with a bitter hatred all who would enlighten or be enlightened," for it is Chinese men who kill the story's hero.

"The Wisdom of the New" and "The Americanization of Pau Tsu" are contrasting stories about the adjustment of Chinese wives who, after years of separation, join their Americanized husbands in the United States. In the first, the husband is insensitive to his wife's jealousy of a young, white American woman, Adah Charleton—with tragic results. In the second, the husband understands his wife's reaction to his friendship with a young, white American woman, Adah Raymond, and, protecting his wife, he distances himself from his friend—with, presumably, happy results. That the white women have the same first name, that Adah was the name Winifred gave Edith in *Marion: The Story of an Artist's Model* (which is a slightly fictionalized biography of their sister and the Eaton family), that the stories are almost identical except for their endings, and that Edith Eaton/Sui Sin Far taught English in Chinatown lead to speculations about the possible autobiographical nature of this story, but, unfortunately, we have no way of verifying such a hypothesis. Many of these stories have tantalizing depths that remain unplumbed: the cross-dressing theme in "The Smuggling of Tie Co," "Tian Shan's Kindred Spirit," and "A Chinese Boy-Girl"; the self-sacrificial element of "The Chinese Lily," "The Story of a Little Chinese Seabird," and "Lin John"; and the nature of friendship between women in "A Chinese Lily" and "The Sing Song Woman."

The stories in the second section, Tales of Chinese Children, with a few exceptions, are less concerned with contemporaneous political and social issues and more in the vein of Aesop's fables, timeless parables shaped around a moral. The exceptions, "Children of Peace" and "Pat and Pan," while stories about children are not particularly stories for children, for their themes are the consequences of hatred, between races and between families, and in "Children of Peace," at least, the healing value of love. "The Banishment of Ming and Mai" embodies the same theme, but, set in a land where tiger and leopard live in harmony with every other animal and insect, this story is very much a literary manifestation of the nineteenth-century naive, utopian paint- ing "The Peaceable Kingdom" by Edward Hicks. Ironic twist endings, employing the element of surprise, contribute to the charm of several stories, while the narratives embody such familiar maxims as "Don't count your chickens before they hatch," the theme of "The Dreams That Failed," and "Don't judge a book by its cover," in "A Chinese Boy-Girl." "What about the Cat?" and "The Heart's Desire" may be read as stories of female independence and friendship.

On balance, the virtues of Sui Sin Far's writings clearly outweigh their failings. Put her Chinese characters beside those Bret Harte's "heathen Chinese" in "Plain Language from Truthful James," and hers are less of a caricature and less ambivalent. Compare her representation of Chinese women with those of Helen Clark in *The Lady of the Lily Feet and Other Tales of Chinatown,*[7] and Sui Sin Far's concern is clearly deep and without ulterior motive, while Clark's reveals a one- dimensional Christianizing zeal. Set Sui Sin Far in her time and place, and we would all have to agree with Elizabeth Ammons: "That Sui Sin Far invented herself—created her own voice—out of such deep silenc- ing and systematic racist repression was one of the triumphs of Ameri- can literature at the turn of the century."[8]

Notes

1. Sui Sin Far (Edith Eaton), *Mrs. Spring Fragrance* (Chicago: A. C. McClurg, 1912).

2. S. E. Solberg, "The Eaton Sisters: Sui Sin Far and Onoto Watanna" (Paper presented at the Pacific Northwest Asian American Writer's Conference, Seattle, Washington, 16 April 1976); S. E. Solberg, "Sui Sin Far/Edith Eaton: First Chinese-American Fictionist," *MELUS* 8 (Spring 1981): 27–39; William F. Wu, *The Yellow Peril: Chinese Americans in American Fiction, 1850–1940* (Hamden, Conn.: Archon Books, 1982); Amy Ling, "Edith Eaton: Pioneer Chinamerican Writer and Feminist," *American Literary Realism* 16 (Autumn 1983): 287–98; Amy Ling, "Writers with a Cause: Sui Sin Far and Han Suyin," *Women's Studies International Forum* 9, no. 4 (1986): 411–19; Linda Popp DiBiase, "A Chinese Lily in Seattle," *Seattle Weekly,* 10 September 1986; Lorraine Dong and Marlon K. Hom, "Defiance or Perpetuation: An Analysis

of Characters in *Mrs. Spring Fragrance,*" in *Chinese America: History and Perspectives,*
ed. Him Mark Lai, Ruthanne Lum McCunn, and Judy Yung (San Francisco:
Chinese Historical Society of America, 1987), 139–68; Amy Ling, "Pioneers
and Paradigms: The Eaton Sisters," in *Between Worlds: Women Writers of
Chinese Ancestry* (New York: Pergamon, 1990), 21–55; Annette White-Parks,
"Sui Sin Far: Writer on the Chinese-Anglo Borders of North America" (Ph.D.
diss., Washington State University, 1991); Annette White-Parks, *Sui Sin Far/Edith
Maude Eaton: A Literary Biography* (Urbana: University of Illinois Press, 1995);
Xiao-Huang Yin, "Between the East and West: Sui Sin Far—The First Chinese
American Woman Writer," *Arizona Quarterly* 7 (Winter 1991): 49–84; Eliza-
beth Ammons, "Audacious Words: Sui Sin Far's *Mrs. Spring Fragrance,*" in
*Conflicting Stories: American Women Writers at the Turn into the Twentieth Cen-
tury* (New York: Oxford University Press, 1992), 105–20.

3. Dong and Hom, "Defiance or Perpetuation," 154.

4. For example, note "Chinese Laundry Checking" in Part 2 in which the
laundry receipt, on which Chinese characters are written, was printed upside
down.

5. Ammons, "Audacious Words."

6. See Jane Tompkins's discussion of Little Eva's death from *Uncle Tom's
Cabin* in *Sensational Designs* (New York: Oxford University Press, 1985),
127–28.

7. Helen Clark, *The Lady of the Lily Feet and Other Tales of Chinatown*
(Philadelphia: Griffith and Rowland Press, under the imprint of the American
Baptist Publication Society, 1900).

8. Ammons, *Conflicting Stories,* 105.

Mrs. Spring Fragrance

When Mrs. Spring Fragrance first arrived in Seattle, she was unacquainted with even one word of the American language. Five years later her husband, speaking of her, said: "There are no more American words for her learning." And everyone who knew Mrs. Spring Fragrance agreed with Mr. Spring Fragrance.

Mr. Spring Fragrance, whose business name was Sing Yook, was a young curio merchant. Though conservatively Chinese in many respects, he was at the same time what is called by the Westerners, "Americanized." Mrs. Spring Fragrance was even more "Americanized."

Next door to the Spring Fragrances lived the Chin Yuens. Mrs. Chin Yuen was much older than Mrs. Spring Fragrance; but she had a daughter of eighteen with whom Mrs. Spring Fragrance was on terms of great friendship. The daughter was a pretty girl whose Chinese name was Mai Gwi Far (a rose) and whose American name was Laura. Nearly everybody called her Laura, even her parents and Chinese friends. Laura had a sweetheart, a youth named Kai Tzu. Kai Tzu, who was American-born, and as ruddy and stalwart as any young Westerner, was noted amongst baseball players as one of the finest pitchers on the Coast. He could also sing, "Drink to me only with thine eyes," to Laura's piano accompaniment.

Now the only person who knew that Kai Tzu loved Laura and that Laura loved Kai Tzu, was Mrs. Spring Fragrance. The reason for this was that, although the Chin Yuen parents lived in a house furnished in American style, and wore American clothes, yet they religiously observed many Chinese customs, and their ideals of life were the ideals of their Chinese forefathers. Therefore, they had betrothed their daughter, Laura, at the age of fifteen, to the eldest son of the Chinese Government school-teacher in San Francisco. The time for the consummation of the betrothal was approaching.

Laura was with Mrs. Spring Fragrance and Mrs. Spring Fragrance was trying to cheer her.

"I had such a pretty walk today," said she. "I crossed the banks above the beach and came back by the long road. In the green grass the daffodils were blowing, in the cottage gardens the currant bushes were flowering, and in the air was the perfume of the wallflower. I wished, Laura, that you were with me."

Laura burst into tears. "That is the walk," she sobbed, "Kai Tzu and I so love; but never, ah, never, can we take it together again."

"Now, Little Sister," comforted Mrs. Spring Fragrance "you really must not grieve like that. Is there not a beautiful American poem written by a noble American named Tennyson, which says:

> "'Tis better to have loved and lost.
> Than never to have loved at all?"

Mrs. Spring Fragrance was unaware that Mr. Spring Fragrance, having returned from the city, tired with the day's business, had thrown himself down on the bamboo settee on the veranda, and that although his eyes were engaged in scanning the pages of the *Chinese World,* his ears could not help receiving the words which were borne to him through the open window.

> "'Tis better to have loved and lost,
> Than never to have loved at all,"

repeated Mr. Spring Fragrance. Not wishing to hear more of the secret talk of women, he arose and sauntered around the veranda to the other side of the house. Two pigeons circled around his head. He felt in his pocket for a li-chi which he usually carried for their pecking. His fingers touched a little box. It contained a jadestone pendant, which Mrs. Spring Fragrance had particularly admired the last time she was down town. It was the fifth anniversary of Mr. and Mrs. Spring Fragrance's wedding day.

Mr. Spring Fragrance pressed the little box down into the depths of his pocket.

A young man came out of the back door of the house at Mr. Spring Fragrance's left. The Chin Yuen house was at his right.

"Good evening," said the young man. "Good evening," returned

Mr. Spring Fragrance. He stepped down from his porch and went and leaned over the railing which separated this yard from the yard in which stood the young man.

"Will you please tell me," said Mr. Spring Fragrance, "the meaning of two lines of an American verse which I have heard?"

"Certainly," returned the young man with a genial smile. He was a star student at the University of Washington, and had not the slightest doubt that he could explain the meaning of all things in the universe. "Well," said Mr. Spring Fragrance, "it is this:

> "'Tis better to have loved and lost,
> Than never to have loved at all."

"Ah!" responded the young man with an air of profound wisdom. "That, Mr. Spring Fragrance, means that it is a good thing to love anyway —even if we can't get what we love, or, as the poet tells us, lose what we love. Of course, one needs experience to feel the truth of this teaching."

The young man smiled pensively and reminiscently. More than a dozen young maidens "loved and lost" were passing before his mind's eye.

"The truth of the teaching!" echoed Mr. Spring Fragrance, a little testily. "There is no truth in it whatever. It is disobedient to reason. Is it not better to have what you do not love than to love what you do not have?"

"That depends," answered the young man, "upon temperament."

"I thank you. Good evening," said Mr. Spring Fragrance. He turned away to muse upon the unwisdom of the American way of looking at things.

Meanwhile, inside the house, Laura was refusing to be comforted.

"Ah, no! no!" cried she. "If I had not gone to school with Kai Tzu, nor talked nor walked with him, nor played the accompaniments to his songs, then I might consider with complacency, or at least without horror, my approaching marriage with the son of Man You. But as it is—oh, as it is—!"

The girl rocked herself to and fro in heartfelt grief.

Mrs. Spring Fragrance knelt down beside her, and clasping her arms around her neck, cried in sympathy:

"Little Sister, oh, Little Sister! Dry your tears—do not despair. A moon has yet to pass before the marriage can take place. Who knows what the stars may have to say to one another during its passing? A little bird has whispered to me—"

For a long time Mrs. Spring Fragrance talked. For a long time Laura listened. When the girl arose to go, there was a bright light in her eyes.

II

Mrs. Spring Fragrance, in San Francisco on a visit to her cousin, the wife of the herb doctor of Clay Street, was having a good time. She was invited everywhere that the wife of an honorable Chinese merchant could go. There was much to see and hear, including more than a dozen babies who had been born in the families of her friends since she last visited the city of the Golden Gate. Mrs. Spring Fragrance loved babies. She had had two herself, but both had been transplanted into the spirit land before the completion of even one moon. There were also many dinners and theatre-parties given in her honor. It was at one of the theatre-parties that Mrs. Spring Fragrance met Ah Oi, a young girl who had the reputation of being the prettiest Chinese girl in San Francisco, and the naughtiest. In spite of gossip, however, Mrs. Spring Fragrance took a great fancy to Ah Oi and invited her to a tête-à-tête picnic on the following day. This invitation Ah Oi joyfully accepted. She was a sort of bird girl and never felt so happy as when out in the park or woods.

On the day after the picnic Mrs. Spring Fragrance wrote to Laura Chin Yuen thus:

MY PRECIOUS LAURA,—May the bamboo ever wave. Next week I accompany Ah Oi to the beauteous town of San José. There will we be met by the son of the Illustrious Teacher, and in a little Mission, presided over by a benevolent American priest, the little Ah Oi and the son of the Illustrious Teacher will be joined together in love and harmony—two pieces of music made to complete one another.

The Son of the Illustrious Teacher, having been through an American Hall of Learning, is well able to provide for his orphan bride and fears not the displeasure of his parents, now that he is assured that your grief at his loss will not be inconsolable. He wishes me to waft to you and to Kai Tzu—and the little Ah Oi joins with him—ten thousand rainbow wishes for your happiness.

My respects to your honorable parents, and to yourself, the heart of your loving friend,

JADE SPRING FRAGRANCE

To Mr. Spring Fragrance, Mrs. Spring Fragrance also indited a letter:

GREAT AND HONORED MAN,—Greeting from your plum blossom,* who is desirous of hiding herself from the sun of your presence for a week of seven days more. My honorable cousin is preparing for the Fifth Moon Festival, and wishes me to compound for the occasion some American "fudge," for which delectable sweet, made by my clumsy hands, you have sometimes shown a slight prejudice. I am enjoying a most agreeable visit, and American friends, as also our own, strive benevolently for the accomplishment of my pleasure. Mrs. Samuel Smith, an American lady, known to my cousin, asked for my accompaniment to a magniloquent lecture the other evening. The subject was "America, the Protector of China!" It was most exhilarating, and the effect of so much expression of benevolence leads me to beg of you to forget to remember that the barber charges you one dollar for a shave while he humbly submits to the American man a bill of fifteen cents. And murmur no more because your honored elder brother, on a visit to this country, is detained under the roof-tree of this great Government instead of under your own humble roof. Console him with the reflection that he is protected under the wing of the Eagle, the Emblem of Liberty. What is the loss of ten hundred years or ten thousand times ten dollars compared with the happiness of knowing oneself so securely sheltered? All of this I have learned from Mrs. Samuel Smith, who is as brilliant and great of mind as one of your own superior sex.

For me it is sufficient to know that the Golden Gate Park is most enchanting, and the seals on the rock at the Cliff House extremely entertaining and amiable. There is much feasting and merrymaking under the lanterns in honor of your Stupid Thorn.

I have purchased for your smoking a pipe with an amber mouth. It is said to be very sweet to the lips and to emit a cloud of smoke fit for the gods to inhale.

Awaiting, by the wonderful wire of the telegram message, your gracious permission to remain for the celebration of the Fifth Moon

---

*The plum blossom is the Chinese flower of virtue. It has been adopted by the Japanese, just in the same way as they have adopted the Chinese national flower, the chrysanthemum.

Festival and the making of American "fudge," I continue for ten thousand times ten thousand years,

> Your ever loving and obedient woman,

> JADE

P.S. Forget not to care for the cat, the birds, and the flowers. Do not
eat too quickly nor fan too vigorously now that the weather is warming.

Mrs. Spring Fragrance smiled as she folded this last epistle. Even if
he were old-fashioned, there was never a husband so good and kind as
hers. Only on one occasion since their marriage had he slighted her
wishes. That was when, on the last anniversary of their wedding, she
had signified a desire for a certain jadestone pendant, and he had failed
to satisfy that desire.

But Mrs. Spring Fragrance, being of a happy nature, and disposed
to look upon the bright side of things, did not allow her mind to dwell
upon the jadestone pendant. Instead, she gazed complacently down
upon her bejeweled fingers and folded in with her letter to Mr. Spring
Fragrance a bright little sheaf of condensed love.

III

Mr. Spring Fragrance sat on his doorstep. He had been reading two
letters, one from Mrs. Spring Fragrance, and the other from an elderly
bachelor cousin in San Francisco. The one from the elderly bachelor
cousin was a business letter, but contained the following postscript:

> Tsen Hing, the son of the Government schoolmaster, seems to be
> much in the company of your young wife. He is a good-looking youth,
> and pardon me, my dear cousin; but if women are allowed to stray at
> will from under their husbands' mulberry roofs, what is to prevent them
> from becoming butterflies?

"Sing Foon is old and cynical," said Mr. Spring Fragrance to himself.
"Why should I pay any attention to him? This is America, where a man
may speak to a woman, and a woman listen, without any thought of evil."

He destroyed his cousin's letter and re-read his wife's. Then he
became very thoughtful. Was the making of American fudge sufficient
reason for a wife to wish to remain a week longer in a city where her
husband was not?

The young man who lived in the next house came out to water the lawn.

"Good evening," said he. "Any news from Mrs. Spring Fragrance?"

"She is having a very good time," returned Mr. Spring Fragrance.

"Glad to hear it. I think you told me she was to return the end of this week."

"I have changed my mind about her," said Mr. Spring Fragrance. "I am bidding her remain a week longer, as I wish to give a smoking party during her absence. I hope I may have the pleasure of your company."

"I shall be delighted," returned the young fellow. "But, Mr. Spring Fragrance, don't invite any other white fellows. If you do not I shall be able to get in a scoop. You know, I'm a sort of honorary reporter for the *Gleaner.*"

"Very well," absently answered Mr. Spring Fragrance.

"Of course, your friend the Consul will be present. I shall call it 'A high-class Chinese stag party!' "

In spite of his melancholy mood, Mr. Spring Fragrance smiled.

"Everything is 'high-class' in America," he observed.

"Sure!" cheerfully assented the young man. "Haven't you ever heard that all Americans are princes and princesses, and just as soon as a foreigner puts his foot upon our shores, he also becomes of the nobility—I mean, the royal family."

"What about my brother in the Detention Pen?" dryly inquired Mr. Spring Fragrance.

"Now, you've got me," said the young man, rubbing his head. "Well, that is a shame—'a beastly shame,' as the Englishman says. But understand, old fellow, we that are real Americans are up against that—even more than you. It is against our principles."

"I offer the real Americans my consolations that they should be compelled to do that which is against their principles."

"Oh, well, it will all come right some day. We're not a bad sort, you know. Think of the indemnity money returned to the Dragon by Uncle Sam."

Mr. Spring Fragrance puffed his pipe in silence for some moments. More than politics was troubling his mind.

At last he spoke. "Love," said he, slowly and distinctly, "comes before the wedding in this country, does it not?"

"Yes, certainly."

Young Carman knew Mr. Spring Fragrance well enough to receive with calmness his most astounding queries.

"Presuming," continued Mr. Spring Fragrance—"presuming that some friend of your father's, living—presuming—in England—has a daughter that he arranges with your father to be your wife. Presuming that you have never seen that daughter, but that you marry her, knowing her not. Presuming that she marries you, knowing you not. —After she marries you and knows you, will that woman love you?"

"Emphatically, no," answered the young man.

"That is the way it would be in America—that the woman who marries the man like that—would not love him?"

"Yes, that is the way it would be in America. Love, in this country, must be free, or it is not love at all."

"In China, it is different!" mused Mr. Spring Fragrance.

"Oh, yes, I have no doubt that in China it is different."

"But the love is in the heart all the same," went on Mr. Spring Fragrance.

"Yes, all the same. Everybody falls in love some time or another. Some"—pensively—"many times."

Mr. Spring Fragrance arose.

"I must go down town," said he.

As he walked down the street he recalled the remark of a business acquaintance who had met his wife and had had some conversation with her: "She is just like an American woman."

He had felt somewhat flattered when this remark had been made. He looked upon it as a compliment to his wife's cleverness; but it rankled in his mind as he entered the telegraph office. If his wife was becoming as an American woman, would it not be possible for her to love as an American woman—a man to whom she was not married? There also floated in his memory the verse which his wife had quoted to the daughter of Chin Yuen. When the telegraph clerk handed him a blank, he wrote this message:

> Remain as you wish, but remember that "'Tis better to have loved and lost, than never to have loved at all."

• • •

When Mrs. Spring Fragrance received this message, her laughter tinkled like falling water. How droll! How delightful! Here was her husband quoting American poetry in a telegram. Perhaps he had been reading her American poetry books since she had left him! She hoped so. They would lead him to understand her sympathy for her dear Laura and Kai Tzu. She need no longer keep from him their secret. How joyful! It had been such a hardship to refrain from confiding in him before. But discreetness had been most necessary, seeing that Mr. Spring Fragrance entertained as old-fashioned notions concerning marriage as did the Chin Yuen parents. Strange that that should be so, since he had fallen in love with her picture before *ever* he had seen her, just as she had fallen in love with his! And when the marriage veil was lifted and each beheld the other for the first time in the flesh, there had been no disillusion—no lessening of the respect and affection, which those who had brought about the marriage had inspired in each young heart.

Mrs. Spring Fragrance began to wish she could fall asleep and wake to find the week flown, and she in her own little home pouring tea for Mr. Spring Fragrance.

IV

Mr. Spring Fragrance was walking to business with Mr. Chin Yuen. As they walked they talked.

"Yes," said Mr. Chin Yuen, "the old order is passing away, and the new order is taking its place, even with us who are Chinese. I have finally consented to give my daughter in marriage to young Kai Tzu."

Mr. Spring Fragrance expressed surprise. He had understood that the marriage between his neighbor's daughter and the San Francisco school-teacher's son was all arranged.

"So 'twas," answered Mr. Chin Yuen; "but it seems the young renegade, without consultation or advice, has placed his affections upon some untrustworthy female, and is so under her influence that he refuses to fulfil his parents' promise to me for him."

"So!" said Mr. Spring Fragrance. The shadow on his brow deepened.

"But," said Mr. Chin Yuen, with affable resignation, "it is all ordained by Heaven. Our daughter, as the wife of Kai Tzu, for whom she has long had a loving feeling, will not now be compelled to dwell with a mother-in-law and where her own mother is not. For that, we are thankful, as she is our only one and the conditions of life in this Western country are not as in China. Moreover, Kai Tzu, though not so much of a scholar as the teacher's son, has a keen eye for business and that, in America, is certainly much more desirable than scholarship. What do you think?"

"Eh! What!" exclaimed Mr. Spring Fragrance. The latter part of his companion's remarks had been lost upon him.

That day the shadow which had been following Mr. Spring Fragrance ever since he had heard his wife quote, "'Tis better to have loved," etc., became so heavy and deep that he quite lost himself within it.

At home in the evening he fed the cat, the bird, and the flowers. Then, seating himself in a carved black chair—a present from his wife on his last birthday—he took out his pipe and smoked. The cat jumped into his lap. He stroked it softly and tenderly. It had been much fondled by Mrs. Spring Fragrance, and Mr. Spring Fragrance was under the impression that it missed her. "Poor thing!" said he. "I suppose you want her back!" When he arose to go to bed he placed the animal carefully on the floor, and thus apostrophized it:

"O Wise and Silent One, your mistress returns to you, but her heart she leaves behind her, with the Tommies in San Francisco."

The Wise and Silent One made no reply. He was not a jealous cat.

Mr. Spring Fragrance slept not that night; the next morning he ate not. Three days and three nights without sleep and food went by.

There was a springlike freshness in the air on the day that Mrs. Spring Fragrance came home. The skies overhead were as blue as Puget Sound stretching its gleaming length toward the mighty Pacific, and all the beautiful green world seemed to be throbbing with springing life.

Mrs. Spring Fragrance was never so radiant.

"Oh," she cried light-heartedly, "is it not lovely to see the sun shining so clear, and everything so bright to welcome me?"

Mr. Spring Fragrance made no response. It was the morning after the fourth sleepless night.

Mrs. Spring Fragrance noticed his silence, also his grave face.

"Everything—everyone is glad to see me but you," she declared, half seriously, half jestingly.

Mr. Spring Fragrance set down her valise. They had just entered the house.

"If my wife is glad to see me," he quietly replied, "I also am glad to see her!"

Summoning their servant boy, he bade him look after Mrs. Spring Fragrance's comfort.

"I must be at the store in half an hour," said he, looking at his watch. "There is some very important business requiring attention."

"What is the business?" inquired Mrs. Spring Fragrance, her lip quivering with disappointment.

"I cannot just explain to you," answered her husband.

Mrs. Spring Fragrance looked up into his face with honest and earnest eyes. There was something in his manner, in the tone of her husband's voice, which touched her.

"Yen," said she, "you do not look well. You are not well. What is it?"

Something arose in Mr. Spring Fragrance's throat which prevented him from replying.

"O darling one! O sweetest one!" cried a girl's joyous voice. Laura Chin Yuen ran into the room and threw her arms around Mrs. Spring Fragrance's neck.

"I spied you from the window," said Laura, "and I couldn't rest until I told you. We are to be married next week, Kai Tzu and I. And all through you, all through you—the sweetest jade jewel in the world!"

Mr. Spring Fragrance passed out of the room.

"So the son of the Government teacher and little Happy Love are already married," Laura went on, relieving Mrs. Spring Fragrance of her cloak, her hat, and her folding fan.

Mr. Spring Fragrance paused upon the doorstep.

"Sit down, Little Sister, and I will tell you all about it," said Mrs. Spring Fragrance, forgetting her husband for a moment.

When Laura Chin Yuen had danced away, Mr. Spring Fragrance came in and hung up his hat.

"You got back very soon," said Mrs. Spring Fragrance, covertly wiping away the tears which had begun to fall as soon as she thought herself alone.

"I did not go," answered Mr. Spring Fragrance. "I have been listening to you and Laura."

"But if the business is very important, do not you think you should attend to it?" anxiously queried Mrs. Spring Fragrance.

"It is not important to me now," returned Mr. Spring Fragrance. "I would prefer to hear again about Ah Oi and Man You and Laura and Kai Tzu."

"How lovely of you to say that!" exclaimed Mrs. Spring Fragrance, who was easily made happy. And she began to chat away to her husband in the friendliest and wifeliest fashion possible. When she had finished she asked him if he were not glad to hear that those who loved as did the young lovers whose secrets she had been keeping, were to be united; and he replied that indeed he was; that he would like every man to be as happy with a wife as he himself had ever been and ever would be.

"You did not always talk like that," said Mrs. Spring Fragrance slyly. "You must have been reading my American poetry books!"

"American poetry!" ejaculated Mr. Spring Fragrance almost fiercely, "American poetry is detestable, *abhorrable!*"

"Why! why!" exclaimed Mrs. Spring Fragrance, more and more surprised.

But the only explanation which Mr. Spring Fragrance vouchsafed was a jadestone pendant.

The Inferior Woman

I

Mrs. Spring Fragrance walked through the leafy alleys of the park, admiring the flowers and listening to the birds singing. It was a beautiful afternoon with the warmth from the sun cooled by a refreshing breeze. As she walked along she meditated upon a book which she had some notion of writing. Many American women wrote books. Why should not a Chinese? She would write a book about Americans for her Chinese women friends. The American people were so interesting and mysterious. Something of pride and pleasure crept into Mrs. Spring Fragrance's heart as she pictured Fei and Sie and Mai Gwi Far listening to Lae-Choo reading her illuminating paragraphs.

As she turned down a by-path she saw Will Carman, her American neighbor's son, coming towards her, and by his side a young girl who seemed to belong to the sweet air and brightness of all the things around her. They were talking very earnestly and the eyes of the young man were on the girl's face.

"Ah!" murmured Mrs. Spring Fragrance, after one swift glance. "It is love."

She retreated behind a syringa bush, which completely screened her from view.

Up the winding path went the young couple.

"It is love," repeated Mrs. Spring Fragrance, "and it is the 'Inferior Woman.'"

She had heard about the Inferior Woman from the mother of Will Carman.

After tea that evening Mrs. Spring Fragrance stood musing at her front window. The sun hovered over the Olympic mountains like a great, golden red-bird with dark purple wings, its long tail of light trailing underneath in the waters of Puget Sound.

"How very beautiful!" exclaimed Mrs. Spring Fragrance; then she sighed.

"Why do you sigh?" asked Mr. Spring Fragrance.

"My heart is sad," answered his wife.

"Is the cat sick?" inquired Mr. Spring Fragrance.

Mrs. Spring Fragrance shook her head. "It is not our Wise One who troubles me today," she replied. "It is our neighbors. The sorrow of the Carman household is that the mother desires for her son the Superior Woman, and his heart enshrines but the Inferior. I have seen them together today, and I know."

"What do you know?"

"That the Inferior Woman is the mate for young Carman."

Mr. Spring Fragrance elevated his brows. Only the day before, his wife's arguments had all been in favor of the Superior Woman. He uttered some words expressive of surprise, to which Mrs. Spring Fragrance retorted:

"Yesterday, O Great Man, I was a caterpillar!"

Just then young Carman came strolling up the path. Mr. Spring Fragrance opened the door to him. "Come in, neighbor," said he. "I have received some new books from Shanghai."

"Good," replied young Carman, who was interested in Chinese literature. While he and Mr. Spring Fragrance discussed the "Odes of Chow" and the "Sorrows of Han," Mrs. Spring Fragrance, sitting in a low easy-chair of rose-colored silk, covertly studied her visitor's countenance. Why was his expression so much more grave than gay? It had not been so a year ago—before he had known the Inferior Woman. Mrs. Spring Fragrance noted other changes, also, both in speech and manner. "He is no longer a boy," mused she. "He is a man, and it is the work of the Inferior Woman."

"And when, Mr. Carman," she inquired, "will you bring home a daughter to your mother?"

"And when, Mrs. Spring Fragrance, do you think I should?" returned the young man.

Mrs. Spring Fragrance spread wide her fan and gazed thoughtfully over its silver edge.

"The summer moons will soon be over," said she. "You should not wait until the grass is yellow."

> "The woodmen's blows responsive ring,
>   As on the trees they fall,
> And when the birds their sweet notes sing,
>   They to each other call.
> From the dark valley comes a bird,
>   And seeks the lofty tree,
> *Ying* goes its voice, and thus it cries:
>   'Companion, come to me.'
> The bird, although a creature small
>   Upon its mate depends,
> And shall we men, who rank o'er all,
>   Not seek to have our friends?"

quoted Mr. Spring Fragrance.

Mrs. Spring Fragrance tapped his shoulder approvingly with her fan.

"I perceive," said young Carman, "that you are both allied against my peace."

"It is for your mother," replied Mrs. Spring Fragrance soothingly. "She will be happy when she knows that your affections are fixed by marriage."

There was a slight gleam of amusement in the young man's eyes as he answered: "But if my mother has no wish for a daughter—at least, no wish for the daughter I would want to give her?"

"When I first came to America," returned Mrs. Spring Fragrance, "my husband desired me to wear the American dress. I protested and declared that never would I so appear. But one day he brought home a gown fit for a fairy, and ever since then I have worn and adored the American dress."

"Mrs. Spring Fragrance," declared young Carman, "your argument is incontrovertible."

II

A young man with a determined set to his shoulders stood outside the door of a little cottage perched upon a bluff overlooking the Sound. The chill sea air was sweet with the scent of roses, and he drew in a deep breath of inspiration before he knocked.

"Are you not surprised to see me?" he inquired of the young person who opened the door.

"Not at all," replied the young person demurely.

He gave her a quick almost fierce look. At their last parting he had declared that he would not come again unless she requested him, and that she assuredly had not done.

"I wish I could make you feel," said he.

She laughed—a pretty infectious laugh which exorcised all his gloom. He looked down upon her as they stood together under the cluster of electric lights in her cozy little sitting-room. Such a slender, girlish figure! Such a soft cheek, red mouth, and firm little chin! Often in his dreams of her he had taken her into his arms and coaxed her into a good humor. But, alas! dreams are not realities, and the calm friendliness of this young person made any demonstration of tenderness well-nigh impossible. But for the shy regard of her eyes, you might have thought that he was no more to her than a friendly acquaintance.

"I hear," said she, taking up some needlework, "that your Welland case comes on tomorrow."

"Yes," answered the young lawyer, "and I have all my witnesses ready."

"So, I hear, has Mr. Greaves," she retorted. "You are going to have a hard fight."

"What of that, when in the end I'll win."

He looked over at her with a bright gleam in his eyes.

"I wouldn't be too sure," she warned demurely. "You may lose on a technicality."

He drew his chair a little nearer to her side and turned over the pages of a book lying on her work-table. On the fly-leaf was inscribed in a man's writing: "To the dear little woman whose friendship is worth a fortune."

Another book beside it bore the inscription: "With the love of all the firm, including the boys," and a volume of poems above it was dedicated to the young person "with the high regards and stanch affection" of some other masculine person.

Will Carman pushed aside these evidences of his sweetheart's popularity with his own kind and leaned across the table.

"Alice," said he, "once upon a time you admitted that you loved me."

A blush suffused the young person's countenance.

"Did I?" she queried.

"You did, indeed."

"Well?"

"Well! If you love me and I love you—"

"Oh, please!" protested the girl, covering her ears with her hands.

"I *will* please," asserted the young man. "I have come here tonight, Alice, to ask you to marry me—and at once."

"Deary me!" exclaimed the young person; but she let her needlework fall into her lap as her lover, approaching nearer, laid his arm around her shoulders and, bending his face close to hers, pleaded his most important case.

If for a moment the small mouth quivered, the firm little chin lost its firmness, and the proud little head yielded to the pressure of a lover's arm, it was only for a moment so brief and fleeting that Will Carman had hardly become aware of it before it had passed.

"No," said the young person sorrowfully but decidedly. She had arisen and was standing on the other side of the table facing him. "I cannot marry you while your mother regards me as beneath you."

"When she knows you she will acknowledge you are above me. But I am not asking you to come to my mother, I am asking you to come to me, dear. If you will put your hand in mine and trust to me through all the coming years, no man or woman born can come between us."

But the young person shook her head.

"No," she repeated. "I will not be your wife unless your mother welcomes me with pride and with pleasure."

The night air was still sweet with the perfume of roses as Will Carman passed out of the little cottage door; but he drew in no deep breath of inspiration. His impetuous Irish heart was too heavy with disappointment. It might have been a little lighter, however, had he known that the eyes of the young person who gazed after him were misty with a love and yearning beyond expression.

III

"Will Carman has failed to snare his bird," said Mr. Spring Fragrance to Mrs. Spring Fragrance.

Their neighbor's son had just passed their veranda without turning to bestow upon them his usual cheerful greeting.

"It is too bad," sighed Mrs. Spring Fragrance sympathetically. She clasped her hands together and exclaimed:

"Ah, these Americans! These mysterious, inscrutable, incomprehensible Americans! Had I the divine right of learning I would put them into an immortal book!"

"The divine right of learning," echoed Mr. Spring Fragrance, "Humph!"

Mrs. Spring Fragrance looked up into her husband's face in wonderment.

"Is not the authority of the scholar, the student, almost divine?" she queried.

"So 'tis said," responded he. "So it seems."

The evening before, Mr. Spring Fragrance, together with several Seattle and San Francisco merchants, had given a dinner to a number of young students who had just arrived from China. The morning papers had devoted several columns to laudation of the students, prophecies as to their future, and the great influence which they would exercise over the destiny of their nation; but no comment whatever was made on the givers of the feast, and Mr. Spring Fragrance was therefore feeling somewhat unappreciated. Were not he and his brother merchants worthy of a little attention? If the students had come to learn things in America, they, the merchants, had accomplished things. There were those amongst them who had been instrumental in bringing several of the students to America. One of the boys was Mr. Spring Fragrance's own young brother, for whose maintenance and education he had himself sent the wherewithal every year for many years. Mr. Spring Fragrance, though well read in the Chinese classics, was not himself a scholar. As a boy he had come to the shores of America, worked his way up, and by dint of painstaking study after working hours acquired the Western language and Western business ideas. He had made money, saved money, and sent money home. The years had flown, his business had grown. Through his efforts trade between his native town and the port city in which he lived had greatly increased.

A school in Canton was being builded in part with funds furnished by him, and a railway syndicate, for the purpose of constructing a line of railway from the big city of Canton to his own native town, was under process of formation, with the name of Spring Fragrance at its head.

No wonder then that Mr. Spring Fragrance muttered "Humph!" when Mrs. Spring Fragrance dilated upon the "divine right of learning," and that he should feel irritated and humiliated, when, after explaining to her his grievances, she should quote in the words of Confutze: "Be not concerned that men do not know you; be only concerned that you do not know them." And he had expected wifely sympathy.

He was about to leave the room in a somewhat chilled state of mind when she surprised him again by pattering across to him and following up a low curtsy with these words:

"I bow to you as the grass bends to the wind. Allow me to detain you for just one moment."

Mr. Spring Fragrance eyed her for a moment with suspicion.

"As I have told you, O Great Man," continued Mrs. Spring Fragrance, "I desire to write an immortal book, and now that I have learned from you that it is not necessary to acquire the 'divine right of learning' in order to accomplish things, I will begin the work without delay. My first subject will be 'The Inferior Woman of America.' Please advise me how I shall best inform myself concerning her."

Mr. Spring Fragrance, perceiving that his wife was now serious, and being easily mollified, sat himself down and rubbed his head. After thinking for a few moments he replied:

"It is the way in America, when a person is to be illustrated, for the illustrator to interview the person's friends. Perhaps, my dear, you had better confer with the Superior Woman."

"Surely," cried Mrs. Spring Fragrance, "no sage was ever so wise as my Great Man."

"But I lack the 'divine right of learning,'" dryly deplored Mr. Spring Fragrance.

"I am happy to hear it," answered Mrs. Spring Fragrance. "If you were a scholar you would have no time to read American poetry and American newspapers."

Mr. Spring Fragrance laughed heartily.

"You are no Chinese woman," he teased. "You are an American."

"Please bring me my parasol and my folding fan," said Mrs. Spring Fragrance. "I am going out for a walk."

And Mr. Spring Fragrance obeyed her.

IV

"This is from Mary Carman, who is in Portland," said the mother of the Superior Woman, looking up from the reading of a letter, as her daughter came in from the garden.

"Indeed," carelessly responded Miss Evebrook.

"Yes, it's chiefly about Will."

"Oh, is it? Well, read it then, dear. I'm interested in Will Carman, because of Alice Winthrop."

"I had hoped, Ethel, at one time that you would have been interested in him for his own sake. However, this is what she writes:

"I came here chiefly to rid myself of a melancholy mood which has taken possession of me lately, and also because I cannot bear to see my boy so changed towards me, owing to his infatuation for Alice Winthrop. It is incomprehensible to me how a son of mine can find any pleasure whatever in the society of such a girl. I have traced her history, and find that she is not only uneducated in the ordinary sense, but her environment, from childhood up, has been the sordid and demoralizing one of extreme poverty and ignorance. This girl, Alice, entered a law office at the age of fourteen, supposedly to do the work of an office boy. Now, after seven years in business, through the friendship and influence of men far above her socially, she holds the position of private secretary to the most influential man in Washington—a position which by rights belongs only to a well-educated young woman of good family. Many such applied. I myself sought to have Jane Walker appointed. Is it not disheartening to our woman's cause to be compelled to realize that girls such as this one can win men over to be their friends and lovers, when there are so many splendid young women who have been carefully trained to be companions and comrades of educated men?"

"Pardon me, mother," interrupted Miss Evebrook, "but I have heard enough. Mrs. Carman is your friend and a well-meaning woman sometimes; but a woman suffragist, in the true sense, she certainly is not. Mark my words: If any young man had accomplished for himself what Alice Winthrop has accomplished, Mrs. Carman could not have said enough in his praise. It is women such as Alice Winthrop who, in spite of every drawback, have raised themselves to the level of those who have had every advantage, who are the pride and glory of America. There are thousands of them, all over this land: women who have been of service to others all their years and who have graduated from the university of life with honor. Women such as I, who are called the Superior Women of America, are after all nothing but schoolgirls in comparison.

Mrs. Evebrook eyed her daughter mutinously. "I don't see why you should feel like that," said she. "Alice is a dear bright child, and it is prejudice engendered by Mary Carman's disappointment about you and Will which is the real cause of poor Mary's bitterness towards her; but to my mind, Alice does not compare with my daughter. She would be frightened to death if she had to make a speech."

"You foolish mother!" rallied Miss Evebrook. "To stand upon a platform at woman suffrage meetings and exploit myself is certainly a great recompense to you and father for all the sacrifices you have made in my behalf. But since it pleases you, I do it with pleasure even on the nights when my beau should 'come a courting.'"

"There is many a one who would like to come, Ethel. You're the handsomest girl in this Western town—and you know it."

"Stop that, mother. You know very well I have set my mind upon having ten years' freedom; ten years in which to love, live, suffer, see the world, and learn about men (not schoolboys) before I choose one."

"Alice Winthrop is the same age as you are, and looks like a child beside you."

"Physically, maybe; but her heart and mind are better developed. She has been out in the world all her life, I only a few months."

"Your lecture last week on 'The Opposite Sex' was splendid."

"Of course. I have studied one hundred books on the subject and attended fifty lectures. All that was necessary was to repeat in an original manner what was not by any means original."

Miss Evebrook went over to a desk and took a paper therefrom.

"This," said she, "is what Alice has written me in reply to my note suggesting that she attend next week the suffrage meeting, and give some of the experiences of her business career. The object I had in view when I requested the relation of her experiences was to use them as illustrations of the suppression and oppression of women by men. Strange to say, Alice and I have never conversed on this particular subject. If we had I would not have made this request of her, nor written her as I did. Listen:

> "I should dearly love to please you, but I am afraid that my experiences, if related, would not help the cause. It may be, as you say, that men prevent women from rising to their level; but if there are such men, I have not met them. Ever since, when a little girl, I walked into a law office and asked for work, and the senior member kindly looked me over through his spectacles and inquired if I thought I could learn to index books, and the junior member glanced under my hat and said: 'This is a pretty little girl and we must be pretty to her,' I have loved and respected the men amongst whom I have worked and wherever I have worked. I may have been exceptionally fortunate, but I know this: the men for whom I have worked and amongst whom I have spent my life, whether they have been business or professional men, students or great lawyers and politicians, all alike have upheld me, inspired me, advised me, taught me, given me a broad outlook upon life for a woman; interested me in themselves and in their work. As to corrupting my mind and my morals, as you say so many men do, when they have young and innocent girls to deal with: As a woman I look back over my years spent amongst business and professional men, and see myself, as I was at first, an impressionable, ignorant little girl, born a Bohemian, easy to lead and easy to win, but borne aloft and morally supported by the goodness of my brother men, the men amongst whom I worked. That is why, dear Ethel, you will have to forgive me, because I cannot carry out your design, and help your work, as otherwise I would like to do."

"That, mother," declared Miss Evebrook, "answers all Mrs. Carman's insinuations, and should make her ashamed of herself. Can any one know the sentiments which little Alice entertains toward men, and wonder at her winning out as she has?"

Mrs. Evebrook was about to make reply, when her glance happening to stray out of the window, she noticed a pink parasol.

"Mrs. Spring Fragrance!" she ejaculated, while her daughter went to the door and invited in the owner of the pink parasol, who was seated in a veranda rocker calmly writing in a note-book.

"I'm so sorry that we did not hear your ring, Mrs. Spring Fragrance," said she.

"There is no necessity for you to sorrow," replied the little Chinese woman. "I did not expect you to hear a ring which rang not. I failed to pull the bell."

"You forgot, I suppose," suggested Ethel Evebrook.

"Is it wise to tell secrets?" ingenuously inquired Mrs. Spring Fragrance.

"Yes, to your friends. Oh, Mrs. Spring Fragrance, you are *so* refreshing."

"I have pleasure, then, in confiding to you. I have an ambition to accomplish an immortal book about the Americans, and the conversation I heard through the window was so interesting to me that I thought I would take some of it down for my book before I intruded myself. With your kind permission I will translate for your correction."

"I shall be delighted—honored," said Miss Evebrook, her cheeks glowing and her laugh rippling, "if you will promise me that you will also translate for our friend, Mrs. Carman."

"Ah, yes, poor Mrs. Carman! My heart is so sad for her," murmured the little Chinese woman.

V

When the mother of Will Carman returned from Portland, the first person upon whom she called was Mrs. Spring Fragrance. Having lived in China while her late husband was in the customs service there, Mrs. Carman's prejudices did not extend to the Chinese, and ever since the Spring Fragrances had become the occupants of the villa beside the Carmans, there had been social good feeling between the American and Chinese families. Indeed, Mrs. Carman was wont to declare that amongst all her acquaintances there was not one more congenial and interesting than little Mrs. Spring Fragrance. So after she had sipped a cup of delicious tea, tasted some piquant candied limes, and told Mrs. Spring Fragrance all about her visit to the Oregon city and the Chinese people she had met there, she reverted to a personal trouble confided to Mrs. Spring Fragrance some months before and dwelt upon it for more than half an hour. Then she checked herself and gazed at Mrs. Spring Fragrance in surprise. Hitherto she had found the little Chinese woman sympathetic and consoling. Chinese ideas of filial duty chimed in with her own. But today Mrs. Spring Fragrance seemed strangely uninterested and unresponsive.

"Perhaps," gently suggested the American woman, who was nothing if not sensitive, "you have some trouble yourself. If so, my dear, tell me all about it."

"Oh, no!" answered Mrs. Spring Fragrance brightly. "I have no troubles to tell; but all the while I am thinking about the book I am writing."

"A book!"

"Yes, a book about Americans, an immortal book."

"My dear Mrs. Spring Frag ance!" exclaimed her visitor in amazement.

"The American woman writes books about the Chinese. Why not a Chinese woman write books about the Americans?"

"I see what you mean. Why, yes, of course. What an original idea!"

"Yes, I think that is what it is. My book I shall take from the words of others."

"What do you mean, my dear?"

"I listen to what is said, I apprehend, I write it down. Let me illustrate by the 'Inferior Woman' subject. The Inferior Woman is most interesting to me because you have told me that your son is in much love with her. My husband advised me to learn about the Inferior Woman from the Superior Woman. I go to see the Superior Woman. I sit on the veranda of the Superior Woman's house. I listen to her converse with her mother about the Inferior Woman. With the speed of flames I write down all I hear. When I enter the house the Superior Woman advises me that what I write is correct. May I read to you?"

"I shall be pleased to hear what you have written; but I do not think you were wise in your choice of subject," returned Mrs. Carman somewhat primly.

"I am sorry I am not wise. Perhaps I had better not read?" said Mrs. Spring Fragrance with humility.

"Yes, yes, do, please."

There was eagerness in Mrs. Carman's voice. What could Ethel Evebrook have to say about that girl!

When Mrs. Spring Fragrance had finished reading, she looked up into the face of her American friend—a face in which there was nothing now but tenderness.

"Mrs. Mary Carman," said she, "you are so good as to admire my husband because he is what the Americans call 'a man who has made himself.' Why then do you not admire the Inferior Woman who is a woman who has made herself?"

"I think I do," said Mrs. Carman slowly.

VI

It was an evening that invited to reverie. The far stretches of the sea were gray with mist, and the city itself, lying around the sweep of the Bay, seemed dusky and distant. From her cottage window Alice Winthrop looked silently at the open world around her. It seemed a long time since she had heard Will Carman's whistle. She wondered if he were still angry with her. She was sorry that he had left her in anger, and yet not sorry. If she had not made him believe that she was proud and selfish, the parting would have been much harder; and perhaps had he known the truth and realized that it was for his sake, and not for her own, that she was sending him away from her, he might have refused to leave her at all. His was such an imperious nature. And then they would have married—right away. Alice caught her breath a little, and then she sighed. But they would not have been happy. No, that could not have been possible if his mother did not like her. When a gulf of prejudice lies between the wife and mother of a man, that man's life is not what it should be. And even supposing she and Will could have lost themselves in each other, and been able to imagine themselves perfectly satisfied with life together, would it have been right? The question of right and wrong was a very real one to Alice Winthrop. She put herself in the place of the mother of her lover—a lonely elderly woman, a widow with an only son, upon whom she had expended all her love and care ever since, in her early youth, she had been bereaved of his father. What anguish of heart would be hers if that son deserted her for one whom she, his mother, deemed unworthy! Prejudices are prejudices. They are like diseases.

The poor, pale, elderly woman, who cherished bitter and resentful feelings towards the girl whom her son loved, was more an object of pity than condemnation to the girl herself.

She lifted her eyes to the undulating line of hills beyond the water. From behind them came a silver light. "Yes," said she aloud to herself—and, though she knew it not, there was an infinite pathos in such philosophy from one so young—"if life cannot be bright and beautiful for me, at least it can be peaceful and contented."

The light behind the hills died away; darkness crept over the sea. Alice withdrew from the window and went and knelt before the open fire in her sitting-room. Her cottage companion, the young woman who rented the place with her, had not yet returned from town.

Alice did not turn on the light. She was seeing pictures in the fire, and in every picture was the same face and form—the face and form of a fine, handsome young man with love and hope in his eyes. No, not always love and hope. In the last picture of all there was an expression which she wished she could forget. And yet she would remember— ever—always—and with it, these words: "Is it nothing to you— nothing—to tell a man that you love him, and then to bid him go?"

Yes, but when she had told him she loved him she had not dreamed that her love for him and his for her would estrange him from one who, before ever she had come to this world, had pillowed his head on her breast.

Suddenly this girl, so practical, so humorous, so clever in every-day life, covered her face with her hands and sobbed like a child. Two roads of life had lain before her and she had chosen the hardest.

The warning bell of an automobile passing the cross-roads checked her tears. That reminded her that Nellie Blake would soon be home. She turned on the light and went to the bedroom and bathed her eyes. Nellie must have forgotten her key. There she was knocking.

• • •

The chill sea air was sweet with the scent of roses as Mary Carman stood upon the threshold of the little cottage, and beheld in the illumination from within the young girl whom she had called "the Inferior Woman."

"I have come, Miss Winthrop," said she, "to beg of you to return home with me. Will, reckless boy, met with a slight accident while out shooting, so could not come for you himself. He has told me that he loves you, and if you love him, I want to arrange for the prettiest wedding of the season. Come, dear!"

"I am so glad," said Mrs. Spring Fragrance, "that Will Carman's bird is in his nest and his felicity is assured."

"What about the Superior Woman?" asked Mr. Spring Fragrance.

"Ah, the Superior Woman! Radiantly beautiful, and gifted with the divine right of learning! I love well the Inferior Woman; but, O Great Man, when we have a daughter, may Heaven ordain that she walk in the groove of the Superior Woman."

The Wisdom of the New

I

Old Li Wang, the peddler, who had lived in the land beyond the sea, was wont to declare: "For every cent that a man makes here, he can make one hundred there."

"Then, why," would ask Sankwei, "do you now have to move from door to door to fill your bowl with rice?"

And the old man would sigh and answer:

"Because where one learns how to make gold, one also learns how to lose it."

"How to lose it!" echoed Wou Sankwei. "Tell me all about it."

So the old man would tell stories about the winning and the losing, and the stories of the losing were even more fascinating than the stories of the winning.

"Yes, that was life," he would conclude. "Life, life."

At such times the boy would gaze across the water with wistful eyes. The land beyond the sea was calling to him.

The place was a sleepy little south coast town where the years slipped by monotonously. The boy was the only son of the man who had been the town magistrate.

Had his father lived, Wou Sankwei would have been sent to complete his schooling in another province. As it was he did nothing but sleep, dream, and occasionally get into mischief. What else was there to do? His mother and sister waited upon him hand and foot. Was he not the son of the house? The family income was small, scarcely sufficient for their needs; but there was no way by which he could add to it, unless, indeed, he disgraced the name of Wou by becoming a common fisherman. The great green waves lifted white arms of foam to him, and the fishes gleaming and lurking in the waters seemed to beseech him to draw them from the deep; but his mother shook her head.

"Should you become a fisherman," said she, "your family would lose face. Remember that your father was a magistrate."

When he was about nineteen there returned to the town one who had been absent for many years. Ching Kee, like old Li Wang, had also lived in the land beyond the sea; but unlike old Li Wang he had accumulated a small fortune.

"'Tis a hard life over there," said he, "but 'tis worth while. At least one can be a man, and can work at what work comes his way without losing face." Then he laughed at Wou Sankwei's flabby muscles, at his soft, dark eyes, and plump, white hands.

"If you lived in America," said he, "you would learn to be ashamed of such beauty."

Whereupon Wou Sankwei made up his mind that he would go to America, the land beyond the sea. Better any life than that of a woman man.

He talked long and earnestly with his mother. "Give me your blessing," said he. "I will work and save money. What I send home will bring you many a comfort, and when I come back to China, it may be that I shall be able to complete my studies and obtain a degree. If not, my knowledge of the foreign language which I shall acquire, will enable me to take a position which will not disgrace the name of Wou."

His mother listened and thought. She was ambitious for her son whom she loved beyond all things on earth. Moreover, had not Sik Ping, a Canton merchant, who had visited the little town two moons ago, declared to Hum Wah, who traded in palm leaves, that the signs of the times were that the son of a cobbler, returned from America with the foreign language, could easier command a position of consequence than the son of a school-teacher unacquainted with any tongue but that of his motherland?

"Very well," she acquiesced; "but before you go I must find you a wife. Only your son, my son, can comfort me for your loss."

II

Wou Sankwei stood behind his desk, busily entering figures in a long yellow book. Now and then he would thrust the hair pencil with which he worked behind his ears and manipulate with deft fingers a Chinese counting machine. Wou Sankwei was the junior partner and bookkeeper of the firm of Leung Tang Wou & Co. of San Francisco. He had been in America seven years and had made good use of his time. Self-improvement had been his object and ambition, even more than the acquirement of a fortune, and who, looking at his fine, intelligent face and listening to his careful English, could say that he had failed?

One of his partners called his name. Some ladies wished to speak to him. Wou Sankwei hastened to the front of the store. One of his callers, a motherly looking woman, was the friend who had taken him under her wing shortly after his arrival in America. She had come to invite him to spend the evening with her and her niece, the young girl who accompanied her.

After his callers had left, Sankwei returned to his desk and worked steadily until the hour for his evening meal, which he took in the Chinese restaurant across the street from the bazaar. He hurried through with this, as before going to his friend's house, he had a somewhat important letter to write and mail. His mother had died a year before, and the uncle, to whom he was writing, had taken his wife and son into his home until such time as his nephew could send for them. Now the time had come.

Wou Sankwei's memory of the woman who was his wife was very faint. How could it be otherwise? She had come to him but three weeks before the sailing of the vessel which had brought him to America, and until then he had not seen her face. But she was his wife and the mother of his son. Ever since he had worked in America he had sent money for her support, and she had proved a good daughter to his mother.

As he sat down to write he decided that he would welcome her with a big dinner to his countrymen.

"Yes," he replied to Mrs. Dean, later on in the evening, "I have sent for my wife."

"I am so glad," said the lady. "Mr. Wou"—turning to her niece—"has not seen his wife for seven years."

"Deary me!" exclaimed the young girl. "What a lot of letters you must have written!"

"I have not written her one," returned the young man somewhat stiffly.

Adah Charlton looked up in surprise. "Why—" she began.

"Mr. Wou used to be such a studious boy when I first knew him," interrupted Mrs. Dean, laying her hand affectionately upon the young man's shoulder. "Now, it is all business. But you won't forget the concert on Saturday evening."

"No, I will not forget," answered Wou Sankwei.

"He has never written to his wife," explained Mrs. Dean when she and her niece were alone, "because his wife can neither read nor write."

"Oh, isn't that sad!" murmured Adah Charlton, her own winsome face becoming pensive.

"They don't seem to think so. It is the Chinese custom to educate only the boys. At least it has been so in the past. Sankwei himself is unusually bright. Poor boy! He began life here as a laundryman, and you may be sure that it must have been hard on him, for, as the son of a petty Chinese Government official, he had not been accustomed to manual labor. But Chinese character is wonderful; and now after seven years in this country, he enjoys a reputation as a business man amongst his countrymen, and is as up to date as any young American."

"But, Auntie, isn't it dreadful to think that a man should live away from his wife for so many years without any communication between them whatsoever except through others."

"It is dreadful to our minds, but not to theirs. Everything with them is a matter of duty. Sankwei married his wife as a matter of duty. He sends for her as a matter of duty."

"I wonder if it is all duty on her side," mused the girl.

Mrs. Dean smiled. "You are too romantic, Adah," said she. "I hope, however, that when she does come, they will be happy together. I think almost as much of Sankwei as I do of my own boy."

III

Pau Lin, the wife of Wou Sankwei, sat in a corner of the deck of the big steamer, awaiting the coming of her husband. Beside her, leaning his little queued head against her shoulder, stood her six-year-old son. He had been ailing throughout the voyage, and his small face was pinched with pain. His mother, who had been nursing him every night since the ship had left port, appeared very worn and tired. This, despite the fact that with a feminine desire to make herself fair to see in the eyes of her husband, she had arrayed herself in a heavily embroidered purple costume, whitened her forehead and cheeks with powder, and tinted her lips with carmine.

He came at last, looking over and beyond her. There were two others of her countrywomen awaiting the men who had sent for them, and each had a child, so that for a moment he seemed somewhat bewildered. Only when the ship's officer pointed out and named her, did he know her as his. Then he came forward, spoke a few words of formal welcome, and, lifting the child in his arms, began questioning her as to its health.

She answered in low monosyllables. At his greeting she had raised her patient eyes to his face—the face of the husband whom she had not seen for seven long years—then the eager look of expectancy which had crossed her own faded away, her eyelids drooped, and her countenance assumed an almost sullen expression.

"Ah, poor Sankwei!" exclaimed Mrs. Dean, who with Adah Charlton stood some little distance apart from the family group.

"Poor wife!" murmured the young girl. She moved forward and would have taken in her own white hands the ringed ones of the Chinese woman, but the young man gently restrained her. "She cannot understand you," said he. As the young girl fell back, he explained to his wife the presence of the stranger women. They were there to bid her welcome; they were kind and good and wished to be her friends as well as his.

Pau Lin looked away. Adah Charlton's bright face, and the tone in her husband's voice when he spoke to the young girl, aroused a suspicion in her mind—a suspicion natural to one who had come from a land where friendship between a man and woman is almost unknown.

"Poor little thing! How shy she is!" exclaimed Mrs. Dean.

Sankwei was glad that neither she nor the young girl understood the meaning of the averted face.

Thus began Wou Sankwei's life in America as a family man. He soon became accustomed to the change, which was not such a great one after all. Pau Lin was more of an accessory than a part of his life. She interfered not at all with his studies, his business, or his friends, and when not engaged in housework or sewing, spent most of her time in the society of one or the other of the merchants' wives who lived in the flats and apartments around her own. She kept up the Chinese custom of taking her meals after her husband or at a separate table, and observed faithfully the rule laid down for her by her late mother-in-law: to keep a quiet tongue in the presence of her man. Sankwei, on his part, was always kind and indulgent. He bought her silk dresses, hair ornaments, fans, and sweetmeats. He ordered her favorite dishes from the Chinese restaurant. When she wished to go out with her women friends, he hired a carriage, and shortly after her advent erected behind her sleeping room a chapel for the ancestral tablet and gorgeous goddess which she had brought over seas with her.

Upon the child both parents lavished affection. He was a quaint, serious little fellow, small for his age and requiring much care. Although naturally much attached to his mother, he became also very fond of his father who, more like an elder brother than a parent, delighted in playing all kinds of games with him, and whom he followed about like a little dog. Adah Charlton took a great fancy to him and sketched him in many different poses for a book on Chinese children which she was illustrating.

"He will be strong enough to go to school next year," said Sankwei to her one day. "Later on I intend to put him through an American college."

"What does your wife think of a Western training for him?" inquired the young girl.

"I have not consulted her about the matter," he answered. "A woman does not understand such things."

"A woman, Mr. Wou," declared Adah, "understands such things as well as and sometimes better than a man."

"An American woman, maybe," amended Sankwei; "but not a Chinese."

From the first Pau Lin had shown no disposition to become Americanized, and Sankwei himself had not urged it.

"I do appreciate the advantages of becoming westernized," said he to Mrs. Dean whose influence and interest in his studies in America had helped him to become what he was, "but it is not as if she had come here as I came, in her learning days. The time for learning with her is over."

One evening, upon returning from his store, he found the little Yen sobbing pitifully.

"What!" he teased, "A man—and weeping."

The boy tried to hide his face, and as he did so, the father noticed that his little hand was red and swollen. He strode into the kitchen where Pau Lin was preparing the evening meal.

"The little child who is not strong—is there anything he could do to merit the infliction of pain?" he questioned.

Pau Lin faced her husband. "Yes, I think so," said she.

"What?"

"I forbade him to speak the language of the white women, and he disobeyed me. He had words in that tongue with the white boy from the next street."

Sankwei was astounded.

"We are living in the white man's country," said he. "The child will have to learn the white man's language."

"Not my child," answered Pau Lin.

Sankwei turned away from her. "Come, little one," said he to his son, "we will take supper tonight at the restaurant, and afterwards Yen shall see a show."

Pau Lin laid down the dish of vegetables which she was straining and took from a hook a small wrap which she adjusted around the boy.

"Now go with thy father," said she sternly.

But the boy clung to her—to the hand which had punished him. "I will sup with you," he cried, "I will sup with you."

"Go," repeated his mother, pushing him from her. And as the two passed over the threshold, she called to the father: "Keep the wrap around the child. The night air is chill."

Late that night, while father and son were peacefully sleeping, the wife and mother arose, and lifting gently the unconscious boy, bore him into the next room where she sat down with him in a rocker. Waking, he clasped his arms around her neck. Backwards and forwards she rocked him, passionately caressing the wounded hand and crooning and crying until he fell asleep again.

The first chastisement that the son of Wou Sankwei had received from his mother, was because he had striven to follow in the footsteps of his father and use the language of the stranger.

"You did perfectly right," said old Sien Tau the following morning, as she leaned over her balcony to speak to the wife of Wou Sankwei. "Had I again a son to rear, I should see to it that he followed not after the white people."

Sien Tau's son had married a white woman, and his children passed their grandame on the street without recognition.

"In this country, she is most happy who has no child," said Lae Choo, resting her elbow upon the shoulder of Sien Tau. "A Toy, the young daughter of Lew Wing, is as bold and free in her ways as are the white women, and her name is on all the men's tongues. What prudent man of our race would take her as wife?"

"One needs not to be born here to be made a fool of," joined in Pau Lin, appearing at another balcony door. "Think of Hum Wah. From sunrise till midnight he worked for fourteen years, then a white man came along and persuaded from him every dollar, promising to return doublefold within the moon. Many moons have risen and waned, and Hum Wah still waits on this side of the sea for the white man and his money. Meanwhile, his father and mother, who looked long for his coming, have passed beyond returning."

"The new religion—what trouble it brings!" exclaimed Lae Choo. "My man received word yestereve that the good old mother of Chee Ping—he who was baptized a Christian at the last baptizing in the Mission around the corner—had her head secretly severed from her body by the steadfast people of the village, as soon as the news reached there. 'Twas the first violent death in the records of the place. This happened to the mother of one of the boys attending the Mission corner of my street."

"No doubt, the poor old mother, having lost face, minded not so much the losing of her head," sighed Pau Lin. She gazed below her curiously. The American Chinatown held a strange fascination for the girl from the seacoast village. Streaming along the street was a motley throng made up of all nationalities. The sing-song voices of girls whom respectable merchants' wives shudder to name, were calling to one another from high balconies up shadowy alleys. A fat barber was laughing hilariously at a drunken white man who had fallen into a gutter; a withered old fellow, carrying a bird in a cage, stood at the corner entreating passersby to have a good fortune told; some children were burning punk on the curbstone. There went by a stalwart Chief of the Six Companies engaged in earnest confab with a yellow-robed priest from the joss house. A Chinese dressed in the latest American style and a very blonde woman, laughing immoderately, were entering a Chinese restaurant together. Above all the hubbub of voices was heard the clang of electric cars and the jarring of heavy wheels over cobblestones.

Pau Lin raised her head and looked her thoughts at the old woman, Sien Tau.

"Yes," nodded the dame, "'tis a mad place in which to bring up a child."

Pau Lin went back into the house, gave little Yen his noonday meal, and dressed him with care. His father was to take him out that afternoon. She questioned the boy, as she braided his queue, concerning the white women whom he visited with his father.

It was evening when they returned—Wou Sankwei and his boy. The little fellow ran up to her in high glee. "See, mother," said he, pulling off his cap, "I am like father now. I wear no queue."

The mother looked down upon him—at the little round head from which the queue, which had been her pride, no longer dangled.

"Ah!" she cried. "I am ashamed of you; I am ashamed!"

The boy stared at her, hurt and disappointed.

"Never mind, son," comforted his father. "It is all right."

Pau Lin placed the bowls of seaweed and chickens' liver before them and went back to the kitchen where her own meal was waiting. But she did not eat. She was saying within herself: "It is for the white woman he has done this; it is for the white woman!"

Later, as she laid the queue of her son within the trunk wherein lay that of his father, long since cast aside, she discovered a picture of Mrs. Dean, taken when the American woman had first become the teacher and benefactress of the youthful laundryman. She ran over with it to her husband. "Here," said she; "it is a picture of one of your white friends."

Sankwei took it from her almost reverently, "That woman," he explained, "has been to me as a mother."

"And the young woman—the one with eyes the color of blue china—is she also as a mother?" inquired Pau Lin gently.

But for all her gentleness, Wou Sankwei flushed angrily.

"Never speak of her," he cried. "Never speak of her!"

"Ha, ha, ha! Ha, ha, ha!" laughed Pau Lin. It was a soft and not unmelodious laugh, but to Wou Sankwei it sounded almost sacrilegious.

Nevertheless, he soon calmed down. Pau Lin was his wife, and to be kind to her was not only his duty but his nature. So when his little boy climbed into his lap and besought his father to pipe him a tune, he reached for his flute and called to Pau Lin to put aside work for that night. He would play her some Chinese music. And Pau Lin, whose heart and mind, undiverted by change, had been concentrated upon Wou Sankwei ever since the day she had become his wife, smothered, for the time being, the bitterness in her heart, and succumbed to the magic of her husband's playing—a magic which transported her in thought to the old Chinese days, the old Chinese days whose impression and influence ever remain with the exiled sons and daughters of China.

IV

That a man should take to himself two wives, or even three, if he thought proper, seemed natural and right in the eyes of Wou Pau Lin. She herself had come from a home where there were two broods of children and where her mother and her father's other wife had eaten their meals together as sisters. In that home there had not always been peace; but each woman, at least, had the satisfaction of knowing that her man did not regard or treat the other woman as her superior. To each had fallen the common lot — to bear children to the man, and the man was master of all.

But, oh! the humiliation and shame of bearing children to a man who looked up to another woman — and a woman of another race — as a being above the common uses of women. There is a jealousy of the mind more poignant than any mere animal jealousy.

When Wou Sankwei's second child was two weeks old, Adah Charlton and her aunt called to see the little one, and the young girl chatted brightly with the father and played merrily with Yen, who was growing strong and merry. The American women could not, of course, converse with the Chinese; but Adah placed beside her a bunch of beautiful flowers, pressed her hand, and looked down upon her with radiant eyes. Secure in the difference of race, in the love of many friends, and in the happiness of her chosen work, no suspicion whatever crossed her mind that the woman whose husband was her aunt's protégé tasted everything bitter because of her.

After the visitors had gone, Pau Lin, who had been watching her husband's face while the young artist was in the room, said to him:

"She can be happy who takes all and gives nothing."

"Takes all and gives nothing," echoed her husband. "What do you mean?"

"She has taken all your heart," answered Pau Lin, "but she has not given you a son. It is I who have had that task."

"You are my wife," answered Wou Sankwei. "And she — oh! how can you speak of her so? She, who is as a pure water-flower — a lily!"

He went out of the room, carrying with him a little painting of their boy, which Adah Charlton had given to him as she bade him goodbye and which he had intended showing with pride to the mother.

It was on the day that the baby died that Pau Lin first saw the little picture. It had fallen out of her husband's coat pocket when he lifted the tiny form in his arms and declared it lifeless. Even in that first moment of loss Pau Lin, stooping to pick up the portrait, had shrunk back in horror, crying: "She would cast a spell! She would cast a spell!"

She set her heel upon the face of the picture and destroyed it beyond restoration.

"You know not what you say and do," sternly rebuked Sankwei. He would have added more, but the mystery of the dead child's look forbade him.

"The loss of a son is as the loss of a limb," said he to his childless partner, as under the red glare of the lanterns they sat discussing the sad event.

"But you are not without consolation," returned Leung Tsao. "Your firstborn grows in strength and beauty."

"True," assented Wou Sankwei, his heavy thoughts becoming lighter.

And Pau Lin, in her curtained balcony overhead, drew closer her child and passionately cried:

"Sooner would I, O heart of my heart, that the light of thine eyes were also quenched, than that thou shouldst be contaminated with the wisdom of the new."

V

The Chinese women friends of Wou Pau Lin gossiped among themselves, and their gossip reached the ears of the American woman friend of Pau Lin's husband. Since the days of her widowhood Mrs. Dean had devoted herself earnestly and whole-heartedly to the betterment of the condition and the uplifting of the young workingmen of Chinese race who came to America. Their appeal and need, as she had told her niece, was for closer acquaintance with the knowledge of the Western people, and *that* she had undertaken to give them, as far as she was able. The rewards and satisfactions of her work had been rich in some cases. Witness Wou Sankwei.

But the gossip had reached and much perturbed her. What was it that they said Wou Sankwei's wife had declared—that her little son should not go to an American school nor learn the American learning. Such bigotry and narrow-mindedness! How sad to think of! Here was a man who had benefited and profited by living in America, anxious to have his son receive the benefits of a Western education—and here was this man's wife opposing him with her ignorance and hampering him with her unreasonable jealousy.

Yes, she had heard that too. That Wou Sankwei's wife was jealous— jealous—and her husband the most moral of men, the kindest and the most generous.

"Of what is she jealous?" she questioned Adah Charlton. "Other Chinese men's wives, I have known, have had cause to be jealous, for it is true some of them are dreadfully immoral and openly support two or more wives. But not Wou Sankwei. And this little Pau Lin. She has everything that a Chinese woman could wish for."

A sudden flash of intuition came to the girl, rendering her for a moment speechless. When she did find words, she said:

"Everything that a Chinese woman could wish for, you say. Auntie, I do not believe there is any real difference between the feelings of a Chinese wife and an American wife. Sankwei is treating Pau Lin as he would treat her were he living in China. Yet it cannot be the same to her as if she were in their own country, where he would not come in contact with American women. A woman is a woman with intuitions and perceptions, whether Chinese or American, whether educated or uneducated, and Sankwei's wife must have noticed, even on the day of her arrival, her husband's manner towards us, and contrasted it with his manner towards her. I did not realize this before you told me that she was jealous. I only wish I had. Now, for all her ignorance, I can see that the poor little thing became more of an American in that one half hour on the steamer than Wou Sankwei, for all your pride in him, has become in seven years."

Mrs. Dean rested her head on her hand. She was evidently much perplexed.

"What you say may be, Adah," she replied after a while; "but even so, it is Sankwei whom I have known so long, who has my sympathies. He has much to put up with. They have drifted seven years of life apart. There is no bond of interest or sympathy between them, save the boy. Yet never the slightest hint of trouble has come to me from his own lips. Before the coming of Pau Lin, he would confide in me every little thing that worried him, as if he were my own son. Now he maintains absolute silence as to his private affairs."

"Chinese principles," observed Adah, resuming her work. "Yes, I admit Sankwei has some puzzles to solve. Naturally, when he tries to live two lives—that of a Chinese and that of an American."

"He is compelled to that," retorted Mrs. Dean. "Is it not what we teach these Chinese boys—to become Americans? And yet, they are Chinese, and must, in a sense, remain so."

Adah did not answer.

Mrs. Dean sighed. "Poor, dear children, both of them," mused she. "I feel very low-spirited over the matter. I suppose you wouldn't care to come down town with me. I should like to have another chat with Mrs. Wing Sing."

"I shall be glad of the change," replied Adah, laying down her brushes.

Rows of lanterns suspended from many balconies shed a mellow, moonshiny radiance. On the walls and doors were splashes of red paper inscribed with hieroglyphics. In the narrow streets, booths decorated with flowers, and banners and screens painted with immense figures of josses diverted the eye; while bands of musicians in gaudy silks, shrilled and banged, piped and fluted.

Everybody seemed to be out of doors—men, women, and children—and nearly all were in holiday attire. A couple of priests, in vivid scarlet and yellow robes, were kotowing before an altar covered with a rich cloth, embroidered in white and silver. Some Chinese students from the University of California stood looking on with comprehending, half-scornful interest; three girls lavishly dressed in colored silks, with their black hair plastered back from their faces and heavily bejewelled behind, chirped and chattered in a gilded balcony above them like birds in a cage. Little children, their hands full of half-moon-shaped cakes, were pattering about, with eyes, for all the hour, as bright as stars.

Chinatown was celebrating the Harvest Moon Festival, and Adah Charlton was glad that she had an opportunity to see something of the celebration before she returned East. Mrs. Dean, familiar with the Chinese people and the mazes of Chinatown, led her around fearlessly, pointing out this and that object of interest and explaining to her its meaning. Seeing that it was a gala night, she had abandoned her idea of calling upon the Chinese friend.

Just as they turned a corner leading up to the street where Wou Sankwei's place of business and residence was situated, a pair of little hands grasped Mrs. Dean's skirt and a delighted little voice piped: "See me! See me!" It was little Yen, resplendent in mauve-colored pantaloons and embroidered vest and cap. Behind him was a tall man whom both women recognized.

"How do you happen to have Yen with you?" Adah asked.

"His father handed him over to me as a sort of guide, counsellor, and friend. The little fellow is very amusing."

"See over here," interrupted Yen. He hopped over the alley to where the priests stood by the altar. The grown people followed him.

"What is that man chanting?" asked Adah. One of the priests had mounted a table, and with arms outstretched towards the moon sailing high in the heavens, seemed to be making some sort of an invocation.

Her friend listened for some moments before replying:

"It is a sort of apotheosis of the moon. I have heard it on a like occasion in Hankow, and the Chinese *bonze* who officiated gave me a translation. I almost know it by heart. May I repeat it to you?"

Mrs. Dean and Yen were examining the screen with the big josses.

"Yes, I should like to hear it," said Adah.

"Then fix your eyes upon Diana."

"Dear and lovely moon, as I watch thee pursuing thy solitary course o'er the silent heavens, heart-easing thoughts steal o'er me and calm my passionate soul. Thou art so sweet, so serious, so serene, that thou causest me to forget the stormy emotions which crash like jarring discords across the harmony of life, and bringest to my memory a voice scarce ever heard amidst the warring of the world—love's low voice.

"Thou art so peaceful and so pure that it seemeth as if naught false or ignoble could dwell beneath thy gentle radiance, and that earnestness— even the earnestness of genius—must glow within the bosom of him on whose head thy beams fall like blessings.

"The magic of thy sympathy disburtheneth me of many sorrows, and thoughts, which, like the songs of the sweetest sylvan singer, are too dear and sacred for the careless ears of day, gush forth with unconscious eloquence when thou art the only listener.

"Dear and lovely moon, there are some who say that those who dwell in the sunlit fields of reason should fear to wander through the moonlit valleys of imagination; but I, who have ever been a pilgrim and a stranger in the realm of the wise, offer to thee the homage of a heart which appreciates that thou graciously shinest—even on the fool."

"Is that really Chinese?" queried Adah.

"No doubt about it—in the main. Of course, I cannot swear to it word for word."

"I should think that there would be some reference to the fruits of the earth—the harvest. I always understood that the Chinese religion was so practical."

"Confucianism is. But the Chinese mind requires two religions. Even the most commonplace Chinese has yearnings for something above everyday life. Therefore, he combines with his Confucianism, Buddhism—or, in this country, Christianity."

"Thank you for the information. It has given me a key to the mind of a certain Chinese in whom Auntie and I are interested."

"And who is this particular Chinese in whom you are interested."

"The father of the little boy who is with us tonight."

"Wou Sankwei! Why, here he comes with Lee Tong Hay. Are you acquainted with Lee Tong Hay?"

"No, but I believe Aunt is. Plays and sings in vaudeville, doesn't he?"

"Yes; he can turn himself into a German, a Scotchman, an Irishman, or an American, with the greatest ease, and is as natural in each character as he is as a Chinaman. Hello, Lee Tong Hay."

"Hello, Mr. Stimson."

While her friend was talking to the lively young Chinese who had answered his greeting, Adah went over to where Wou Sankwei stood speaking to Mrs. Dean.

"Yen begins school next week," said her aunt, drawing her arm within her own. It was time to go home.

Adah made no reply. She was settling her mind to do something quite out of the ordinary. Her aunt often called her romantic and impractical. Perhaps she was.

VI

Auntie went out of town this morning," said Adah Charlton. "I, 'phoned for you to come up, Sankwei because I wished to have a personal and private talk with you."

"Any trouble, Miss Adah," inquired the young merchant. "Anything I can do for you?"

Mrs. Dean often called upon him to transact little business matters for her or to consult with him on various phases of her social and family life.

"I don't know what I would do without Sankwei's head to manage for me," she often said to her niece.

"No," replied the girl, "you do too much for us. You always have, ever since I've known you. It's a shame for us to have allowed you."

"What are you talking about, Miss Adah? Since I came to America your aunt has made this house like a home to me, and, of course, I take an interest in it and like to do anything for it that a man can. I am always happy when I come here."

"Yes, I know you are, poor old boy," said Adah to herself.

Aloud she said: "I have something to say to you which I would like you to hear. Will you listen, Sankwei?"

"Of course I will," he answered.

"Well then," went on Adah, "I asked you to come here today because I have heard that there is trouble at your house and that your wife is jealous of you."

"Would you please not talk about that, Miss Adah. It is a matter which you cannot understand."

"You promised to listen and heed. I do understand, even though I cannot speak to your wife nor find out what she feels and thinks. I know you, Sankwei, and I can see just how the trouble has arisen. As soon as I heard that your wife was jealous I knew why she was jealous."

"Why?" he queried.

"Because," she answered unflinchingly, "you are thinking far too much of other women."

"Too much of other women?" echoed Sankwei dazedly. "I did not know that."

"No, you didn't. That is why I am telling you. But you are, Sankwei. And you are becoming too Americanized. My aunt encourages you to become so, and she is a good woman, with the best and highest of motives; but we are all liable to make mistakes, and it is a mistake to try and make a Chinese man into an American—if he has a wife who is to remain as she always has been. It would be different if you were not married and were a man free to advance. But you are not."

"What am I to do then, Miss Adah? You say that I think too much of other women besides her, and that I am too much Americanized. What can I do about it now that it is so?"

"First of all you must think of your wife. She has done for you what no American woman would do—came to you to be your wife, love you and serve you without even knowing you—took you on trust altogether. You must remember that for many years she was chained in a little cottage to care for your ailing and aged mother—a hard task indeed for a young girl. You must remember that you are the only man in the world to her, and that you have always been the only one that she has ever cared for. Think of her during all the years you are here, living a lonely hard-working life—a baby and an old woman her only companions. For this, she had left all her own relations. No American woman would have sacrificed herself so.

"And, now, what has she? Only you and her housework. The white woman reads, plays, paints, attends concerts, entertainments, lectures, absorbs herself in the work she likes, and in the course of her life thinks of and cares for a great many people. She has much to make her happy besides her husband. The Chinese woman has him only."

"And her boy."

"Yes, her boy," repeated Adah Charlton, smiling in spite of herself, but lapsing into seriousness the moment after. "There's another reason for you to drop the American for a time and go back to being a Chinese. For sake of your darling little boy, you and your wife should live together kindly and cheerfully. That is much more important for his welfare than that he should go to the American school and become Americanized."

"It is my ambition to put him through both American and Chinese schools."

"But what he needs most of all is a loving mother."

"She loves him all right."

"Then why do you not love her as you should? If I were married I would not think my husband loved me very much if he preferred spending his evenings in the society of other women than in mine, and was so much more polite and deferential to other women than he was to me. Can't you understand now why your wife is jealous?"

Wou Sankwei stood up.

"Goodbye," said Adah Charlton, giving him her hand.

"Goodbye," said Wou Sankwei.

Had he been a white man, there is no doubt that Adah Charlton's little lecture would have had a contrary effect from what she meant it to have. At least, the lectured would have been somewhat cynical as to her sincerity. But Wou Sankwei was not a white man. He was a Chinese, and did not see any reason for insincerity in a matter as important as that which Adah Charlton had brought before him. He felt himself exiled from Paradise, yet it did not occur to him to question, as a white man would have done, whether the angel with the flaming sword had authority for her action. Neither did he lay the blame for things gone wrong upon any woman. He simply made up his mind to make the best of what was.

VII

It had been a peaceful week in the Wou household—the week before little Yen was to enter the American school. So peaceful indeed that Wou Sankwei had begun to think that his wife was reconciled to his wishes with regard to the boy. He whistled softly as he whittled away at a little ship he was making for him. Adah Charlton's suggestions had set coursing a train of thought which had curved around Pau Lin so closely that he had decided that, should she offer any further opposition to the boy's attending the American school, he would not insist upon it. After all, though the American language might be useful during this century, the wheel of the world would turn again, and then it might not be necessary at all. Who could tell? He came very near to expressing himself thus to Pau Lin.

And now it was the evening before the morning that little Yen was to march away to the American school. He had been excited all day over the prospect, and to calm him, his father finally told him to read aloud a little story from the Chinese book which he had given him on his first birthday in America and which he had taught him to read. Obediently the little fellow drew his stool to his mother's side and read in his childish sing-song the story of an irreverent lad who came to great grief because he followed after the funeral of his grandfather and regaled himself on the crisply roasted chickens and loose-skinned oranges which were left on the grave for the feasting of the spirit.

Wou Sankwei laughed heartily over the story. It reminded him of some of his own boyish escapades. But Pau Lin stroked silently the head of the little reader, and seemed lost in reverie.

A whiff of fresh salt air blew in from the Bay. The mother shivered, and Wou Sankwei, looking up from the fastening of the boat's rigging, bade Yen close the door. As the little fellow came back to his mother's side, he stumbled over her knee.

"Oh, poor mother!" he exclaimed with quaint apology. "'Twas the stupid feet, not Yen."

"So," she replied, curling her arm around his neck, "'tis always the feet. They are to the spirit as the cocoon to the butterfly. Listen, and I will sing you the song of the Happy Butterfly."

She began singing the old Chinese ditty in a fresh birdlike voice. Wou Sankwei, listening, was glad to hear her. He liked having everyone around him cheerful and happy. That had been the charm of the Dean household.

The ship was finished before the little family retired. Yen examined it, critically at first, then exultingly. Finally, he carried it away and placed it carefully in the closet where he kept his kites, balls, tops, and other treasures. "We will set sail with it tomorrow after school," said he to his father, hugging gratefully that father's arm.

Sankwei rubbed the little round head. The boy and he were great chums.

• • •

What was that sound which caused Sankwei to start from his sleep? It was just on the border land of night and day, an unusual time for Pau Lin to be up. Yet, he could hear her voice in Yen's room. He raised himself on his elbow and listened. She was softly singing a nursery song about some little squirrels and a huntsman. Sankwei wondered at her singing in that way at such an hour. From where he lay he could just perceive the child's cot and the silent child figure lying motionless in the dim light. How very motionless! In a moment Sankwei was beside it.

The empty cup with its dark dregs told the tale.

The thing he loved the best in all the world—the darling son who had crept into his heart with his joyousness and beauty—had been taken from him—by her who had given.

Sankwei reeled against the wall. The kneeling figure by the cot arose. The face of her was solemn and tender.

"He is saved," smiled she, "from the Wisdom of the New."

In grief too bitter for words the father bowed his head upon his hands.

"Why! Why!" queried Pau Lin, gazing upon him bewilderedly. "The child is happy. The butterfly mourns not o'er the shed cocoon." Sankwei put up his shutters and wrote this note to Adah Charlton:

> I have lost my boy through an accident. I am returning to China with my wife whose health requires a change.

"Its Wavering Image"

I

Pan was a half white, half Chinese girl. Her mother was dead, and Pan lived with her father who kept an Oriental Bazaar on Dupont Street. All her life had Pan lived in Chinatown, and if she were different in any sense from those around her, she gave little thought to it. It was only after the coming of Mark Carson that the mystery of her nature began to trouble her.

They met at the time of the boycott of the Sam Yups by the See Yups. After the heat and dust and unsavoriness of the highways and byways of Chinatown, the young reporter who had been sent to find a story, had stepped across the threshold of a cool, deep room, fragrant with the odor of dried lilies and sandalwood, and found Pan.

She did not speak to him, nor he to her. His business was with the spectacled merchant, who, with a pointed brush, was making up accounts in brown paper books and rolling balls in an abacus box. As to Pan, she always turned from whites. With her father's people she was natural and at home; but in the presence of her mother's she felt strange and constrained, shrinking from their curious scrutiny as she would from the sharp edge of a sword.

When Mark Carson returned to the office, he asked some questions concerning the girl who had puzzled him. What was she? Chinese or white? The city editor answered him, adding: "She is an unusually bright girl, and could tell more stories about the Chinese than any other person in this city—if she would."

Mark Carson had a determined chin, clever eyes, and a tone to his voice which easily won for him the confidence of the unwary. In the reporter's room he was spoken of as "a man who would sell his soul for a story."

After Pan's first shyness had worn off, he found her bewilderingly frank and free with him; but he had all the instincts of a gentleman save one, and made no ordinary mistake about her. He was Pan's first white friend. She was born a Bohemian, exempt from the conventional restrictions imposed upon either the white or Chinese woman; and the Oriental who was her father mingled with his affection for his child so great a respect for and trust in the daughter of the dead white woman, that everything she did or said was right to him. And Pan herself! A white woman might pass over an insult; a Chinese woman fail to see one. But Pan! He would be a brave man indeed who offered one to childish little Pan.

All this Mark Carson's clear eyes perceived, and with delicate tact and subtlety he taught the young girl that, all unconscious until his coming, she had lived her life alone. So well did she learn this lesson that it seemed at times as if her white self must entirely dominate and trample under foot her Chinese.

Meanwhile, in full trust and confidence, she led him about Chinatown, initiating him into the simple mystery and history of many things, for which she, being of her father's race, had a tender regard and pride. For her sake he was received as a brother by the yellow-robed priest in the joss house, the Astrologer of Prospect Place, and other conservative Chinese. The Water Lily Club opened its doors to him when she knocked, and the Sublimely Pure Brothers' organization admitted him as one of its honorary members, thereby enabling him not only to see but to take part in a ceremony in which no American had ever before participated. With her by his side, he was welcomed wherever he went. Even the little Chinese women in the midst of their babies, received him with gentle smiles, and the children solemnly munched his candies and repeated nursery rhymes for his edification.

He enjoyed it all, and so did Pan. They were both young and light-hearted. And when the afternoon was spent, there was always that high room open to the stars, with its China bowls full of flowers and its big colored lanterns, shedding a mellow light.

Sometimes there was music. A Chinese band played three evenings a week in the gilded restaurant beneath them, and the louder the gongs sounded and the fiddlers fiddled, the more delighted was Pan. Just below the restaurant was her father's bazaar. Occasionally Mun You would stroll upstairs and inquire of the young couple if there was anything needed to complete their felicity, and Pan would answer: "Thou only." Pan was very proud of her Chinese father. "I would rather have a Chinese for a father than a white man," she often told Mark Carson. The last time she had said that he had asked whom she would prefer for a husband, a white man or a Chinese. And Pan, for the first time since he had known her, had no answer for him.

II

It was a cool, quiet evening, after a hot day. A new moon was in the sky.

"How beautiful above! How unbeautiful below!" exclaimed Mark Carson involuntarily.

He and Pan had been gazing down from their open retreat into the lantern-lighted, motley-thronged street beneath them.

"Perhaps it isn't very beautiful," replied Pan, "but it is here I live. It is my home." Her voice quivered a little.

He leaned towards her suddenly and grasped her hands.

"Pan," he cried, "you do not belong here. You are white—white."

"No! no!" protested Pan.

"You are," he asserted. "You have no right to be here."

"I was born here," she answered, "and the Chinese people look upon me as their own."

"But they do not understand you," he went on. "Your real self is alien to them. What interest have they in the books you read—the thoughts you think?"

"They have an interest in me," answered faithful Pan. "Oh, do not speak in that way any more."

"But I must," the young man persisted. "Pan, don't you see that you have got to decide what you will be—Chinese or white? You cannot be both."

"Hush! Hush!" bade Pan. "I do not love you when you talk to me like that."

A little Chinese boy brought tea and saffron cakes. He was a picturesque little fellow with a quaint manner of speech. Mark Carson jested merrily with him, while Pan holding a tea-bowl between her two small hands laughed and sipped.

When they were alone again, the silver stream and the crescent moon became the objects of their study. It was a very beautiful evening.

After a while Mark Carson, his hand on Pan's shoulder, sang:

> "And forever, and forever,
> As long as the river flows,
> As long as the heart has passions,
> As long as life has woes,
> The moon and its broken reflection,
> And its shadows shall appear,
> As the symbol of love in heaven,
> And its wavering image here."

Listening to that irresistible voice singing her heart away, the girl broke down and wept. She was so young and so happy.

"Look up at me," bade Mark Carson. "Oh, Pan! Pan! Those tears prove that you are white."

Pan lifted her wet face.

"Kiss me, Pan," said he. It was the first time.

Next morning Mark Carson began work on the special-feature article which he had been promising his paper for some weeks.

III

Cursed be his ancestors," bayed Man You.

He cast a paper at his daughter's feet and left the room.

Startled by her father's unwonted passion, Pan picked up the paper, and in the clear passionless light of the afternoon read that which forever after was blotted upon her memory.

"Betrayed! Betrayed! Betrayed to be a betrayer!"

It burnt red hot; agony unrelieved by words, unassuaged by tears.

So till evening fell. Then she stumbled up the dark stairs which led to the high room open to the stars and tried to think it out. Someone had hurt her. Who was it? She raised her eyes. There shone: "Its Wavering Image." It helped her to lucidity. He had done it. Was it unconsciously dealt—that cruel blow? Ah, well did he know that the sword which pierced her through others, would carry with it to her own heart, the pain of all those others. None knew better than he that she, whom he had called "a white girl, a white woman," would rather that her own naked body and soul had been exposed, than that things, sacred and secret to those who loved her, should be cruelly unveiled and ruthlessly spread before the ridiculing and uncomprehending foreigner. And knowing all this so well, so well, he had carelessly sung her heart away, and with her kiss upon his lips, had smilingly turned and stabbed her. She, who was of the race that remembers.

IV

Mark Carson, back in the city after an absence of two months, thought of Pan. He would see her that very evening. Dear little Pan, pretty Pan, clever Pan, amusing Pan; Pan, who was always so frankly glad to have him come to her; so eager to hear all that he was doing; so appreciative, so inspiring, so loving. She would have forgotten that article by now. Why should a white woman care about such things? Her true self was above it all. Had he not taught her *that* during the weeks in which they had seen so much of one another? True, his last lesson had been a little harsh, and as yet he knew not how she had taken it; but even if its roughness had hurt and irritated, there was a healing balm, a wizard's oil which none knew so well as he how to apply.

But for all these soothing reflections, there was an undercurrent of feeling which caused his steps to falter on his way to Pan. He turned into Portsmouth Square and took a seat on one of the benches facing the fountain erected in memory of Robert Louis Stevenson. Why had Pan failed to answer the note he had written telling her of the assignment which would keep him out of town for a couple of months and giving her his address? Would Robert Louis Stevenson have known why? Yes—and so did Mark Carson. But though Robert Louis Stevenson would have boldly answered himself the question, Mark Carson thrust it aside, arose, and pressed up the hill.

"I knew they would not blame you, Pan!"

"Yes."

"And there was no word of you, dear. I was careful about that, not only for your sake, but for mine."

Silence.

"It is mere superstition anyway. These things have got to be exposed and done away with."

Still silence.

Mark Carson felt strangely chilled. Pan was not herself tonight. She did not even look herself. He had been accustomed to seeing her in American dress. Tonight she wore the Chinese costume. But for her clear-cut features she might have been a Chinese girl. He shivered.

"Pan," he asked, "why do you wear that dress?"

Within her sleeves Pan's small hands struggled together; but her face and voice were calm.

"Because I am a Chinese woman," she answered.

"You are not," cried Mark Carson, fiercely. "You cannot say that now, Pan. You are a white woman—white. Did your kiss not promise me that?"

"A white woman!" echoed Pan her voice rising high and clear to the stars above them. "I would not be a white woman for all the world. *You* are a white man. And *what* is a promise to a white man!"

• • •

When she was lying low, the element of Fire having raged so fiercely within her that it had almost shriveled up the childish frame, there came to the house of Man You a little toddler who could scarcely speak. Climbing upon Pan's couch, she pressed her head upon the sick girl's bosom. The feel of that little head brought tears.

"Lo!" said the mother of the toddler. "Thou wilt bear a child thyself some day, and all the bitterness of this will pass away."

And Pan, being a Chinese woman, was comforted.

The Story of One White Woman Who Married a Chinese

I

Why did I marry Liu Kanghi, a Chinese? Well, in the first place, because I loved him; in the second place, because I was weary of working, struggling and fighting with the world; in the third place, because my child needed a home.

My first husband was an American fifteen years older than myself. For a few months I was very happy with him. I had been a working girl—a stenographer. A home of my own filled my heart with joy. It was a pleasure to me to wait upon James, cook him nice little dinners and suppers, read to him little pieces from the papers and magazines, and sing and play to him my little songs and melodies. And for a few months he seemed to be perfectly contented. I suppose I was a novelty to him, he having lived a bachelor existence until he was thirty-four. But it was not long before he left off smiling at my little jokes, grew restive and cross when I teased him, and when I tried to get him to listen to a story in which I was interested and longed to communicate, he would bid me not bother him. I was quick to see the change and realize that there was a gulf of differences between us. Nevertheless, I loved and was proud of him. He was considered a very bright and well-informed man, and although his parents had been uneducated working people he had himself been through the public schools. He was also an omnivorous reader of socialistic and new-thought literature. Woman suffrage was one of his particular hobbies. Whenever I had a magazine around he would pick it up and read aloud to me the columns of advice to women who were ambitious to become com-rades to men and walk shoulder to shoulder with their brothers. Once I ventured to remark that much as I admired a column of men keeping step together, yet men and women thus ranked would, to my mind, make a very unbeautiful and disorderly spectacle. He frowned and answered that I did not understand him, and was too frivolous. He would often draw my attention to newspaper reports concerning women of marked business ability and enterprise. Once I told him that I did not admire clever business women, as I had usually found them, and so had other girls of my acquaintance, not nearly so kind-hearted, generous, and helpful as the humble drudges of the world—the ordinary working women. His answer to this was that I was jealous and childish.

But, in spite of his unkind remarks and evident contempt for me, I wished to please him. He was my husband and I loved him. Many an afternoon, when through with my domestic duties, did I spend in trying to acquire a knowledge of labor politics, socialism, woman suffrage, and baseball, the things in which he was most interested.

It was hard work, but I persevered until one day. It was about six months after our marriage. My husband came home a little earlier than usual, and found me engaged in trying to work out problems in subtraction and addition. He laughed sneeringly. "Give it up, Minnie," said he. "You weren't built for anything but taking care of kids. Gee! But there's a woman at our place who has a head for figures that makes her worth over a hundred dollars a month. *Her* husband would have a chance to develop himself."

This speech wounded me. I knew it was James' ambition to write a book on social reform.

The next day, unknown to my husband, I called upon the wife of the man who had employed me as stenographer before I was married, and inquired of her whether she thought I could get back my old position.

"But, my dear," she exclaimed, "your husband is receiving a good salary! Why should you work?"

I told her that my husband had in mind the writing of a book on social reform, and I wished to help him in his ambition by earning some money towards its publication.

"Social reform!" she echoed. "What sort of social reformer is he who would allow his wife to work when he is well able to support her!"

She bade me go home and think no more of an office position. I was disappointed. I said: "Oh! I wish I could earn some money for James. If I were earning money, perhaps he would not think me so stupid."

"Stupid, my dear girl! You are one of the brightest little women I know," kindly comforted Mrs. Rogers.

But I knew differently and went on to tell her of my inability to figure with my husband how much he had made on certain sales, of my lack of interest in politics, labor questions, woman suffrage, and world reformation. "Oh! I cried, "I am a narrow-minded woman. All I care for is for my husband to love me and be kind to me, for life to be pleasant and easy, and to be able to help a wee bit the poor and sick around me."

Mrs. Rogers looked very serious as she told me that there were differences of opinion as to what was meant by "narrow-mindedness," and that the majority of men had no wish to drag their wives into all their business perplexities, and found more comfort in a woman who was unlike rather than like themselves. Only that morning her husband had said to her: "I hate a woman who tries to get into every kink of a man's mind, and who must be forever at his elbow meddling with all his affairs."

I went home comforted. Perhaps after a while James would feel and see as did Mr. Rogers. Vain hope!

My child was six weeks old when I entered business life again as stenographer for Rutherford & Rutherford. My salary was fifty dollars a month—more than I had ever earned before, and James was well pleased, for he had feared that it would be difficult for me to obtain a paying place after having been out of practise for so long. This fifty dollars paid for all our living expenses, with the exception of rent, so that James would be able to put by his balance against the time when his book would be ready for publication.

He began writing his book, and Miss Moran the young woman bookkeeper at his place collaborated with him. They gave three evenings a week to the work, sometimes four. She came one evening when the baby was sick and James had gone for the doctor. She looked at the child with the curious eyes of one who neither loved nor understood children. "There is no necessity for its being sick," said she. "There must be an error somewhere." I made no answer, so she went on: "Sin, sorrow, and sickness all mean the same thing. We have no disease that we do not deserve, no trouble which we do not bring upon ourselves."

I did not argue with her. I knew that I could not; but as I looked at her standing there in the prime of her life and strength, broad-shouldered, masculine-featured, and, as it seemed to me, heartless, I disliked her more than I had ever disliked anyone before. My own father had died after suffering for many years from a terrible malady, contracted while doing his duty as a physician and surgeon. And my little innocent child! What had sin to do with its measles?

When James came in she discussed with him the baseball game which had been played that afternoon, and also a woman suffrage meeting which she had attended the evening before.

After she had gone he seemed to be quite exhilarated. "That's a great woman!" he remarked.

"I do not think so!" I answered him. "One who would take from the sorrowful and suffering their hope of a happier existence hereafter, and add to their trials on earth by branding them as objects of aversion and contempt, is not only not a great woman but, to my mind, no woman at all."

He picked up a paper and walked into another room.

"What do you think now?" I cried after him.

"What would be the use of my explaining to you?" he returned. "You wouldn't understand."

How my heart yearned over my child those days! I would sit before the typewriter and in fancy hear her crying for her mother. Poor, sick little one, watched over by a strange woman, deprived of her proper nourishment. While I took dictation from my employer I thought only of her. The result, of course, was, that I lost my place. My husband showed his displeasure at this in various ways, and as the weeks went by and I was unsuccessful in obtaining another position, he became colder and more indifferent. He was neither a drinking nor an abusive man; but he could say such cruel and cutting things that I would a hundred times rather have been beaten and ill-used than compelled, as I was, to hear them. He even made me feel it a disgrace to be a woman and a mother. Once he said to me: "If you had had ambition of the right sort you would have perfected yourself in your stenography so that you could have taken cases in court. There's a little fortune in that business."

I was acquainted with a woman stenographer who reported divorce cases and who had described to me the work, so I answered: "I would rather die of hunger, my baby in my arms, then report divorce proceedings under the eyes of men in a court house."

"Other women, as good as you, have done and are doing it," he retorted.

"Other women, perhaps better than I, have done and are doing it," I replied, "but all women are not alike. I am not that kind."

"That's so," said he. "Well, they are the kind who are up to date. You are behind the times."

One evening I left James and Miss Moran engaged with their work and went across the street to see a sick friend. When I returned I let myself into the house very softly for fear of awakening the baby whom I had left sleeping. As I stood in the hall I heard my husband's voice in the sitting-room. This is what he was saying:

"I am a lonely man. There is no companionship between me and my wife."

"Nonsense!" answered Miss Moran, as I thought a little impatiently. "Look over this paragraph, please, and tell me if you do not think it would be well to have it follow after the one ending with the words 'ultimate concord,' in place of that beginning with 'These great principles.'"

"I cannot settle my mind upon the work tonight," said James in a sort of thick, tired voice. "I want to talk to you—to win your sympathy—your love."

I heard a chair pushed back. I knew Miss Moran had arisen.

"Good night!" I heard her say. "Much as I would like to see this work accomplished, I shall come no more!"

"But, my God! You cannot throw the thing up at this late date."

"I can and I will. Let me pass, sir."

"If there were no millstone around my neck, you would not say, 'Let me pass, sir, in that tone of voice.'"

The next I heard was a heavy fall. Miss Moran had knocked my big husband down.

I pushed open the door. Miss Moran, cool and collected, was pulling on her gloves. James was struggling to his feet.

"Oh, Mrs. Carson!" exclaimed the former. "Your husband fell over the stool. Wasn't it stupid of him!"

• • •

James, of course, got his divorce six months after I deserted him. He did not ask for the child, and I was allowed to keep it.

II

I was on my way to the waterfront, the baby in my arms. I was walking quickly, for my state of mind was such that I could have borne twice my burden and not have felt it. Just as I turned down a hill which led to the docks, someone touched my arm and I heard a voice say:

"Pardon me, lady; but you have dropped your baby's shoe!"

"Oh, yes!" I answered, taking the shoe mechanically from an outstretched hand, and pushing on.

I could hear the waves lapping against the pier when the voice again fell upon my ear.

"If you go any further, lady, you will fall into the water!"

My answer was a step forward.

A strong hand was laid upon my arm and I was swung around against my will.

"Poor little baby," went on the voice, which was unusually soft for a man's. "Let me hold him!"

I surrendered my child to the voice.

"Better come over where it is light and you can see where to walk!"

I allowed myself to be led into the light.

Thus I met Liu Kanghi, the Chinese who afterwards became my husband. I followed him, obeyed him, trusted him from the very first. It never occurred to me to ask myself what manner of man was succoring me. I only knew that he was a man, and that I was being cared for as no one had ever cared for me since my father died. And my grim determination to leave a world which had been cruel to me, passed away—and in its place I experienced a strange calmness and content.

"I am going to take you to the house of a friend of mine," he said as he preceded me up the hill, the baby in his arms.

"You will not mind living with Chinese people?" he added.

An electric light under which we were passing flashed across his face.

I did not recoil—not even at first. It may have been because he was wearing American clothes, wore his hair cut, and, even to my American eyes, appeared a good-looking young man—and it may have been because of my troubles; but whatever it was I answered him, and I meant it: "I would much rather live with Chinese than Americans."

He did not ask me why, and I did not tell him until long afterwards the story of my unhappy marriage, my desertion of the man who had made it impossible for me to remain under his roof; the shame of the divorce, the averted faces of those who had been my friends; the cruelty of the world; the awful struggle for an existence for myself and child; sickness followed by despair.

The Chinese family with which he placed me were kind, simple folk. The father had been living in America for more than twenty years. The family consisted of his wife, a grown daughter, and several small sons and daughters, all of whom had been born in America. They made me very welcome and adored the baby. Liu Jusong, the father, was a working jeweler; but, because of an accident by which he had lost the use of one hand, was partially incapacitated for work. Therefore, their family depended for maintenance chiefly upon their kinsman, Liu Kanghi, the Chinese who had brought me to them.

"We love much our cousin," said one of the little girls to me one day. "He teaches us so many games and brings us toys and sweets."

As soon as I recovered from the attack of nervous prostration which laid me low for over a month after being received into the Liu home, my mind began to form plans for my own and my child's maintenance. One morning I put on my hat and jacket and told Mrs. Liu I would go down town and make an application for work as a stenographer at the different typewriting offices. She pleaded with me to wait a week longer — until, as she said, "your limbs are more fortified with strength"; but I assured her that I felt myself well able to begin to do for myself, and that I was anxious to repay some little part of the expense I had been to them.

"For all we have done for you," she answered, "our cousin has paid us doublefold."

"No money can recompense your kindness to myself and child," I replied; "but if it is your cousin to whom I am indebted for board and lodging, all the greater is my anxiety to repay what I owe."

When I returned to the house that evening, tired out with my quest for work, I found Liu Kanghi tossing ball with little Fong in the front porch.

Mrs. Liu bustled out to meet me and began scolding in motherly fashion.

"Oh, why you go down town before you strong enough? See! You look all sick again!" said she.

She turned to Liu Kanghi and said something in Chinese. He threw the ball back to the boy and came toward me, his face grave and concerned.

"Please be so good as to take my cousin's advice," he urged.

"I am well enough to work now," I replied, "and I cannot sink deeper into your debt."

"You need not," said he. "I know a way by which you can quickly pay me off and earn a good living without wearing yourself out and leaving the baby all day. My cousin tells me that you can create most beautiful flowers on silk, velvet, and linen. Why not then you do some of that work for my store? I will buy all you can make."

"Oh!" I exclaimed, "I should be only too glad to do such work! But do you really think I can earn a living in that way?"

"You certainly can," was his reply. "I am requiring an embroiderer, and if you will do the work for me I will try to pay you what it is worth."

So I gladly gave up my quest for office work. I lived in the Liu Jusong house and worked for Liu Kanghi. The days, weeks, and months passed peacefully and happily. Artistic needlework had always been my favorite occupation, and when it became a source both of remuneration and pleasure, I began to feel that life was worth living, after all. I watched with complacency my child grow amongst the little Chinese children. My life's experience had taught me that the virtues do not all belong to the whites. I was interested in all that concerned the Liu household, became acquainted with all their friends, and lost altogether the prejudice against the foreigner in which I had been reared.

I had been living thus more than a year when, one afternoon as I was walking home from Liu Kanghi's store on Kearney Street, a parcel of silks and floss under my arm, and my little girl trudging by my side, I came face to face with James Carson.

"Well, now," said he, planting himself in front of me, "you are looking pretty well. How are you making out?"

I caught up my child and pushed past him without a word. When I reached the Liu house I was trembling in every limb, so great was my dislike and fear of the man who had been my husband.

About a week later a letter came to the house addressed to me. It read:

204 BUCHANAN STREET

DEAR MINNIE, — If you are willing to forget the past and make up, I am, too. I was surprised to see you the other day, prettier than ever — and much more of a woman. Let me know your mind at an early date.

Your affectionate husband,

JAMES

I ignored this letter, but a heavy fear oppressed me. Liu Kanghi, who called the evening of the day I received it, remarked as he arose to greet me that I was looking troubled, and hoped that it was not the embroidery flowers.

"It is the shadow from my big hat," I answered lightly. I was dressed for going down town with Mrs. Liu who was preparing her eldest daughter's trousseau.

"Some day," said Liu Kanghi earnestly, "I hope that you will tell to me all that is in your heart and mind."

I found comfort in his kind face.

"If you will wait until I return, I will tell you all tonight," I answered.

Strange as it may seem, although I had known Liu Kanghi now for more than a year, I had had little talk alone with him, and all he knew about me was what he had learned from Mrs. Liu; namely, that I was a divorced woman who, when saved from self-destruction, was homeless and starving.

That night, however, after hearing my story, he asked me to be his wife. He said: "I love you and would protect you from all trouble. Your child shall be as my own."

I replied: "I appreciate your love and kindness, but I cannot answer you just yet. Be my friend for a little while longer."

"Do you have for me the love feeling?" he asked.

"I do not know," I answered truthfully.

Another letter came. It was written in a different spirit from the first and contained a threat about the child.

There seemed but one course open to me. That was to leave my Chinese friends. I did. With much sorrow and regret I bade them goodbye, and took lodgings in a part of the city far removed from the outskirts of Chinatown where my home had been with the Lius. My little girl pined for her Chinese playmates, and I myself felt strange and lonely; but I knew that if I wished to keep my child I could no longer remain with my friends.

I still continued working for Liu Kanghi, and carried my embroidery to his store in the evening after the little one had been put to sleep. He usually escorted me back; but never asked to be allowed, and I never invited him, to visit me, or even enter the house. I was a young woman, and alone, and what I had suffered from scandal since I had left James Carson had made me wise.

It was a cold, wet evening in November when he accosted me once again. I had run over to a delicatessen store at the corner of the block where I lived. As I stepped out, his burly figure loomed up in the gloom before me. I started back with a little cry, but he grasped my arm and held it.

"Walk beside me quietly if you do not wish to attract attention," said he, "and by God, if you do, I will take the kid tonight!"

"You dare not!" I answered. "You have no right to her whatever. She is my child and I have supported her for the last two years alone."

"Alone! What will the judges say when I tell them about the Chinaman?"

"What will the judges say!" I echoed. "What can they say? Is there any disgrace in working for a Chinese merchant and receiving pay for my labor?"

"And walking in the evening with him, and living for over a year in a house for which he paid the rent. Ha! ha! ha! Ha! ha! ha!"

His laugh was low and sneering. He had evidently been making enquiries concerning the Liu family, and also watching me for some time. How a woman can loathe and hate the man she has once loved!

We were nearing my lodgings. Perhaps the child had awakened and was crying for me. I would not, however, have entered the house, had he not stopped at the door and pushed it open.

"Lead the way upstairs!" said he. "I want to see the kid."

"You shall not," I cried. In my desperation I wrenched myself from his grasp and faced him, blocking the stairs.

"If you use violence," I declared, "the lodgers will come to my assistance. They know me!"

He released my arm.

"Bah!" said he. "I've no use for the kid. It is you I'm after getting reconciled to. Don't you know, Minnie, that once your husband, always your husband? Since I saw you the other day on the street, I have been more in love with you than ever before. Suppose we forget all and begin over again!"

Though the tone of his voice had softened, my fear of him grew greater. I would have fled up the stairs had he not again laid his hand on my arm.

"Answer me, girl," said he.

And in spite of my fear, I shook off his hand and answered him: "No husband of mine are you, either legally or morally. And I have no feeling whatever for you other than contempt."

"Ah! So you have sunk!"—his expression was evil—"The oily little Chink has won you!"

I was no longer afraid of him.

"Won me!" I cried, unheeding who heard me. "Yes, honorably and like a man. And what are you that dare sneer at one like him. For all your six feet of grossness, your small soul cannot measure up to his great one. You were unwilling to protect and care for the woman who was your wife or the little child you caused to come into this world; but he succored and saved the stranger woman, treated her as a woman, with reverence and respect; gave her child a home, and made them both independent, not only of others but of himself. Now, hearing you insult him behind his back, I know, what I did not know before—that I love him, and all I have to say to you is, Go!"

And James Carson went. I heard of him again but once. That was when the papers reported his death of apoplexy while exercising at a public gymnasium.

Loving Liu Kanghi, I became his wife, and though it is true that there are many Americans who look down upon me for so becoming, I have never regretted it. No, not even when men cast upon me the glances they cast upon sporting women. I accept the lot of the American wife of an humble Chinaman in America. The happiness of the man who loves me is more to me than the approval or disapproval of those who in my dark days left me to die like a dog. My Chinese husband has his faults. He is hot-tempered and, at times, arbitrary; but he is always a man, and has never sought to take away from me the privilege of being but a woman. I can lean upon and trust in him. I feel him behind me, protecting and caring for me, and that, to an ordinary woman like myself, means more than anything else.

Only when the son of Liu Kanghi lays his little head upon my bosom do I question whether I have done wisely. For my boy, the son of the Chinese man, is possessed of a childish wisdom which brings the tears to my eyes; and as he stands between his father and myself, like yet unlike us both, so will he stand in after years between his father's and his mother's people. And if there is no kindliness nor understanding between them, what will my boy's fate be?

Her Chinese Husband

Sequel to the Story of the White Woman Who Married a Chinese

Now that Liu Kanghi is no longer with me, I feel that it will ease my heart to record some memories of him—if I can. The task, though calling to me, is not an easy one, so throng to my mind the invincible proofs of his love for me, the things he has said and done. My memories of him are so vivid and pertinacious, my thoughts of him so tender.

To my Chinese husband I could go with all my little troubles and perplexities; to him I could talk as women love to do at times of the past and the future, the mysteries of religion, of life and death. He was not above discussing such things with me. With him I was never strange or embarrassed. My Chinese husband was simple in his tastes. He liked to hear a good story, and though unlearned in a sense, could discriminate between the good and bad in literature. This came of his Chinese education. He told me one day that he thought the stories in the Bible were more like Chinese than American stories, and added: "If you had not told me what you have about it, I should say that it was composed by the Chinese." Music had a soothing though not a deep influence over him. It could not sway his mind, but he enjoyed it just as he did a beautiful picture. Because I was interested in fancy work, so also was he. I can see his face, looking so grave and concerned, because one day by accident I spilt some ink on a piece of embroidery I was working. If he came home in the evenings and found me tired and out of sorts, he would cook the dinner himself, and go about it in such a way that I felt that he rather enjoyed showing off his skill as a cook. The next evening, if he found everything ready, he would humorously declare himself much disappointed that I was so exceedingly well.

At such times a gray memory of James Carson would arise. How his cold anger and contempt, as exhibited on like occasions, had shrivelled me up in the long ago. And then—I would fall to musing on the difference between the two men as lovers and husbands.

James Carson had been much more of an ardent lover than ever had been Liu Kanghi. Indeed it was his passion, real or feigned, which had carried me off my feet. When wooing he had constantly reproached me with being cold, unfeeling, a marble statue, and so forth; and I, poor, ignorant little girl, would wonder how it was I appeared so when I felt so differently. For I had given James Carson my first love. Upon him my life had been concentrated as it has never been concentrated upon any other. Yet—!

There was nothing feigned about my Chinese husband. Simple and sincere as he was before marriage, so was he afterwards. As my union with James Carson had meant misery, bitterness, and narrowness, so my union with Liu Kanghi meant, on the whole, happiness, health, and development. Yet the former, according to American ideas, had been an educated broad-minded man; the other, just an ordinary Chinaman.

But the ordinary Chinaman that I would show to you was the sort of man that children, birds, animals, and some women love. Every morning he would go to the window and call to his pigeons, and they would flock around him, hearing and responding to his whistling and cooing. The rooms we lived in had been his rooms ever since he had come to America. They were above his store, and large and cool. The furniture had been brought from China, but there was nothing of tinsel about it. Dark wood, almost black, carved and antique, some of the pieces set with mother-of-pearl. On one side of the inner room stood a case of books and an ancestral tablet. I have seen Liu Kanghi touch the tablet with reverence, but the faith of his fathers was not strong enough to cause him to bow before it. The elegant simplicity of these rooms had surprised me much when I was first taken to them. I looked at him then, standing for a moment by the window, a solitary pigeon peeking in at him, perhaps wondering who had come to divert from her her friend's attention. So had he lived since he had come to this country—quietly and undisturbed—from twenty years of age to twenty-five. I felt myself an intruder. A feeling of pity for the boy— for such he seemed in his enthusiasm—arose in my breast. Why had I come to confuse his calm? Was it ordained, as he declared?

My little girl loved him better than she loved me. He took great pleasure in playing with her, curling her hair over his fingers, tying her sash, and all the simple tasks from which so many men turn aside.

Once the baby got hold of a set rat trap, and was holding it in such a way that the slightest move would have released the spring and plunged the cruel steel into her tender arms. Kanghi's eyes and mine beheld her thus at the same moment. I stood transfixed with horror. Kanghi quietly went up to the child and took from her the trap. Then he asked me to release his hand. I almost fainted when I saw it. "It was the only way," said he. We had to send for the doctor, and even as it was, came very near having a case of blood poisoning.

I have heard people say that he was a keen business man, this Liu Kanghi, and I imagine that he was. I did not, however, discuss his business with him. All I was interested in were the pretty things and the women who would come in and jest with him. He could jest too. Of course, the women did not know that I was his wife. Once a woman in rich clothes gave him her card and asked him to call upon her. After she had left he passed the card to me. I tore it up. He took those things as a matter of course, and was not affected by them. "They are a part of Chinatown life," he explained.

He was a member of the Reform Club, a Chinese social club, and the Chinese Board of Trade. He liked to discuss business affairs and Chinese and American politics with his countrymen, and occasionally enjoyed an evening away from me. But I never needed to worry over him.

He had his littlenesses as well as his bignesses, had Liu Kanghi. For instance, he thought he knew better about what was good for my health and other things, purely personal, than I did myself, and if my ideas opposed or did not tally with his, he would very vigorously denounce what he called "the foolishness of women." If he admired a certain dress, he would have me wear it on every occasion possible, and did not seem to be able to understand that it was not always suitable.

"Wear the dress with the silver lines," he said to me one day somewhat authoritatively. I was attired for going out, but not as he wished to see me. I answered that the dress with the silver lines was unsuitable for a long and dusty ride on an open car.

"Never mind," said he, "whether it is unsuitable or not. I wish you to wear it."

"All right," I said. "I will wear it, but I will stay at home."

I stayed at home, and so did he.

At another time, he reproved me for certain opinions I had expressed in the presence of some of his countrymen. "You should not talk like that," said he. "They will think you are a bad woman."

My white blood rose at that, and I answered him in a way which grieves me to remember. For Kanghi had never meant to insult or hurt me. Imperious by nature, he often spoke before he thought—and he was so boyishly anxious for me to appear in the best light possible before his own people.

There were other things too: a sort of childish jealousy and suspicion which it was difficult to allay. But a woman can forgive much to a man, the sincerity and strength of whose love makes her own, though true, seem slight and mean.

Yes, life with Liu Kanghi was not without its trials and tribulations. There was the continual uncertainty about his own life here in America, the constant irritation caused by the assumption of the white men that a white woman does not love her Chinese husband, and their actions accordingly; also sneers and offensive remarks. There was also on Liu Kanghi's side an acute consciousness that, though belonging to him as his wife, yet in a sense I was not his, but of the dominant race, which claimed, even while it professed to despise me. This consciousness betrayed itself in words and ways which filled me with a passion of pain and humiliation. "Kanghi," I would sharply say, for I had to cloak my tenderness, "do not talk to me like that. You *are* my superior. . . . I would not love you if you were not."

But in spite of all I could do or say, it was there between us: that strange, invisible—what? Was it the barrier of race—that consciousness?

Sometimes he would talk about returning to China. The thought filled me with horror. I had heard rumors of secondary wives. One afternoon the cousin of Liu Kanghi, with whom I had lived, came to see me, and showed me a letter which she had received from a little Chinese girl who had been born and brought up in America until the age of ten. The last paragraph in the letter read: "Emma and I are very sad and wish we were back in America." Kanghi's cousin explained that the father of the little girls, having no sons, had taken to himself another wife, and the new wife lived with the little girls and their mother.

That was before my little boy was born. That evening I told Kanghi that he need never expect me to go to China with him.

"You see," I began, "I look upon you as belonging to me."

He would not let me say more. After a while he said: "It is true that in China a man may and occasionally does take a secondary wife, but that custom is custom, not only because sons are denied to the first wife, but because the first wife is selected by parents and guardians before a man is hardly a man. If a Chinese marries for love, his life is a filled-up cup, and he wants no secondary wife. No, not even for sake of a son. Take, for example, me, your great husband."

I sometimes commented upon his boyish ways and appearance, which was the reason why, when he was in high spirits, he would call himself my "great husband." He was not boyish always. I have seen him, when shouldering the troubles of kinfolk, the quarrels of his clan, and other responsibilities, acting and looking like a man of twice his years.

But for all the strange marriage customs of my husband's people I considered them far more moral in their lives than the majority of Americans. I expressed myself thus to Liu Kanghi, and he replied: "The American people think higher. If only more of them lived up to what they thought, the Chinese would not be so confused in trying to follow their leadership."

If ever a man rejoiced over the birth of his child, it was Liu Kanghi. The boy was born with a veil over his face. "A prophet!" cried the old mulatto Jewess who nursed me. "A prophet has come into the world."

She told this to his father when he came to look upon him, and he replied: "He is my son; that is all I care about." But he was so glad, and there was feasting and rejoicing with his Chinese friends for over two weeks. He came in one evening and found me weeping over my poor little boy. I shall never forget the expression on his face.

"Oh, shame!" he murmured, drawing my head down to his shoulder. "What is there to weep about? The child is beautiful! The feeling heart, the understanding mind is his. And we will bring him up to be proud that he is of Chinese blood; he will fear none and, after him, the name of half-breed will no longer be one of contempt."

Kanghi as a youth had attended a school in Hong Kong, and while there had made the acquaintance of several half Chinese half English lads. "They were the brightest of all," he told me, "but they lowered themselves in the eyes of the Chinese by being ashamed of their Chinese blood and ignoring it."

His theory, therefore, was that if his own son was brought up to be proud instead of ashamed of his Chinese half, the boy would become a great man.

Perhaps he was right, but he could not see as could I, an American woman, the conflict before our boy.

After the little Kanghi had passed his first month, and we had found a reliable woman to look after him, his father began to take me around with him much more than formerly, and life became very enjoyable.

We dined often at a Chinese restaurant kept by a friend of his, and afterwards attended theatres, concerts, and other places of entertainment. We frequently met Americans with whom he had become acquainted through business, and he would introduce them with great pride in me shining in his eyes. The little jealousies and suspicions of the first year seemed no longer to irritate him, and though I had still cause to shrink from the gaze of strangers, I know that my Chinese husband was for several years a very happy man.

· · ·

Now, I have come to the end. He left home one morning, followed to the gate by the little girl and boy (we had moved to a cottage in the suburbs).

"Bring me a red ball," pleaded the little girl.

"And me too," cried the boy.

"All right, chickens," he responded, waving his hand to them.

He was brought home at night, shot through the head. There are some Chinese, just as there are some Americans, who are opposed to all progress, and who hate with a bitter hatred all who would enlighten or be enlightened.

But that I have not the heart to dwell upon. I can only remember that when they brought my Chinese husband home there were two red balls in his pocket. Such was Liu Kanghi—a man.

The Americanizing of Pau Tsu

I

When Wan Hom Hing came to Seattle to start a branch of the merchant business which his firm carried on so successfully in the different ports of China, he brought with him his nephew, Wan Lin Fo, then eighteen years of age. Wan Lin Fo was a well-educated Chinese youth, with bright eyes and keen ears. In a few years' time he knew as much about the business as did any of the senior partners. Moreover, he learned to speak and write the American language with such fluency that he was never at a loss for an answer, when the white man, as was sometimes the case, sought to pose him. "All work and no play," however, is as much against the principles of a Chinese youth as it is against those of a young American, and now and again Lin Fo would while away an evening at the Chinese Literary Club, above the Chinese restaurant, discussing with some chosen companions the works and merits of Chinese sages—and some other things. New Year's Day, or rather, Week, would also see him, business forgotten, arrayed in national costume of finest silk, and color "the blue of the sky after rain," visiting with his friends, both Chinese and American, and scattering silver and gold coin amongst the youngsters of the families visited.

It was on the occasion of one of these New Year's visits that Wan Lin Fo first made known to the family of his firm's silent American partner, Thomas Raymond, that he was betrothed. It came about in this wise: One of the young ladies of the house, who was fair and frank of face and friendly and cheery in manner, observing as she handed him a cup of tea that Lin Fo's eyes wore a rather wistful expression, questioned him as to the wherefore:

"Miss Adah," replied Lin Fo, "may I tell you something?"

"Certainly, Mr. Wan," replied the girl. "You know how I enjoy hearing your tales."

"But this is no tale. Miss Adah, you have inspired in me a love—"

Adah Raymond started. Wan Lin Fo spake slowly.

"For the little girl in China to whom I am betrothed."

"Oh, Mr. Wan! That is good news. But what have I to do with it?"

"This, Miss Adah! Every time I come to this house, I see you, so good and so beautiful, dispensing tea and happiness to all around, and I think, could I have in my home and ever by my side one who is also both good and beautiful, what a felicitious life mine would be!"

"You must not flatter me, Mr. Wan!"

"All that I say is founded on my heart. But I will speak not of you. I will speak of Pau Tsu."

"Pau Tsu?"

"Yes. That is the name of my future wife. It means a pearl."

"How pretty! Tell me all about her!"

"I was betrothed to Pau Tsu before leaving China. My parents adopted her to be my wife. As I remember, she had shining eyes and the good-luck color was on her cheek. Her mouth was like a red vine leaf, and her eyebrows most exquisitely arched. As slender as a willow was her form, and when she spoke, her voice lilted from note to note in the sweetest melody."

Adah Raymond softly clapped her hands.

"Ah! You were even then in love with her."

"No," replied Lin Fo thoughtfully. "I was too young to be in love—sixteen years of age. Pau Tsu was thirteen. But, as I have confessed, you have caused me to remember and love her."

Adah Raymond was not a self-conscious girl, but for the life of her she could think of no reply to Lin Fo's speech.

"I am twenty-two years old now," he continued. "Pau Tsu is eighteen. Tomorrow I will write to my parents and persuade them to send her to me at the time of the spring festival. My elder brother was married last year, and his wife is now under my parents' roof, so that Pau Tsu, who has been the daughter of the house for so many years, can now be spared to me."

"What a sweet little thing she must be," commented Adah Raymond.

"You will say that when you see her," proudly responded Lin Fo. "My parents say she is always happy. There is not a bird or flower or dewdrop in which she does not find some glad meaning."

"I shall be so glad to know her. Can she speak English?"

Lin Fo's face fell.

"No," he replied, "but,"—brightening—"when she comes I will have her learn to speak like you—and be like you."

II

Pau Tsu came with the spring, and Wan Lin Fo was one of the happiest and proudest of bridegrooms. The tiny bride was really very pretty—even to American eyes. In her peach and plum colored robes, her little arms and hands sparkling with jewels, and her shiny black head decorated with wonderful combs and pins, she appeared a bit of Eastern coloring amidst the Western lights and shades.

Lin Fo had not been forgotten, and her eyes under their downcast lids discovered him at once, as he stood awaiting her amongst a group of young Chinese merchants on the deck of the vessel.

The apartments he had prepared for her were furnished in American style, and her birdlike little figure in Oriental dress seemed rather out of place at first. It was not long, however, before she brought forth from the great box, which she had brought over seas, screens and fans, vases, panels, Chinese matting, artificial flowers and birds, and a number of exquisite carvings and pieces of antique porcelain. With these she transformed the American flat into an Oriental bower, even setting up in her sleeping-room a little chapel, enshrined in which was an image of the Goddess of Mercy, two ancestral tablets, and other emblems of her faith in the Gods of her fathers.

The Misses Raymond called upon her soon after arrival, and she smiled and looked pleased. She shyly presented each girl with a Chinese cup and saucer, also a couple of antique vases, covered with whimsical pictures, which Lin Fo tried his best to explain.

The girls were delighted with the gifts, and having fallen, as they expressed themselves, in love with the little bride, invited her through her husband to attend a launch party, which they intended giving the following Wednesday on Lake Washington.

Lin Fo accepted the invitation in behalf of himself and wife. He was quite at home with the Americans and, being a young man, enjoyed their rather effusive appreciation of him as an educated Chinaman. Moreover, he was of the opinion that the society of the American young ladies would benefit Pau Tsu in helping her to acquire the ways and language of the land in which he hoped to make a fortune.

Wan Lin Fo was a true son of the Middle Kingdom and secretly pitied all those who were born far away from its influences; but there was much about the Americans that he admired. He also entertained sentiments of respect for a motto which hung in his room which bore the legend: "When in Rome, do as the Romans do."

"What is best for men is also best for women in this country," he told Pau Tsu when she wept over his suggestion that she should take some lessons in English from a white woman.

"It may be best for a man who goes out in the street," she sobbed, "to learn the new language, but of what importance is it to a woman who lives only within the house and her husband's heart?"

It was seldom, however, that she protested against the wishes of Lin Fo. As her mother-in-law had said, she was a docile, happy little creature. Moreover, she loved her husband.

But as the days and weeks went by the girl bride whose life hitherto had been spent in the quiet retirement of a Chinese home in the performance of filial duties, in embroidery work and lute playing, in sipping tea and chatting with gentle girl companions, felt very much bewildered by the novelty and stir of the new world into which she had been suddenly thrown. She could not understand, for all Lin Fo's explanations, why it was required of her to learn the strangers' language and adopt their ways. Her husband's tongue was the same as her own. So also her little maid's. It puzzled her to be always seeing this and hearing that—sights and sounds which as yet had no meaning for her. Why also was it necessary to receive visitors nearly every evening? —visitors who could neither understand nor make themselves understood by her, for all their curious smiles and stares, which she bore like a second Vashti—or rather, Esther. And why, oh! why should she be constrained to eat her food with clumsy, murderous looking American implements instead of with her own elegant and easily manipulated ivory chopsticks?

Adah Raymond, who at Lin Fo's request was a frequent visitor to the house, could not fail to observe that Pau Tsu's small face grew daily smaller and thinner, and that the smile with which she invariably greeted her, though sweet, was tinged with melancholy. Her woman's instinct told her that something was wrong, but what it was the light within her failed to discover. She would reach over to Pau Tsu and take within her own firm, white hand the small, trembling fingers, pressing them lovingly and sympathetically; and the little Chinese woman would look up into the beautiful face bent above hers and think to herself: "No wonder he wishes me to be like her!"

If Lin Fo happened to come in before Adah Raymond left he would engage the visitor in bright and animated conversation. They had so much of common interest to discuss, as is always the way with young people who have lived any length of time in a growing city of the West. But to Pau Tsu, pouring tea and dispensing sweetmeats, it was all Greek, or rather, all American.

"Look, my pearl, what I have brought you," said Lin Fo one afternoon as he entered his wife's apartments, followed by a messenger-boy, who deposited in the middle of the room a large cardboard box.

With murmurs of wonder Pau Tsu drew near, and the messenger-boy having withdrawn Lin Fo cut the string, and drew forth a beautiful lace evening dress and dark blue walking costume, both made in American style.

For a moment there was silence in the room. Lin Fo looked at his wife in surprise. Her face was pale and her little body was trembling, while her hands were drawn up into her sleeves.

"Why, Pau Tsu!" he exclaimed, "I thought to make you glad."

At these words the girl bent over the dress of filmy lace, and gathering the flounce in her hand smoothed it over her knee; then lifting a smiling face to her husband, replied: "Oh, you are too good, too kind to your unworthy Pau Tsu. My speech is slow, because I am overcome with happiness."

Then with exclamations of delight and admiration she lifted the dresses out of the box and laid them carefully over the couch.

"I wish you to dress like an American woman when we go out or receive," said her husband. "It is the proper thing in America to do as the Americans do. You will notice, light of my eyes, that it is only on New Year and our national holidays that I wear the costume of our country and attach a queue. The wife should follow the husband in all things."

A ripple of laughter escaped Pau Tsu's lips.

"When I wear that dress," said she, touching the walking costume, "I will look like your friend, Miss Raymond."

She struck her hands together gleefully, but when her husband had gone to his business she bowed upon the floor and wept pitifully.

III

During the rainy season Pau Tsu was attacked with a very bad cough. A daughter of Southern China, the chill, moist climate of the Puget Sound winter was very hard on her delicate lungs. Lin Fo worried much over the state of her health, and meeting Adah Raymond on the street one afternoon told her of his anxiety. The kind-hearted girl immediately returned with him to the house. Pau Tsu was lying on her couch, feverish and breathing hard. The American girl felt her hands and head.

"She must have a doctor," said she, mentioning the name of her family's physician.

Pau Tsu shuddered. She understood a little English by this time.

"No! No! Not a man, *not* a man!" she cried.

Adah Raymond looked up at Lin Fo.

"I understand," said she. "There are several women doctors in this town. Let us send for one."

But Lin Fo's face was set.

"No!" he declared. "We are in America. Pau Tsu shall be attended to by your physician."

Adah Raymond was about to protest against this dictum when the sick wife, who had also heard it, touched her hand and whispered: "I not mind now. Man all right."

So the other girl closed her lips, feeling that if the wife would not dispute her husband's will it was not her place to do so; but her heart ached with compassion as she bared Pau Tsu's chest for the stethoscope.

"It was like preparing a lamb for slaughter," she told her sister afterwards. "Pau Tsu was motionless, her eyes closed and her lips sealed, while the doctor remained; but after he had left and we two were alone she shuddered and moaned like one bereft of reason. I honestly believe that the examination was worse than death to that little Chinese woman. The modesty of generations of maternal ancestors was crucified as I rolled down the neck of her silk tunic."

It was a week after the doctor's visit, and Pau Tsu, whose cough had yielded to treatment, though she was still far from well, was playing on her lute, and whisperingly singing this little song, said to have been written on a fan which was presented to an ancient Chinese emperor by one of his wives:

> "Of fresh new silk,
> All snowy white,
> And round as a harvest moon,
> A pledge of purity and love,
> A small but welcome boon.
>
> While summer lasts,
> When borne in hand,
> Or folded on thy breast,
> 'Twill gently soothe thy burning brow,
> And charm thee to thy rest.
>
> But, oh, when Autumn winds blow chill,
> And days are bleak and cold,
> No longer sought, no longer loved,
> 'Twill lie in dust and mould.
>
> This silken fan then deign accept,
> Sad emblem of my lot,

Caressed and cherished for an hour,
Then speedily forgot."

"Why so melancholy, my pearl?" asked Lin Fo, entering from the street.

"When a bird is about to die, its notes are sad," returned Pau Tsu.

"But thou art not for death—thou art for life," declared Lin Fo, drawing her towards him and gazing into a face which day by day seemed to grow finer and more transparent.

IV

A Chinese messenger-boy ran up the street, entered the store of Wan Hom Hing & Co. and asked for the junior partner. When Lin Fo came forward he handed him a dainty, flowered missive, neatly folded and addressed. The receiver opened it and read:

> DEAR AND HONORED HUSBAND,—Your unworthy Pau Tsu lacks the courage to face the ordeal before her. She has, therefore, left you and prays you to obtain a divorce, as is the custom in America, so that you may be happy with the Beautiful One, who is so much your Pau Tsu's superior. This, she acknowledges, for she sees with your eyes, in which, like a star, the Beautiful One shineth. Else, why should you have your Pau Tsu follow in her footsteps? She has tried to obey your will and to be as an American woman; but now she is very weary, and the terror of what is before her has overcome.
>
> Your stupid thorn,
>
> PAU TSU

Mechanically Lin Fo folded the letter and thrust it within his breast pocket. A customer inquired of him the price of a lacquered tray. "I wish you good morning," he replied, reaching for his hat. The customer and clerks gaped after him as he left the store.

Out in the street, as fate would have it, he met Adah Raymond. He would have turned aside had she not spoken to him.

"Whatever is the matter with you, Mr. Wan?" she inquired. "You don't look yourself at all."

"The density of my difficulties you cannot understand," he replied, striding past her.

But Adah Raymond was persistent. She had worried lately over Pau Tsu.

"Something is wrong with your wife," she declared.

Lin Fo wheeled around.

"Do you know where she is?" he asked with quick suspicion.

"Why, no!" exclaimed the girl in surprise.

"Well, she has left me."

Adah Raymond stood incredulous for a moment, then with indignant eyes she turned upon the deserted husband.

"You deserve it!" she cried, "I have seen it for some time: your cruel, arbitrary treatment of the dearest, sweetest little soul in the world."

"I beg your pardon, Miss Adah," returned Lin Fo, "but I do not understand. Pau Tsu is heart of my heart. How then could I be cruel to her?"

"Oh, you stupid!" exclaimed the girl. "You're a Chinaman, but you're almost as stupid as an American. Your cruelty consisted in forcing Pau Tsu to be—what nature never intended her to be—an American woman; to adapt and adopt in a few months' time all our ways and customs. I saw it long ago, but as Pau Tsu was too sweet and meek to see any faults in her man I had not the heart to open her eyes—or yours. Is it not true that she has left you for this reason?"

"Yes," murmured Lin Fo. He was completely crushed. "And some other things."

"What other things?"

"She—is—afraid—of—the—doctor."

"She is!"—fiercely—"Shame upon you!"

Lin Fo began to walk on, but the girl kept by his side and continued:

"You wanted your wife to be an American woman while you remained a Chinaman. For all your clever adaptation of our American ways you are a thorough Chinaman. Do you think an American would dare treat his wife as you have treated yours?"

Wan Lin Fo made no response. He was wondering how he could ever have wished his gentle Pau Tsu to be like this angry woman. Now his Pau Tsu was gone. His anguish for the moment made him oblivious to the presence of his companion and the words she was saying. His silence softened the American girl. After all, men, even Chinamen, were nothing but big, clumsy boys, and she didn't believe in kicking a man after he was down.

"But, cheer up, you're sure to find her," said she, suddenly changing her tone. "Probably her maid has friends in Chinatown who have taken them in."

"If I find her," said Lin Fo fervently, "I will not care if she never speaks an American word, and I will take her for a trip to China, so that our son may be born in the country that Heaven loves."

"You cannot make too much amends for all she has suffered. As to Americanizing Pau Tsu—that will come in time. I am quite sure that were I transferred to your country and commanded to turn myself into a Chinese woman in the space of two or three months I would prove a sorry disappointment to whomever built their hopes upon me."

Many hours elapsed before any trace could be found of the missing one. All the known friends and acquaintances of little Pau Tsu were called upon and questioned; but if they had knowledge of the young wife's hiding place they refused to divulge it. Though Lin Fo's face was grave with an unexpressed fear, their sympathies were certainly not with him.

The seekers were about giving up the search in despair when a little boy, dangling in his hands a string of blue beads, arrested the attention of the young husband. He knew the necklace to be a gift from Pau Tsu to the maid, A–Toy. He had bought it himself. Stopping and questioning the little fellow he learned to his great joy that his wife and her maid were at the boy's home, under the care of his grandmother, who was a woman learned in herb lore.

Adah Raymond smiled in sympathy with her companion's evident great relief.

"Everything will now be all right," said she, following Lin Fo as he proceeded to the house pointed out by the lad. Arrived there, she suggested that the husband enter first and alone. She would wait a few moments.

"Miss Adah," said Lin Fo, "ten thousand times I beg your pardon, but perhaps you will come to see my wife some other time—not today?"

He hesitated, embarrassed and humiliated.

In one silent moment Adah Raymond grasped the meaning of all the morning's trouble—of all Pau Tsu's sadness.

"Lord, what fools we mortals be!" she soliloquized as she walked home alone. "I ought to have known. What else could Pau Tsu have thought?—coming from a land where women have no men friends save their husbands. How she must have suffered under her smiles! Poor, brave little soul!"

In the Land of the Free

"See, Little One—the hills in the morning sun. There is thy home for years to come. It is very beautiful and thou wilt be very happy there."

The Little One looked up into his mother's face in perfect faith. He was engaged in the pleasant occupation of sucking a sweetmeat; but that did not prevent him from gurgling responsively.

"Yes, my olive bud; there is where thy father is making a fortune for thee. Thy father! Oh, wilt thou not be glad to behold his dear face. 'Twas for thee I left him."

The Little One ducked his chin sympathetically against his mother's knee. She lifted him on to her lap. He was two years old, a round, dimple-cheeked boy with bright brown eyes and a sturdy little frame.

"Ah! Ah! Ah! Ooh! Ooh! Ooh!" puffed he, mocking a tugboat steaming by.

San Francisco's waterfront was lined with ships and steamers, while other craft, large and small, including a couple of white transports from the Philippines, lay at anchor here and there off shore. It was some time before the *Eastern Queen* could get docked, and even after that was accomplished, a lone Chinaman who had been waiting on the wharf for an hour was detained that much longer by men with the initials U.S.C. on their caps, before he could board the steamer and welcome his wife and child.

"This is thy son," announced the happy Lae Choo.

Hom Hing lifted the child, felt of his little body and limbs, gazed into his face with proud and joyous eyes; then turned inquiringly to a customs officer at his elbow.

"That's a fine boy you have there," said the man. "Where was he born?"

"In China," answered Hom Hing, swinging the Little One on his right shoulder, preparatory to leading his wife off the steamer.

"Ever been to America before?"

"No, not he," answered the father with a happy laugh.

The customs officer beckoned to another.

"This little fellow," said he, "is visiting America for the first time."

The other customs officer stroked his chin reflectively.

"Good day," said Hom Hing.

"Wait!" commanded one of the officers. "You cannot go just yet."

"What more now?" asked Hom Hing.

"I'm afraid," said the first customs officer, "that we cannot allow the boy to go ashore. There is nothing in the papers that you have shown us—your wife's papers and your own—having any bearing upon the child."

"There was no child when the papers were made out," returned Hom Hing. He spoke calmly; but there was apprehension in his eyes and in his tightening grip on his son.

"What is it? What is it?" quavered Lae Choo, who understood a little English.

The second customs officer regarded her pityingly.

"I don't like this part of the business," he muttered.

The first officer turned to Hom Hing and in an official tone of voice, said:

"Seeing that the boy has no certificate entitling him to admission to this country you will have to leave him with us."

"Leave my boy!" exclaimed Hom Hing.

"Yes; he will be well taken care of, and just as soon as we can hear from Washington he will be handed over to you."

"But," protested Hom Hing, "he is my son."

"We have no proof," answered the man with a shrug of his shoulders; "and even if so we cannot let him pass without orders from the Government."

"He is my son," reiterated Hom Hing, slowly and solemnly. "I am a Chinese merchant and have been in business in San Francisco for many years. When my wife told to me one morning that she dreamed of a green tree with spreading branches and one beautiful red flower growing thereon, I answered her that I wished my son to be born in our country, and for her to prepare to go to China. My wife complied with my wish. After my son was born my mother fell sick and my wife nursed and cared for her; then my father, too, fell sick, and my wife also nursed and cared for him. For twenty moons my wife care for and nurse the old people, and when they die they bless her and my son, and I send for her to return to me. I had no fear of trouble. I was a Chinese merchant and my son was my son."

"Very good, Hom Hing," replied the first officer. "Nevertheless, we take your son."

"No, you not take him; he my son too."

It was Lae Choo. Snatching the child from his father's arms she held and covered him with her own.

The officers conferred together for a few moments; then one drew Hom Hing aside and spoke in his ear.

Resignedly Hom Hing bowed his head, then approached his wife. "'Tis the law," said he, speaking in Chinese, "and 'twill be but for a little while—until tomorrow's sun arises."

"You, too," reproached Lae Choo in a voice eloquent with pain. But accustomed to obedience she yielded the boy to her husband, who in turn delivered him to the first officer. The Little One protested lustily against the transfer; but his mother covered her face with her sleeve and his father silently led her away. Thus was the law of the land complied with.

II

Day was breaking. Lae Choo, who had been awake all night, dressed herself, then awoke her husband.

"'Tis the morn," she cried. "Go, bring our son."

The man rubbed his eyes and arose upon his elbow so that he could see out of the window. A pale star was visible in the sky. The petals of a lily in a bowl on the windowsill were unfurled.

"'Tis not yet time," said he, laying his head down again.

"Not yet time. Ah, all the time that I lived before yesterday is not so much as the time that has been since my little one was taken from me."

The mother threw herself down beside the bed and covered her face.

Hom Hing turned on the light, and touching his wife's bowed head with a sympathetic hand inquired if she had slept.

"Slept!" she echoed, weepingly. "Ah, how could I close my eyes with my arms empty of the little body that has filled them every night for more than twenty moons! You do not know—man—what it is to miss the feel of the little fingers and the little toes and the soft round limbs of your little one. Even in the darkness his darling eyes used to shine up to mine, and often have I fallen into slumber with his pretty babble at my ear. And now, I see him not; I touch him not; I hear him not. My baby, my little fat one!"

"Now! Now! Now!" consoled Hom Hing, patting his wife's shoulder reassuringly; "there is no need to grieve so; he will soon gladden you again. There cannot be any law that would keep a child from its mother!"

Lae Choo dried her tears.

"You are right, my husband," she meekly murmured. She arose and stepped about the apartment, setting things to rights. The box of presents she had brought for her California friends had been opened the evening before; and silks, embroideries, carved ivories, ornamental lacquer-ware, brasses, camphorwood boxes, fans, and chinaware were scattered around in confused heaps. In the midst of unpacking the thought of her child in the hands of strangers had overpowered her, and she had left everything to crawl into bed and weep.

Having arranged her gifts in order she stepped out on to the deep balcony.

The star had faded from view and there were bright streaks in the western sky. Lae Choo looked down the street and around. Beneath the flat occupied by her and her husband were quarters for a number of bachelor Chinamen, and she could hear them from where she stood, taking their early morning breakfast. Below their dining-room was her husband's grocery store. Across the way was a large restaurant. Last night it had been resplendent with gay colored lanterns and the sound of music. The rejoicings over "the completion of the moon," by Quong Sum's firstborn, had been long and loud, and had caused her to tie a handkerchief over her ears. She, a bereaved mother, had it not in her heart to rejoice with other parents. This morning the place was more in accord with her mood. It was still and quiet. The revellers had dispersed or were asleep.

A roly-poly woman in black sateen, with long pendant earrings in her ears, looked up from the street below and waved her a smiling greeting. It was her old neighbor, Kuie Hoe, the wife of the gold embosser, Mark Sing. With her was a little boy in yellow jacket and lavender pantaloons. Lae Choo remembered him as a baby. She used to like to play with him in those days when she had no child of her own. What a long time ago that seemed! She caught her breath in a sigh, and laughed instead.

"Why are you so merry?" called her husband from within.

"Because my Little One is coming home," answered Lae Choo. "I am a happy mother—a happy mother."

She pattered into the room with a smile on her face.

• • •

The noon hour had arrived. The rice was steaming in the bowls and a fragrant dish of chicken and bamboo shoots was awaiting Hom Hing. Not for one moment had Lae Choo paused to rest during the morning hours; her activity had been ceaseless. Every now and again, however, she had raised her eyes to the gilded clock on the curiously carved mantelpiece. Once, she had exclaimed:

"Why so long, oh! why so long?" Then apostrophizing herself: "Lae Choo, be happy. The Little One is coming! The Little One is coming!" Several times she burst into tears and several times she laughed aloud.

Hom Hing entered the room; his arms hung down by his side.

"The Little One!" shrieked Lae Choo.

"They bid me call tomorrow."

With a moan the mother sank to the floor.

The noon hour passed. The dinner remained on the table.

III

The winter rains were over: the spring had come to California, flushing the hills with green and causing an ever-changing pageant of flowers to pass over them. But there was no spring in Lae Choo's heart, for the Little One remained away from her arms. He was being kept in a mission. White women were caring for him, and though for one full moon he had pined for his mother and refused to be comforted he was now apparently happy and contented. Five moons or five months had gone by since the day he had passed with Lae Choo through the Golden Gate; but the great Government at Washington still delayed sending the answer which would return him to his parents.

• • •

Hom Hing was disconsolately rolling up and down the balls in his abacus box when a keen-faced young man stepped into his store.

"What news?" asked the Chinese merchant.

"This!" The young man brought forth a typewritten letter. Hom Hing read the words:

Re Chinese child, alleged to be the son of Hom Hing, Chinese
merchant, doing business at 425 Clay street, San Francisco.
Same will have attention as soon as possible.

Hom Hing returned the letter, and without a word continued his
manipulation of the counting machine.

"Have you anything to say?" asked the young man.

"Nothing. They have sent the same letter fifteen times before. Have
you not yourself showed it to me?"

"True!" The young man eyed the Chinese merchant furtively. He
had a proposition to make and he was pondering whether or not the
time was opportune.

"How is your wife?" he inquired solicitously—and diplomatically.

Hom Hing shook his head mournfully.

She seems less every day," he replied. "Her food she takes only when
I bid her and her tears fall continually. She finds no pleasure in dress or
flowers and cares not to see her friends. Her eyes stare all night. I think
before another moon she will pass into the land of spirits."

"No!" exclaimed the young man, genuinely startled.

"If the boy not come home I lose my wife sure," continued Hom
Hing with bitter sadness.

"It's not right," cried the young man indignantly. Then he made his
proposition.

The Chinese father's eyes brightened exceedingly.

"Will I like you to go to Washington and make them give you the
paper to restore my son?" cried he. "How can you ask when you know
my heart's desire?"

"Then," said the young fellow, "I will start next week. I am anxious
to see this thing through if only for the sake of your wife's peace of
mind."

"I will call her. To hear what you think to do will make her glad,"
said Hom Hing.

He called a message to Lae Choo upstairs through a tube in the wall.

In a few moments she appeared, listless, wan, and hollow-eyed; but
when her husband told her the young lawyer's suggestion she became
as one electrified; her form straightened, her eyes glistened; the color
flushed to her cheeks.

"Oh," she cried, turning to James Clancy, "You are a hundred man
good!"

The young man felt somewhat embarrassed; his eyes shifted a little under the intense gaze of the Chinese mother.

"Well, we must get your boy for you," he responded. "Of course"— turning to Hom Hing—"it will cost a little money. You can't get fellows to hurry the Government for you without gold in your pocket."

Hom Hing stared blankly for a moment. Then: "How much do you want, Mr. Clancy?" he asked quietly.

"Well, I will need at least five hundred to start with."

Hom Hing cleared his throat.

"I think I told to you the time I last paid you for writing letters for me and seeing the Custom boss here that nearly all I had was gone!"

"Oh, well then we won't talk about it, old fellow. It won't harm the boy to stay where he is, and your wife may get over it all right."

"What that you say?" quavered Lae Choo.

James Clancy looked out of the window.

"He says," explained Hom Hing in English, "that to get our boy we have to have much money."

"Money! Oh, yes."

Lae Choo nodded her head.

"I have not got the money to give him."

For a moment Lae Choo gazed wonderingly from one face to the other; then, comprehension dawning upon her, with swift anger, pointing to the lawyer, she cried: "You not one hundred man good; you just common white man."

"Yes, ma'am," returned James Clancy, bowing and smiling ironically.

Hom Hing pushed his wife behind him and addressed the lawyer again: "I might try," said he, "to raise something; but five hundred—it is not possible."

"What about four?"

"I tell you I have next to nothing left and my friends are not rich."

"Very well!"

The lawyer moved leisurely toward the door, pausing on its threshold to light a cigarette.

"Stop, white man; white man, stop!"

Lae Choo, panting and terrified, had started forward and now stood beside him, clutching his sleeve excitedly.

"You say you can go to get paper to bring my Little One to me if Hom Hing give you five hundred dollars?"

The lawyer nodded carelessly; his eyes were intent upon the cigarette which would not take the fire from the match.

"Then you go get paper. If Hom Hing not can give you five hundred dollars—I give you perhaps what more that much."

She slipped a heavy gold bracelet from her wrist and held it out to the man. Mechanically he took it.

"I go get more!"

She scurried away, disappearing behind the door through which she had come.

"Oh, look here, I can't accept this," said James Clancy, walking back to Hom Hing and laying down the bracelet before him.

"It's all right," said Hom Hing, seriously, "pure China gold. My wife's parent give it to her when we married."

"But I can't take it anyway," protested the young man.

"It is all same as money. And you want money to go to Washington," replied Hom Hing in a matter of fact manner.

"See, my jade earrings—my gold buttons—my hairpins—my comb of pearl and my rings—one, two, three, four, five rings; very good—very good—all same much money. I give them all to you. You take and bring me paper for my Little One."

Lae Choo piled up her jewels before the lawyer.

Hom Hing laid a restraining hand upon her shoulder. "Not all, my wife," he said in Chinese. He selected a ring—his gift to Lae Choo when she dreamed of the tree with the red flower. The rest of the jewels he pushed toward the white man.

"Take them and sell them," said he. "They will pay your fare to Washington and bring you back with the paper."

For one moment James Clancy hesitated. He was not a sentimental man; but something within him arose against accepting such payment for his services.

"They are good, good," pleadingly asserted Lae Choo, seeing his hesitation.

Whereupon he seized the jewels, thrust them into his coat pocket, and walked rapidly away from the store.

IV

Lae Choo followed after the missionary woman through the mission nursery school. Her heart was beating so high with happiness that she could scarcely breathe. The paper had come at last—the precious paper which gave Hom Hing and his wife the right to the possession of their own child. It was ten months now since he had been taken from them—ten months since the sun had ceased to shine for Lae Choo.

The room was filled with children—most of them wee tots, but none so wee as her own. The mission woman talked as she walked. She told Lae Choo that little Kim, as he had been named by the school, was the pet of the place, and that his little tricks and ways amused and delighted every one. He had been rather difficult to manage at first and had cried much for his mother; "but children so soon forget, and after a month he seemed quite at home and played around as bright and happy as a bird."

"Yes," responded Lae Choo. "Oh, yes, yes!"

But she did not hear what was said to her. She was walking in a maze of anticipatory joy.

"Wait here, please," said the mission woman, placing Lae Choo in a chair. "The very youngest ones are having their breakfast."

She withdrew for a moment—it seemed like an hour to the mother—then she reappeared leading by the hand a little boy dressed in blue cotton overalls and white-soled shoes. The little boy's face was round and dimpled and his eyes were very bright.

"Little One, ah, my Little One!" cried Lae Choo.

She fell on her knees and stretched her hungry arms toward her son.

But the Little One shrunk from her and tried to hide himself in the folds of the white woman's skirt.

"Go'way, go'way!" he bade his mother.

The Chinese Lily

Mermei lived in an upstairs room of a Chinatown dwelling-house. There were other little Chinese women living on the same floor, but Mermei never went amongst them. She was not as they were. She was a cripple. A fall had twisted her legs so that she moved around with difficulty and scarred her face so terribly that none save Lin John cared to look upon it. Lin John, her brother, was a laundryman, working for another of his countrymen. Lin John and Mermei had come to San

Francisco with their parents when they were small children. Their mother had died the day she entered the foreign city, and the father the week following, both having contracted a fever on the steamer. Mermei and Lin John were then taken in charge by their father's brother, and although he was a poor man he did his best for them until called away by death.

Long before her Uncle died Mermei had met with the accident that had made her not as other girls; but that had only strengthened her brother's affection, and old Lin Wan died happy in the knowledge that Lin John would ever put Mermei before himself.

So Mermei lived in her little upstairs room, cared for by Lin John, and scarcely an evening passed that he did not call to see her. One evening, however, Lin John failed to appear, and Mermei began to feel very sad and lonely. Mermei could embroider all day in contented silence if she knew that in the evening someone would come to whom she could communicate all the thoughts that filled a small black head that knew nothing of life save what it saw from an upstairs window. Mermei's window looked down upon the street, and she would sit for hours, pressed close against it, watching those who passed below and all that took place. That day she had seen many things which she had put into her mental portfolio for Lin John's edification when evening should come. Two yellow-robed priests had passed below on their way to the joss house in the next street; a little bird with a white breast had fluttered against the window pane; a man carrying an image of a Gambling Cash Tiger had entered the house across the street; and six young girls of about her own age, dressed gaily as if to attend a wedding, had also passed over the same threshold.

But when nine o'clock came and no Lin John, the girl began to cry softly. She did not often shed tears, but for some reason unknown to Mermei herself, the sight of those joyous girls caused sad reflections. In the midst of her weeping a timid knock was heard. It was not Lin John. He always gave a loud rap, then entered without waiting to be bidden. Mermei hobbled to the door, pulled it open, and there, in the dim light of the hall without, beheld a young girl—the most beautiful young girl that Mermei had ever seen—and she stood there extending to Mermei a blossom from a Chinese lily plant. Mermei understood the meaning of the offered flower, and accepting it, beckoned for her visitor to follow her into her room.

What a delightful hour that was to Mermei! She forgot that she was scarred and crippled, and she and the young girl chattered out their little hearts to one another. "Lin John is dear, but one can't talk to a man, even if he is a brother, as one can to one the same as oneself," said Mermei to Sin Far—her new friend, and Sin Far, the meaning of whose name was Pure Flower, or Chinese Lily, answered:

"Yes, indeed. The woman must be the friend of the woman, and the man the friend of the man. Is it not so in the country that Heaven loves?"

"What beneficent spirit moved you to come to my door?" asked Mermei.

"I know not," replied Sin Far, "save that I was lonely. We have but lately moved here, my sister, my sister's husband, and myself. My sister is a bride, and there is much to say between her and her husband. Therefore, in the evening, when the day's duties are done, I am alone. Several times, hearing that you were sick, I ventured to your door; but failed to knock, because always when I drew near, I heard the voice of him whom they call your brother. Tonight, as I returned from an errand for my sister, I heard only the sound of weeping—so I hastened to my room and plucked the lily for you."

The next evening when Lin John explained how he had been obliged to work the evening before Mermei answered brightly that that was all right. She loved him just as much as ever and was just as glad to see him as ever; but if work prevented him from calling he was not to worry. She had found a friend who would cheer her loneliness.

Lin John was surprised, but glad to hear such news, and it came to pass that when he beheld Sin Far, her sweet and gentle face, her pretty drooped eyelids and arched eyebrows, he began to think of apple and peach and plum trees showering their dainty blossoms in the country that Heaven loves.

• • •

It was about four o'clock in the afternoon. Lin John, working in his laundry, paid little attention to the street uproar and the clang of the engines rushing by. He had no thought of what it meant to him and would have continued at his work undisturbed had not a boy put his head into the door and shouted:

"Lin John, the house in which your sister lives is on fire!"

The tall building was in flames when Lin John reached it. The uprising tongues licked his face as he sprung up the ladder no other man dared ascend.

"I will not go. It is best for me to die," and Mermei resisted her friend with all her puny strength.

"The ladder will not bear the weight of both of us. You are his sister," calmly replied Sin Far.

"But he loves you best. You and he can be happy together. I am not fit to live."

"May Lin John decide, Mermei?"

"Yes, Lin John may decide."

Lin John reached the casement. For one awful second he wavered. Then his eyes sought the eyes of his sister's friend.

"Come, Mermei," he called.

• • •

"Where is Sin Far?" asked Mermei when she became conscious.

"Sin Far is in the land of happy spirits."

"And I am still in this sad, dark world."

"Speak not so, little one. Your brother loves you and will protect you from the darkness."

"But you loved Sin Far better—and she loved you."

Lin John bowed his head.

"Alas!" wept Mermei. "That I should live to make others sad!"

"Nay," said Lin John, "Sin Far is happy. And I—I did my duty with her approval, aye, at her bidding. How then, little sister, can I be sad?"

The Smuggling of Tie Co

Amongst the daring men who engage in contrabanding Chinese from Canada into the United States Jack Fabian ranks as the boldest in deed, the cleverest in scheming, and the most successful in outwitting Government officers.

Uncommonly strong in person, tall and well built, with fine features and a pair of keen, steady blue eyes, gifted with a sort of rough eloquence and of much personal fascination, it is no wonder that we fellows regard him as our chief and are bound to follow where he leads. With Fabian at our head we engage in the wildest adventures and find such places of concealment for our human goods as none but those who take part in a desperate business would dare to dream of.

Jack, however, is not in search of glory—money is his object. One day when a romantic friend remarked that it was very kind of him to help the poor Chinamen over the border, a cynical smile curled his moustache.

"Kind!" he echoed. "Well, I haven't yet had time to become sentimental over the matter. It is merely a matter of dollars and cents, though, of course, to a man of my strict principles, there is a certain pleasure to be derived from getting ahead of the Government. A poor devil does now and then like to take a little out of those millionaire concerns."

It was last summer and Fabian was somewhat down on his luck. A few months previously, to the surprise of us all, he had made a blunder, which resulted in his capture by American officers, and he and his companion, together with five uncustomed Chinamen, had been lodged in a county jail to await trial.

But loafing behind bars did not agree with Fabian's energetic nature, so one dark night, by means of a saw which had been given to him by a very innocent-looking visitor the day before, he made good his escape, and after a long, hungry, detective-hunted tramp through woods and bushes, found himself safe in Canada.

He had had a three months' sojourn in prison, and during that time some changes had taken place in smuggling circles. Some ingenious lawyers had devised a scheme by which any young Chinaman on payment of a couple of hundred dollars could procure a father which father would swear the young Chinaman was born in America—thus proving him to be an American citizen with the right to breathe United States air. And the Chinese themselves, assisted by some white men, were manufacturing certificates establishing their right to cross the border, and in that way were crossing over in large batches.

That sort of trick naturally spoiled our fellows' business, but we all know that "Yankee sharper" games can hold good only for a short while; so we bided our time and waited in patience.

Not so Fabian. He became very restless and wandered around with glowering looks. He was sitting one day in a laundry, the proprietor of which had sent out many a boy through our chief's instrumentality. Indeed, Fabian is said to have "rushed over" to "Uncle Sam" himself some five hundred Celestials, and if Fabian had not been an exceedingly generous fellow he might now be a gentleman of leisure instead of an unimmortalized Rob Roy.

Well, Fabian was sitting in the laundry of Chen Ting Lung & Co., telling a nice-looking young Chinaman that he was so broke that he'd be willing to take over even one man at a time.

The young Chinaman looked thoughtfully into Fabian's face. "Would you take me?" he inquired.

"Take you!" echoed Fabian. "Why, you are one of the 'bosses' here. You don't mean to say that you are hankering after a place where it would take you years to get as high up in the 'washee, washee' business as you are now?"

"Yes, I want go," replied Tie Co. "I want go to New York and I will pay you fifty dollars and all expense if you take me, and not say you take me to my partners."

"There's no accounting for a Chinaman," muttered Fabian; but he gladly agreed to the proposal and a night was fixed.

"What is the name of the firm you are going to?" inquired the white man.

Chinamen who intend being smuggled always make arrangements with some Chinese firm in the States to receive them.

Tie Co hesitated, then mumbled something which sounded like "Quong Wo Yuen" or "Long Lo Toon," Fabian was not sure which, but did not repeat the question, not being sufficiently interested.

He left the laundry, nodding goodbye to Tie Co as he passed outside the window, and the Chinaman nodded back, a faint smile on his small, delicate face lingering until Fabian's receding form was lost to view.

It was a pleasant night on which the two men set out. Fabian had a rig waiting at the corner of the street; Tie Co, dressed in citizen's clothes, stepped into it unobserved, and the smuggler and would-be-smuggled were soon out of the city. They had a merry drive, for Fabian's liking for Tie Co was very real; he had known him for several years, and the lad's quick intelligence interested him.

The second day they left their horse at a farmhouse, where Fabian would call for it on his return trip, crossed a river in a rowboat before the sun was up, and plunged into a wood in which they would remain till evening. It was raining, but through mud and wind and rain they trudged slowly and heavily.

Tie Co paused now and then to take breath. Once Fabian remarked:

"You are not a very strong lad, Tie Co. It's a pity you have to work as you do for your living," and Tie Co had answered:

"Work velly good! No work, Tie Co die."

Fabian looked at the lad protectingly, wondering in a careless way why this Chinaman seemed to him so different from the others.

"Wouldn't you like to be back in China?" he asked.

"No," said Tie Co decidedly.

"Why?"

"I not know why," answered Tie Co.

Fabian laughed.

"Haven't you got a nice little wife at home?" he continued. "I hear you people marry very young."

"No, I no wife," asserted his companion with a choky little laugh. "I never have no wife."

"Nonsense," joked Fabian. "Why, Tie Co, think how nice it would be to have a little woman cook your rice and to love you."

"I not have wife," repeated Tie Co seriously. "I not like woman, I like man."

"You confirmed old bachelor!" ejaculated Fabian.

"I like you," said Tie Co, his boyish voice sounding clear and sweet in the wet woods. "I like you so much that I want go to New York, so you make fifty dollars. I no flend in New York."

"What!" exclaimed Fabian.

"Oh, I solly I tell you, Tie Co velly solly," and the Chinese boy shuffled on with bowed head.

"Look here, Tie Co," said Fabian; "I won't have you do this for my sake. You have been very foolish, and I don't care for your fifty dollars. I do not need it half as much as you do. Good God! how ashamed you make me feel—I who have blown in my thousands in idle pleasures cannot take the little you have slaved for. We are in New York State now. When we get out of this wood we will have to walk over a bridge which crosses a river. On the other side, not far from where we cross, there is a railway station. Instead of buying you a ticket for the city of New York I shall take train with you for Toronto."

Tie Co did not answer—he seemed to be thinking deeply. Suddenly he pointed to where some fallen trees lay.

"Two men run away behind there," cried he.

Fabian looked round them anxiously; his keen eyes seemed to pierce the gloom in his endeavor to catch a glimpse of any person; but no man was visible, and, save the dismal sighing of the wind among the trees, all was quiet.

"There's no one," he said somewhat gruffly—he was rather startled, for they were a mile over the border and he knew that the Government officers were on a sharp lookout for him, and felt, despite his strength, if any trick or surprise were attempted it would go hard with him.

"If they catch you with me it be too bad," sententiously remarked Tie Co. It seemed as if his words were in answer to Fabian's thoughts.

"But they will not catch us; so cheer up your heart, my boy," replied the latter, more heartily than he felt.

"If they come, and I not with you, they not take you and it be all lite."

"Yes," assented Fabian, wondering what his companion was thinking about.

They emerged from the woods in the dusk of the evening and were soon on the bridge crossing the river. When they were near the centre Tie Co stopped and looked into Fabian's face.

"Man come for you, I not here, man no hurt you." And with the words he whirled like a flash over the rail.

In another flash Fabian was after him. But though a first-class swimmer, the white man's efforts were of no avail, and Tie Co was borne away from him by the swift current.

Cold and dripping wet, Fabian dragged himself up the bank and found himself a prisoner.

"So your Chinaman threw himself into the river. What was that for?" asked one of the Government officers.

"I think he was out of his head," replied Fabian. And he fully believed what he uttered.

"We tracked you right through the woods," said another of the captors. "We thought once the boy caught sight of us."

Fabian remained silent.

• • •

Tie Co's body was picked up the next day. Tie Co's body, and yet not Tie Co, for Tie Co was a youth, and the body found with Tie Co's face and dressed in Tie Co's clothes was the body of a girl—a woman.

Nobody in the laundry of Chen Ting Lung & Co.—no Chinaman

in Canada or New York—could explain the mystery. Tie Co had come out to Canada with a number of other youths. Though not very strong he had always been a good worker and "very smart." He had been quiet and reserved among his own countrymen; had refused to smoke tobacco or opium, and had been a regular attendant at Sunday schools and a great favorite with Mission ladies.

Fabian was released in less than a week. "No evidence against him," said the Commissioner, who was not aware that the prisoner was the man who had broken out of jail but a month before.

Fabian is now very busy; there are lots of boys taking his helping hand over the border, but none of them are like Tie Co; and sometimes, between whiles, Fabian finds himself pondering long and earnestly over the mystery of Tie Co's life—and death.

The God of Restoration

"He that hath wine hath many friends," muttered Koan-lo the Second, as he glanced backwards into the store out of which he was stepping. It was a Chinese general store, well stocked with all manner of quaint wares, and about a dozen Chinamen were sitting around; whilst in an adjoining room could be seen the recumbent forms of several smokers who were discussing business and indulging in the fascinating pipe during the intervals of conversation.

Noticeable amongst the smokers was Koan-lo the First, a tall, middle-aged Chinaman, wearing a black cap with a red button. Koan-lo the First was cousin to Koan-lo the Second, but whereas Koan-lo the Second was young and penniless, Koan-lo the First was one of the wealthiest Chinese merchants in San Francisco and a mighty man amongst the people of his name in that city, who regarded him as a father.

Koan-lo the Second had been instructed by Koan-lo the First to meet Sie, the latter's bride, who was arriving that day by steamer from China. Koan-lo the First was too busy a man to go down himself to the docks.

So Koan-lo the Second and Sie met—though not for the first time.

Five years before in a suburb of Canton City they had said to one another: "I love you."

Koan-lo the Second was an orphan and had been educated and cared for from youth upwards by Koan-lo the First.

Sie was the daughter of a slave, which will explain why she and Koan-lo the Second had had the opportunity to know one another before the latter left with his cousin for America. In China the daughters of slaves are allowed far more liberty than girls belonging to a higher class of society.

"Koan-lo, ah Koan-lo," cooed Sie softly and happily as she recognized her lover.

"Sie, my sweetest heart," returned Koan-lo the Second, his voice both glad and sad.

He saw that a mistake had been made—that Sie believed that the man who was to be her husband was himself—Koan-lo the Second.

And all the love that was in him awoke, and he became dizzy thinking of what might yet be.

Could he explain that the Koan-lo who had purchased Sie for his bride, and to whom she of right belonged, was his cousin and not himself? Could he deliver to the Koan-lo who had many friends and stores of precious valuables the only friend, the only treasure he had ever possessed? And was it likely that Sie would be happy eating the rice of Koan-lo the First when she loved him, Koan-lo the Second?

Sie's little fingers crept into his. She leaned against him. "I am tired. Shall we soon rest?" said she.

"Yes, very soon, my Sie," he murmured, putting his arm around her.

"I was too glad when my father told me that you had sent for me," she whispered.

"I said: 'How good of Koan-lo to remember me all these years.'"

"And did you not remember me, my jess'mine flower?"

"Why need you ask? You know the days and nights have been filled with you."

"Having remembered me, why should you have dreamt that I might have forgotten you?"

"There is a difference. You are a man; I am a woman."

"You have been mine now for over two weeks," said Koan-lo the Second. "Do you still love me, Sie?"

"Look into mine eyes and see," she answered.

"And are you happy?"

"Happy! Yes, and this is the happiest day of all, because today my father obtains his freedom."

"How is that, Sie?"

"Why, Koan-lo, you know. Does not my father receive today the balance of the price you pay for me, and is not that, added to what you sent in advance, sufficient to purchase my father's freedom? My dear, good father—he has worked so hard all these years. He has ever been so kind to me. How glad am I to think that through me the God of Restoration has decreed that he shall no longer be a slave. Yes, I am the happiest woman in the world today."

Sie kissed her husband's hand.

He drew it away and hid with it his face.

"Ah, dear husband!" cried Sie. "You are very sick."

"No, not sick," replied the miserable Koan-lo—"but, Sie, I must tell you that I am a very poor man, and we have got to leave this pretty house in the country and go to some city where I will have to work hard and you will scarcely have enough to eat."

"Kind, generous Koan-lo," answered Sie, "you have ruined yourself for my sake; you paid too high a price for me. Ah, unhappy Sie, who has pulled Koan-lo into the dust! Now let me be your servant, for gladly would I starve for your sake. I care for Koan-lo, not riches."

And she fell on her knees before the young man, who raised her gently, saying:

"Sie, I am unworthy of such devotion, and your words drive a thousand spears into my heart. Hear my confession. I am your husband, but I am not the man who bought you. My cousin, Koan-lo the First, sent for you to come from China. It was he who bargained for you, and paid half the price your father asked whilst you were in Canton, and agreed to pay the balance upon sight of your face. Alas! the balance will never be paid, for as I have stolen you from my cousin, he is not bound to keep to the agreement, and your father is still a slave."

Sie stood motionless, overwhelmed by the sudden and terrible news. She looked at her husband bewilderedly.

"Is it true, Koan-lo? Must my father remain a slave?" she asked.

"Yes, it is true," replied her husband. "But we have still one another, and you say you care not for poverty. So forgive me and forget your father. I forgot all for love of you."

He attempted to draw her to him, but with a pitiful cry she turned and fled.

. . .

Koan-lo the First sat smoking and meditating.

Many moons had gone by since Koan-lo the Second had betrayed the trust of Koan-lo the First, and Koan-lo the First was wondering what Koan-lo the Second was doing, and how he was living. "He had little money and was unused to working hard, and with a woman to support what will the dog do?" thought the old man. He felt injured and bitter, but towards the evening, after long smoking, his heart became softened, and he said to his pipe: "Well, well, he had a loving feeling for her, and the young I suppose must mate with the young. I think I could overlook his ungratefulness were he to come and seek forgiveness."

"Great and honored sir, the dishonored Sie kneels before you and begs you to put your foot on her head."

These words were uttered by a young Chinese girl of rare beauty who had entered the room suddenly and prostrated herself before Koan-lo the First. He looked up angrily.

"Ah, I see the false woman who made her father a liar!" he cried.

Tears fell from the downcast eyes of Sie, the kneeler.

"Good sir," said she, "ere I had become a woman or your cousin a man, we loved one another, and when we met after a long separation, we both forgot our duty. But the God of Restoration worked with my heart. I repented and now am come to you to give myself up to be your slave, to work for you until the flesh drops from my bones, if such be your desire, only asking that you will send to my father the balance of my purchase price, for he is too old and feeble to be a slave. Sir, you are known to be a more than just man. Oh, grant my request! 'Tis for my father's sake I plead. For many years he nourished me, with trouble and care; and my heart almost breaks when I think of him. Punish me for my misdeeds, dress me in rags, and feed me on the meanest food! Only let me serve you and make myself of use to you, so that I may be worth my father's freedom."

"And what of my cousin? Are you now false to him?"

"No, not false to Koan-lo, my husband—only true to my father."

"And you wish me, whom you have injured, to free your father?"

Sie's head dropped lower as she replied:

"I wish to be your slave. I wish to pay with the labor of my hands the debt I owe you and the debt I owe my father. For this I have left my husband."

Koan-lo the First arose, lifted Sie's chin with his hand, and contemplated with earnest eyes her face.

"Your heart is not all bad," he observed. "Sit down and listen. I will not buy you for my slave, for in this country it is against the law to buy a woman for a slave; but I will hire you for five years to be my servant, and for that time you will do my bidding, and after that you will be free. Rest in peace concerning your father."

"May the sun ever shine on you, most gracious master!" cried Sie.

Then Koan-lo the First pointed out to her a hallway leading to a little room, which room he said she could have for her own private use while she remained with him.

Sie thanked him and was leaving his presence when the door was burst open and Koan-lo the Second, looking haggard and wild, entered. He rushed up to Sie and clutched her by the shoulder.

"You are mine!" he shouted. "I will kill you before you become another man's!"

"Cousin," said Koan-lo the First, "I wish not to have the woman to be my wife, but I claim her as my servant. She has already received her wages—her father's freedom."

Koan-lo the Second gazed bewilderedly into the faces of his wife and cousin. Then he threw up his hands and cried:

"Oh, Koan-lo, my cousin, I have been evil. Always have I envied you and carried bitter thoughts of you in my heart. Even your kindness to me in the past has provoked my ill-will, and when I have seen you surrounded by friends, I have said scornfully: 'He that hath wine hath many friends,' although I well knew the people loved you for your good heart. And Sie I have deceived. I took her to myself, knowing that she thought I was what I was not. I caused her to believe she was mine by all rights."

"So I am yours," broke in Sie tremblingly.

"So she shall be yours—when you are worthy of such a pearl and can guard and keep it," said Koan-lo the First. Then waving his cousin away from Sie, he continued:

"This is your punishment; the God of Restoration demands it. For five years you shall not see the face of Sie, your wife. Meanwhile, study, think, be honest, and work."

• • •

"Your husband comes for you today. Does the thought make you glad?" questioned Koan-lo the First.

Sie smiled and blushed.

"I shall be sorry to leave you," she replied.

"But more glad than sad," said the old man. "Sie, your husband is now a fine fellow. He has changed wonderfully during his years of probation."

"Then I shall neither know nor love him," said Sie mischievously. "Why, here he—"

"My sweet one!"

"My husband!"

"My children, take my blessing; be good and be happy. I go to my pipe, to dream of bliss if not to find it."

With these words Koan-lo the First retired.

"Is he not almost as a god?" said Sie.

"Yes," answered her husband, drawing her on to his knee. "He has been better to me than I have deserved. And you—ah, Sie, how can you care for me when you know what a bad fellow I have been?"

"Well," said Sie contentedly, "it is always our best friends who know how bad we are."

The Prize China Baby

The baby was the one gleam of sunshine in Fin Fan's life, and how she loved it no words can tell. When it was first born, she used to lie with her face turned to its little soft, breathing mouth and think there was nothing quite so lovely in the world as the wee pink face before her, while the touch of its tiny toes and fingers would send wonderful thrills through her whole body. Those were delightful days, but, oh, how quickly they sped. A week after the birth of the little Jessamine Flower, Fin Fan was busy winding tobacco leaves in the dark room behind her husband's factory. Winding tobacco leaves had been Fin Fan's occupation ever since she had become Chung Kee's wife, and hard and dreary work it was. Now, however, she did not mind it quite so much, for in a bunk which was built on one side of the room was a most precious bundle, and every now and then she would go over to that bunk and crow and coo to the baby therein.

But though Fin Fan prized her child so highly, Jessamine Flower's father would rather she had not been born, and considered the babe a nuisance because she took up so much of her mother's time. He would rather that Fin Fan spent the hours in winding tobacco leaves than in nursing baby. However, Fin Fan managed to do both, and by dint of getting up very early in the morning and retiring very late at night, made as much money for her husband after baby was born as she ever did before. And it was well for her that that was so, as the baby would otherwise have been taken from her and given to some other more fortunate woman. Not that Fin Fan considered herself unfortunate. Oh, no! She had been a hard-working little slave all her life, and after her mistress sold her to be wife to Chung Kee, she never dreamt of complaining, because, though a wife, she was still a slave.

When Jessamine Flower was about six months old one of the ladies of the Mission, in making her round of Chinatown, ran in to see Fin Fan and her baby.

"What a beautiful child!" exclaimed the lady. "And, oh, how cunning," she continued, noting the amulets on the little ankles and wrists, the tiny, quilted vest and gay little trousers in which Fin Fan had arrayed her treasure.

Fin Fan sat still and shyly smiled, rubbing her chin slowly against the baby's round cheek. Fin Fan was scarcely more than a child herself in years.

"Oh, I want to ask you, dear little mother," said the lady, "if you will not send your little one to the Chinese baby show which we are going to have on Christmas Eve in the Presbyterian Mission schoolroom."

Fin Fan's eyes brightened.

"What you think? That my baby get a prize?" she asked hesitatingly.

"I think so, indeed," answered the lady, feeling the tiny, perfectly shaped limbs and peeping into the brightest of black eyes.

From that day until Christmas Eve, Fin Fan thought of nothing but the baby show. She would be there with her baby, and if it won a prize, why, perhaps its father might be got to regard it with more favor, so that he would not frown so blackly and mutter under his breath at the slightest cry or coo.

On the morning of Christmas Eve, Chung Kee brought into Fin

Fan's room a great bundle of tobacco which he declared had to be rolled by the evening, and when it was time to start for the show, the work was not nearly finished. However, Fin Fan dressed her baby, rolled it in a shawl, and with it in her arms, stealthily left the place.

It was a bright scene that greeted her upon arrival at the Mission house. The little competitors, in the enclosure that had been arranged for them, presented a peculiarly gorgeous appearance. All had been carefully prepared for the beauty test and looked as pretty as possible, though in some cases bejewelled head dresses and voluminous silken garments almost hid the competitors. Some small figures quite blazed in gold and tinsel, and then there were solemn cherubs almost free from clothing. The majority were plump and well-formed children, and there wasn't a cross or crying baby in the forty-five. Fin Fan's baby made the forty-sixth, and it was immediately surrounded by a group of admiring ladies.

How Fin Fan's eyes danced. Her baby would get a prize, and she would never more need to fear that her husband would give it away. That terrible dread had haunted her ever since its birth. "But surely," thought the little mother, "if it gets a prize he will be so proud that he will let me keep it forever."

And Fin Fan's baby did get a prize—a shining gold bit—and Fin Fan, delighted and excited, started for home. She was so happy and proud.

· · ·

Chung Kee was very angry. Fin Fan was not in her room, and the work he had given her to do that morning was lying on the table undone. He said some hard words in a soft voice, which was his way sometimes, and then told the old woman who helped the men in the factory to be ready to carry a baby to the herb doctor's wife that night. "Tell her," said he, "that my cousin, the doctor, says that she long has desired a child, and so I send her one as a Christmas present, according to American custom."

Just then came a loud knocking at the door. Chung Kee slowly unbarred it, and two men entered, bearing a stretcher upon which a covered form lay.

"Why be you come to my store?" asked Chung Kee in broken English.

The men put down their burden, and one pulled down the covering from that which lay on the stretcher and revealed an unconscious woman and a dead baby.

"It was on Jackson Street. The woman was trying to run with the baby in her arms, and just as she reached the crossing a butcher's cart came around the corner. Some Chinese who knows you advised me to bring them here. Your wife and child, eh?"

Chung Kee stared speechlessly at the still faces—an awful horror in his eyes.

A curious crowd began to fill the place. A doctor was in the midst of it and elbowed his way to where Fin Fan was beginning to regain consciousness.

"Move back all of you; we want some air here!" he shouted authoritatively, and Fin Fan, roused by the loud voice, feebly raised her head, and looking straight into her husband's eyes, said:

"Chung Kee's baby got first prize. Chung Kee let Fin Fan keep baby always."

That was all. Fin Fan's eyes closed. Her head fell back beside the prize baby's—hers forever.

Lin John

It was New Year's Eve. Lin John mused over the brightly burning fire. Through the beams of the roof the stars shone, far away in the deep night sky they shone down upon him, and he felt their beauty, though he had no words for it. The long braid which was wound around his head lazily uncoiled and fell down his back; his smooth young face was placid and content. Lin John was at peace with the world. Within one of his blouse sleeves lay a small bag of gold, the accumulated earnings of three years, and that gold was to release his only sister from a humiliating and secret bondage. A sense of duty done led him to dream of the To-Come. What a fortunate fellow he was to have been able to obtain profitable work, and within three years to have saved four hundred dollars! In the next three years, he might be able to establish a little business and send his sister to their parents in China to live like an honest woman. The sharp edges of his life were forgotten in the drowsy warmth and the world faded into dreamland.

The latch was softly lifted; with stealthy step a woman approached the boy and knelt beside him. By the flickering gleam of the dying fire she found that for which she searched, and hiding it in her breast swiftly and noiselessly withdrew.

• • •

Lin John arose. His spirits were light—and so were his sleeves. He reached for his bowl of rice, then set it down, and suddenly his chopsticks clattered on the floor. With hands thrust into his blouse he felt for what was not there. Thus, with bewildered eyes for a few moments. Then he uttered a low cry and his face became old and gray.

• • •

A large apartment, richly carpeted; furniture of dark and valuable wood artistically carved; ceiling decorated with beautiful Chinese ornaments and gold incense burners; walls hung from top to bottom with long bamboo panels covered with silk, on which were printed Chinese characters; tropical plants, on stands; heavy curtains draped over windows. This, in the heart of Chinatown. And in the midst of these surroundings a girl dressed in a robe of dark blue silk worn over a full skirt richly embroidered. The sleeves fell over hands glittering with rings, and shoes of light silk were on her feet. Her hair was ornamented with flowers made of jewels; she wore three or four pairs of bracelets; her jewel earrings were over an inch long.

The girl was fair to see in that her face was smooth and oval, eyes long and dark, mouth small and round, hair of jetty hue, and figure petite and graceful.

Hanging over a chair by her side was a sealskin sacque, such as is worn by fashionable American women. The girl eyed it admiringly and every few moments stroked the soft fur with caressing fingers.

"Pau Sang," she called.

A curtain was pushed aside and a heavy, broad-faced Chinese woman in blouse and trousers of black sateen stood revealed.

"Look," said the beauty. "I have a cloak like the American ladies. Is it not fine?"

Pau Sang nodded. "I wonder at Moy Loy," said she. "He is not in favor with the Gambling Cash Tiger and is losing money."

"Moy Loy gave it not to me. I bought it myself."

"But from whom did you obtain the money?"

"If I let out a secret, will you lock it up?"

Pau Sang smiled grimly, and her companion, sidling closer to her, said: "I took the money from my brother—it was my money; for years he had been working to make it for me, and last week he told me that he had saved four hundred dollars to pay to Moy Loy, so that I might be free. Now, what do I want to be free for? To be poor? To have no one to buy me good dinners and pretty things—to be gay no more? Lin John meant well, but he knows little. As to me, I wanted a sealskin sacque like the fine American ladies. So two moons gone by I stole away to the country and found him asleep. I did not awaken him—and for the first day of the New Year I had this cloak. See?"

• • •

"Heaven frowns on me," said Lin John sadly, speaking to Moy Loy. "I made the money with which to redeem my sister and I have lost it. I grieve, and I would have you say to her that for her sake, I will engage myself laboriously and conform to virtue till three more New Years have grown old, and that though I merit blame for my carelessness, yet I am faithful unto her."

And with his spade over his shoulder he shuffled away from a house, from an upper window of which a woman looked down and under her breath called "Fool!"

Tian Shan's Kindred Spirit

Had Tian Shan been an American and China to him a forbidden country, his daring exploits and thrilling adventures would have furnished inspiration for many a newspaper and magazine article, novel, and short story. As a hero, he would certainly have far outshone Dewey, Peary, or Cook. Being, however, a Chinese, and the forbidden country America, he was simply recorded by the American press as "a wily Oriental, who 'by ways that are dark and tricks that are vain,' is eluding the vigilance of our brave customs officers." As to his experiences, the only one who took any particular interest in them was Fin Fan.

Fin Fan was Tian Shan's kindred spirit. She was the daughter of a

Canadian Chinese storekeeper and the object of much concern to both Protestant Mission ladies and good Catholic sisters.

"I like learn talk and dress like you," she would respond to attempts to bring her into the folds, "but I not want think like you. Too much discuss." And when it was urged upon her that her father was a convert—the Mission ladies declaring, to the Protestant faith, and the nuns, to the Catholic—she would calmly answer: "That so? Well, I not my father. Beside I think my father just say he Catholic (or Protestant) for sake of be amiable to you. He good-natured man and want to please you."

This independent and original stand led Fin Fan to live, as it were, in an atmosphere of outlawry even amongst her own countrywomen, for all proper Chinese females in Canada and America, unless their husbands are men of influence in their own country, conform upon request to the religion of the women of the white race.

• • •

Fin Fan sat on her father's doorstep amusing herself with a ball of yarn and a kitten. She was a pretty girl, with the delicate features, long slanting eyes, and pouting mouth of the women of Soo Chow, to which province her dead mother had belonged.

Tian Shan came along.

"Will you come for a walk around the mountain?" asked he.

"I don't know," answered Fin Fan.

"Do!" he urged.

The walk around the mountain is enjoyable at all seasons, but particularly so in the fall of the year when the leaves on the trees are turning all colors, making the mount itself look like one big posy.

The air was fresh, sweet, and piny. As Tian Shan and Fin Fan walked, they chatted gaily—not so much of Tian Shan or Fin Fan as of the brilliant landscape, the sun shining through a grove of black-trunked trees with golden leaves, the squirrels that whisked past them, the birds twittering and soliloquizing over their vanishing homes, and many other objects of nature. Tian Shan's roving life had made him quite a woodsman, and Fin Fan—well, Fin Fan was his kindred spirit.

A large oak, looking like a smouldering pyre, invited them to a seat under its boughs.

After happily munching half a dozen acorns, Fin Fan requested to be told all about Tian Shan's last adventure. Every time he crossed the border, he was obliged to devise some new scheme by which to accomplish his object, and as he usually succeeded, there was always a new story to tell whenever he returned to Canada.

This time he had run across the river a mile above the Lachine Rapids in an Indian war canoe, and landed in a cove surrounded by reefs, where pursuit was impossible. It had been a perilous undertaking, for he had had to make his way right through the swift current of the St. Lawrence, the turbulent rapids so near that it seemed as if indeed he must yield life to the raging cataract. But with indomitable courage he had forged ahead, the canoe, with every plunge of his paddles, rising on the swells and cutting through the whitecaps, until at last he reached the shore for which he had risked so much.

Fin Fan was thoughtful for a few moments after listening to his narration.

"Why," she queried at last, "when you can make so much more money in the States than in Canada, do you come so often to this side and endanger your life as you do when returning?"

Tian Shan was puzzled himself. He was not accustomed to analyzing the motives for his actions.

Seeing that he remained silent, Fin Fan went on:

"I think," said she, "that it is very foolish of you to keep running backwards and forwards from one country to another, wasting your time and accomplishing nothing."

Tian Shan dug up some soft, black earth with the heels of his boots.

"Perhaps it is," he observed.

That night Tian Shan's relish for his supper was less keen than usual, and when he laid his head upon his pillow, instead of sleeping, he could only think of Fin Fan. Fin Fan! Fin Fan! Her face was before him, her voice in his ears. The clock ticked Fin Fan; the cat purred it; a little mouse squeaked it; a night-bird sang it. He tossed about, striving to think what ailed him. With the first glimmer of morning came knowledge of his condition. He loved Fin Fan, even as the American man loves the girl he would make his wife.

Now Tian Shan, unlike most Chinese, had never saved money and, therefore, had no home to offer Fin Fan. He knew, also, that her father had his eye upon a young merchant in Montreal, who would make a very desirable son-in-law.

In the early light of the morning Tian Shan arose and wrote a letter. In this letter, which was written with a pointed brush on long yellow

sheets of paper, he told Fin Fan that, as she thought it was foolish, he
was going to relinquish the pleasure of running backwards and forwards across the border, for some time at least. He was possessed of a
desire to save money so that he could have a wife and a home. In a
year, perhaps, he would see her again.

• • •

Lee Ping could hardly believe that his daughter was seriously
opposed to becoming the wife of such a good-looking, prosperous
young merchant as Wong Ling. He tried to bring her to reason, but
instead of yielding her will to the parental, she declared that she would
take a place as a domestic to some Canadian lady with whom she had
become acquainted at the Mission sooner than wed the man her father
had chosen.

"Is not Wong Ling a proper man?" inquired the amazed parent.

"Whether he is proper or improper makes no difference to me,"
returned Fin Fan. "I will not marry him, and the law in this country is
so that you cannot compel me to wed against my will."

Lee Ping's good-natured face became almost pitiful as he regarded
his daughter. Only a hen who has hatched a duckling and sees it take
to the water for the first time could have worn such an expression.

Fin Fan's heart softened. She was as fond of her father as he of her.
Sidling up to him, she began stroking his sleeve in a coaxing fashion.

"For a little while longer I wish only to stay with you," said she.

Lee Ping shook his head, but gave in.

"You must persuade her yourself," said he to Wong Ling that
evening. "We are in a country where the sacred laws and customs of
China are as naught."

So Wong Ling pressed his own suit. He was not a bad-looking
fellow, and knew well also how to honey his speech. Moreover, he
believed in paving his way with offerings of flowers, trinkets, sweetmeats.

Fin Fan looked, listened, and accepted. Every gift that could be kept
was carefully put by in a trunk which she hoped some day to take to
New York. "They will help to furnish Tian Shan's home," said she.

• • •

Twelve moons had gone by since Tian Shan had begun to think of
saving and once again he was writing to Fin Fan.

"I have made and I have saved," wrote he. "Shall I come for you?"

And by return mail came an answer which was not "No."

Of course, Fin Fan's heart beat high with happiness when Tian Shan walked into her father's store; but to gratify some indescribable feminine instinct she simply nodded coolly in his direction, and continued what might be called a flirtation with Wong Ling, who had that morning presented her with the first Chinese lily of the season and a box of the best preserved ginger.

Tian Shan sat himself down on a box of dried mushrooms and glowered at his would-be rival, who, unconscious of the fact that he was making a third when there was needed but a two, chattered on like a running stream. Thoughtlessly and kittenishly Fin Fan tossed a word, first to this one, and next to that; and whilst loving with all her heart one man, showed much more favor to the other.

Finally Tian Shan arose from the mushrooms and marched over to the counter.

"These yours?" he inquired of Wong Ling, indicating the lily and the box of ginger.

"Miss Fin Fan has done me the honor of accepting them," blandly replied Wong Ling.

"Very good," commented Tian Shan. He picked up the gifts and hurled them into the street.

A scene of wild disorder followed. In the midst of it the father of Fin Fan, who had been downtown, appeared at the door.

"What is the meaning of this?" he demanded.

"Oh, father, father, they are killing one another! Separate them, oh, separate them!" pleaded Fin Fan.

But her father's interference was not needed. Wong Ling swerved to one side, and falling, struck the iron foot of the stove. Tian Shan, seeing his rival unconscious, rushed out of the store.

• • •

The moon hung in the sky like a great yellow pearl and the night was beautiful and serene. But Fin Fan, miserable and unhappy, could not rest.

"All your fault! All your fault!" declared the voice of conscience.

"Fin Fan," spake a voice near to her.

Could it be? Yes, it surely was Tian Shan.

She could not refrain from a little scream.

"Sh! Sh!" bade Tian Shan. "Is he dead?"

"No," replied Fin Fan, "he is very sick, but he will recover."

"I might have been a murderer," mused Tian Shan. "As it is I am liable to arrest and imprisonment for years."

"I am the cause of all the trouble," wept Fin Fan.

Tian Shan patted her shoulder in an attempt at consolation, but a sudden footfall caused her to start away from him.

"They are hunting you!" she cried. "Go! Go!"

And Tian Shan, casting upon her one long farewell look, strode with rapid steps away.

• • •

Poor Fin Fan! She had indeed lost every one, and added to that shame, was the secret sorrow and remorse of her own heart. All the hopes and the dreams which had filled the year that was gone were now as naught, and he, around whom they had been woven, was, because of her, a fugitive from justice, even in Canada.

One day she picked up an American newspaper which a customer had left on the counter, and, more as a habit than for any other reason, began spelling out the paragraphs.

> A Chinese, who has been unlawfully breathing United States air for several years, was captured last night crossing the border, a feat which he is said to have successfully accomplished more than a dozen times during the last few years. His name is Tian Shan, and there is no doubt whatever that he will be deported to China as soon as the necessary papers can be made out.

Fin Fan lifted her head. Fresh air and light had come into her soul. Her eyes sparkled. In the closet behind her hung a suit of her father's clothes. Fin Fan was a tall and well-developed young woman.

• • •

"You are to have company," said the guard, pausing in front of Tian Shan's cage. "A boy without certificate was caught this morning by two of our men this side of Rouse's Point. He has been unable to give an account of himself, so we are putting him in here with you. You will probably take the trip to China together."

Tian Shan continued reading a Chinese paper which he had been allowed to retain. He was not at all interested in the companion thrust upon him. He would have preferred to be left alone. The face of the absent one is so much easier conjured in silence and solitude. It was a foregone conclusion with Tian Shan that he would never again behold Fin Fan, and with true Chinese philosophy he had begun to reject realities and accept dreams as the stuff upon which to live. Life itself was hard, bitter, and disappointing. Only dreams are joyous and smiling.

One star after another had appeared until the heavens were patterned with twinkling lights. Through his prison bars Tian Shan gazed solemnly upon the firmament.

Some one touched his elbow. It was his fellow-prisoner.

So far the boy had not intruded himself, having curled himself up in a corner of the cell and slept soundly apparently, ever since his advent.

"What do you want?" asked Tian Shan not unkindly.

"To go to China with you and to be your wife," was the softly surprising reply.

"Fin Fan!" exclaimed Tian Shan. "Fin Fan!"

The boy pulled off his cap.

"Aye," said he. "'Tis Fin Fan!"

The Sing Song Woman

I

Ah Oi, the Chinese actress, threw herself down on the floor of her room and, propping her chin on her hands, gazed up at the narrow strip of blue sky which could be seen through her window. She seemed to have lost her usually merry spirits. For the first time since she had left her home her thoughts were seriously with the past, and she longed with a great longing for the Chinese Sea, the boats, and the wet, blowing sands. She had been a fisherman's daughter, and many a spring had she watched the gathering of the fishing fleet to which her father's boat belonged. Well could she remember clapping her hands as the vessels steered out to sea for the season's work, her father's amongst them, looking as bright as paint could make it, and flying a neat little flag at its stern; and well could she also remember how her mother had taught her to pray to "Our Lady of Pootoo," the goddess of sailors. One does not need to be a Christian to be religious, and Ah Oi's parents had carefully instructed their daughter according to their light, and it was not their fault if their daughter was a despised actress in an American Chinatown.

The sound of footsteps outside her door seemed to chase away Ah Oi's melancholy mood, and when a girl crossed her threshold, she was gazing amusedly into the street below—a populous thoroughfare of Chinatown.

The newcomer presented a strange appearance. She was crying so hard that red paint, white powder, and carmine lip salve were all besmeared over a naturally pretty face.

Ah Oi began to laugh.

"Why, Mag-gee," said she, "how odd you look with little red rivers running over your face! What is the matter?"

"What is the matter?" echoed Mag-gee, who was a half-white girl. "The matter is that I wish that I were dead! I am to be married tonight to a Chinaman whom I have never seen, and whom I can't bear. It isn't natural that I should. I always took to other men, and never could put up with a Chinaman. I was born in America, and I'm not Chinese in looks nor in any other way. See! My eyes are blue, and there is gold in my hair; and I love potatoes and beef, and every time I eat rice it makes me sick, and so does chopped up food. He came down about a week ago and made arrangements with father, and now everything is fixed and I'm going away forever to live in China. I shall be a Chinese woman next year—I commenced to be one today, when father made me put the paint and powder on my face, and dress in Chinese clothes. Oh! I never want anyone to feel as I do. To think of having to marry a Chinaman! How I hate the Chinese! And the worst of it is, loving somebody else all the while."

The girl burst into passionate sobs. The actress, who was evidently accustomed to hearing her compatriots reviled by the white and half-white denizens of Chinatown, laughed—a light, rippling laugh. Her eyes glinted mischievously.

"Since you do not like the Chinese men," said she, "why do you give yourself to one? And if you care so much for somebody else, why do you not fly to that somebody?"

Bold words for a Chinese woman to utter! But Ah Oi was not as other Chinese women, who all their lives have been sheltered by a husband or father's care.

The half-white girl stared at her companion.

"What do you mean?" she asked.

"This," said Ah Oi. The fair head and dark head drew near together; and two women passing the door heard whispers and suppressed laughter.

"Ah Oi is up to some trick," said one.

II

"The Sing Song Woman! The Sing Song Woman!" It was a wild cry of anger and surprise.

The ceremony of unveiling the bride had just been performed, and Hwuy Yen, the father of Mag-gee, and his friends, were in a state of great excitement, for the unveiled, brilliantly clothed little figure standing in the middle of the room was not the bride who was to have been; but Ah Oi, the actress, the Sing Song Woman.

Every voice but one was raised. The bridegroom, a tall, handsome man, did not understand what had happened, and could find no words to express his surprise at the uproar. But he was so newly wedded that it was not until Hwuy Yen advanced to the bride and shook his hand threateningly in her face, that he felt himself a husband, and interfered by placing himself before the girl.

"What is all this?" he inquired. "What has my wife done to merit such abuse?"

"Your wife!" scornfully ejaculated Hwuy Yen. "She is no wife of yours. You were to have married my daughter, Mag-gee. This is not my daughter; this is an impostor, an actress, a Sing Song Woman. Where is my daughter?"

Ah Oi laughed her peculiar, rippling, amused laugh. She was in no wise abashed, and, indeed, appeared to be enjoying the situation. Her bright, defiant eyes met her questioner's boldly as she answered:

"Mag-gee has gone to eat beef and potatoes with a white man. Oh, we had such a merry time making this play!"

"See how worthless a thing she is," said Hwuy Yen to the young bridegroom.

The latter regarded Ah Oi compassionately. He was a man, and perhaps a little tenderness crept into his heart for the girl towards whom so much bitterness was evinced. She was beautiful. He drew near to her.

"Can you not justify yourself?" he asked sadly.

For a moment Ah Oi gazed into his eyes—the only eyes that had looked with true kindness into hers for many a moon.

"You justify me," she replied with an upward, pleading glance.

Then Ke Leang, the bridegroom, spoke. He said: "The daughter of Hwuy Yen cared not to become my bride and has sought her happiness with another. Ah Oi, having a kind heart, helped her to that happiness, and tried to recompense me my loss by giving me herself. She has been unwise and indiscreet; but the good that is in her is more than the evil, and now that she is my wife, none shall say a word against her."

Ah Oi pulled at his sleeve.

"You give me credit for what I do not deserve," said she. "I had no kind feelings. I thought only of mischief, and I am not your wife. It is but a play like the play I shall act tomorrow."

"Hush!" bade Ke Leang. "You shall act no more. I will marry you again and take you to China."

Then something in Ah Oi's breast, which for a long time had been hard as stone, became soft and tender, and her eyes ran over with tears.

"Oh, sir," said she, "it takes a heart to make a heart, and you have put one today in the bosom of a Sing Song Woman."

Children of Peace

I

They were two young people with heads hot enough and hearts true enough to believe that the world was well lost for love, and they were Chinese.

They sat beneath the shade of a cluster of tall young pines forming a perfect bower of greenness and coolness on the slope of Strawberry hill. Their eyes were looking oceanwards, following a ship nearing the misty horizon. Very serious were their faces and voices. That ship, sailing from west to east, carried from each a message to his and her kin—a message which humbly but firmly set forth that they were resolved to act upon their belief and to establish a home in the new country, where they would ever pray for blessings upon the heads of those who could not see as they could see, nor hear as they could hear.

"My mother will weep when she reads," sighed the girl.

"Pau Tsu," the young man asked, "do you repent?"

"No," she replied, "but—"

She drew from her sleeve a letter written on silk paper.

The young man ran his eye over the closely penciled characters.

"'Tis very much in its tenor like what my father wrote to me," he commented.

"Not that."

Pau Tsu indicated with the tip of her pink forefinger a paragraph which read:

> Are you not ashamed to confess that you love a youth who is not yet your husband? Such disgraceful boldness will surely bring upon your head the punishment you deserve. Before twelve moons go by you will be an Autumn Fan.

The young man folded the missive and returned it to the girl, whose face was averted from his.

"Our parents," said he, "knew not love in its springing and growing, its bud and blossom. Let us, therefore, respectfully read their angry letters, but heed them not. Shall I not love you dearer and more faithfully because you became mine at my own request and not at my father's? And Pau Tsu, be not ashamed."

The girl lifted radiant eyes.

"Listen," said she. "When you, during vacation, went on that long journey to New York, to beguile the time I wrote a play. My heroine is very sad, for the one she loves is far away and she is much tormented by enemies. They would make her ashamed of her love. But this is what she replies to one cruel taunt:

> "When Memory sees his face and hears his voice,
> The Bird of Love within my heart sings sweetly,
> So sweetly, and so clear and jubilant,
> That my little Home Bird, Sorrow,
> Hides its head under its wing,
> And appeareth as if dead.

Shame! Ah, speak not that word to one who loves!
For loving, all my noblest, tenderest feelings are awakened,
And I become too great to be ashamed."

"You do love me then, eh, Pau Tsu?" queried the young man.
"If it is not love, what is it?" softly answered the girl.
Happily chatting they descended the green hill. Their holiday was over. A little later Liu Venti was on the ferry-boat which leaves every half hour for the Western shore, bound for the Berkeley Hills opposite the Golden Gate, and Pau Tsu was in her room at the San Francisco Seminary, where her father's ambition to make her the equal in learning of the son of Liu Jusong had placed her.

II

The last little scholar of Pau Tsu's free class for children was pattering out of the front door when Liu Venti softly entered the schoolroom. Pau Tsu was leaning against her desk, looking rather weary. She did not hear her husband's footstep, and when he approached her and placed his hand upon her shoulder she gave a nervous start.

"You are tired, dear one," said he, leading her towards the door where a seat was placed.

"Teacher, the leaves of a flower you gave me are withering, and mother says that is a bad omen."

The little scholar had turned back to tell her this.

"Nay," said Pau Tsu gently. "There are no bad omens. It is time for the flower to wither and die. It cannot live always."

"Poor flower!" compassionated the child.

"Not so poor!" smiled Pau Tsu. "The flower has seed from which other flowers will spring, more beautiful than itself!"

"Ah, I will tell my mother!"

The little child ran off, her queue dangling and flopping as she loped along. The teachers watched her join a group of youngsters playing on the curb in front of the quarters of the Six Companies. One of the Chiefs in passing had thrown a handful of firecrackers amongst the children, and the result was a small bonfire and great glee.

It was seven years since Liu Venti and Pau Tsu had begun their work in San Francisco's Chinatown; seven years of struggle and hardship, working and waiting, living, learning, fighting, failing, loving—and conquering. The victory, to an onlooker, might have seemed small; just a modest school for adult pupils of their own race, a few white night pupils, and a free school for children. But the latter was in itself evidence that Liu Venti and Pau Tsu had not only sailed safely through the waters of poverty, but had reached a haven from which they could enjoy the blessedness of stretching out helping hands to others.

During the third year of their marriage twin sons had been born to them, and the children, long looked for and eagerly desired, were welcomed with joy and pride. But mingled with this joy and pride was much serious thought. Must their beloved sons ever remain exiles from the land of their ancestors? For their little ones Liu Venti and Pau Tsu were much more worldly than they had ever been themselves, and they could not altogether stifle a yearning to be able to bestow upon them the brightest and best that the world has to offer. Then, too, memories of childhood came thronging with their children, and filial affection reawakened. Both Liu Venti and Pau Tsu had been only children; both had been beloved and had received all the advantages which wealth in their own land could obtain; both had been the joy and pride of their homes. They might, they sometimes sadly mused, have been a little less assured in their declarations to the old folk; a little kinder, a little more considerate. It was a higher light and a stronger motive than had ever before influenced their lives which had led them to break the ties which had bound them; yet those from whom they had cut away were ignorant of such forces; at least, unable, by reason of education and environment, to comprehend them. There were days when everything seemed to taste bitter to Pau Tsu because she could not see her father and mother. And Liu's blood would tingle and his heart swell in his chest in the effort to banish from his mind the shadows of those who had cared for him before ever he had seen Pau Tsu.

"I was a little fellow of just about that age when my mother first taught me to kotow to my father and run to greet him when he came into the house," said he, pointing to Little Waking Eyes, who came straggling after them, a kitten in his chubby arms.

"Oh, Liu Venti," replied Pau Tsu, "you are thinking of home—even as I. This morning I thought I heard my mother's voice, calling to me as I have so often heard her on sunny mornings in the Province of the Happy River. She would flutter her fan at me in a way that was peculiarly her own. And my father! Oh, my dear father!"

"Aye," responded Liu Venti. "Our parents loved us, and the love of parents is a good thing. Here, we live in exile, and though we are happy in each other, in our children, and in the friendships which the new light has made possible for us, yet I would that our sons could be brought up in our own country and not in an American Chinatown."

He glanced comprehensively up the street as he said this. A motley throng, made up, not only of his own countrymen, but of all nationalities, was scuffling along. Two little children were eating rice out of a tin dish on a near-by door-step. The sing song voices of girls were calling to one another from high balconies up a shadowy alley. A boy, balancing a wooden tray of viands on his head, was crossing the street. The fat barber was laughing hilariously at a drunken white man who had fallen into a gutter. A withered old fellow, carrying a bird in a cage, stood at a corner entreating passers-by to pause and have a good fortune told. A vender of dried fish and bunches of sausages held noisy possession of the corner opposite.

Liu Venti's glance travelled back to the children eating rice on the doorstep, then rested on the head of his own young son.

"And our fathers' mansions," said he, "are empty of the voices of little ones."

● ● ●

"Let us go home," said Pau Tsu suddenly. Liu Venti started. Pau Tsu's words echoed the wish of his own heart. But he was not as bold as she.

"How dare we?" he asked. "Have not our fathers sworn that they will never forgive us?"

"The light within me this evening," replied Pau Tsu, "reveals that our parents sorrow because they have this sworn. Oh, Liu Venti, ought we not to make our parents happy, even if we have to do so against their will?"

"I would that we could," replied Liu Venti. "But before we can approach them, there is to be overcome your father's hatred for my father and my father's hatred for thine."

A shadow crossed Pau Tsu's face. But not for long. It lifted as she softly said: "Love is stronger than hate."

Little Waking Eyes clambered upon his father's knee.

"Me too," cried Little Sleeping Eyes, following him. With chubby fists he pushed his brother to one side and mounted his father also.

Pau Tsu looked across at her husband and sons. "Oh, Liu Venti," she said, "for the sake of our children; for the sake of our parents; for the sake of a broader field of work for ourselves, we are called upon to make a sacrifice!"

Three months later, Liu Venti and Pau Tsu, with mingled sorrow and hope in their hearts, bade goodbye to their little sons and sent them across the sea, offerings of love to parents of whom both son and daughter remembered nothing but love and kindness, yet from whom that son and daughter were estranged by a poisonous thing called Hate.

III

Two little boys were playing together on a beach. One gazed across the sea with wondering eyes. A thought had come—a memory.

"Where are father and mother?" he asked, turning to his brother.

The other little boy gazed bewilderedly back at him and echoed: "Where are father and mother?"

Then the two little fellows sat down in the sand and began to talk to one another in a queer little old-fashioned way of their own.

"Grandfathers and grandmothers are very good," said Little Waking Eyes.

"Very good," repeated Little Sleeping Eyes.

"They give us lots of nice things."

"Lots of nice things!"

"Balls and balloons and puff puffs and kitties."

"Balls and balloons and puff puffs and kitties."

"The puppet show is very beautiful!"

"Very beautiful!"

"And grandfathers fly kites and puff fire flowers!"

"Fly kites and puff fire flowers!"

"And grandmothers have cakes and sweeties."

"Cakes and sweeties!"

"But where are father and mother?"

Little Waking Eyes and Little Sleeping Eyes again searched each other's faces; but neither could answer the other's question. Their little mouths drooped pathetically; they propped their chubby little faces in their hands and heaved queer little sighs.

There were father and mother one time—always, always; father and mother and Sung Sung. Then there was the big ship and Sung Sung only, and the big water. After the big water, grandfathers and grandmothers; and Little Waking Eyes had gone to live with one grandfather and grandmother, and Little Sleeping Eyes had gone to live with another grandfather and grandmother. And the old Sung Sung had gone away and two new Sung Sungs had come. And Little Waking Eyes and Little Sleeping Eyes had been good and had not cried at all. Had not father and mother said that grandfathers and grandmothers were just the same as fathers and mothers?

"Just the same as fathers and mothers," repeated Little Waking Eyes to Little Sleeping Eyes, and Little Sleeping Eyes nodded his head and solemnly repeated: "Just the same as fathers and mothers."

Then all of a sudden Little Waking Eyes stood up, rubbed his fists into his eyes and shouted: "I want my father and mother; I want my father and mother!" And Little Sleeping Eyes also stood up and echoed strong and bold: "I want my father and mother; I want my father and mother."

It was the day of rebellion of the sons of Liu Venti and Pau Tsu.

When the two new Sung Sungs who had been having their fortunes told by an itinerant fortune-teller whom they had met some distance down the beach, returned to where they had left their young charges, and found them not, they were greatly perturbed and rent the air with their cries. Where could the children have gone? The beach was a lonely one, several miles from the seaport city where lived the grand-parents of the children. Behind the beach, the bare land rose for a little way back up the sides and across hills to meet a forest dark and dense.

Said one Sung Sung to another, looking towards this forest: "One might as well search for a pin at the bottom of the ocean as search for the children there. Besides, it is haunted with evil spirits."

"A-ya, A-ya, A-ya!" cried the other, "Oh, what will my master and mistress say if I return home without Little Sleeping Eyes, who is the golden plum of their hearts?"

"And what will my master and mistress do to me if I enter their presence without Little Waking Eyes? I verily believe that the sun shines for them only when he is around."

For over an hour the two distracted servants walked up and down the beach, calling the names of their little charges; but there was no response.

IV

"Thy grandson—the beloved of my heart, is lost, is lost! Go forth, old man, and find him."

Liu Jusong, who had just returned from the Hall, where from morn till eve he adjusted the scales of justice, stared speechlessly at the old lady who had thus accosted him. The loss of his grandson he scarcely realized; but that his humble spouse had suddenly become his superior officer, surprised him out of his dignity.

"What meaneth thy manner?" he bewilderedly inquired.

"It meaneth," returned the old lady, "that I have borne all I can bear. Thy grandson is lost through thy fault. Go, find him!"

"How my fault? Surely, thou art demented!"

"Hadst thou not hated Li Wang, Little Waking Eyes and Little Sleeping Eyes could have played together in our own grounds or within the compound of Li Wang. But this is no time to discourse on spilt plums. Go, follow Li Wang in the search for thy grandsons. I hear that he has already left for the place where the stupid thorns who had them in charge, declare they disappeared."

The old lady broke down.

"Oh, my little Bright Eyes! Where art thou wandering?" she wailed.

Liu Jusong regarded her sternly. "If my enemy," said he, "searcheth for my grandsons, then will not I."

With dignified step he passed out of the room. But in the hall was a child's plaything. His glance fell upon it and his expression softened. Following the servants despatched by his wife, the old mandarin joined in the search for Little Waking Eyes and Little Sleeping Eyes.

·   ·   ·

Under the quiet stars they met—the two old men who had quarrelled in student days and who ever since had cultivated hate for each other. The cause of their quarrel had long been forgotten; but in the fertile soil of minds irrigated with the belief that the superior man hates well and long, the seed of hate had germinated and flourished. Was it not because of that hate that their children were exiles from the homes of their fathers—those children who had met in a foreign land, and in spite of their fathers' hatred, had linked themselves in love.

They spread their fans before their faces, each pretending not to see the other, while their servants inquired: "What news of the honorable little ones?"

"No news," came the answer from each side.

The old men pondered sternly. Finally Liu Jusong said to his servants: "I will search in the forest."

"So also will I," announced Li Wang.

Liu Jusong lowered his fan. For the first time in many years he allowed his eyes to rest on the countenance of his quondam friend, and that quondam friend returned his glance. But the servant men shuddered.

"It is the haunted forest," they cried. "Oh, honorable masters, venture not amongst evil spirits!"

But Li Wang laughed them to scorn, as also did Liu Jusong.

"Give me a lantern," bade Li Wang. "I will search alone since you are afraid."

He spake to his servants; but it was not his servants who answered: "Nay, not alone. Thy grandson is my grandson and mine is thine!"

• • •

"Oh, grandfather," cried Little Waking Eyes, clasping his arms around Liu Jusong's neck, "where are father and mother?"

And Little Sleeping Eyes murmured in Li Wang's ear, "I want my father and mother!"

Liu Jusong and Li Wang looked at each other. "Let us send for our children," said they.

V

"How many moons, Liu Venti, since our little ones went from us?" asked Pau Tsu.

She was very pale, and there was a yearning expression in her eyes.

"Nearly five," returned Liu Venti, himself stifling a sigh.

"Sometimes," said Pau Tsu, "I feel I cannot any longer bear their absence."

She drew from her bosom two little shoes, one red, one blue.

"Their first," said she. "Oh, my sons, my little sons!"

A messenger boy approached, handed Liu Venti a message, and slipped away.

Liu Venti read:

> May the bamboo ever wave. Son and daughter, return to your parents and your children.
>
> LIU JUSONG,
> LI WANG.

"The answer to our prayer," breathed Pau Tsu. "Oh Liu Venti, love is indeed stronger than hate!"

The Banishment of Ming and Mai

I

Many years ago in the beautiful land of China, there lived a rich and benevolent man named Chan Ah Sin. So kind of heart was he that he could not pass through a market street without buying up all the live fish, turtles, birds, and animals that he saw, for the purpose of giving them liberty and life. The animals and birds he would set free in a cool green forest called the Forest of the Freed, and the fish and turtles he would release in a moon-loved pool called the Pool of Happy Life. He also bought up and set free all animals that were caged for show, and even remembered the reptiles.

Some centuries after this good man had passed away, one of his descendants was accused of having offended against the laws of the land, and he and all of his kin were condemned to be punished therefor. Amongst his kin were two little seventh cousins named Chan Ming and Chan Mai, who had lived very happily all their lives with a kind uncle as guardian and a good old nurse. The punishment meted out to this little boy and girl was banishment to a wild and lonely forest, which forest could only be reached by travelling up a dark and mysterious river in a small boat. The journey was long and perilous, but on the evening of the third day a black shadow loomed before

Ming and Mai. This black shadow was the forest, the trees of which grew so thickly together and so close to the river's edge that their roots interlaced under the water.

The rough sailors who had taken the children from their home, beached the boat, and without setting foot to land themselves, lifted the children out, then quickly pushed away. Their faces were deathly pale, for they were mortally afraid of the forest, which was said to be inhabited by innumerable wild animals, winged and crawling things.

Ming's lip trembled. He realized that he and his little sister were now entirely alone, on the edge of a fearsome forest on the shore of a mysterious river. It seemed to the little fellow, as he thought of his dear Canton, so full of bright and busy life, that he and Mai had come, not to another province, but to another world.

One great, big tear splashed down his cheek. Mai, turning to weep on his sleeve, saw it, checked her own tears, and slipping a little hand into his, murmured in his ear:

"Look up to the heavens, O brother. Behold, the Silver Stream floweth above us here as bright as it flowed above our own fair home." (The Chinese call the Milky Way the Silver Stream.)

While thus they stood, hand in hand, a moving thing resembling a knobby log of wood was seen in the river. Strange to say, the children felt no fear and watched it float towards them with interest. Then a watery voice was heard. "Most honorable youth and maid," it said, "go back to the woods and rest."

It was a crocodile. Swimming beside it were a silver and a gold fish, who leaped in the water and echoed the crocodile's words; and following in the wake of the trio, was a big green turtle mumbling: "To the woods, most excellent, most gracious, and most honorable."

Obediently the children turned and began to find their way among the trees. The woods were not at all rough and thorny as they had supposed they would be. They were warm and fragrant with aromatic herbs and shrubs. Moreover, the ground was covered with moss and grass, and the bushes and young trees bent themselves to allow them to pass through. But they did not wander far. They were too tired and sleepy. Choosing a comfortable place in which to rest, they lay down side by side and fell asleep.

When they awoke the sun was well up. Mai was the first to open her eyes, and seeing it shining through the trees, exclaimed: "How beautiful is the ceiling of my room!" She thought she was at home and had forgotten the river journey. But the next moment Ming raised his head and said: "The beauty you see is the sun filtering through the trees and the forest where—"

He paused, for he did not wish to alarm his little sister, and he had nearly said: "Where wild birds and beasts abound."

"Oh, dear!" exclaimed Mai in distress. She also thought of the wild birds and beasts, but like Ming, she also refrained from mentioning them.

"I am impatiently hungry," cried Ming. He eyed enviously a bright little bird hopping near. The bird had found a good, fat grasshopper for its breakfast, but when it heard Ming speak, it left the grasshopper and flew quickly away.

A moment later there was a great trampling and rustling amongst the grasses and bushes. The hearts of the children stood still. They clasped hands. Under every bush and tree, on the branches above them, in a pool near by, and close beside them, almost touching their knees, appeared a great company of living things from the animal, fish, fowl, and insect kingdoms.

It was true then—what the sailors had told them—only worse; for whereas they had expected to meet the denizens of the forest, either singly or in couples, here they were all massed together.

A tiger opened its mouth. Ming put his sister behind him and said: "Please, honorable animals, birds, and other kinds of living things, would some of you kindly retire for a few minutes. We expected to meet you, but not so many at once, and are naturally overwhelmed with the honor."

"Oh, yes, please your excellencies," quavered Mai, "or else be so kind as to give us space in which to retire ourselves, so that we may walk into the river and trouble you no more. Will we not, honorable brother?"

"Nay, sister," answered Ming. "These honorable beings have to be subdued and made to acknowledge that man is master of this forest. I am here to conquer them in fight, and am willing to take them singly, in couples, or even three at a time; but as I said before, the honor of all at once is somewhat overwhelming."

"Oh! ah!" exclaimed Mai, gazing awestruck at her brother. His words made him more terrible to her than any of the beasts of the field. Just then the tiger, who had politely waited for Ming and Mai to say their say, made a strange purring sound, loud, yet strangely soft;

fierce, yet wonderfully kind. It had a surprising effect upon the children, seeming to soothe them and drive away all fear. One of little Mai's hands dropped upon the head of a leopard crouching near, whilst Ming gazed straight into the tiger's eyes and smiled as at an old friend. The tiger smiled in return, and advancing to Ming, laid himself down at his feet, the tip of his nose resting on the boy's little red shoes. Then he rolled his body around three times. Thus in turn did every other animal, bird, fish, and insect present. It took quite a time and Mai was glad that she stood behind her brother and received the obeisances by proxy.

This surprising ceremony over, the tiger sat back upon his haunches and, addressing Ming, said:

"Most valorous and honorable descendant of Chan Ah Sin the First: Your coming and the coming of your exquisite sister will cause the flowers to bloom fairer and the sun to shine brighter for us. There is, therefore, no necessity for a trial of your strength or skill with any here. Believe me, Your Highness, we were conquered many years ago—and not in fight."

"Why! How?" cried Ming.

"Why! How?" echoed Mai.

And the tiger said:

"Many years ago in the beautiful land of China, there lived a rich and benevolent man named Chan Ah Sin. So kind of heart was he that he could not pass through a market street without buying up all the live fish, turtles, birds, and animals that he saw, for the purpose of giving them liberty and life. These animals and birds he would set free in a cool green forest called the Forest of the Freed, and the fish and turtles he would release in a moon-loved pool called the Pool of Happy Life. He also bought up and set free all animals that were caged for show, and even remembered the reptiles."

The tiger paused.

"And you," observed Ming, "you, sir tiger, and your forest companions, are the descendants of the animals, fish, and turtles thus saved by Chan Ah Sin the First."

"We are, Your Excellency," replied the tiger, again prostrating himself. "The beneficent influence of Chan Ah Sin the First, extending throughout the centuries, has preserved the lives of his young descendants, Chan Ming and Chan Mai."

II: The Tiger's Farewell

Many a moon rose and waned over the Forest of the Freed and the Moon-loved Pool of Happy Life, and Ming and Mai lived happily and contentedly amongst their strange companions. To be sure, there were times when their hearts would ache and their tears would flow for their kind uncle and good old nurse, also for their little playfellows in far-away Canton; but those times were few and far between. Full well the children knew how much brighter and better was their fate than it might have been.

One day, when they were by the river, amusing themselves with the crocodiles and turtles, the water became suddenly disturbed, and lashed and dashed the shore in a very strange manner for a river naturally calm and silent.

"Why, what can be the matter?" cried Ming.

"An honorable boat is coming," shouted a goldfish.

Ming and Mai clasped hands and trembled.

"It is the sailors," said they to one another; then stood and watched with terrified eyes a large boat sail majestically up the broad stream.

Meanwhile down from the forest had rushed the tiger with his tigress and cubs, the leopard with his leopardess and cubs, and all the other animals with their young, and all the birds, and all the insects, and all the living things that lived in the Forest of the Freed and the Moon-loved Pool. They surrounded Ming and Mai, crouched at their feet, swarmed in the trees above their heads, and crowded one another on the beach and in the water.

The boat stopped in the middle of the stream, in front of the strip of forest thus lined with living things. There were two silk-robed men on it and a number of sailors, also an old woman carrying a gigantic parasol and a fan whose breeze fluttered the leaves in the Forest of the Freed.

When the boat stopped, the old woman cried: "Behold, I see my precious nurslings surrounded by wild beasts. A-ya, A-ya, A-ya." Her cries rent the air and Ming and Mai, seeing that the old woman was Woo Ma, their old nurse, clapped their little hands in joy.

"Come hither," they cried. "Our dear friends will welcome you. They are not wild beasts. They are elegant and accomplished superior beings."

Then one of the men in silken robes commanded the sailors to steer for the shore, and the other silk-robed man came and leaned over the side of the boat and said to the tiger and leopard:

"As I perceive, honorable beings, that you are indeed the friends of my dear nephew and niece, Chan Ming and Chan Mai, I humbly ask your permission to allow me to disembark on the shore of this river on the edge of your forest."

The tiger prostrated himself, so also did his brother animals, and all shouted:

"Welcome, O most illustrious, most benevolent, and most excellent Chan Ah Sin the Ninth."

So Mai crept into the arms of her nurse and Ming hung on to his uncle's robe, and the other silk-robed man explained how and why they had come to the Forest of the Freed and the Moon-loved Pool.

A fairy fish, a fairy duck, a fairy butterfly, and a fairy bird, who had seen the children on the river when the cruel sailors were taking them from their home, had carried the news to the peasants of the rice fields, the tea plantations, the palm and bamboo groves. Whereupon great indignation had prevailed, and the people of the province, who loved well the Chan family, arose in their might and demanded that an investigation be made into the charges against that Chan who was reputed to have broken the law, and whose relatives as well as himself had been condemned to suffer therefor. So it came to pass that the charges, which had been made by some malicious enemy of high official rank, were entirely disproved, and the edict of banishment against the Chan family recalled.

The first thought of the uncle of Ming and Mai, upon being liberated from prison, was for his little nephew and niece, and great indeed was his alarm and grief upon learning that the two tender scions of the house of Chan had been banished to a lonely forest by a haunted river, which forest and river were said to be inhabited by wild and cruel beings. Moreover, since the sailors who had taken them there, and who were the only persons who knew where the forest was situated, had been drowned in a swift rushing rapid upon their return journey, it seemed almost impossible to trace the little ones, and Chan Ah Sin the Ninth was about giving up in despair, when the fairy bird, fish, and butterfly, who had aroused the peasants, also aroused the uncle by appearing to him and telling him where the forest of banishment lay and how to reach it.

"Yes," said Chan Ah Sin the Ninth, when his friend ceased speaking, "but they did not tell me that I should find my niece and nephew so tenderly cared for. Heaven alone knows why you have been so good to my beloved children."

He bowed low to the tiger, leopard, and all the living things around him.

"Most excellent and honorable Chan Ah Sin the Ninth," replied the Tiger, prostrating himself, "we have had the pleasure and privilege of being good to these little ones, because many years ago in the beautiful land of China, your honorable ancestor, Chan Ah Sin the First, was good and kind to our forefathers."

Then arising upon his hind legs, he turned to Ming and Mai and tenderly touching them with his paws, said:

"Honorable little ones, your banishment is over, and those who roam the Forest of the Freed, and dwell in the depths of the Pool of Happy Life, will behold no more the light of your eyes. May heaven bless you and preserve you to be as good and noble ancestors to your descendants as your ancestor, Chan Ah Sin the First, was to you."

The Story of a Little Chinese Seabird

A little Chinese seabird sat in the grass which grew on a rocky island. The little Chinese seabird was very sad. Her wing was broken and all her brothers and sisters had flown away, leaving her alone. Why, oh why, had she broken her wing? Why, oh why, were brothers and sisters so?

The little Chinese seabird looked over the sea. How very beautiful its life and movement! The sea was the only consolation the little Chinese seabird had. It was always lovely and loving to the little Chinese seabird. No matter how often the white-fringed waves spent themselves for her delight, there were always more to follow. Changeably unchanged, they never deserted her nor her island home. Not so with her brothers and sisters. When she could fly with them, circle in the air, float upon the water, dive for little fish, and be happy and gay—then indeed she was one of them and they loved her. But since she had broken her wing, it was different. The little Chinese seabird shook her little head mournfully.

But what was that which the waves were bearing towards her island? The little Chinese seabird gave a quick glance, then put her little head under the wing that was not broken.

Now, what the little Chinese seabird had seen was a boat. Within the boat were three boys—and these boys were coming to the island to hunt for birds' eggs. The little Chinese seabird knew this, and her bright, wild little eyes glistened like jewels, and she shivered and shuddered as she spread herself as close to the ground as she could.

The boys beached the boat and were soon scrambling over the island, gathering all the eggs that they could find. Sometimes they passed so near to the little Chinese seabird that she thought she must surely be trampled upon, and she set her little beak tight and close so that she might make no sound, should so painful an accident occur. Once, however, when the tip of a boy's queue dangled against her head and tickled it, the little Chinese seabird forgot entirely her prudent resolve to suffer in silence, and recklessly pecked at the dangling queue. Fortunately for her, the mother who had braided the queue of the boy had neglected to tie properly the bright red cord at the end thereof. Therefore when the little Chinese seabird pecked at the braid, the effect of the peck was not to cause pain to the boy and make him turn around, as might otherwise have been the case, but to pull out of his queue the bright red cord. This, the little Chinese seabird held in her beak for quite a long time. She enjoyed glancing down at its bright red color, and was afraid to let it fall in case the boys might hear.

Meanwhile, the boys, having gathered all the eggs they could find, plotted together against the little Chinese seabird and against her brothers and sisters, and the little seabird, holding the red cord in her beak, listened with interest. For many hours after the boys had left the island, the little Chinese seabird sat meditating over what she had heard. So deeply did she meditate that she forgot all about the pain of her broken wing.

Towards evening her brothers and sisters came home and settled over the island like a wide-spreading mantle of wings.

For some time the little Chinese seabird remained perfectly still and quiet. She kept saying to herself, "Why should I care? Why should I care?" But as she did care, she suddenly let fall the bright red cord and opened and closed her beak several times.

"What is all that noise?" inquired the eldest seabird.

"Dear brother," returned the little Chinese seabird, "I hope I have not disturbed you; but is not this a very lovely night? See how radiant the moon."

"Go to sleep! Go to sleep!"

"Did you have an enjoyable flight today, brother?"

"Tiresome little bird, go to sleep, go to sleep."

It was the little Chinese seabird's eldest sister that last spoke.

"Oh, sister, is that you?" replied the little Chinese seabird. "I could see you last of the flock as you departed from our island, and I did so admire the satin white of your underwings and tail."

"Mine is whiter," chirped the youngest of all the birds.

"Go to sleep, go to sleep!" snapped the eldest brother.

"What did you have to eat today?" inquired the second brother of the little Chinese seabird.

"I had a very tasty worm porridge, dear brother," replied the little Chinese seabird. "I scooped it out of the ground beside me, because you know I dared not move any distance for fear of making worse my broken wing?"

"Your broken wing? Ah, yes, your broken wing!" murmured the second brother.

"Ah, yes, your broken wing!" faintly echoed the others.

Then they all, except the very youngest one, put their heads under their own wings, for they all, except the very youngest one, felt a little bit ashamed of themselves.

But the little Chinese seabird did not wish her brothers and sisters to feel ashamed of themselves. It embarrassed her, so she lifted up her little voice again, and said:

"But I enjoyed the day exceedingly. The sea was never so lovely nor the sky either. When I was tired of watching the waves chase each other, I could look up and watch the clouds. They sailed over the blue sky so soft and white."

"There's no fun in just watching things," said the youngest of all the birds: "we went right up into the clouds and then deep down into the waves. How we splashed and dived and swam! When I fluttered my wings after a bath in silver spray, it seemed as if a shower of jewels dropped therefrom."

"How lovely!" exclaimed the little Chinese seabird. Then she remembered that if her brothers and sisters were to have just as good a time the next day, she must tell them a story—a true one.

So she did.

After she had finished speaking, there was a great fluttering of wings, and all her brothers and sisters rose in the air above her, ready for flight.

"To think," they chattered to one another, "that if we had remained an hour longer, those wicked boys would have come with lighted torches and caught us and dashed us to death against stones."

"Yes, and dressed us and salted us!"

"And dressed us and salted us!"

"And dried us!"

"And dried us!"

"And eaten us!"

"And eaten us!"

"How rude!"

"How inconsiderate!"

"How altogether uncalled for!"

"Are you quite sure?" inquired the eldest brother of the little Chinese seabird.

"See," she replied, "here is the red cord from the queue of one of the boys. I picked it out as his braid dangled against my head!"

The brothers and sisters looked at one another.

"How near they must have come to her!" exclaimed the eldest sister.

"They might have trampled her to death in a very unbecoming manner!" remarked the second.

"They will be sure to do it tonight when they search with torchlight," was the opinion of the second brother.

And the eldest brother looked sharply down upon the little Chinese seabird, and said:

"If you had not told us what these rude boys intended doing, you would not have had to die alone."

"I prefer to die alone!" proudly replied the little Chinese seabird. "It will be much pleasanter to die in quiet than with wailing screams in my ears."

"Hear her, oh, hear her!" exclaimed the second sister.

But the eldest sister, she with the satin-white under-wings and spreading tail, descended to the ground, and began pulling up some tough grass. "Come," she cried to the other birds, "let us make a strong nest for our broken-winged little sister—a nest in which we can bear away to safety one who tonight has saved our lives without thought of her own."

"We will, with pleasure," answered the other birds."

Whereupon they fluttered down and helped to build the most wonderful nest that ever was built, weaving in and out of it the bright red cord, which the little Chinese seabird had plucked out of the boy's queue. This made the nest strong enough to bear the weight of the little Chinese seabird, and when it was finished they dragged it beside her and tenderly pushed her in. Then they clutched its sides with their beaks, flapped their wings, and in a moment were soaring together far up in the sky, the little Chinese seabird with the broken wing happy as she could be in the midst of them.

What about the Cat?

"What about the cat?" asked the little princess of her eldest maid.

"It is sitting on the sunny side of the garden wall, watching the butterflies. It meowed for three of the prettiest to fall into its mouth, and would you believe it, that is just what happened. A green, a blue, a pink shaded with gold, all went down pussy's red throat."

The princess smiled. "What about the cat?" she questioned her second maid.

"She is seated in your honorable father's chair of state, and your honorable father's first body-slave is scratching her back with your father's own back-scratcher, made of the purest gold and ivory."

The princess laughed outright. She pattered gracefully into another room. There she saw the youngest daughter of her foster-mother.

"What about the cat?" she asked for the third time.

"The cat! Oh, she has gone to Shinku's duck farm. The ducks love her so that when they see her, they swim to shore and embrace her with their wings. Four of them combined to make a raft and she got upon their backs and went down-stream with them. They met some of the ducklings on the way and she patted them to death with her paws. How the big ducks quacked!"

"That is a good story," quoth the princess.

She went into the garden and, seeing one of the gardeners, said: "What about the cat?"

"It is frisking somewhere under the cherry tree, but you would not know it if you saw it," replied the gardener.

"Why?" asked the princess.

"Because, Your Highness, I gave it a strong worm porridge for its dinner, and as soon as it ate it, its white fur coat became a glossy green, striped with black. It looks like a giant caterpillar, and all the little caterpillars are going to hold a festival tonight in its honor."

"Deary me! What a great cat!" exclaimed the princess.

A little further on she met one of the chamberlains of the palace. "What about the cat?" she asked.

"It is dancing in the ballroom in a dress of elegant cobwebs and a necklace of pearl rice. For partner, she has the yellow dragon in the hall, come to life, and they take such pretty steps together that all who behold them shriek in ecstasy. Three little mice hold up her train as she dances, and another sits perched on the tip of the dragon's curled tail."

At this the princess quivered like a willow tree and was obliged to seek her apartments. When there, she recovered herself, and placing a blossom on her exquisite eyebrow, commanded that all those of whom she had inquired concerning the cat should be brought before her. When they appeared she looked at them very severely and said:

"You have all told me different stories when I have asked you: 'What about the cat?' Which of these stories is true?"

No one answered. All trembled and paled.

"They are all untrue," announced the princess.

She lifted her arm and there crawled out of her sleeve her white cat. It had been there all the time.

Then the courtly chamberlain advanced towards her, kotowing three times. "Princess," said he, "would a story be a story if it were true? Would you have been as well entertained this morning if, instead of our stories, we, your unworthy servants, had simply told you that the cat was up your sleeve?"

The princess lost her severity in hilarity.

"Thank you, my dear servants," said she. "I appreciate your desire to amuse me."

She looked at her cat, thought of all it had done and been in the minds of her servants, and laughed like a princess again and again.

The Dreams That Failed

Ping Sik and Soon Yen sat by the roadside under a spreading olive tree. They were on their way to market to sell two little pigs. With the money to be obtained from the sale of the little pigs, they were to buy caps and shoes with which to attend school.

"When I get to be a man," said Ping Sik, "I will be so great and so glorious that the Emperor will allow me to wear a three-eyed peacock feather, and whenever I walk abroad, all who meet me will bow to the ground."

"And I," said Soon Yen, "will be a great general. The reins of my steeds will be purple and scarlet, and in my cap will wave a bright blue plume."

"I shall be such a great poet and scholar," continued Ping Sik, "that the greatest university in the Middle Kingdom will present me with a vase encrusted with pearls."

"And I shall be so valiant and trustworthy that the Pearly Emperor will appoint me commander-in-chief of his army, and his enemies will tremble at the sound of my name."

"I shall wear a yellow jacket with the names of three ancestors inscribed thereon in seven colors."

"And I shall wear silk robes spun by princesses, and a cloak of throat skins of sables."

"And I shall live in a mansion of marble and gold."

"And I in halls of jadestone."

"And I will own silk and tea plantations and tens of thousands of rice farms."

"All the bamboo country shall be mine, and the rivers and sea shall be full of my fishing boats, junks, and craft of all kinds."

"People will bow down before me and cry: 'Oh, most excellent, most gracious, most beautiful!'"

"None will dare offend so mighty a man as I shall be!"

"O ho! You good-for-nothing rascals!" cried the father of Ping Sik. "What are you doing loafing under a tree when you should be speeding to market?"

"And the little pigs, where are they?" cried the father of Soon Yen.

The boys looked down at the baskets which had held the little pigs. While they had been dreaming of future glories, the young porkers had managed to scramble out of the loosely woven bamboo thatch of which the baskets were made.

The fathers of Ping Sik and Soon Yen produced canes.

"Without shoes and caps," said they, "you cannot attend school. Therefore, back to the farm and feed pigs."

The Heart's Desire

She was dainty, slender, and of waxen pallor. Her eyes were long and drooping, her eyebrows finely arched. She had the tiniest Golden Lily feet and the glossiest black hair. Her name was Li Chung O'Yam, and she lived in a sad, beautiful old palace surrounded by a sad, beautiful old garden, situated on a charming island in the middle of a lake. This lake was spanned by marble bridges, entwined with green creepers, reaching to the mainland. No boats were ever seen on its waters, but the pink lotus lily floated thereon and swans of marvellous whiteness.

Li Chung O'Yam wore priceless silks and radiant jewels. The rarest flowers bloomed for her alone. Her food and drink were of the finest flavors and served in the purest gold and silver plates and goblets. The sweetest music lulled her to sleep.

Yet Li Chung O'Yam was not happy. In the midst of the grandeur of her enchanted palace, she sighed for she knew not what.

"She is weary of being alone," said one of the attendants. And he who ruled all within the palace save Li Chung O'Yam, said: "Bring her a father!"

A portly old mandarin was brought to O'Yam. She made humble obeisance, and her august father inquired ceremoniously as to the state of her health, but she sighed and was still weary.

"We have made a mistake; it is a mother she needs," said they.

A comely matron, robed in rich silks and waving a beautiful peacock feather fan, was presented to O'Yam as her mother. The lady delivered herself of much good advice and wise instruction as to deportment and speech, but O'Yam turned herself on her silken cushions and wished to say goodbye to her mother.

Then they led O'Yam into a courtyard which was profusely illuminated with brilliant lanterns and flaring torches. There were a number of little boys of about her own age dancing on stilts. One little fellow, dressed all in scarlet and flourishing a small sword, was pointed out to her as her brother. O'Yam was amused for a few moments, but in a little while she was tired of the noise and confusion.

In despair, they who lived but to please her consulted amongst themselves. O'Yam, overhearing them, said: "Trouble not your minds. I will find my own heart's ease."

Then she called for her carrier dove, and had an attendant bind under its wing a note which she had written. The dove went forth and flew with the note to where a little girl named Ku Yum, with a face as round as a harvest moon, and a mouth like a red vine leaf, was hugging a cat to keep her warm and sucking her finger to prevent her from being hungry. To this little girl the dove delivered O'Yam's message, then returned to its mistress.

"Bring me my dolls and my cats, and attire me in my brightest and best," cried O'Yam.

When Ku Yum came slowly over one of the marble bridges towards the palace wherein dwelt Li Chung O'Yam, she wore a blue cotton blouse, carried a peg doll in one hand and her cat in another. O'Yam ran to greet her and brought her into the castle hall. Ku Yum looked at O'Yam, at her radiant apparel, at her cats and her dolls.

"Ah!" she exclaimed. "How beautifully you are robed! In the same colors as I. And behold, your dolls and your cats, are they not much like mine?"

"Indeed they are," replied O'Yam, lifting carefully the peg doll and patting the rough fur of Ku Yum's cat.

Then she called her people together and said to them:

"Behold, I have found my heart's desire—a little sister."

And forever after O'Yam and Ku Yum lived happily together in a glad, beautiful old palace, surrounded by a glad, beautiful old garden, on a charming little island in the middle of a lake.

Misunderstood

The baby was asleep. Ku Yum looked curiously at her little brother as he lay in placid slumber. His head was to be shaved for the first time that afternoon,* and he was dressed for the occasion in three padded silk vests, sky-blue trousers and an embroidered cap, which was surmounted by a little gold god and a sprig of evergreen for good luck. This kept its place on his head, even in sleep. On his arms and ankles were hung many amulets and charms, and on the whole he appeared a very resplendent baby. To Ku Yum, he was simply gorgeous, and she longed to get her little arms around him and carry him to some place where she could delight in him all by herself.

Ku Yum's mind had been in a state of wonder concerning the boy, Ko Ku, ever since he had been born. Why was he so very small and so very noisy? What made his fingers and toes so pink? Why did her mother always smile and sing whenever she had the baby in her arms? Why did her father, when he came in from his vegetable garden, gaze so long at Ko Ku? Why did grandmother make so much fuss over him? And yet, why, oh why, did they give him nothing nice to eat?

The baby was sleeping very soundly. His little mouth was half open and a faint, droning sound was issuing therefrom. He had just completed his first moon and was a month old. Poor baby! that never got any rice to eat, nor nice sweet cakes. Ku Yum's heart swelled with compassion. In her hand was a delicious half-moon cake. It was the time of the harvest-moon festival and Ku Yum had already eaten three. Surely, the baby would like a taste. She hesitated. Would she dare, when it lay upon that silken coverlet? Ku Yum had a wholesome regard for her mother's bamboo slipper.

The window blind was torn on one side. A vagrant wind lifted it, revealing an open window. There was a way out of that window to the vegetable garden. Beyond the vegetable garden was a cool, green spot under a clump of trees; also a beautiful puddle of muddy water.

An inspiration came to Ku Yum, born of benevolence. She lifted

---

*The ceremony of the "Completion of the Moon" takes place when a Chinese boy child attains to a month old. His head is then shaved for the first time amidst much rejoicing. The foundation of the babe's future fortune is laid on that day, for every guest invited to the shaving is supposed to present the baby with a gold piece, no matter how small.

the sleeping babe in her arms, and with hushed, panting breaths, bore him slowly and laboriously to where her soul longed to be. He opened his eyes once and gave a faint, disturbed cry, but lapsed again into dreamland.

Ku Yum laid him down on the grass, adjusted his cap, smoothed down his garments, ran her small fingers over his brows, or where his brows ought to have been, tenderly prodded his plump cheeks, and ruffled his straight hair. Little sighs of delight escaped her lips. The past and the future were as naught to her. She revelled only in the present.

For a few minutes thus: then a baby's cries filled the air. Ku Yum sat up. She remembered the cake. It had been left behind. She found a large green leaf, and placing that over the baby's mouth in the hope of mellowing its tones, cautiously wended her way back between the squash and cabbages.

All was quiet and still. It was just before sundown and it was very warm. Her mother still slept her afternoon sleep. Hastily seizing the confection, she returned to the babe, her face beaming with benevolence and the desire to do good. She pushed some morsels into the child's mouth. It closed its eyes, wrinkled its nose and gurgled; but its mouth did not seem to Ku Yum to work just as a proper mouth should under such pleasant conditions.

"Behold me! Behold me!" she cried, and herself swallowed the remainder of the cake in two mouthfuls. Ko Ku, however, did not seem to be greatly edified by the example set him. The crumbs remained, half on his tongue and half on the creases of his cheek. He still emitted explosive noises.

Ku Yum sadly surveyed him.

"He doesn't know how to eat. That's why they don't give him anything," she said to herself, and having come to this logical conclusion, she set herself to benefit him in other ways than the one in which she had failed.

She found some worms and ants, which she arranged on leaves and stones, meanwhile keeping up a running commentary on their charms.

"See! This very small brown one—how many legs it has, and how fast it runs. This one is so green that I think its father and mother must have been blades of grass, don't you? And look at the wings on this worm. That one has no wings, but its belly is pretty pink. Feel how nice and slimy it is. Don't you just love slimy things that creep on their bellies, and things that fly in the air, and things with four legs? Oh, all kinds of things except grown-up things with two legs."

She inclined the baby's head so that his eyes would be on a level with her collection, but he screamed the louder for the change.

> "Oh, hush thee, baby, hush thee,
> And never, never fear
> The bogies of the dark land,
> When the green bamboo is near,"

she chanted in imitation of her mother. But the baby would not be soothed.

She wrinkled her childish brow. Her little mind was perplexed. She had tried her best to amuse her brother, but her efforts seemed in vain.

Her eyes fell on the pool of muddy water. They brightened. Of all things in the world Ku Yum loved mud, real, good, clean mud. What bliss to dip her feet into that tempting pool, to feel the slow brown water oozing into her little shoes! Ku Yum had done that before and the memory thrilled her. But with that memory came another—a memory of poignant pain; the cause, a bamboo cane, which bamboo cane had been sent from China by her father's uncle, for the express purpose of helping Ku Yum to walk in the straight and narrow path laid out for a proper little Chinese girl living in Santa Barbara.

Still the baby cried. Ku Yum looked down on him and the cloud on her brow lifted. Ko Ku should have the exquisite pleasure of dipping his feet into that soft velvety water. There would be no bamboo cane for him. He was loved too well. Ku Yum forgot herself. Her thoughts were entirely for Ko Ku. She half dragged, half carried him to the pool. In a second his feet were immersed therein and small wiggling things were wandering up his tiny legs. He gave a little gasp and ceased crying. Ku Yum smiled. Ah! Ko Ku was happy at last! Then:

Before Ku Yum's vision flashed a large, cruel hand. Twice, thrice it appeared, after which, for a space of time, Ku Yum could see nothing but twinkling stars.

"My son! My son! the evil spirit in your sister had almost lost you to me!" cried her mother.

"That this should happen on the day of the completion of the moon, when the guests from San Francisco are arriving with the gold coins. Verily, my son, your sister is possessed of a devil," declared her father.

And her grandmother, speaking low, said: "'Tis fortunate the child is alive. But be not too hard on Ku Yum. The demon of jealousy can best be exorcised by kindness."

And the sister of Ko Ku wailed low in the grass, for there were none to understand.

A Chinese Boy-Girl

I

The warmth was deep and all-pervading. The dust lay on the leaves of the palms and the other tropical plants that tried to flourish in the Plaza. The persons of mixed nationalities lounging on the benches within and without the square appeared to be even more listless and unambitious than usual. The Italians who ran the peanut and fruit stands at the corners were doing no business to speak of. The Chinese merchants' stores in front of the Plaza looked as quiet and respectable and drowsy as such stores always do. Even the bowling alleys, billiard halls, and saloons seemed under the influence of the heat, and only a subdued clinking of glasses and roll of balls could be heard from behind the half-open doors. It was almost as hot as an August day in New York City, and that is unusually sultry for Southern California.

A little Chinese girl, with bright eyes and round cheeks, attired in blue cotton garments, and wearing her long, shining hair in a braid interwoven with silks of many colors, paused beside a woman tourist who was making a sketch of the old Spanish church. The tourist and the little Chinese girl were the only persons visible who did not seem to be affected by the heat. They might have been friends; but the lady, fearing for her sketch, bade the child run off. Whereupon the little thing shuffled across the Plaza, and in less than five minutes was at the door of the Los Angeles Chinatown school for children.

"Come in, little girl, and tell me what they call you," said the young American teacher, who was new to the place.

"Ku Yum be my name," was the unhesitating reply; and said Ku Yum walked into the room, seated herself complacently on an empty bench in the first row, and informed the teacher that she lived on

Apablaza street, that her parents were well, but her mother was dead, and her father, whose name was Ten Suie, had a wicked and tormenting spirit in his foot.

The teacher gave her a slate and pencil, and resumed the interrupted lesson by indicating with her rule ten lichis (called "Chinese nuts" by people in America) and counting them aloud.

"One, two, three, four, five, six, seven, eight, nine, ten," the baby class repeated.

After having satisfied herself by dividing the lichis unequally among the babies, that they might understand the difference between a singular and a plural number, Miss Mason began a catechism on the features of the face. Nose, eyes, lips, and cheeks were properly named, but the class was mute when it came to the forehead.

"What is this?" Miss Mason repeated, posing her finger on the fore part of her head.

"Me say, me say," piped a shrill voice, and the new pupil stepped to the front, and touching the forehead of the nearest child with the tips of her fingers, christened it "one," named the next in like fashion "two," a third "three," then solemnly pronounced the fourth a "four head."

Thus Ku Yum made her debut in school, and thus began the trials and tribulations of her teacher.

Ku Yum was bright and learned easily, but she seemed to be possessed with the very spirit of mischief; to obey orders was to her an impossibility, and though she entered the school a voluntary pupil, one day at least out of every week found her a truant.

"Where is Ku Yum?" Miss Mason would ask on some particularly alluring morning, and a little girl with the air of one testifying to having seen a murder committed, would reply: "She is running around with the boys." Then the rest of the class would settle themselves back in their seats like a jury that has found a prisoner guilty of some heinous offense, and, judging by the expression on their faces, were repeating a silent prayer somewhat in the strain of "O Lord, I thank thee that I am not as Ku Yum is!" For the other pupils were demure little maidens who, after once being gathered into the fold, were very willing to remain.

But if ever the teacher broke her heart over any one it was over Ku Yum. When she first came, she took an almost unchildlike interest in the rules and regulations, even at times asking to have them repeated to her; but her study of such rules seemed only for the purpose of finding a means to break them, and that means she never failed to discover and put into effect.

After a disappearance of a day or so she would reappear, bearing a gorgeous bunch of flowers. These she would deposit on Miss Mason's desk with a little bow; and though one would have thought that the sweetness of the gift and the apparent sweetness of the giver needed but a gracious acknowledgment, something like the following conversation would ensue:

"Teacher, I plucked these flowers for you from the Garden of Heaven." (They were stolen from some park.)

"Oh, Ku Yum, whatever shall I do with you?"

"Maybe you better see my father."

"You are a naughty girl. You shall be punished. Take those flowers away."

"Teacher, the eyebrow over your little eye is very pretty."

But the child was most exasperating when visitors were present. As she was one of the brightest scholars, Miss Mason naturally expected her to reflect credit on the school at the examinations. On one occasion she requested her to say some verses which the little Chinese girl could repeat as well as any young American, and with more expression than most. Great was the teacher's chagrin when Ku Yum hung her head and said only: "Me 'shamed, me 'shamed!"

"Poor little thing," murmured the bishop's wife. "She is too shy to recite in public."

But Miss Mason, knowing that of all children Ku Yum was the least troubled with shyness, was exceedingly annoyed.

Ku Yum had been with Miss Mason about a year when she became convinced that some steps would have to be taken to discipline the child, for after school hours she simply ran wild on the streets of Chinatown, with boys for companions. She felt that she had a duty to perform towards the motherless little girl; and as the father, when apprised of the fact that his daughter was growing up in ignorance of all home duties, and, worse than that, shared the sports of boy children on the street, only shrugged his shoulders and drawled: "Too bad! Too bad!" she determined to act.

She interested in Ku Yum's case the president of the Society for the Prevention of Cruelty to Children, the matron of the Rescue Home, and the most influential ministers, and the result, after a month's work, was that an order went forth from the Superior Court of the State decreeing that Ku Yum, the child of Ten Suie, should be removed from the custody of her father, and, under the auspices of the Society for the Prevention of Cruelty to Children, be put into a home for Chinese girls in San Francisco.

Her object being accomplished, strange to say, Miss Mason did not experience that peaceful content which usually follows a benevolent action. Instead, the question as to whether, after all, it was right, under the circumstances, to deprive a father of the society of his child, and a child of the love and care of a parent, disturbed her mind, morning, noon, and night. What had previously seemed her distinct duty no longer appeared so, and she began to wish with all her heart that she had not interfered in the matter.

II

Ku Yum had not been seen for weeks and those who were deputed to bring her into the sheltering home were unable to find her. It was suspected that the little thing purposely kept out of the way—no difficult matter, all Chinatown being in sympathy with her and arrayed against Miss Mason. Where formerly the teacher had met with smiles and pleased greetings, she now beheld averted faces and downcast eyes, and her school had within a week dwindled from twenty-four scholars to four. Verily, though acting with the best of intentions, she had shown a lack of diplomacy.

It was about nine o'clock in the evening. She had been visiting little Lae Choo, who was lying low with typhoid fever. As she wended her way home through Chinatown, she did not feel at all easy in mind; indeed, as she passed one of the most unsavory corners and observed some men frown and mutter among themselves as they recognized her, she lost her dignity in a little run. As she stopped to take breath, she felt her skirt pulled from behind and heard a familiar little voice say:

"Teacher, be you afraid?"

"Oh, Ku Yum," she exclaimed, "is that you?" Then she added reprovingly: "Do you think it is right for a little Chinese girl to be out alone at this time of the night?"

"I be not alone," replied the little creature, and in the gloom Miss Mason could distinguish behind her two boyish figures.

She shook her head.

"Ku Yum, will you promise me that you will try to be a good little girl?" she asked.

Ku Yum answered solemnly:

"Ku Yum *never* be a good girl."

Her heart hardened. After all, it was best that the child should be placed where she would be compelled to behave herself.

"Come, see my father," said Ku Yum pleadingly.

Her voice was soft, and her expression was so subdued that the teacher could hardly believe that the moment before she had defiantly stated that she would never be a good girl. She paused irresolutely. Should she make one more appeal to the parent to make her a promise which would be a good excuse for restraining the order of the Court? Ah, if he only would, and she only could prevent the carrying out of that order!

They found Ten Suie among his curiosities, smoking a very long pipe with a very small, ivory bowl. He calmly surveyed the teacher through a pair of gold-rimmed goggles, and under such scrutiny it was hard indeed for her to broach the subject that was on her mind. However, after admiring the little carved animals, jars, vases, bronzes, dishes, pendants, charms, and snuff-boxes displayed in his handsome showcase, she took courage.

"Mr. Ten Suie," she began, "I have come to speak to you about Ku Yum."

Ten Suie laid down his pipe and leaned over the counter. Under his calm exterior some strong excitement was working, for his eyes glittered exceedingly.

"Perhaps you speak too much about Ku Yum alleady," he said. "Ku Yum be my child. I bling him up as I please. Now, teacher, I tell you something. One, two, three, four, five, seven, eight, nine years go by, I have five boy. One, two, three, four, five, six, seven years go, I have four boy. One, two, three, four, five, six years go by, I have one boy. Every year for three year evil spirit come, look at my boy, and take him. Well, one, two, three, four, five, six years go by, I see but one boy, he four year old. I say to me: Ten Suie, evil spirit be jealous. I be 'flaid he want my one boy. I dless him like one girl. Evil spirit think him one girl, and go away; no want girl."

Ten Suie ceased speaking, and settled back into his seat.

For some moments Miss Mason stood uncomprehending. Then the

full meaning of Ten Suie's words dawned upon her, and she turned to Ku Yum, and taking the child's little hand in hers, said:

"Goodbye, Ku Yum. Your father, by passing you off as a girl, thought to keep an evil spirit away from you; but just by that means he brought another, and one which nearly took you from him too."

"Goodbye, teacher," said Ku Yum, smiling wistfully. "I never be good girl, but perhaps I be good boy."

Pat and Pan

I

They lay there, in the entrance to the joss house, sound asleep in each other's arms. Her tiny face was hidden upon his bosom and his white, upturned chin rested upon her black, rosetted head.

It was that white chin which caused the passing Mission woman to pause and look again at the little pair. Yes, it was a white boy and a little Chinese girl; he, about five, she, not more than three years old.

"Whose is that boy?" asked the Mission woman of the peripatetic vender of Chinese fruits and sweetmeats.

"That boy! Oh, him is boy of Lum Yook that make the China gold ring and bracelet."

"But he is white."

"Yes, him white; but all same, China boy. His mother, she not have any white flend, and the wife of Lum Yook give her lice and tea, so when she go to the land of spilit, she give her boy to the wife of Lum Yook. Lady, you want buy lichi?"

While Anna Harrison was extracting a dime from her purse the black, rosetted head slowly turned and a tiny fist began rubbing itself into a tiny face.

"Well, chickabiddy, have you had a nice nap?"

"Tjo ho! tjo ho!"

The black eyes gazed solemnly and disdainfully at the stranger.

"She tell you to be good," chuckled the old man.

"Oh, you quaint little thing!"

The quaint little thing hearing herself thus apostrophized, turned herself around upon the bosom of the still sleeping boy and, reaching her arms up to his neck, buried her face again under his chin. This, of course, awakened him. He sat up and stared bewilderedly at the Mission woman.

"What is the boy's name?" she asked, noting his gray eyes and rosy skin.

His reply, though audible, was wholly unintelligible to the American woman.

"He talk only Chinese talk," said the old man.

Anna Harrison was amazed. A white boy in America talking only Chinese talk! She placed her bag of lichis beside him and was amused to see the little girl instantly lean over her companion and possess herself of it. The boy made no attempt to take it from her, and the little thing opened the bag and cautiously peeped in. What she saw evoked a chirrup of delight. Quickly she brought forth one of the browny-red fruit nuts, crushed and pulled off its soft shell. But to the surprise of the Mission woman, instead of putting it into her own mouth, she thrust the sweetish, dried pulp into that of her companion. She repeated this operation several times, then cocking her little head on one side, asked:

"Ho 'm ho? Is it good or bad?"

"Ho! ho!" answered the boy, removing several pits from his mouth and shaking his head to signify that he had had enough. Whereupon the little girl tasted herself of the fruit.

"Pat! Pan! Pat! Pan!" called a woman's voice, and a sleek-headed, kindly-faced matron in dark blue pantalettes and tunic, wearing double hooped gold earrings, appeared around the corner. Hearing her voice, the boy jumped up with a merry laugh and ran out into the street. The little girl more seriously and slowly followed him.

"Him mother!" informed the lichi man.

II

When Anna Harrison, some months later, opened her school for white and Chinese children in Chinatown, she determined that Pat, the adopted son of Lum Yook, the Chinese jeweller, should learn to speak his mother tongue. For a white boy to grow up as a Chinese was unthinkable. The second time she saw him, it was some kind of a Chinese holiday, and he was in great glee over a row of red Chinese candles and punk which he was burning on the curb of the street, in company with a number of Chinese urchins. Pat's candle was giving a brighter and bigger flame than any of the others, and he was jumping up and down with his legs doubled under him from the knees like an india-rubber ball, while Pan, from the doorstep of her father's store, applauded him in vociferous, infantile Chinese.

Miss Harrison laid her hand upon the boy's shoulder and spoke to him. It had not been very difficult for her to pick up a few Chinese phrases. Would he not like to come to her school and see some pretty pictures? Pat shook his ruddy curls and looked at Pan. Would Pan come too? Yes, Pan would. Pan's memory was good, and so were lichis and shredded cocoanut candy.

Of course Pan was too young to go to school—a mere baby; but if Pat could not be got without Pan, why then Pan must come too. Lum Yook and his wife, upon being interviewed, were quite willing to have Pat learn English. The foster-father could speak a little of the language himself; but as he used it only when in business or when speaking to Americans, Pat had not benefited thereby. However, he was more eager than otherwise to have Pat learn "the speech of his ancestors," and promised that he would encourage the little ones to practise "American" together when at home.

So Pat and Pan went to the Mission school, and for the first time in their lives suffered themselves to be divided, for Pat had to sit with the boys and tiny Pan had a little red chair near Miss Harrison, beside which were placed a number of baby toys. Pan was not supposed to learn, only to play.

But Pan did learn. In a year's time, although her talk was more broken and babyish, she had a better English vocabulary than had Pat. Moreover, she could sing hymns and recite verses in a high, shrill voice; whereas Pat, though he tried hard enough, poor little fellow, was unable to memorize even a sentence. Naturally, Pat did not like school as well as did Pan, and it was only Miss Harrison's persistent ambition for him that kept him there.

One day, when Pan was five and Pat was seven, the little girl, for the first time, came to school alone.

"Where is Pat?" asked the teacher.

"Pat, he is sick today," replied Pan.

"Sick!" echoed Miss Harrison. "Well, that is too bad. Poor Pat! What is the matter with him?"

"A big dog bite him."

That afternoon, the teacher, on her way to see the bitten Pat, beheld him up an alley busily engaged in keeping five tops spinning at one time, while several American boys stood around, loudly admiring the Chinese feat.

The next morning Pat received five strokes from a cane which Miss Harrison kept within her desk and used only on special occasions. These strokes made Pat's right hand tingle smartly; but he received them with smiling grace.

Miss Harrison then turned to five year old Pan, who had watched the caning with tearful interest.

"Pan!" said the teacher, "you have been just as naughty as Pat, and you must be punished too."

"I not stay away flom school!" protested Pan.

"No,"—severely—"you did not stay away from school; but you told me a dog had bitten Pat, and that was not true. Little girls must not say what is not true. Teacher does not like to slap Pan's hands, but she must do it, so that Pan will remember that she must not say what is not true. Come here!"

Pan, hiding her face in her sleeve, sobbingly arose.

The teacher leaned forward and pulling down the uplifted arm, took the small hand in her own and slapped it. She was about to do this a second time when Pat bounded from his seat, pushed Pan aside, and shaking his little fist in the teacher's face, dared her in a voice hoarse with passion:

"You hurt my Pan again! You hurt my Pan again!"

They were not always lovers—those two. It was aggravating to Pat, when the teacher finding he did not know his verse, would turn to Pan and say:

"Well, Pan, let us hear you."

And Pan, who was the youngest child in school and unusually small for her years, would pharisaically clasp her tiny fingers and repeat word for word the verse desired to be heard.

"I hate you, Pan!" muttered Pat on one such occasion.

Happily Pan did not hear him. She was serenely singing:

> "Yesu love me, t'is I know,
> For the Bible tell me so."

But though a little seraph in the matter of singing hymns and repeating verses, Pan, for a small Chinese girl, was very mischievous. Indeed, she was the originator of most of the mischief which Pat carried out with such spirit. Nevertheless, when Pat got into trouble, Pan, though sympathetic, always had a lecture for him. "Too bad, too bad! Why not you be good like me?" admonished she one day when he was suffering "consequences."

Pat looked down upon her with wrathful eyes.

"Why," he asked, "is bad people always so good?"

III

The child of the white woman, who had been given a babe into the arms of the wife of Lum Yook, was regarded as their own by the Chinese jeweller and his wife, and they bestowed upon him equal love and care with the little daughter who came two years after him. If Mrs. Lum Yook showed any favoritism whatever, it was to Pat. He was the first she had cradled to her bosom; the first to gladden her heart with baby smiles and wiles; the first to call her Ah Ma; the first to love her. On his eighth birthday, she said to her husband: "The son of the white woman is the son of the white woman, and there are many tongues wagging because he lives under our roof. My heart is as heavy as the blackest heavens."

"Peace, my woman," answered the easygoing man. "Why should we trouble before trouble comes?"

When trouble did come it was met calmly and bravely. To the comfortably off American and wife who were to have the boy and "raise him as an American boy should be raised," they yielded him without protest. But deep in their hearts was the sense of injustice and outraged love. If it had not been for their pity for the unfortunate white girl, their care and affection for her helpless offspring, there would have been no white boy for others to "raise."

And Pat and Pan? "I will not leave my Pan! I will not leave my Pan!" shouted Pat.

"But you must!" sadly urged Lum Yook. "You are a white boy and Pan is Chinese."

"I am Chinese too! I am Chinese too!" cried Pat.

"He Chinese! He Chinese!" pleaded Pan. Her little nose was swollen with crying; her little eyes red-rimmed.

But Pat was driven away.

. . .

Pat, his schoolbooks under his arm, was walking down the hill, whistling cheerily. His roving glance down a side street was suddenly arrested.

"Gee!" he exclaimed. "If that isn't Pan! Pan, oh, Pan!" he shouted.

Pan turned. There was a shrill cry of delight, and Pan was clinging to Pat, crying: "Nice Pat! Good Pat!"

Then she pushed him away from her and scanned him from head to foot.

"Nice coat! Nice boot! How many dollars?" she queried.

Pat laughed good-humoredly. "I don't know," he answered. "Mother bought them."

"Mother!" echoed Pan. She puckered her brows for a moment.

"You are grown big, Pat," was her next remark.

"And you have grown little, Pan," retorted Pat. It was a year since they had seen one another and Pan was much smaller than any of his girl schoolfellows.

"Do you like to go to the big school?" asked Pan, noticing the books.

"I don't like it very much. But, say, Pan, I learn lots of things that you don't know anything about."

Pan eyed him wistfully. Finally she said: "O Pat! A–Toy, she die."

"A–Toy! Who is A–Toy?"

"The meow, Pat; the big gray meow! Pat, you have forgot to remember."

Pat looked across A–Toy's head and far away.

"Chinatown is very nice now," assured Pan. "Hum Lock has two trays of brass beetles in his store and Ah Ma has many flowers!"

"I would like to see the brass beetles," said Pat.

"And father's new glass case?"

"Yes."

"And Ah Ma's flowers?"

"Yes."

"Then come, Pat."

"I can't, Pan!"

"Oh!"

Again Pat was walking home from school, this time in company with some boys. Suddenly a glad little voice sounded in his ear. It was Pan's.

"Ah, Pat!" cried she joyfully. "I find you! I find you!"

"Hear the China kid!" laughed one of the boys.

Then Pat turned upon Pan. "Get away from me," he shouted. "Get away from me!"

And Pan did get away from him—just as fast as her little legs could carry her. But when she reached the foot of the hill, she looked up and shook her little head sorrowfully. "Poor Pat!" said she. "He Chinese no more; he Chinese no more!"

Part 2

Other Writings:

Journalism, Essays, Short Fiction

Introduction

Annette White-Parks

The selections from Sui Sin Far's uncollected writings that follow range from the writer's earliest sketches and journalism, through her later journalism and essays, to her last located fiction, published after *Mrs. Spring Fragrance.* It is important to understand that these are only selections, a representative few from among the numerous pieces that Sui Sin Far wrote. Since she often wrote for little-known publications that many nineteenth-century women who supported themselves by the pen were forced to use—railway brochures or newspapers or small magazines—her works went out of print almost as soon as they were published. In the past twenty years, many of Sui Sin Far's writings have been located; equivalent pages, I conjecture, are still to be found.[1] Because most of these pieces are being seen publicly for the first time since Sui Sin Far published them, some knowledge of background, especially of the early pieces, is important to understanding them. It is with this in mind that I begin by sharing notes on my research and sources.

The clues that I started with came mainly form S. E. Solberg's paper "Eaton Sisters: Sui Sin Far and Onoto Watanna" and Sui Sin Far's autobiography, "Leaves from the Mental Portfolio of an Eurasian."[2] The former led me to Montreal, Sui Sin Far's home; the latter I came to rely on as a map—impressionistic, surely, in terms of dates, names, or places, but each detail a gem in suggesting direction. As I read and reread her essay throughout my research, small clues in the text came to interweave with materials uncovered in the archives, each folding back on and expanding the other. For instance, the simple passage in "Leaves," "When I have been working for some years I open an office of my own. The local papers patronize me and give me . . . most of the local Chinese reporting," was confirmed by the entry "Eaton, Miss Edith, stenographer and typewriter, 147 St. James" in Montreal's 1894–97 city directories and pointed me to these dates in microfilms of local papers. In such ways did the autobiography, written in 1909, and my research, conducted in 1989, continue to verify and complement one another. Like a puzzle with matching numbers, art and life opened joint doors, each leading to a new possibility. The result was a packet of articles that I identify as authored by Sui Sin Far.

The authorship of most of this early journalism had to be proven because nineteenth-century newspapers rarely gave bylines to unknown writers and because Sui Sin Far was ingenuous at trickster stylistics, often masking her personal identity under various guises.[3] My major criteria for establishing authorship were, first, that the pieces be written during the 1894–97 time period when Sui Sin Far had her office; second, that the pieces were "Chinese reporting," that is, about Chinese Americans or Chinese Canadians; and, third, that the reporter's attitude toward Chinese North American populations was noticeably sympathetic, in contrast to the racist attitudes of most reporters who were Sui Sin Far's contemporaries. With time and my increasing awareness of Sui Sin Far's ironic wit and sense of juxtaposition, stylistic parallels began to stand out. The skills at reversing unjust but socially accepted images that aided Sui Sin Far in later fictional battles with stereotypes appear also in her journalism. In addition, several of the pieces gave themselves away with themes and diction that duplicate, almost line for line, themes and diction in Sui Sin Far's essays and fiction. We can compare, for instance, the ironic stance the writer casts on the media's rhetoric of "freedom" in the two newspieces "The Land of the Free" and " 'The Ching Song Episode,' " published in the *Montreal Daily Witness* in the spring of 1890, with Sui Sin Far's exposure of similar ironies in her 1909 short story "In the Land of the Free"—the common titles were the first tip-off.[4] "A Chinese Party: A Singular Scene at the Windsor Street Depot," published in the fall of 1890 in the *Montreal Daily Witness,* similarly disparages popular assumptions about Chinese Americans forced to travel in bond and satirizes the integrity of a white Canadian official who holds them en route.[5]

The experiences and descriptions of "Half-Chinese Children: Those of American Mothers and Chinese Fathers" in New York, published in the *Montreal Daily Star* in 1895, reverberate with the experiences and descriptions Sui Sin Far later recollects about her siblings and herself in "Leaves." As with the Eaton siblings, in the news story the children's "peculiar cast about the face" calls forth mocking cries of " 'Chinese'

'Chinese' " and gives rise to street fights waged by the white children with whom they come into contact.[6] "Girl Slave in Montreal: Our Chinese Colony Cleverly Described," published a year earlier in the *Montreal Daily Witness* and introduced as written by "a lady reporter," hints at the hide-and-seek games of Sui Sin Far, the trickster, as does our knowledge that, had her reading audience known about Sui Sin Far, her mother, and her eight sisters, "the only [three] Chinese females in Montreal" described in the article would have increased by ten.[7]

It is worth noting that these two articles, plus "A Plea for the Chinaman: A Correspondent's Argument in His Favor," published in the *Montreal Daily Star* in 1896,[8] were written during an era of severe Chinese witch-hunts in both Canada and the United States, after each nation had completed the transcontinental railroad. While it was being built, labor contractors had urged people from China to migrate for work, but as soon as their work was finished, there was a flurry of racist laws and social abuse to drive Chinese immigrants out of North America. The 1890s saw the second decade of the Chinese Exclusion Act, passed by the United States government in 1882 to prevent Chinese from entering the country. It also saw the gradual increase in head taxes, initially imposed by the Canadian Parliament in 1885 on Chinese seeking to enter Canada. At the time of "A Plea," there was a petition to increase the tax to five hundred dollars.

Sui Sin Far's "Plea," cast in letter form but indeed her most persuasive essay, protests this increase and points out the injustice, illogic, and inconsistency when a nation uses the rhetoric of equality yet persecutes people because of their race. Responding to a Mr. Maxwell, the representative of a commission from British Columbia who is pushing the tax, her argument is classic and brilliantly tongue-in-cheek. This writing dramatically illustrates her claim in "Leaves" to have fought the battles of the Chinese in the papers. It is also significant because it is the first located writing where she openly speaks in her own name for the Chinese. Her tone is that of the sympathetic outsider, and she signs the letter "E.E.," initials that stand for "Edith Eaton," the name she is known by professionally; the piece is written while she still lives with her parents and is generally seen as an "English woman."[9] Desmond Wu translated the piece into Chinese in 1992, when approximately three hundred Chinese Canadians rallied on Ottawa's Parliament Hill demanding restitution for the head tax against which "E.E." had protested. The inspiration this letter offered the protesters almost one hundred years after it was originally written testifies to Sui Sin Far's contemporaneity and the continuance of her dream to fight the battles of the Chinese in print.

To appreciate the evolution of Sui Sin Far's ethnic-racial identification, we can compare this letter with "Spring Impressions: A Medley of Poetry and Prose," the seventh in a series of eight sketches she wrote between 1888 and 1890 for the Canadian *Dominion Illustrated,* all signed "Edith Eaton" and with English and French Canadian subjects and settings.[10] Though in these pieces the author shows no literal awareness of the Chinese Canadians and Chinese Americans to whose voices her future writings would be dedicated, there is a continuity in language and theme between these pieces and her later work. Amy Ling interprets "Spring Impressions" as "key to Sui Sin Far's later work," for here the phrase that entitles her 1912 book is first introduced: "When the spring fragrance and freshness fill the air." Further, her empathetic stance toward "those who have suffered wrongs, perchance beyond the righting," anticipate her dedication to a cause larger than herself.[11]

The *Los Angeles Express* pieces, seven in number, were written from 2 October to 3 November 1903, after Sui Sin Far moved to the West Coast in the United States and was traveling between San Francisco and Seattle and Los Angeles, trying to live by her pen.[12] In them, Sui Sin Far takes us to the heart of Los Angeles's Chinatown, where we see not the swamp of depravity depicted by "yellow peril" authors of the era but the daily affairs of functioning families and neighborhoods. All presumably are based on interviews with local populations—though knowing that Sui Sin Far plays tricks with her audience, we cannot always tell. In "Chinatown Boys and Girls," for example, she introduces a poem with this comment: "A Chinese mother says the following verses are her daughter's." Only the reader familiar with Sui Sin Far's earlier career would recognize that these verses had been published in 1890 in the *Dominion Illustrated* by another Chinese daughter—Sui Sin Far herself.[13] The diversity of the titles of these pieces illustrates Sui Sin Far's range of acquaintance with Chinese North American issues and interests, as well as her growing commitment to those interests on a personal level. "Leung Ki Chu and His Wife," a piece on the visit to Los Angeles by the reformist leader in China's revolution, indicates her awareness of global issues. Two themes familiar to her fiction are ventured here: China as "the country that Heaven loves," and Chinese as citizens of the world. She positions herself as a sympathetic but objective observer, and the pieces are bylined "Sui Sin Far."

Set in China, "Aluteh" is Sui Sin Far's last located story before the four-year publishing hiatus that would be broken by "Leaves from the Mental Portfolio of an Eurasian" in 1909.[14] The Chinese daughter, Aluteh, who saves her father and a local magistrate from disgrace, foreshadows Sui Sin Far's later "Woman Warrior" figures. Aluteh's courage, independence, and assertive self-will and her determination to break through the stereotypes society has made for her create a model for the Chinese American women characters of Sui Sin Far's mature fiction in *Mrs. Spring Fragrance* and the *New England Magazine.* In "The Sugar Cane Baby," Sui Sin Far explores her recurrent theme of the results of assimilation at the personal level but diversifies her cultural focus from Chinese families in North America to Hindu families in the West Indies.[15] Here the satirical look Sui Sin Far casts on colonization comes through at its most scathing, through a baby who is taken from his parents by Catholic missionaries and, in his near death, expresses the life threat to an entire culture.

Published in 1909, both "Leaves from the Mental Portfolio of an Eurasian" and the *Westerner* sketches illustrate Sui Sin Far's increasing identification with the Chinese American community; these writings are the first in which she explicitly identifies herself as a Eurasian and speaks with an insider's voice. "Leaves," published in the New York *Independent* and bylined "Sui Sin Far," can be seen as a turning point in the writer's career—coming after a long publishing silence, evidencing a new sophistication in style, and initiating a period when Sui Sin Far will openly present herself as a person of Chinese heritage. Omitting dates and all but the most general place settings, "Leaves" is structured as a montage of incidents out of memory, arranged in more or less chronological sequence. Sui Sin Far's voice in "Leaves" is not that of a sympathetic outsider but that of a Eurasian, an insider to the experiences she relates, as we hear in the question, "Why are we what we are? I and my brothers and sisters. Why did God make us to be hooted and stared at?" Although the form of "Leaves" is autobiographical, its voice addresses dual reading audiences, just as her fiction does. On one level, Sui Sin Far announces to the public her Eurasian identity and protests what people in her position are being put through: "The unfortunate Chinese Eurasians! Are not those who compel them to thus cringe more to be blamed than they?" On another, she announces to her own family that she will not "cringe" behind an English mask, as do they.

The *Westerner* series, entitled "The Chinese in America," was published out of Earlington, in western Washington, between May and August 1909.[16] In her introduction, Sui Sin Far declares her interest in Chinese was "perpetual since the day I learned that I was of their race." The series, based on interviews during the era when the immigrant station, Port Townsend, was open, focused on a diversity of characters and had an ironic wit, which make the pieces read like miniature short stories as she plays out her views between a variety of oppositions. Many sketches foreshadow fictional ideas and plots; for instance, Go Ek Yu, in "A Chinese Book on Americans," dreams of writing a book on the curious ways of the Americans for the Chinese, just as the title character of "Mrs. Spring Fragrance" does. In the *Westerner* sketches, we thus see glimpses of the historical sources upon which some of Sui Sin Far's fiction is based. We also see her using the term *Chinese American,* which appears in print perhaps for the first time.

"Chinese Workmen in America," an article published in the *Independent* just nine months before her death, picks up on concerns for Chinese Americans that she articulated in the *Westerner* series.[17] In this piece, she plays havoc with notions of class as they pertain to Chinese immigrant laborers: "Many of the Chinese laundrymen I know are not laundrymen only, but artists and poets, often the sons of good families." She also chastises white Americans for their failure to recognize the achievements of these pioneers and the influence they wield in Chinese-U.S. relations when they go back to China. One passage, describing Chinese American as laborers who are "stalwart, self-respecting countrymen from the district around Canton city and province, or are American-born descendants of the pioneer Chinese who came to this coast long before our transcontinental railways were built, and helped the American to mine his ore, build his railways and cause the Pacific coast to blossom as the rose," we recognize as duplicated from Sui Sin Far's introductory comments in the *Westerner* series.

The short stories "An Autumn Fan," "A Love Story from the Rice Fields of China," "Who's Game," and "Chan Hen Yen, Chinese Student" were all published in the *New England Magazine* between 1910 and 1912 and were presumably written during the same period that Sui Sin Far was working on *Mrs. Spring Fragrance.*[18] The first two reveal Sui Sin Far's skill with a theme with which readers of *Mrs. Spring Fragrance* are familiar—using marriage to treat intercultural and intergenerational themes. The third, Sui Sin Far's only found mature fiction to deal with a white American community and characters, illustrates that Christianity does not confine its assimilationist tactics to immigrant cultures or colonized races but marches out against any stray sheep that does not join the fold. In "Who's Game," the writer's trickster stance operates on multiple levels to achieve the ironically layered vision evident in Sui Sin Far's mature fiction. The fourth addresses the issue of miscegenation, at the same time it casts a scathing eye at the mission movement: a Chinese student falls in love with a teenage white missionary and is torn between romantic ideals and allegiance to his native country. Power relationships among the characters in these stories, which often involve courtship and family matters, become analogues to hegemonic issues in early twentieth-century American—Chinese or Victorian—society.

"Sui Sin Far, the Half Chinese Writer, Tells of Her Career" was published in the *Boston Globe* in May 1912, a month before *Mrs. Spring Fragrance* came out and was clearly intended as a promotional piece for the book.[19] Presented in what sounds like replies to an interview, it is told in the first-person voice of Sui Sin Far, the author, and includes many heretofore unseen bits of autobiography. Its central focus, though, is Sui Sin Far's writing life, and it thus offers a rare and invaluable glimpse into her evolution as an artist. We hear of the stories her parents told her when she was four; of her "ambition to write a book about the half Chinese" at age eight; of the "secret doggerel verse" she created as a counterpoint to the Irish lace she crocheted and sold on Montreal streets when she was taken from school at age ten to help earn the family's living. We learn of the chain of mentors who urged her to write, from Mrs. William Darling, her teacher during her primary years in Hochelaga, who "inspired me with the belief that the spirit is more than the body"; to John Archibald, the Montreal attorney who read and commented on her first articles; to the managing editor of the New York *Independent,* whom she credits with encouraging her to complete *Mrs. Spring Fragrance* and to plant, in her words, "a few Eurasian thoughts in Western literature." In its disclosures of continual conflict between creativity and family demands, between earning a living and reserving some time and energy for her own work, the *Globe* piece, more than any other, sets Sui Sin Far in the tradition of all women who have undergone similar struggles.

In the article's concluding lines, Sui Sin far expresses how excited she is at the publication of *Mrs. Spring Fragrance:* "Would not any one be who had worked as hard as I have—and waited as long as I have—for a book?" That excitement becomes contagious. Following its energy some eighty years after Sui Sin Far's death, I have felt it in every piece of her writing that has emerged from a newspaper, journal, or microfilm. "Free from the long dust of the century," each seems to say—a liberation long overdue considering the effort Sui Sin Far expended to get them printed originally. Unique portraits of Chinese North American life at the turn of the last century yet still highly contemporary in the issues they present, each tantalizes us with the possibility of more, waiting in some out-of-sight archive for us to discover.

Notes

1. Linda DiBiase found the *Westerner* series; Amy Ling discovered "Spring Impressions. A Medley of Poetry and Prose"; Anite Malhotra recovered "A Plea for the Chinaman"; S. E. Solberg located "Leaves from the Mental Portfolio of an Eurasian," "Autumn Fan," "A Love Story from the Rice Fields of China," "Who's Game?" "Chan Hen Yen, Chinese Student," and "Chinese Workmen in America"; and I ferreted out "The Land of the Free," "The Ching Song Episode," "A Chinese Party," "Girl Slave in Montreal," "Half-Chinese Children," the *Los Angeles Express* series, and the *Boston Globe* article. I collected and compiled them.

2. S. E. Solberg. "The Eaton Sisters: Sui Sin Far and Ōnoto Watanna" (Paper presented at the Pacific Northwest Asian American Writer's Conference, Seattle, Washington, 16 April 1976); Sui Sin Far, "Leaves from the Mental Portfolio of an Eurasian," *Independent* 66 (21 January 1909): 125–32.

3. For an examination of Sui Sin Far's skills with tricksterism, see Annette White-Parks, "We Wear the Mask: Sui Sin Far as One Example of Trickster Authorship," in *Tricksterism in Turn-of-the-Century American Literature: A Multicultural Perspective,* ed. Elizabeth Ammons and Annette White-Parks (Hanover, N.H.: University Press of New England, 1994).

4. "The Land of the Free," *Montreal Daily Witness,* 15 March 1890; " 'The Ching Song Episode': The Crazy Chinaman Regains His Senses and Stays in Canada," *Montreal Daily Witness,* 17 April 1890; Sui Sin Far, "In the Land of the Free," *Independent* 76 (2 September 1909): 504–8.

5. "A Chinese Party: A Singular Scene at the Windsor Street Depot," *Montreal Daily Witness,* 7 November 1890.

6. "Half-Chinese Children: Those of American Mothers and Chinese Fathers," *Montreal Daily Star,* 20 April 1895.

7. "Girl Slave in Montreal: Our Chinese Colony Cleverly Described," *Montreal Daily Witness*, 4 May 1894.

8. E.E. "A Plea for the Chinaman: A Correspondent's Argument in His Favor," *Montreal Daily Star*, 21 September 1898.

9. For a study of how Sui Sin Far's bylines change with her evolving racial-ethnic identity, see Annette White-Parks, "Naming as Identity," in *A Gathering of Voices on the Asian-American Experience*, ed. Annette White-Parks, Deborah Buffton, Ursula Chiu, Catherine Currier, Decilia Manrique, and Marsha Momoi-Pieh (Fort Atkinson, Wis.: Highsmith Press, forthcoming).

10. Edith Eaton, "A Trip in a Horse Car," *Dominion Illustrated* 1 (13 October 1888): 235; "Misunderstood: The Story of a Young Man," *Dominion Illustrated* 1 (17 November 1888): 314; "A Fatal Tug of War," *Dominion Illustrated* 1 (8 December 1888): 362–63; "The Origin of a Broken Nose," *Dominion Illustrated* 2 (11 May 1889): 302; "Robin," *Dominion Illustrated* 2 (22 June 1889): 394; "Albemarle's Secret," *Dominion Illustrated* 3 (19 October 1889): 254; "Spring Impressions: A Medley of Poetry and Prose," *Dominion Illustrated* 4 (June 1890): 358–59; "In Fairyland," *Dominion Illustrated* 5 (18 October 1890): 270.

11. As cited in Amy Ling, "Edith Eaton: Pioneer Chinamerican Writer and Feminist," *American Literary Realism* 16 (Autumn 1983): 290.

12. Sui Sin Far, "In Los Angeles' Chinatown," *Los Angeles Express*, 2 October 1903; "Betrothals in Chinatown," *Los Angeles Express*, 8 October 1903; "Chinatown Needs a School," *Los Angeles Express*, 14 October 1903; "Chinatown Boys and Girls," *Los Angeles Express*, 15 October 1903; "Leung Ki Chu and His Wife," *Los Angeles Express*, 22 October 1903; "Chinese in Business Here," *Los Angeles Express*, 23 October 1903; "Chinese Laundry Checking," *Los Angeles Express*, 3 November 1903.

13. Edith Eaton, "In Fairyland," 270.

14. Sui Sin Far (Edith Eaton), "Aluteh," *Chautauquan* 42 (December 1905): 338–42.

15. Sui Sin Far, "The Sugar Cane Baby," *Good Housekeeping* 50 (May 1910): 50–72.

16. Sui Sin Far (Edith Eaton), "The Chinese in America," *Westerner* 10, 11 (May, June, July, August 1909).

17. Sui Sin Far, "Chinese Workmen in America," *Independent* 75 (3 July 1913): 56–58.

18. Sui Sin Far, "An Autumn Fan," *New England Magazine* 42 (August 1910): 700–702; "A Love Story from the Rice Fields of China," *New England Magazine* 45 (December 1911): 343–45; "Who's Game?" *New England Magazine* 45 (February 1912): 573–79; "Chan Hen Yen, Chinese Student," *New England Magazine* 45 (June 1912): 462–66.

19. Sui Sin Far, "Sui Sin Far, the Half Chinese Writer, Tells of Her Career," *Boston Globe*, 5 May 1912.

The Land of the Free

"Goon" was a Chinaman from New York, desirous of taking up his residence in Montreal. He was sent through in bond like a box of traps, and the moment he touched the free soil of Canada he was pounced upon by customs officer, A. Pare, who demanded in the name of the Queen of his marvelously free country, $50 or his immediate departure from the country.

"Goon" gave the officer to understand that if he took him to Hop Sing, 1316 Notre Dame St., that generous compatriot would put up the amount and, sure enough, Hop Sing did, and "Goon" is now "washee-washee" as happy as a King.

Montreal Daily Witness, 15 March 1890

The Ching Song Episode

The Crazy Chinaman Regains His Senses and Stays in Canada

Ching Song is free once more. He had a narrow escape. He was just on the eve of being declared insane. But he suddenly ceased to talk about desiring to go to "China or heaven," and expressed his intention of becoming a good Canadian citizen, and engaging prosaically in "washee-washee." So, after being a few days in gaol for safety, Ching Song was liberated, and at once went to pay his respects to the C.P.R. officials, who had suffered greatly on his account last week, not knowing what to do with him. "Tom Lee" came along, and handed Ching Song's $153 to Mr. McNicoll, out of which the Custom's people will have to get $50 before they allow the foreign gentleman to wash as much as a ten cent handkerchief in the Queen's Dominions.

Montreal Daily Witness, 17 April 1890

A Chinese Party

A Singular Scene at the Windsor Street Depot

Nineteen Chinamen, having made their "pile" in Boston in the tea and "washee-washee" business, hungered to go back to the land of their fathers and paralyze the natives. It is rather mortifying to have to travel in bond, like a Saratoga trunk, from Boston to Vancouver, but that's what these 19 successful merchants are doing. The philosophy of the Chinese is—silence, but no doubt, when they get home they will have a few rather vigorous remarks to make about the bountiful laws of this great country. At the Windsor Street depot this morning there was quite an entertainment. The 19 Chinamen arrived in charge of a Custom's officer, and when they were informed that they could not leave until 8 o'clock this evening they proceeded to make themselves comfortable. Squatting upon their luggage, of which they had an enormous quantity, they produced the daintiest little teakettles and teapots, and tiny little cups, about the size of a thimble, hand-painted, so fragile that a breath would reduce them to nothingness—things of beauty that would have been the despair of the aesthetic boarder, accustomed to vessels as thick as boiler-plate. Then they dived into their valises and got out hams and canned salmon and bread, and three large turkeys with the heads still inviolate whose glossy eyes, as the Chinamen selected toothsome morsels from the breasts, regarded them with mild reproach. So, the tea having been warmed in the refreshment room and all being in readiness, the Chinamen fell to with such dispatch and evident enjoyment as made the mouths of the C.P.R. pages water. They drank more cups of tea than could well be counted, and when they had done Mr. Ching Pah, dressed in irreproachable European costume and speaking good English, "and worth," said a

C.P.R. official in an awestruck whisper, "at least a million dollars," went over to the Customs officer and said, "Look here, a few of us want to go downtown to see some friends. Now here's a thousand dollars (pulling out the bills) as a guarantee for our safe return, and you can also come along with us." Red tape and human nature had a terrible struggle in the breast of that officer. Human nature knocked red tape out with a right-hander. The officer remembered that he was a man and that visit was allowed. He took that $1,000 all the same.

Montreal Daily Witness, 7 November 1890

Girl Slave in Montreal

Our Chinese Colony Cleverly Described

Only Two Women from the Flowery Land in Town

There is a slave in Montreal—a ten-year-old Chinese girl—the property of Mrs. Sam Kee.

There are quite a number of Chinese in Montreal. Mr. Chan Tung, who lives in the hotel on Lagauchetiere street, says there are three hundred. Most of them are occupied in the Laundry business and the rest are merchants or transient visitors. Messrs. Wing Sing and Sam Kee keep the hotel on Lagauchetiere street. Mr. Cheeping is a well-to-do, well dressed individual. The "Witness" recently printed his official declaration that he was starting a grocery business. He is well informed, talks English quite fluently and has polite manners. He has a cousin, a lad of about sixteen, who goes to school, and whose face is as bright and intelligent as any you could wish to see.

Mr. Wing Sing has a wife—Mrs. Wing Sing. Not many people can see Mrs. Wing Sing—she is very exclusive, but a lady reporter of the "Witness" saw her recently, and gives this interesting account of her visit.

Mrs. Wing Sing received me very graciously, her round face beaming with smiles. She is considered by her countrymen to be quite a beauty. Her hair is worn drawn tightly back from her forehead, pinned to the back or top of her head and falls in a large spreading loop on her neck. She wore the Chinese costume, pyjamas and blouse of dark blue stuff, a combination of silk and cotton. From out the bell sleeves hung pretty little hands, which were somewhat spoiled, however, by long nails. On her wrists were very handsome greenish-blue jadestone bracelets, in her ears were long silver ear-rings, very delicately enamelled. Her feet are of natural size.

With Mrs. Wing Sing was Mrs. Sam Kee, a bride of a few months, and a little Chinese girl of about ten years old, both of whom where in their native dress. Sam Kee's bride "is but a lassie yet" and when I first made my appearance she was demolishing with great gusto some "crisped rice." After shaking hands she disappeared into an adjoining room. All that I can remember of her is that she was very dark, very small, and very much unlike a bride.

As to the child. She is a slave. Well, poor little thing; her face is by no means her fortune. She belongs to Mrs. Sam Kee, and came over with her from China. She is treated more like a sister than a slave, indeed it is the custom in China to look upon slaves as family, and they are treated accordingly.

These three, Mrs. Wing Sing, Mrs. Sam Kee, and the little girl are the only Chinese females in Montreal.

After taking this fact in, and not wishing to appear too curious and personal, I withdrew my eyes from Mrs. Wing Sing and cast them around the room. It was an ordinarily furnished apartment, very much in appearance like the living room of a European family in moderate circumstances, the only difference being that the walls were hung from top to bottom with long bamboo panels covered with paper, on which were printed Chinese characters, signifying good luck. A sewing machines was visible and in use, a proof that the Chinese do march forward in the van of civilization. Mrs. Wing Sing is quite an expert operator.

That little woman is evidently very amiable, quite jolly, in fact, for she laughed at every sound we uttered, at every movement we made. I couldn't imagine her in a fury. The only words she can say in English are "good, good," "thank you," "nice boy," "nice girl," "come again," "how do you do," "yes," "no."

It's "good, good" with her nearly all the time.

I looked around the four walls within which her life is spent and I wondered how it was she could laugh and be merry. Is it custom or nature that makes her contented with a life that to the daughters of Europe and America seems worse than death? Obedience, never-failing obedience, is the characteristic of the Chinese woman. She loves her parents and those who are put in authority over her because she is taught to do so; she loves her husband because she has been given to him to be his wife; she comes when she's called and does what she's bid. No question of "woman's rights" perplexes her little brains. She takes no responsibilities upon herself, and wishes for none. She has perfect confidence in her man.

So much for what I saw in the hotel on Lagauchetiere street. When coming out I met several Chinese men who spoke to me in English and said that they attended the Chinese Sunday-school of the American Presbyterian Church. They all spoke in most grateful terms of Mr. Baikie, the superintendent of the Sunday-school, Mr. George Lighthall, Miss Lighthall, Miss Hastings, the superintendents of Emmanuel and other Sunday-schools and the many ladies who so kindly interest themselves in teaching them Sunday after Sunday.

The majority of the Chinese in the hotel, including Mrs. Wing Sing and Mrs. Sam Kee, have nothing whatever to do with the Christian faith, but despite that, the converted and unconverted get on very peaceably and comfortably together.

There are people who say that the Chinese merely go to Sunday-school for the sake of learning the English language. That may be so. The Chinese see that it will benefit them to be able to speak English and they go to learn. The religion that is taught them does not at first strike them as of any importance. They swallow it like a sugar-coated pill, but by and by, when they can understand and read a little English, they become more interested in what is so perseveringly poured into their ears, and in some cases the teachings have gone deep to the heart and been honestly accepted.

The Montreal Chinese mostly hail from Canton, which is situated in the Province of Quang-Tong, south-west China. They are by no means aristocrats, these Chinese. In fact, they belong to the very lowest class of Chinese. Perhaps that is the reason why they are so looked down upon here, but they are very industrious, very persevering, and they have one immeasurable superiority over other foreigners—they are a peaceable people.

Montreal Daily Witness, 4 May 1894

Spring Impressions

A Medley of Poetry and Prose

The morning sun throws an emerald radiance over woods and fields, enchanting in their spring-tide beauty. Happy, silvery-winged birds are skimming o'er a pure blue sky, and some sober-coloured little songsters, merry for all their quakery looks, are twittering on the hedges and tree tops. The leaf buds are bursting and swelling, and the flowers are unfolding their long hidden loveliness. The water music of rippling streams purls in our ears, and the soft winds caress us with murmurs of delight.

'Tis spring, and the spring feeling, the gladness of spring is in our heart.

We are not always happy. Man was not made to be always happy; but when the spring sun shines upon us; when the spring voices sound in our ears; when the spring fragrance and freshness fill the air; when all nature rejoices in returning life, then that elusive bird called "happiness," which we are forever pursuing, tarries with us of its own sweet will and sings a song so loud and clear that our little home bird, "Sorrow," hides its head under its wing and appeareth as if dead.

Our love for Spring has ever been deep and true, although until now, until we could obtain the sanction of Time to prove its worth, we made no protestations of affection, finding, as many young lovers find, more charm and romance in a secret love than in one known to the world.

Be that as it may, the communicativeness of our nature will no longer be repressed, and though to us be not given the "faculty divine," the power of expressing all that we feel and see in words which sound melodious to the ear and create for Fancy's eye scenes of beauty, yet out of a heart which hath ever been open to the sweet charm of Spring there cannot but escape a few earnest words in acknowledgment of that charm.

Then let earnestness be the substitute of eloquence, and believe us when we say that no true Irishman's breast, when beholding a display of his national colour on St. Patrick's Day, throbs with more enthusiastic pleasure than ours when our eyes are gladdened with the sight of woods and fields so fair and young in their greenness that they seem to grow greener even as we gaze.

Another lease of life and hope is given us "when the robin nests again"; for the spring time of the year recalls the spring-time of life and the glory of the fresh young earth brings back to us the hopes and dreams of youth. And, oh, what rainbow hopes have been ours, what bright, and to doubting minds, what impossible dreams we have dreamt! Even when too young, perhaps to *think* seriously, did we love the hours of solitude in which we could dream, could look into the Future through Fancy's magic mirror and see therein beings which were to exist for us, flowers which were to bloom for us, birds which were to sing for us, — some day — some day.

And though we are no longer a nonsensical child, and though our human sympathies are as warm as it is needful for them to be without inconveniencing us by their heat (he that hath a taste for solitude is generally considered misanthropic), yet there are times even now when we love to wander alone into a realm of hopes and dreams very little different from the fairyland To-Come of our childhood.

And tell us not on such a bright day as this that 'tis unwise to be so sanguine and hopeful. 'Tis spring-time now, and though Despondency may visit us during the other seasons of the year, in the happy, buoyant, life-giving spring it seemeth impossible to be too hopeful, too joyous, too trustful.

We hope for blessings, and we believe that we shall get them, and to those who talk of "Blighted Hopes" we would say: There is enough pleasure in anticipation; there is enough charm in things hoped for though not possessed, and there is enough cheerfulness and courage given us through hoping to recompense us for all the "Blighted Hopes" that this world has to blight.

What a dreary, hopeless, effortless being is he who will not hope because he fears his hopes may be disappointed; who seeth nothing in the future worth striving for!

We can suffer with those who have suffered wrongs, perchance beyond the righting; we can weep for those whose hearts unnoticed broke amidst this world's great traffic; we can mourn for those whom the grave hath robbed of all that was dear to them, and can sympathize with those remorse-tortured ones, who, gifted with utmost divine wisdom, yet, willfully turned from the guiding light and with eyes that saw all the horror and shame before them walked into the arms of sin.

Yes, we can feel for all these, for we have often gazed (though not in the spring time) into the melancholy deep of life; but we cannot, no, we cannot waste our sympathy on one who can stand in the beneficial, wholesome spring sunshine and ask us despondently the question, "Is life worth living?" To such a one we can only reply, "The question is not whether life is worth living, but it is whether you are worthy to have the gift of life bestowed on you. The worth of life depends upon your own worth, and if, with all the spring influences around you, you can find nothing better to do than to ask that question, then your worth is, indeed, small.

And, now look up, all ye who are weary, sorrow-stricken and broken-hearted; look up, as the sky raiseth itself in spring; look up and believe and feel that just as the flowers are blooming afresh over the graves of sister flowers of other years, so also is it possible for hope, faith and love to rise again in the heart in which they once withered and died.

> For thee, who knowest how to love;
> For thee, who weavest fancies bright,
> There is a glory in the Spring,
> There is a rapturous delight.
> For thee, there's music in the wind,
> Whose unseen chords the green trees bind,
> And Nature's smiles are more than kind
> For thee. Ah, yes for thee.
> For thee, the sunbeams haunt the streams,
> Bewitch the leaves, dance in the air;
> For thee, the sapphire sky of Spring
> Hath charms with which no charms compare.
> For thee, the sweet wild flowerest spring;
> For thee, the joyous song-birds sing;
> For thee, rejoiceth everything.
> For thee! Ah, yes for thee.

May 1890   Edith Eaton

Dominion Illustrated, 7 June 1890

Half-Chinese Children

Those of American Mothers and Chinese Fathers

Some of Their Troubles and Discomforts—They Are Taken Entirely in Charge by the Fathers and Generally Marry Chinese

An American lady, the wife of a Chinese merchant, now of this city, but formerly residing in the United States of America, gives some very interesting information concerning the children of Chinese fathers and white mothers of whom there are a large number in Boston and New York. She says that these children, who, for the most part live in the Chinatown of the Cities, are not by any means to be envied, for the white people with whom they come in contact that is, the lower-class, jibe and jeer at the poor little things continually, and their pure and unadulterated Chinese cousins look down upon them as being neither one thing nor the other—neither Chinese nor white.

The Chinese fathers, however, are, as a rule, very kind and good to their offspring, and so also are those mothers who are respectable women, having a true affection for their Chinese husbands; but there are a great many women whose characters would not stand much investigation, and who have married Chinamen simply for their money and they do not seem to feel any natural maternal tenderness for their little ones and are only too glad to give them away or sell them for adoption whenever they have the chance. To some this unnaturalness might almost seem natural, for the true cause often lies in the fact that the majority of Chinamen who come to the States have left behind them wives in their own country, and therefore, the children of the American woman can hardly be called legitimate. They would not be considered so in China were their father to return to that country, taking them with him. The conditions therefore under which the American Chinese child is "dragged up" are not, to say the least, favorable, to either its mental, physical or moral welfare, and it is not to be expected (although the unexpected sometimes does happen) that we will ever have a celebrated bishop whose father is a Chinaman, whose mother is an American woman. Still, the blighting atmosphere of Chinatown and its vicinity, the sneers and taunting words which are their birthright, the superstitions of their fathers and the careless, indifferent lives (with some exceptions) of the mothers, do not prevent these children from developing and becoming as fine a lot as a globe trotter could wish to see.

There is occasionally to be seen a half Chinese child with bright complexion and fair hair, and these combined with a straight nose, small mouth and wide eyes might easily deceive a stranger, but a person who has been informed of the child's parentage, notices at once a peculiar cast about the face. This cast is over the face of every child who has a drop of Chinese blood in its veins. It is indescribable—but it is there. In some families, there are children with blue eyes, fair hair and Mongolian features, and other children with Chinese hair and complexion and features which are purely caucasian. Not all of these children are "fair to see"—many are very homely, but some are "as pretty as pictures." They are by nature proud and reserved (some say, sullen and hardened). They are quick to understand and appreciate book-lore and the little girls are particularly clever with their needles and can be easily taught the most difficult patterns in embroidery. Numberless humorous and pathetic stories are related of these children. One is of a little boy, who after having been persecuted for nearly an hour by a crowd of roughs, turned upon them in a fury, and not being conscious, in his excitement, of what he said, echoed their mocking cry of "Chinese," "Chinese." But almost before the words had died on his lips, a full sense of his terrible mistake overpowered him and he rushed away from his tormentors who were shrieking derisively and hid himself where his father found him and comforted him with a thrashing.

There are a few children, the sons and daughters of wealthy and perhaps Christianized Chinamen who live in more respectable parts of the cities than Chinatown, who attend Sunday schools and day schools and who associate freely with other children. These children certainly appear to be fortunate, for a certain class of people consider them "interesting" and patronize and make much of them. And those of the children who are merry hearted and light-natured enjoy such treatment and, basking in the sunshine of "patronage," possibly benefit by it. But others who are not susceptible to such petting, feel like a little girl who is recorded to have said to her mother, "Mamma, I'm not going to see Mrs. G— today." "Why not?" said the mother, "she is always so kind to you and gives you more toys than you know what to do with." "Yes!" said the child, "but I don't care for the toys. It is just because I'm Chinese that she likes to have me there. When I'm in her parlor she whispers to some people about me, and then they try to make me talk and pick up all that I say and I hear them whisper 'her father's a Chinese' 'Did you know' 'Isn't it curious'—and they examine me from head to toe as if I was a wild animal—and just because father is a Chinese. I'd rather be dead than be a 'show.'"

A Chinese American child cannot really be said to have any religion. The father may have an idol in a private room before which he performs idolatrous rites, the mother may attend some Protestant or Catholic Church, but the child has no religion. There are certainly a few boys and girls who are brought up to be Christians—but these are the exception and not the rule. A Chinese father has sole control of his children. He orders their life as he pleases and disposes of them whenever so inclined. That is Chinese law and it has not yet been contested in the United States of America. The boys of a family, however, often drift away from parental influence in American cities and marry American women, but the daughters are usually married to Chinamen, sons of friends of the father. As an instance, there is Lee Fee's daughter. Lee Fee is a New York Chinaman who married a German woman. Lee Fee's daughter was handsome and intelligent. She had been brought up very much like an ordinary American girl in the land of the free,[1] but she was married with all the rites and ceremonies of her father's country to a Chinaman. In some families, one daughter is married to a Chinaman, another to an American. It gives food for thought—the fact, that a couple of centuries from now, the great grand children of the woman who married an American will be Americans and nothing else, whilst the descendents of her sister, who married a Chinaman and probably followed her husband to his own country will be Chinamen, pure and simple.

Chinese Marriages

Even in America the tedious Chinese marriage formalities, as far as possible, are observed by the Chinese. The following will give an idea of what an immense amount of trouble and anxiety the ceremonies of betrothal and marriage are to them. The young man's family begins the negotiations. They engage a go-between to go to some family

[1]The phrasing "in the land of the free" duplicates the title of Sui Sin Far's short story "In the Land of the Free," *Independent* 67 (2 September 1909): 504–8.

indicated by them and tender a proposal of marriage in regard to a daughter in behalf of the party employing him. If the young man is considered eligible by the parents of the girl, they consult a fortune teller, who decides after consulting some characters, whether the betrothal would be proper. If the fortune teller decides favorably, the go-between is given a card on which is marked the hour, day, month, and year when the child they wish to betroth was born, which he delivers to the young man's family, who in their turn consult a fortune teller as to the proposed betrothal. If the second fortune teller also pronounces favorably, a formal assent by all parties is made to the betrothment. The betrothal however, is not considered binding until a kind of pasteboard card has been interchanged by the families. The family of the bridegroom provides two of these cards, one having a gilt dragon on it and the other a gilt phoenix. The phoenix card is retained by the young man's family as evidence of his engagement whilst the card with the dragon on is preserved by the girl's family for the same reason. After this, the betrothal is considered consummated.[2]

At the time when the cards are sent to the family to which the girl belongs, it is also customary to send as a present to her a pair of silver or gold bracelets and for her family various articles of food, such as pig's feet, a pair of fowls, fish, etc. When the engagement card is sent back to the family to which the bridegroom belongs, there is sent as a present a quantity of artificial flowers, some vermicelli and bread cakes. The flowers are for distribution amongst the female members and relatives of the family. These articles are regarded as omens of good.

From one to five months before the marriage a fortunate day is selected for its celebration. Generally a relative of the bridegroom or a trustworthy friend takes the eight honorary characters which denote the birth time of each of the affianced parties to a fortune teller who selects lucky days for the marriage, for the making of the wedding garments, etc. These items are written out on a sheet of red paper, which is sent to the family of the girl through a go-between. If accepted, the time specified is fixed for the performance of the particulars indicated. The next thing is the presentation of wedding cakes and material for bridal dress to the family of the bride by the other family.

[2]Compare Sui Sin Far's description of betrothal and marriage customs in "Betrothals in Chinatown," *Los Angeles Express,* 8 October 1903.

The family of the girl on receiving the wedding cakes proceeds to distribute them amongst their relatives and intimate friends. There is also sent with these cakes a sum of money sometimes a large sum, sometimes a small, a quantity of red silk, dried fruits, a cock and a hen, a gander and a goose. Rich families, of course, make more costly presents than the poorer.

At the time mentioned on the betrothal card, the bride's dowry is carried through the streets with as much parade as possible. The wedding day is considered a great day and everything is designed to "show off" *a la,* some Westerners. The day before the wedding, the bride tries on the clothes she is to wear for a time after she arrives at her future home. She also has her hair done up for the first time in the style of a married woman.

A Chinese bridegroom is not supposed to behold the face of his wife on the wedding day until the marriage dinner which takes place in the evening, is set before him, for although the marriage ceremonies may have commenced in the morning early, the bride wears until the evening a thick veil which completely covers her face. When they sit down to dinner, the husband looks at the wife, but says nothing and then gives his attention to the good things provided. The bride, however, sits unveiled, quiet and still. According to custom, she must not touch a particle of food. Refreshments are offered to her by friends and attendants, but she is supposed to decline them with thanks. The ordeal of being married, is, in fact, a very trying one to the Chinese girl, or half Chinese girl, for after removing the veil, all the neighbors, guest[s] who were not invited and strangers even, are allowed to enter the house and stare at her. She is obliged to stand and bear with composure all sorts of criticism. She dares not laugh nor give the slightest evidence of anger. Her duty is to be quiet, pleasant looking and calm—even when at her expense jokes and impertinences are indulged in. The bride's toilet is generally very gorgeous and her hair is decked out with pearls and other jewel ornaments.

Montreal Daily Star, 20 April 1895

A Plea for the Chinaman

A Correspondent's Argument in His Favor

The Mongolian Defended from the Charges Made against Him by Members of Parliament from British Columbia

To the Editor of the Star:

Sir,—Every just person must feel his or her sense of justice outraged by the attacks which are being made by public men upon the Chinese who come to this country. It is a shame because the persecutors have every weapon in their hands and the persecuted are defenceless. They do not understand in a full sense all that their revilers charge them with and they have no representative men to answer the charges. Sir Henri Joly de Lotbiniere and Mr. Fraser are nobly fighting on their side, but neither of these gentlemen are Chinese, nor have they lived for any length of time amongst the Chinese, and so, of course, it is impossible for either of them to give back blow for blow. It needs a Chinaman to stand up for a Chinese cause. The people who are persecuting them send one of themselves, nay, a dozen of themselves, men who are just as prejudiced as their constituents, just as worked up over fancied wrongs and just as incapable of judging fairly. They are all, Mr. Maxwell, Mr. Charlton, Mr. Mcinness, Mr. Smith, etc., etc., equipped with self-interest which is the strongest of weapons.

It makes one's cheeks burn to read about men of high office standing up and abusing a lot of poor foreigners behind their backs and calling them all the bad names their tongues can utter. They know that the Chinese cannot answer them and they go on fully armed, using all their weapons. It's very brave, I must say, to fight with the air. A fine spectacle for the world to look at. But I suppose they don't care. They've got a party at home to cheer them.

I will now go over the ground a little. I speak from experience, because I know the Chinamen in all characters, merchants, laundrymen, laborers, servants, smugglers and smuggled, also as Sunday School scholars and gamblers. They have faults, but they also have virtues. Nations are made up of all sorts.

It is proposed to impose a tax of five hundred dollars upon every Chinaman coming into the Dominion of Canada. The reasons urged for imposing such a tax are that the presence of the Chinese affects the material and moral interests of the Canadian people, that the Chinese work cheap and therefore white men cannot compete with them, that they are gamblers and grossly immoral, that they introduce disease, cost the public much money and delay the development of the country.

The presence of the Chinaman does affect the material interests of this country, for he is a good and steady workman and has helped and is still helping to build our railways, mine our ores and in various branches of agriculture and manufacturing is proving a source of wealth to those who employ him. He does good to our laboring class for he acts as an incentive to them to be industrious and honest. I say honest, because he seeks to gain no advantage over other laborers, simply comes to compete with them—and competition is always good. The Chinaman stands on his merits; if he were of no benefit to this country he would soon have no reason to wish to remain here, for you may be sure, if incapable of performing the tasks required of him, he would not be given employment, for Canadians do not employ Chinamen for love; they take them for the use they can make of them.

As to working cheap, I believe if the matter was investigated, you would find out that the white men are willing to accept the same wages per week as the Chinamen, but they refuse to put in as much work for the wages. If the white man has to live, so also has the Chinaman, and I know that in Montreal the Chinese live well, and a great many of those I am acquainted with are former residents of British Columbia and have not changed their manner of living since coming East. I have seen on their breakfast tables great bowls of rice and dishes of beautiful light omelet, besides many European comestibles and I have noticed and have been told by themselves that they frequently order fowl and fish from the markets and the best of meats and vegetables. I am speaking of laundrymen, not merchants. Of course, the very poor one[s] are more frugal, but I can assure you a Chinaman lives merrily when he has the means.

Now, as to the charges of immorality brought against the Chinese. There are over five hundred Chinamen in Montreal, besides a transient population, and I have never heard during a residence here of many years of any one of these Chinese being accused of saying or doing that which was immoral, in the sense in which I understand the word "immoral." It is true some of the Chinamen who have been contaminated by white men and American lawyers, become swindlers and perjurers, and help their contaminators, who are just like leeches, to bleed the poor Chinese laborers who are desirous of passing into the States, and from which by a disgraceful law they are barred out, but the main body of the Chinamen are straightforward, hard-working fellows. Their worst fault is that they are somewhat cynical with regard to the honesty of white men, but that is not surprising when we consider that nearly all the white men with whom they come in contact think of nothing but squeezing money out of them by some means or other. Even the law restricting them from entering America looks as if it was got up for the sole purpose of giving unprincipled lawyers and corrupt Government officers a chance to do some boodling.

I am surprised at the moral tone of the Chinese population of Canada. These men, far away from their homes and children and womankind, are well behaved and self-respecting. Our magistrates' hair would stand on end with surprise were a Chinaman to be brought before them charged with assault or the use of insulting language.

When Mr. Maxwell speaks of the vices of the Chinese corrupting the whole body politic of British Columbia one has to smile. It is so absurd. Surely those who are "controlled by the higher influences of civilization" cannot succumb to those who obey "the lower forces of barbarism." The Chinaman may be willing to attend Sunday school and learn all that you can teach him, but I am quite certain that it never enters his head to convert you to his way of thinking.

I am afraid Mr. Maxwell knew very little about what he was speaking when he took up the Chinese question. He knew that he wanted to get certain advantages for a party of British Columbians, and he put all his heart and soul into gaining his object, forgetting that there are two sides to every story, or if he did remember, assuring himself that no one else would.

"I have but to say the word, and it will be believed," said he to his constituents on the eve of his departure for Ottawa.

The influence of the Chinese people in a moral sense is null, and I have yet to meet the man or woman who will tell me that a Chinaman influenced him or her to do that against which moral sense rebelled.

The Chinese receive instruction gladly when it comes their way, but they do not ask for it, and as to imparting to others their opinions and beliefs, the pride or humility of the race forbids anything approaching that. The quiet dignity of the Chinese is worthy of admiration, and Mr. Maxwell ought to be ashamed of himself for sneering at them for being docile and easily managed. Perhaps he does not know that the

Chinese are taught to treat the rude with silent contempt. A Chinaman does not knock a man down or stab him for the sake of an insult. He will stand and reason, but unless forced, though not by any means a coward, he will not fight. In China a man who unreasonably insults another has public opinion against him, whilst he who bears and despises the insult is respected. There are signs that in the future we in this country may attain to the high degree of civilization which the Chinese have reached, but for the present we are far away behind them in that respect.

"No self-respecting people," said Mr. Maxwell, "wish to have dumped into their midst the scum of eastern barbarism."

I am sorry to have to again show up Mr. Maxwell's ignorance of his subject. The Chinese who come to our shores are not "scum." They are mostly steady, healthy country boys from the Canton district. There are none of them paupers. They come here furnished with a modest sum of money and with the hope of adding thereto by honest labor. I can prove all I say.

And do you think Li Hung Chang, who knows all about the standing of his countrymen here would have met them as courteously as he did, and send them personally kind messages, had he considered them the "riff-raff" of China.

We are not impoverished by the Chinese immigrants, for they offer a good value for our money and if any of them fall sick they are not thrown upon our hands to be cared for; they are looked after by their own countrymen.

Of course, there are a few black sheep. There are exceptions in all cases, but the Government knows that I speak soberly and Mr. Maxwell fanatically when I say that the Chinese boys who come to Canada are in the main good boys, and he declares they are "the accumulated filth of Chinese goals and dens of vice and crime."

The Chinese have many worthy characteristics; they are good natured—all the world knows that. They have a keen sense of humor—I could tell many good stories showing that up. They easily forgive those who insult or wrong them that is proved every day. They are hospitable and are at heart gentlemen. In the spring of this year I visited New York's Chinatown. I went alone, and though a woman and a perfect stranger was received by the Chinese there with the greatest kindness and courtesy. For two weeks I dwelt amongst them, trotted up and down Mott, Pell and Doyer streets, saw the Chinese theatres and Joss Houses, visited all the little Chinese women, talked pigeon English to them, examined their babies, dined with a Chinese actress, darted hither and thither through the tenements of Chinatown, and during that time not the slightest disrespect or unkindness was shown to me. I was surprised, for I was in the slum portion of the city of New York, and dreadful tales had been told me of what I should meet and see there. I had been told that Chinatown was a dangerously wicked place; I had been warned that if I went in there alone I would never come out alive or sound in mind or body. My warders were like Mr. Maxwell and his colleagues—they did not know the Chinese people. I went there and returned the better for my visit. I had proved to my satisfaction what I had always believed, that the Chinese people are a more moral and a much happier lot than those who are strangers to them make them out to be.

Human nature is the same all the world over, and the Chinaman is as much a human being as those who now presume to judge him; and if he is a human being, he must be treated like one, and that we should not be doing were we to fine him five hundred dollars simply for being himself—a Chinaman. If a Chinaman breaks a law—a just law—a law which is a law to all Canadians, and which all Canadians are liable to be punished for, I would say at once that he should pay the penalty, but there is no justice in fining him just for what he is—a Chinaman. We should be broader-minded. What does it matter whether a man be a Chinaman, an Irishman, an Englishman or an American. Individuality is more than nationality. "A man's a man for all that." Let us admire a clever Chinaman more than a stupid Englishman, and a bright Englishman more than a dull Chinaman.

Why should Canadians in their own land fear to compete with foreigners, when they know that the foreigners are not liked, and if they, the Canadians, worked as well, there would be no chance for the Chinese whatever. If they really want to keep the Chinese out, let them do so by fair means, not by foul. Let the Canadians make an agreement with Canadians that Chinese labor will not be utilized in Canada. Then the Chinese would soon make themselves scarce; but so long as Canadian employers employ Chinese laborers, so long is a sign up telling all the world that Chinese labor is needed and wanted in Canada, and it is only a desire on the part of Mr. Maxwell to please the rowdy element of the Dominion which leads him to pretend that the Chinese are not of benefit to the country in which they are sojourning.

Some complain that they object to the Chinese because they will not settle here, nor associate with other races. That objection is also a pretence, for we well know that if such a notion as settling here ever entered the Chinaman's head, our treatment of him would soon knock it out. "He does not associate with our race at all," they cry. Well, we don't and we won't associate with him. "He comes here to make money, and with the intention of returning sooner or later," says another. In that he follows the example set him by the westerners; there are many foreigners in China, and, with the exception of the missionaries, they are all there with the avowed purpose of making money. The ports of China are full of foreign private adventurers. After they have made their "pile" they will return to their homes—which are not in China.

I believe the chief reason for the prejudice against the Chinese, I may call it the real and only solid reason for all the dislike shown to the Chinese people is that they are not considered good looking by white men; that is, they are not good looking according to a Canadian or American standard for looks. This reason may be laughed at and considered womanish, but it is not a woman's reason, it is a man's. Women do not care half as much for personal appearance as do men. I am speaking very seriously, and if you will send a commission to investigate the Chinese trouble in British Columbia—if the Government will—they will find the matter to be as I say. That the Chinese do not please our artistic taste is really at the root of all the evil there, and from it springs the other objections to the Chinese. It is a big shame, I feel, and I think it is the duty of all enlightened men to combat with and overcome this very real and serious prejudice. Do not the sages say that beauty is a matter of opinion, and so if Wong Change does not appear to our eyes as lovely to behold as Mr. Maxwell, there are those in his own land who would probably think the reverse. Besides, Wong Chang is here for utility and not for ornament.

I am convinced that an honest commission will find no real cause to further tax the Chinese. Indeed, if as conscientious as a commission can be, it will advise the fifty dollar tax already imposed be lifted.

Of course, there will be found many to stand up as witnesses against the Chinamen, but if watched closely it will be discovered that such witnesses belong to a class which is determined to find fault with the Chinaman no matter what he does or does not do.

Will the Government of Canada pander to that certain class? Will it forget the debt of gratitude America and British America owes to China—China, who sent her men to work for us when other labor was not obtainable.

If it is loyal to that England, whose shores, as Mr. Fraser says, "are free to all comers, irrespective of race, creed or color," it will answer decidedly, No.

Montreal, September 19   E.E.

Montreal Daily Star, 21 September 1896

In Los Angeles' Chinatown

In Los Angeles the Chinese are by no means neglected by Christian home missionaries, for there are said to be nine missions in that unattractive and unsavory but interesting part of the city called Chinatown. Nearly all of these missions are in a flourishing condition. It matters not what the denomination—Methodist-Episcopal, Baptist, Presbyterian—all have their following. Four native Chinese preachers backed by American church people, gather in the flock and a Christian Chinese sermon preached to a heathen Chinese congregation can be heard every Sunday.

Attached to these missions are night schools for the Chinamen and a kindergarten for children. The brightest spot in Chinatown is this modest little hall of learning. It is run on philanthropic lines, the children being mostly gathered in from the streets by their teacher, but a few of the well-to-do Chinese merchants are glad to send their sons and daughters to learn to talk the white man's language. After once coming into the fold the little ones are quite willing to remain and become much interested in the proceedings and fond of their teacher. They are the cutest of cute things, in their coats of many colors, purple trouserettes and wooden shoes with turned-up toes.

Many of the little girls dress in American garments, but the majority wear the dress of the Chinese woman, which is the same today as centuries ago, when the first non-fabulous empress of China asked her husband to buy her a costume, which was to consist of a tunic, a pair of trousers and a divided skirt. Chinese children are bright scholars and learn quickly. They take pleasure in singing hymns. Following are the Chinese words of "Now I Lay Me Down to Sleep:"

> Tsoi Ch'ong chi ghung,
> Ka ngo fan,
> K'au shan po yau
> Chan t'al ling wan
> Wak mi ts'ang sing
> Fat in kwo shan
> K'au chu ye soo
> Tsip ngo ling wan.

At New Year and Christmas animated gatherings are held in these school rooms, which are made most inviting, Chinese lanterns being swung overhead and tables spread with all kinds of good things and beautifully decorated with plants and flowers. The flutist brings his flute, the banjo man his banjo and right merrily are visitors entertained, for all the talent of Chinatown turns out, while the little ones, like birds and butterflies, hover around.

There are several Christian Chinese families in Chinatown, noticeably the Sing family of East Commercial street. For those Chinamen who adhere to the worship of their ancestors three joss houses stand conspicuous and the smoke of the burning incense daily ascends to the nostrils of the wrathful or benevolent deities who preside. These joss houses are not so rich in draperies or carvings as are the San Francisco temples, nevertheless it took money to build them and they are well worth seeing.

Chinese restaurants are interesting. Chinese food, though rather insipid to the palate, is good and nutritious. The chief article of diet of a Chinaman, as everybody knows, is rice. It is a wholesome grain and the Chinaman cooks it cleanly and beautifully. A bowl of rice flavored with a little soy often forms the dinner of a Chinaman. Sun-dried comestibles are much used in Chinese cooking and in their soups and stews are to be detected various kinds of dried nuts, dried fish and dried vegetables. A favorite dish and a most appetizing one is small dumplings filled with minced meat and boiled in a big caldron. There is nothing on a Chinaman's table to remind one of living animals and birds—no legs, heads, limbs, wings or loins—every thing is cut up small. The Chinaman comes to the table to eat—not to work.

Shell fish stew is excellent, though it looks suspicious; so are shark fins and gelatinous preserved ducks' tongues. Balls of crab and tripe cooked to a tenderness hard to express are much favored by the Chinese, so also are prawn, ground nuts, preserved ginger and candied fruits.

Notwithstanding what is said to the contrary, the Chinese are good livers, and there are few dyspeptics among them, their food being the kind that digests easily. According to Chinese statistics there are about 4,000 Chinese in Los Angeles, including about seventy-five women and from fifty to sixty children.

Los Angeles Express, 2 October 1903

Betrothals in Chinatown

Mrs. Sing of East Commercial street has gone to San Francisco to negotiate for a husband for her eldest daughter. The Sing family is much respected in Chinatown and the daughters are attractive girls who have been carefully reared. When Mrs. Sing finds a suitable young man and negotiations between the Sing family and the family of the prospective bridegroom are completed there will be great doings in Los Angeles' Chinatown.

After Mrs. Sing has made known her business in San Francisco, the family to which the eligible young man belongs will send a go-between to see her. This go-between will be furnished a card stating the ancestral name and the eight characters which note the hour, day, month and year of birth of the prospective son-in-law, and a proposal of marriage will be made for the girl in due form.

If Mrs. Sing, after instituting inquiries about the family tendering the proposal, is willing to entertain it, she will consult a fortune teller, who will decide, after considering the eight characters which indicate the time of the birth of the applicant, whether the betrothal would be fitting and auspicious. If a favorable decision is rendered the go-between will be furnished with a card indicating the hour, day, month and year when the girl was born, which he delivers to the family employing him.

Then the parents of the would-be benedict will consult a fortune teller in regard to the betrothals. If this seer pronounces favorably and the two families agree in regard to details, a formal assent is made to the match. If, for the space of three days while the betrothal is under consideration in each of the families, anything reckoned unlucky—such as breaking a teacup or a bowl, or the losing of an article—should occur, the negotiations might be terminated.

This, however, though a Chinese custom, is not likely to be the case in the Sing family, its members having lived so long in America, and if little Miss Sing should lose a pearl from her head-dress it is to be hoped that she will not also lose her prospective husband. It is better, however, when an engagement is formed, that both parties should take great care that they neither lose nor break articles of personal value.

This betrothal is not binding upon the parties until a kind of pasteboard card has been interchanged between them. On one of these cards is painted a dragon or a phoenix, according as it is designed for a boy or a girl. Occasionally the dragon or phoenix is made out of gilt paper. There are also provided two long and large threads of red silk and four large needles. These needles and thread are stuck and worked into the cards in a particular manner and are passed between the two families.

One of these cards is carefully kept as evidence of the boy's engagement; the other is proof of the girl's. There is writing on each of these documents which is performed in front of the ancestral tablets of the family to which it relates, incense and candles burning meanwhile.

After these cards have been exchanged the betrothal is declared legal, and it is not likely to be broken, for among the Chinese an engagement cannot be broken save for the gravest of reasons. The Chinese firmly believe that heaven decides who are to be husband and wife, which is one reason why the parties most concerned have little, if anything to say, concerning the event, and why it is left so much in the hands of the fortune tellers and go-betweens.

Miss Sing does not yet know the name of her future life partner, yet it is announced in Chinatown that her marriage will take place before long. The red thread running through the cards signifies that the feet of the boy and girl have been tied together by Fate.

Among the Chinese, wedding cakes are sent before, not after marriage. They are called "cakes of ceremony," and are more like mince pies than ordinary wedding cake. There are samples on view in the Sing restaurant in this city.

Among the presents, which will be given as soon as the engagement is formally declared, will be a quantity of red cloth, many kinds of dried fruit, a cock and a hen, a gander and a goose.

Los Angeles Express, 8 October 1903

Chinatown Needs a School

Mrs. Sing, the most prominent Chinese woman in Los Angeles, who lives in a pretty house on East Commercial street, surrounded by a family of ten bright children, says I was misinformed as to her visit to San Francisco, and that she did not go there with the intention of conferring with a San Francisco Chinese family regarding the betrothal of their son to her daughter. As she says, there are just as many good and respectable Chinamen in Los Angeles as there are in San Francisco, and as a matter of fact, her daughter is and has been for several years engaged to a Chinese merchant in this city and preparations are being made for the marriage.

Mrs. Sing is a Christian Chinese who has been educated in America. Her history is interesting. Kidnapped as a little child from her parents in China, she was brought to this country by her captors. Here good people became interested in her and a lady in Baltimore became her benefactress and had her placed in a mission school, where she received a liberal education and from which she was finally married to a young Chinamen of ability and character, who is now one of the best known merchants in Los Angeles' Chinatown, doing business under the firm name of Soo Hoo Lee on Apablasa street.

Mrs. Sing, though educated a Christian and Americanized, is loyal to her own country and people, and she and her husband always have worked for the good of the Chinese with whom they come in contact. Mrs. Sing's great hope is that before long a government school will be established in Chinatown for the Chinese boys and girls who are above the age of 10 or 12. There is a crying need for such a school, as there is a large number of families with children who ought not to be playing on the streets during the greater part of the day. These children will be admitted into the American schools if they were dressed in American fashion, but not otherwise, and this is a great hardship and inconvenience to Chinese mothers who in many cases are unable to make their children's clothes in American style and occasionally are too poor to afford the change.

In the Sing family the children range in age from 4 to 20 years. Their names are Charles, Henry, Mill, Johnson, Anna, Mansie, Clara, Frances, Laura and Carrie. All these children are native sons and daughters of the Golden West and speak both Chinese and English fluently. They are a bright, happy little flock with good will radiating from their faces. All wear the comfortable Chinese dress, and the baby, little Toe, is as winsome a tot as can be seen anywhere. The eldest Miss Sing is a particularly pretty girl, and she and two of her sisters often are invited to sing in concerts and churches, as they have considerable talent for music. In needlework and embroidery they also excel.

Mrs. Sing's house is furnished tastefully in a semi-eastern, semi-western style. Upon the wall of her sitting room are conspicuous two large pictures—one the portrait of her late benefactress, the lady in Baltimore, who has been translated to another land; the other, a family group consisting of Mrs. Sing, her husband and her children, the mother, a handsome dowager, her head adorned with gold and pearls and heavy gold rings in her ears. The girls are dressed in embroidered tunics with wide, full sleeves and silken trousers.

It is a picture of which the Sings have good reason to be proud, for it is well understood among the Chinese that it is a good thing for a man to have many children. In China to have a large family is a religious as well as a natural political duty.

Los Angeles Express, 14 October 1903

Chinatown Boys and Girls

While there are many boys and girls in Chinatown of Chinese parentage, but of American birth, their earliest recollections are associated with the observance of ceremonies to other American children unknown. They play as other children, have bells, rattles, toys and nick-knacks of all sorts, but at certain times and seasons these miniature men and women are called upon to perform their part in religious feasts and ceremonies such as the "Completion of the Moon," "Passing Through the Door" or the "Worship of Ancestors." On such occasions the parents pray that the child may grow to be good-natured and easy to take care of, that it may not be given to crying, that it may sleep well at night and keep in good health.

Ceremony of the "Completion of the Moon" takes place a month after the birth of a son. It is the time for the first shaving of the head and is one of the customs which is supposed to relate to the future well-being of the child. The hair is all shaved off except a small tuft in the middle of the head, which remains as the embryo of the queue of the future. I saw one little fellow, the first young Chinaman to be born in Montreal, go through the operation quite complacently, his father, San Kee, acting himself as barber. A bright-hued silk Chinese cap decorated in front with a little gold god and a sprig of evergreen gave the distinguished young person a most imposing appearance, and amulets of silver on his wrists and ankles insured his future happiness. After a sumptuous feast congratulations in the shape of rich cloths, silks, jewelry and sweetmeats were evident in abundance, and manifestations of pleasure in the shape of "joyous money," gold, silver and copper pieces wrapped in red paper on which good luck characters were inscribed literally poured in upon the child.

In Los Angeles' Chinatown there are a number of little fellows who have just attained to the "Completion of the Moon," and their small shaved heads bobbing up and down in the arms of their mothers or sisters are very cute and sets one's mind wondering why it is that a custom which was at one time forced upon the Chinese as evidence of their submission to Tartar rule should be adhered to so affectionately.

Little girls of Chinatown wear their hair hanging down on each side in a sort of ringlets, and the back braided with colored silks intermixed. Many wear but a large braid; others wear a knot of hair on the side of their heads. The older girls have their hair parted or braided smoothly back from their faces and gathered in a clump behind their heads. They adorn their hair with gold and jeweled bodkins and imitation flowers. A Chinese mother says the following verses are her daughter's:

The Lost Fairy

We wait and weep in sorrow,
   We weep and wait in vain
For thou art gone to the mortals' world
   Where all thy love is pain;
The moon still shines as o'er us all
   It shone so long ago,
But tears bedim its radiance now,
   For thy head lies sad and low.

Hast thou forgotten fairyland,
   The maze of golden light,
The flower-gemmed bowers,
The crystal founts,
   The skies forever bright—
Save when the evening shadows crept
   Athwart the roseal blue,
And the pale moon whispered to the sun,
   "Say to the earth, Adieu!"

Hast thou forgotten how the stars,
   Were thine own evening glories?
And how their poetry taught to thee,
   The loveliest of love stories?
Oh, then thy spirit leapt beyond,
   The bounds of human gladness,
But now it soundeth o'er and o'er,
   The depths of human sadness.

Hast thou forgot the fairy isles,
   Where laughing flowers display
Their varied hues and blush and glow,
   Beneath the eye of day?
So thoughts like fairest flowers arose
   Within thy verdent mind;
But now thy thoughts are naught but weeds
   And shadows round them wind.

Hast thou forgotten how the breath
  Of morning, fresh and clear,
Called thee across the mountains high,
  And we who loved thee, dear,
Were with thee in thy joyous flight,
  And hand in hand we flew,
To peaks of beauty and delight,
  Known to the free and true?

For thou wert like the summer breeze,
  That kissed thy happy brow,
And sang and wandered where thou woulds't, —
  Oh, for that freedom now!
And thou were true to thine own heart,
  For t'was a trusty guide,
But now thou know'st not what is truth,
  And e'en thy heart's belied.

Los Angeles Express, 15 October 1909

Leung Ki Chu and His Wife ·

Today witnessed the advent in Los Angeles of Leung Ki Chu, the leader of the reform party in China, who though not out of his thirties, is and has been for many years the hero of thousands of the most enlightened Chinese people. For the cause in which he has enlisted many have lost their lives and their liberties, others have had their property confiscated by the Chinese government, their homes made desolate, their families driven into exile and poverty. Leung Ki Chu himself dares not, at the cost of his life, enter his native land, and his wife and family are obliged to make their home in Japan.

Yet Leung Ki Chu's cause is not a lost cause, as his compatriots in America are ready to testify. In Los Angeles, which is a stronghold of the reform party, the Chinamen who by their hearing and intelligence reflect the most credit on their race, are those who believe in Leung Ki Chu and uphold his standard. They are men of education, but though entertaining advanced ideas, they are not Americanized Chinamen—

they are Chinese Chinamen of the sort that a citizen of the world can be proud to know.

Chief among these is Dr. Thom Leung of South Olive street, and the members of the Kwong On company and China Oriental company on North Los Angeles street. One of the reformer's most ardent supporters is Ho Lee of Apablaza street, a merchant who has lately come to this city from San Francisco.

Dr. Thom Leung, who is a brother of Dr. J. C. Thoms of Brooklyn, N. Y. (Thoms is the family name, but while the Chinese doctor in New York adopts the American fashion of having the surname follow the Christian, the Chinese doctor in Los Angeles merely signifies his surname by the initial T), is a schoolfellow and classmate of the reformer. He says of his friend that he is a particularly bright fellow with a wonderful memory. In college he was noted for his retentive mind and the facility with which he mastered the Chinese Classics, the Four Books and the Odes. He attained to the Third literary degree, which entitled him to wear a red sash and a hat with gold flowers. In China, very little attention is paid to history or mathematics, but the young Ki Chu considered these studies as worthy of research and pursued them for his own benefit without any particular aid from his teachers. He also gave his attention to military studies.

Leung Ki Chu, who is a native of the province of Quang-tung, married young, as is the case with most Chinamen. His wife is said to be a charming woman, who has shared her husband's vicissitudes with a brave and cheery spirit. She has full faith that a brighter day will dawn for China, and when it does she hopes to see her husband reinstated with honor. His work is such that it naturally necessitates lengthy periods of separation from his family, but though anxiety for his welfare is ever present with his wife, she has never been heard to repine or reproach. She devotes her life to her children, to whom she daily teaches the lessons of patience and fortitude. Those who believe in ideals and hero worship may picture her—when her children are in bed and her husband over the sea—stretching her arms Chinaward and crying:

"Oh, China! Unhappy country! What would I not sacrifice to see thee uphold thyself among the nations? Far bitterer than death it is to know that thou who wert more glorious than all now liest as low as the lowest, while the feet of those whom thou didst despise rest insolently upon thy limbs. The Middle Kingdom wert thou called, the country that heaven loved. Thou wert the birthplace of the arts and the sciences. Thy princes rested in benevolence, thy wise men were revered, thy people happy. And now, the empire, which is the oldest under the heavens, is falling and other nations stand ready to smite the nation that first smote itself. Truly Mencius said, 'The losing of the empires comes through losing the people.' The government, being foolish and correct, has lost the hearts of the people. Who shall restore them?"

Los Angeles Express, 22 October 1903

Chinese in Business Here

If one will visit the stores, and other places of business of the Chinese of Los Angeles, he will gain a clearer idea of the industry and ingenuity of these people than the most learned books and treatises on the Chinese, both at home and abroad, could give. I have passed many a pleasant half hour or longer in the Chinese stores, taking a cup of tea, here and there and a pinch of instruction in between whiles, and I have in mind as I write, Wong Doong How of the China Oriental Curio company; Heng Lee, dealer in Chinese and Japanese fancy goods; Me Lung, the tailor, of Marchessault street, and Soo Hoo Le, dealer in produce and general merchandise.

These are tradesmen, who are well known in their respective callings. Besides these, there are medicine venders, who comprise with their business fortune telling, undertakers, barbers, cobblers, tinkers, vegetable venders, and last but by no means the least, the laundry man. Many of the poorest business man work at their trade or profession in the streets of Chinatown and sit with their tools, materials or compounds around them as if they were in a workshop.

Nearly all the articles that are to be found in a Chinese curio store are hand made. It has been truly said that the arts which contribute chiefly to the comforts and conveniences of life are but imperfectly understood by the Chinese. The Westerners, by their treatment of these people, have not encouraged them to appreciate the result of

Western science, nevertheless, no one can gainsay that the Chinese certainly excel in work that depends upon fancy and neatness of execution. Not a few of the creations that are to be seen in these curio stores are marvelous results of attention to detail and have a beauty all their own.

There is also this to be said in favor of Chinese ornaments. They are made of good and lasting material and are meant to please the eye for more than a day, which cannot be said of American manufactured knick-knacks. The history of many a Chinese curio is interesting. Numbers of them have been made by Chinese boys and girls living in small, isolated farm houses and cottages of the Middle Kingdom. Much of the beautiful embroidery work that we see is done by Chinese women in their own homes, and has provided many a poor family with rice and tea.

I find the produce man and general merchant are one and the same thing. It seems to be a comfortable business, as the "boss" of the place (he generally has a number of clerks) is usually a chatty fellow with a long pipe in his mouth. There is a fascination in watching him manipulate the abacus, an ancient Chinese invention, which answers all the purposes of numerical figures, and by means of which, the Chinese merchant adds, deducts or multiplies, as the case may be. The abacus is a long box divided into compartments, the balls in one division being units, the others fives. The Chinese did their bookkeeping by the abacus system when the forefathers of the present "Anglo-Saxon" Americans were living as savages in the British Isles or thereabouts.

Chinese vegetable sellers, vegetable venders and vegetable gardeners are the happiest of all Chinamen, for among fruit and vegetables a Chinaman is in his sphere. He is a natural-born gardener and to help the fruits of the earth to flourish is his delight. A Chinaman can grow vegetables where no one else can.

Los Angeles Express, 23 October 1903

Chinese Laundry Checking

Washing clothes does not appear to be an agreeable occupation, yet I have seen a Chinaman making merry with his fellows over his wash tub or his ironing table. Several times have I heard sounds of laughter issuing from the big laundry of Quong Chung & Co., on East Third street, and paused to wonder why these homeless, childless, wifeless sons of labor, far from country and kindred, could carry with them into their exile the spirit of content.

It is interesting to note the ingenious method of checking the clothes left with them to be washed. By it they are able to tell exactly to whom the different bundles of washing which come into the laundry belong. In making these checks the Chinaman fixes upon the name of a person, place or thing, as the sign word of a batch of checks for the week, the heavenly bodies, such as the sun, moon or stars, being generally the favorite signs. The word selected is then drawn on the top of the left hand corner of the check, and after that, the checks are numbered, say, from one to a hundred, according to how many the laundryman thinks he will require during the week. This, for instance, may be one of Wing Wah's checks showing where it is torn in half:

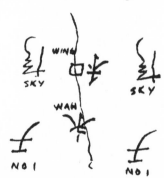

That first figure on the left means "sky;" underneath is No. 1 (that is the number of the first check that goes out during the week).[1]

These signs are duplicated on the right hand side of the check and

[1]The entire set of figures was printed upside down. Sui Sin Far here displays her ignorance of Chinese, for even when the figures are inverted, the sky character is incomplete and the lower left and lower right character is not the number 1 but *wan,* or "bay."

in the center is Wing Wah's name. When a customer brings in his parcel, the check is torn from the center; the customer is given one-half of the check and the other half is attached to the parcel left in the laundry. In this way both customer and laundryman have checks in duplicate. When demand is made for the parcel, the given check is matched to the one attached to the washing. The foregoing is the custom in general use but each laundryman varies it according to different ideas of convenience and speed. For instance, in place of a name in the center, the number is repeated.

Should there by any checks left over at the end of the week, they are destroyed and a new batch of checks with a sign word is made. If a customer fails to keep his check or loses it, the laundryman, unless he knows the person well, and is certain he is the customer to whom the clothes belong will not give them up, that is, not until he has made inquiries and satisfied himself that the person claiming the clothes is by right entitled to them. It is said, that even according to law a person who does not present a check corresponding with the one that the laundry man holds cannot recover anything if the Chinaman refused to stand and deliver. There is, however, very little need to go to law about the matter, as the system described in most cases works admirably.

Los Angeles Express, 3 November 1903

Aluteh

Pih-Yuh was a magistrate who was anxious to see clearly and hear distinctly—a Mandarin who loved the truth and hated insincerity. Yen Yuen, his superior officer, was crafty and mean; but possessed of a certain talent for governing and transacting business. As Governor of the Province, he exercised great power, and used it in such a way that his subordinates trembled at his frown and shook at the sound of his voice. Such was the man under whom the high minded Pih-Yuh was obliged to serve, and it would have been contrary to the order of nature had harmony existed between the two.

Living in the city in which Pih-Yuh's Yamen was situated, was a very old and wealthy merchant named Yenfoh. He was a man of peculiar disposition, quarrelsome, eccentric and vain; but a sincere friend to those who were his friends. This Yenfoh, one unlucky day, dragged a poor poultry farmer into court, and after accusing him of stuffing his fowls with mud or sand to increase their weight, and in particular, of having rammed mud down the throat of a duck, which he, Yenfoh, had purchased, demanded the Pih-Yuh, the presiding magistrate, should send the poultry farmer to the stocks. Pih-Yuh, however, deemed it necessary to make some investigation before sentencing the man, and as upon investigation, no proof was adduced beyond the fact that Yenfoh believed the man guilty, the request of the arbitrary merchant was not complied with. Enraged, Yenfoh appealed to the Governor to redress, what he was pleased to call his "wrong," and Yen Yuen, who had long wished for an opportunity to bring Pih-Yuh's name into disrepute with the Imperial Court, affected to believe in the "wrong," and assured the old man that he had for many months had reason to believe that Pih-Yuh was in league with a gang of poultry swindlers who paid the Magistrate a large sum annually for discharging them whenever they were arrested.

This, of course, was pure fiction on the part of the Governor, but Yenfoh was in a state to believe almost any charge against the Magistrate, and boiling over with spleen, he cried, "That explains why he would not do me justice. He should be fined, degraded in rank and expelled from office."

"Yes," assented Yen Yuen, "but, that will necessitate bringing him before the Tribunal of Punishment, and you will have to appear as principal witness."

"Why, your Excellency," stammered Yenfoh, somewhat taken aback, "what can I say beyond stating that he refused to punish the poultry seller, unless he had more evidence than my simple belief that the duck had been stuffed. Of course, my belief, to myself, and to any one I may wish to imbue with it, is sufficient to establish the poultry man's guilt, and Pih-Yuh has wronged me be refusing to administer punishment; but if it has to be proved that Pih-Yuh is in league with other poultry men, I'm afraid my belief in his guilt—the guilt of a man whom common fame calls just and honorable—will also be refused as evidence by the Tribunal of Punishment.

"Yet you wish Pih-Yuh punished for branding you a liar and a perjurer, which he assuredly did, when he allowed the poultry man to go free."

"Yes, your Excellency, I do," replied Yenfoh, wincing under the Governor's guileful words, "and I will pay you a goodly sum of money if you will see that I am avenged."

The Governor's mouth opened greedily. "Well, then," he said drawing his chair nearer to the old merchant's and eying him steadily, "you must find a man who saw Him Wie putting mud down that duck's throat, and you must testify that Pih-Yuh refused to accept your witness,—which he certainly would have done, had any such witness been offered by you. Do you understand?"

"Yes," replied Yenfoh, "to catch a dishonest man, one has to be dishonest oneself."

"You've got the idea exactly," said the Governor, with an encouraging smile; "it takes a thief to catch a thief."

So it came to pass that Pih-Yuh was arrested, chained and sent to Peking, where he was tried by the officers of the Tribunal of Punishment, and from evidence taken from witnesses by Yen Yuen, the Governor of the Province in which his Mandarinate had been situated, found guilty of fraud and mal-administration, deprived of all honors and titles and expelled from office. Moreover, his paternal and ancestral home in another province was desecrated and his parents made homeless in their old age.

Shortly after these deplorable happenings, Yenfoh, whose evidence in the case had certainly accomplished its ends, received a letter which threw him into a great state of perturbation. So disturbed and excited was he at its contents, that in order to relieve himself, he confided them to his young daughter, Aluteh.

"Behold the sun is eaten, swallowed in the belly of the clouds," he cried. "My dearest friend, Pih-Hwuy, he whom I have loved from my youth up, has been made homeless through my instrumentality."

He tore the buttons from his cap and gown and threw himself on the floor.

Little Aluteh looked serious, and when it was explained to her that Yenfoh had only just learned that Pih-Hwuy was the father of Pih-Yuh, the lately degraded Mandarin, she seemed even more impressed.

"Then, father," said she, "the charges against the good Mandarin were groundless."

Yenfoh had said nothing to lead his daughter to believe what she evidently did, but the girl was gifted with quick perceptions and had heard from others all about her father's case with the poultry man. Moreover, ever since Pih-Yuh had held office in that city, she had listened with girlish interest to tales of his kindness of heart and deeds of justice and mercy. Once, when out walking with her Aunt, the Mandarin had passed them in his sedan chair, and before Aluteh could lower her eyes, her mind had received the impression of a young man of a thoughtful and sedate cast of countenance and clear eyes.

"There goes the good Mandarin," remarked the aunt, and Aluteh had marvelled greatly that one who was so learned and held in such high esteem, should be so youthful in appearance.

The old merchant ignored his daughter's question. Absorbed in his thoughts, he sat rocking his head silently between his hands. Aluteh gazed at him in great distress, but finally fell on her knees by his side and began stroking and soothing him in a very pretty and daughterlike manner. After a while, the influence of her little hands and cooing voice caused the old man to lean his head against her shoulder and pour into her ears the whole story,—how he had gone to the Governor in his wrath against Pih-Yuh and how the Governor had incited him to testify falsely.

"Alas!" cried the girl, "when such men as Yen Yuen hold high office, is it any wonder that dishonor like a swelling flood, spreads over the Province?"

Yenfoh sighed heavily, then suddenly roused himself and started to his feet.

"Something must be done at once; something must be done," he cried. "Pih-Hwuy will soon learn that I am the chief cause of his son's ruin and his own, and the thought is a thousand daggers in my heart; for when we were boys, he saved my life twice, once form death by drowning and once from fire—And I have loved him more than my brothers, though we have been separated these latter years."

"Can you not send them some money?" suggested Aluteh. She had forgotten the Mandarin for the time being and all her anxiety was for her father.

"Money for injuring his son!" cried Yenfoh. "What could be more of an insult? Ah, you don't know Pih-Hwuy. He is like Pih-Yuh."

Thus Yenfoh, unconsciously commending the Mandarin he had ruined.

Then Aluteh reached up her father's sleeve, and finding his hand, held it fast in her own whilst she whispered words of consolation.

Some years before, Tze Loo, Viceroy of the Province, but then a plain citizen, had his place of residence in the same city as Yenfoh. Living with him was his aged mother, who was both blind and deaf, but to whom he was devotedly attached. One day the old lady strayed from her son's house and would probably have met with some terrible accident had it not been for little Aluteh, the daughter of Yenfoh, then but twelve years old, who had observed the old woman wandering aimlessly around and taking her in charge had brought her to Tze Loo, who by way of reward for the service she had rendered had bestowed upon the little girl a gold bracelet and promised that if ever it was in his power to grant some wish of hers, he would gladly do so.

So Aluteh consoled her father with the remembrance of the Viceroy's promise, and suggested that accompanied by her nurse, she should journey to the palace of Tze Loo in the next city, secure an audience with the Viceroy, show him her bracelet, and relate the story of the conspiracy against Pih-Yuh, claiming the exemption of her father from punishment, as a false witness, on the strength of the Viceroy's promise. It would then devolve upon Tze Loo to recommend to the Tribunal of Punishment the degradation of the Governor, Yen Yuen, and the reinstatement in office of Pih-Yuh. That being accomplished, Pih-Yuh's parents would have restored to them their own and ever after live in peace and comfort.

"Now, father, what think you of my plan?" asked the girl with shining eyes.

Yenfoh demurred. What! was his own child eager to uncover her father's shortcomings?

"Heaven knows my heart," answered Aluteh; "and to bend the knee to one to whom one owes one's life seems not to me so difficult."

She arose form her knees and began sorting some sprays of jessamine which she had brought into the room with her.

"Is not their fragrance sweet, my father?" she asked, lifting a spray and tapping his cheek lightly with it. Evidently the matter they had been discussing had passed from her mind.

Yenfoh caught the spray roughly and crushed it.

"Oh, my pretty flower!" cried Aluteh in reproachful accents.

"Daughter, be not so frivolous," said the old man testily. "I am pondering a weighty matter and it is your duty to try to follow my thoughts. Ah! that you had been a man child."

With a smile and a sigh Aluteh turned a patient face to her father.

"Listen!" continued Yenfoh, "female intelligence, though inferior to male, sometimes brings forth good results. I will, therefore, that in the morning early, accompanied by your nurse, you go forth to the Viceroy's Palace."

• • •

Pih-Yuh wandered beside the river and looked through the eyes of his soul. He was homeless and degraded—so also were his parents. For himself, he could have borne much, but that his father and mother in their declining years, should become acquainted with poverty and disgrace, was anguish indeed to the filial young man. And it was all so manifestly unjust. He, who had loved to exercise justice for justice's sake and had kept himself aloof from the gross material life of his brother mandarins, was stirred to the depths of his soul.

Whilst Pih-Yuh thus wandered beside the river, search was being made for him in the city. Foremost amongst the searchers was Yenfoh, and there was no place too dark or vile for him to enter in the hope of finding Pih-Hwuy's son. Yenfoh was now keenly alive to the fact that he had wronged Pih-Yuh grievously, and was more than anxious to find him and rectify the wrong.

The old merchant was recovering from a feeling of faintness, after emerging from some filthy hole, when someone who had known Pih-Yuh inquired why they searched for the Mandarin in such noisome places.

"Because," answered Yenfoh, "it is only amongst the wretched and poverty stricken that those who have been despoiled of all, can hide their heads."

"But Pih-Yuh was of too lofty a mind to wish to hide his head in any case," answered the friend who had known him; "moreover, he was a poet and would find balm for his spirit only where he could have free communion with nature. I suggest that we seek him in the green forest on the other side of the river."

So they took a boat and sailed, and when they were half way across the water, they beheld Pih-Yuh on the other shore. He waited calmly until they came near unto him, when he greeted then with a benign countenance and respectful words.

"Men," said he, "if you have come to imprison me, I surrender myself into your hands, but have a care for my father and my mother."

Before he could say more, Yenfoh threw himself at his feet and cried, "O, man of talents and virtues, we come not to further degrade you, but to restore you to honor."

Then they brought Pih-Yuh to where the Viceroy of the Province, in full view of the people, took him by the hand, placed him in a chair of state, and read aloud an Imperial Edict, proclaiming that Pih-Yuh was reinstated in office with greater honors than he had ever before enjoyed, and that a goodly income from the Imperial Treasury was the portion of his aged parents, with the restoration of their ancestral home.

Hearing this, all the people rejoiced.

Later, in his own private palace, the Viceroy communicated to the Mandarin how the daughter of Yenfoh had been the means of dispelling the clouds which hid the sun of truth and justice, and the maiden who was loved by the wife of Tze Loo, and had been made her friend, was brought in and presented to Pih-Yuh. Modestly she cast down her eyes and fell on her knees; but Pih-Yuh calling himself her "stupid younger brother" raised her with his hand and thanked her for all she had done.

After the maiden had retired, his thoughts dwelt with her so continually that he spake to the Viceroy and said:

"I have been too close a student all my life to have had leisure for the society of women, and when my parents, time and again, have urged me to take unto myself a wife, I have quoted Confucius, who has said, 'Of all people, girls and servants are most difficult to behave to. If you are familiar with them, they lose their humility. If you are reserved, they are discontented.' Yet the soul that shines through the eyes of this maiden haunts me, and I would know whether she is betrothed, as I could unfeignedly love and honor her."

The Viceroy assured him that Aluteh knew not the binding cord, and added that Yenfoh would undoubtedly be glad to betroth the maiden to one whose father was so dear a friend.

So Pih-Yuh returned to his Yamen with a happy heart and in proper time Aluteh became his wife.

Chautauquan, December 1905

Leaves from the Mental Portfolio of an Eurasian

When I look back over the years I see myself, a little child of scarcely four years of age, walking in front of my nurse, in a green English lane, and listening to her tell another of her kind that my mother is Chinese. "Oh, Lord!" exclaims the informed. She turns around and scans me curiously from head to foot. Then the two women whisper together. Tho the word "Chinese" conveys very little meaning to my mind, I feel that they are talking about my father and mother and my heart swells with indignation. When we reach home I rush to my mother and try to tell her what I have heard. I am a young child. I fail to make myself intelligible. My mother does not understand, and when the nurse declares to her, "Little Miss Sui is a story-teller," my mother slaps me.

Many a long year has past over my head since that day—the day on which I first learned that I was something different and apart from other children, but tho my mother has forgotten it, I have not.

I see myself again, a few years older. I am playing with another child in a garden. A girl passes by outside the gate. "Mamie," she cries to my companion. "I wouldn't speak to Sui if I were you. Her mamma is Chinese."

"I don't care," answers the little one beside me. And then to me, "Even if your mamma is Chinese, I like you better than I like Annie."

"But I don't like you," I answer, turning my back on her. It is my first conscious lie.

I am at a children's party, given by the wife of an Indian officer whose children were schoolfellows of mine. I am only six years of age, but have attended a private school for over a year, and have already learned that China is a heathen country, being civilized by England. However, for the time being, I am a merry romping child. There are quite a number of grown people present. One, a white haired old man, has his attention called to me by the hostess. He adjusts his eyeglasses and surveys me critically. "Ah, indeed!" he exclaims. "Who would have thought it at first glance. Yet now I see the difference between her and other children. What a peculiar coloring! Her mother's eyes and hair and her father's features, I presume. Very interesting little creature!"

I had been called from my play for the purpose of inspection. I do not return to it. For the rest of the evening I hide myself behind a hall door and refuse to show myself until it is time to go home.

My parents have come to America. We are in Hudson City, N.Y., and we are very poor. I am out with my brother, who is ten months older than myself. We pass a Chinese store, the door of which is open. "Look!" says Charlie. "Those men in there are Chinese!" Eagerly I gaze into the long low room. With the exception of my mother, who is English bred with English ways and manner of dress, I have never seen a Chinese person. The two men within the store are uncouth specimens of their race, drest in working blouses and pantaloons with queues hanging down their backs. I recoil with a sense of shock.

"Oh, Charlie," I cry. "Are we like that?"

"Well, we're Chinese, and they're Chinese, too, so we must be!" returns my seven-year-old brother.

"Of course you are," puts in a boy who has followed us down the street, and who lives near us and has seen my mother: "Chinky, Chinky, Chinaman, yellow-face, pig-tail, rat-eater." A number of other boys and several little girls join in with him.

"Better than you," shouts my brother, facing the crowd. He is younger and smaller than any there, and I am even more insignificant than he; but my spirit revives.

"I'd rather be Chinese than anything else in the world," I scream.

They pull my hair, they tear my clothes, they scratch my face, and all but lame my brother; but the white blood in our veins fights valiantly for the Chinese half of us. When it is all over, exhausted and bedraggled, we crawl home, and report to our mother that we have "won the battle."

"Are you sure?" asks my mother doubtfully.

"Of course. They ran from us. They were frightened," returns my brother.

My mother smiles with satisfaction.

"Do you hear?" she asks my father.

"Umm," he observes, raising his eyes from his paper for an instant. My childish instinct, however, tells me that he is more interested than he appears to be.

It is tea time, but I cannot eat. Unobserved I crawl away. I do not sleep that night. I am too excited and I ache all over. Our opponents had been so very much stronger and bigger than we. Toward morning, however, I fall into a doze from which I awake myself, shouting:

> "Sound the battle cry;
> See the foe is nigh."

My mother believes in sending us to Sunday school. She has been brought up in a Presbyterian college.

The scene of my life shifts to Eastern Canada. The sleigh which has carried us from the station stops in front of a little French Canadian hotel. Immediately we are surrounded by a number of villagers, who stare curiously at my mother as my father assists her to alight from the sleigh. Their curiosity, however, is tempered with kindness, as they watch, one after another, the little black heads of my brothers and sisters and myself emerge out of the buffalo robe, which is part of the sleigh's outfit. There are six of us, four girls and two boys; the eldest, my brother, being only seven years of age. My father and mother are still in their twenties. "Les pauvres enfants," the inhabitants murmur, as they help to carry us into the hotel. Then in lower tones: "Chinoise, Chinoise."

For some time after our arrival, whenever we children are sent for a walk, our footsteps are dogged by a number of young French and English Canadians, who amuse themselves with speculations as to whether, we being Chinese, are susceptible to pinches and hair pulling, while older persons pause and gaze upon us, very much in the same way that I have seen people gaze upon strange animals in a menagerie. Now and then we are stopt and plied with questions as to what we eat and drink, how we go to sleep, if my mother understands what my father says to her, if we sit on chairs or squat on floors, etc., etc., etc.

There are many pitched battles, of course, and we seldom leave the house without being armed for conflict. My mother takes a great interest in our battles, and usually cheers us on; tho I doubt whether she understands the depth of the troubled waters thru which her little children wade. As to my father, peace is his motto, and he deems it wisest to be blind and deaf to many things.

School days are short, but memorable. I am in the same class with my brother, my sister next to me in the class below. The little girl whose desk my sister shares shrinks close against the wall as my sister takes her place. In a little while she raises her hand.

"Please, teacher!"

"Yes, Annie."

"May I change my seat?"

"No, you may not!"

The little girl sobs. "Why should she have to sit beside a ———"

Happily my sister does not seem to hear, and before long the two little girls become great friends. I have many such experiences.

My brother is remarkably bright; my sister next to me has a wonderful head for figures, and when only eight years of age helps my father with his night work accounts. My parents compare her with me. She is of sturdier build than I, and, as my father says, "Always has her wits about her." He thinks her more like my mother, who is very bright and interested in every little detail of practical life. My father tells me that I will never make half the woman that my mother is or that my sister will be. I am not as strong as my sisters, which makes me feel somewhat ashamed, for I am the eldest little girl, and more is expected of me. I have no organic disease, but the strength of my feelings seems to take from me the strength of my body. I am prostrated at times with attacks of nervous sickness. The doctor says that my heart is unusually large; but in the light of the present I know that the cross of the Eurasian bore too heavily upon my childish shoulders. I usually hide my weakness from the family until I cannot stand. I do not understand myself, and I have an idea that the others will despise me for not being as strong as they. Therefore, I like to wander away alone, either by the river or in the bush. The green fields and flowing water have a charm for me. At the age of seven, as it is today, a bird on the wing is my emblem of happiness.

I have come from a race on my mother's side which is said to be the most stolid and insensible to feeling of all races, yet I look back over the years and see myself so keenly alive to every shade of sorrow and suffering that it is almost a pain to live.

If there is any trouble in the house in the way of a difference between my father and mother, or if any child is punished, how I suffer! And when harmony is restored, heaven seems to be around me. I can be sad, but I can also be glad. My mother's screams of agony when a baby is born almost drive me wild, and long after her pangs have subsided I feel them in my own body. Sometimes it is a week before I can get to sleep after such an experience.

A debt owing by my father fills me with shame. I feel like a criminal when I pass the creditor's door. I am only ten years old. And all the while the question of nationality perplexes my little brain. Why are we what we are? I and my brothers and sisters. Why did God make us to be hooted and stared at? Papa is English, mamma is Chinese. Why couldn't we have been either one thing or the other? Why is my mother's race despised? I look into the faces of my father and mother. Is she not every bit as dear and good as he? Why? Why? She sings us the songs she learned at her English school. She tells us tales of China. Tho a child when she left her native land she remembers it well, and I am never tired of listening to the story of how she was stolen from her home. She tells us over and over again of her meeting with my father in Shanghai and the romance of their marriage. Why? Why?

I do not confide in my father and mother. They would not understand. How could they? He is English, she is Chinese. I am different to both of them—a stranger, tho their own child. "What are we?" I ask my brother. "It doesn't matter, sissy," he responds. But it does. I love poetry, particularly heroic pieces. I also love fairy tales. Stories of everyday life do not appeal to me. I dream dreams of being great and noble; my sisters and brothers also. I glory in the idea of dying at the stake and a great genie arising from the flames and declaring to those who have scorned us: "Behold, how great and glorious and noble are the Chinese people!"

My sisters are apprenticed to a dressmaker; my brother is entered in an office. I tramp around and sell my father's pictures, also some lace which I make myself. My nationality, if I had only know it at that time, helps to make sales. The ladies who are my customers call me "The Little Chinese Lace Girl." But it is a dangerous life for a very young girl. I come near to "mysteriously disappearing" many a time. The greatest temptation was in the thought of getting far away from where I was known, to where no mocking cries of "Chinese!" "Chinese!" could reach.

Whenever I have the opportunity I steal away to the library and read every book I can find on China and the Chinese. I learn that China is the oldest civilized nation on the face of the earth and a few other things. At eighteen years of age what troubles me is not that I am what I am, but that others are ignorant of my superiority. I am small, but my feelings are big—and great is my vanity.

My sisters attend dancing classes, for which they pay their own fees. In spite of covert smiles and sneers, they are glad to meet and mingle with other young folk. They are not sensitive in the sense that I am. And yet they understand. One of them tells me that she overheard a young man say to another that he would rather marry a pig than a girl with Chinese blood in her veins.

In course of time I too learn shorthand and take a position in an office. Like my sister, I teach myself, but, unlike my sister, I have neither the perseverance nor the ability to perfect myself. Besides, to a temperament like mine, it is torture to spend the hours in transcribing other people's thoughts. Therefore, altho I can always earn a moderately good salary, I do not distinguish myself in the business world as does she.

When I have been working for some years I open an office of my own. The local papers patronize me and give me a number of assignments, including most of the local Chinese reporting. I meet many Chinese persons, and when they get into trouble am often called upon to fight their battles in the papers. This I enjoy. My heart leaps for joy when I read one day an article by a New York Chinese in which he declares, "The Chinese in America owe an everlasting debt of gratitude to Sui Sin Far for the bold stand she has taken in their defense."

The Chinaman who wrote the article seeks me out and calls upon me. He is a clever and witty man, a graduate of one of the American colleges and as well a Chinese scholar. I learn that he has an American wife and several children. I am very much interested in these children, and when I meet them my heart throbs in sympathetic tune with the tales they relate of their experiences as Eurasians. "Why did papa and mamma born us?" asks one. Why?

I also meet other Chinese men who compare favorably with the white men of my acquaintance in mind and heart qualities. Some of them are quite handsome. They have not as finely cut noses and as well developed chins as the white men, but they have smoother skins and their expression is more serene; their hands are better shaped and their voices softer.

Some little Chinese women whom I interview are very anxious to know whether I would marry a Chinaman. I do not answer No. They clap their hands delightedly, and assure me that the Chinese are much the finest and best of all men. They are, however, a little doubtful as to whether one could be persuaded to care for me, full-blooded Chinese people having a prejudice against the half white.

Fundamentally, I muse, all people are the same. My mother's race is as prejudiced as my father's. Only when the whole world becomes as one family will human beings be able to see clearly and hear distinctly. I believe that some day a great part of the world will be Eurasian. I cheer myself with the thought that I am but a pioneer. A pioneer should glory in suffering.

"You were walking with a Chinaman yesterday," accuses an acquaintance.

"Yes, what of it?"

"You ought not to. It isn't right."

"Not right to walk with one of my mother's people? Oh, indeed!"

I cannot reconcile his notion of righteousness with my own.

• • •

I am living in a little town away off on the north shore of a big lake. Next to me at the dinner table is the man for whom I work as a stenographer. There are also a couple of business men, a young girl and her mother.

Some one makes a remark about the cars full of Chinamen that past that morning. A transcontinental railway runs thru the town.

My employer shakes his rugged head. "Somehow or other," says he, "I cannot reconcile myself to the thought that the Chinese are humans like ourselves. They may have immortal souls, but their faces seem to be so utterly devoid of expression that I cannot help but doubt."

"Souls," echoes the town clerk. "Their bodies are enough for me. A Chinaman is, in my eyes, more repulsive than a nigger."

"They always give me such a creepy feeling," puts in the young girl with a laugh.

"I wouldn't have one in my house," declares my landlady.

"Now, the Japanese are different altogether. There is something bright and likeable about those men," continues Mr. K.

A miserable, cowardly feeling keeps me silent. I am in a Middle West town. If I declare what I am, every person in the place will hear about it the next day. The population is in the main made up of working folks with strong prejudices against my mother's countrymen. The prospect before me is not an enviable one—if I speak. I have no longer an ambition to die at the stake for the sake of demonstrating the greatness and nobleness of the Chinese people.

Mr. K. turns to me with a kindly smile.

"What makes Miss Far so quiet?" he asks.

"I don't suppose she finds the 'washee washee men' particularly interesting subjects of conversation," volunteers the young manager of the local bank.

With a great effort I raise my eyes from my plate. "Mr. K.," I say, addressing my employer, "the Chinese people may have no souls, no expression on their faces, be altogether beyond the pale of civilization, but whatever they are, I want you to understand that I am—I am a Chinese."

There is silence in the room for a few minutes. Then Mr. K. pushes back his plate and standing up beside me, says:

"I should not have spoken as I did. I know nothing whatever about the Chinese. It was pure prejudice. Forgive me!"

I admire Mr. K.'s moral courage in apologizing to me; he is a conscientious Christian man, but I do not remain much longer in the little town.

● ● ●

I am under a tropic sky, meeting frequently and conversing with persons who are almost as high up in the world as birth, education and money can set them. The environment is peculiar, for I am also surrounded by a race of people, the reputed descendants of Ham, the son of Noah, whose offspring, it was prophesied, should be the servants of the songs of Shem and Japheth. As I am a descendant, according to the Bible, of both Shem and Japheth, I have a perfect right to set my heel upon the Ham people; but tho I see others around me following out the Bible suggestion, it is not in my nature to be arrogant to any but those who seek to impress me with their superiority, which the poor black maid who has been assigned to me by the hotel certainly does not. My employer's wife takes me to task for this. "It is unnecessary," she says, "to thank a black person for service."

The novelty of life in the West Indian island is not without its charm. The surroundings, people, manner of living, are so entirely different from what I have been accustomed to up North that I feel as if I were "born again." Mixing with people of fashion, and yet not of them, I am not of sufficient importance to create comment or curiosity. I am busy nearly all day and often well into the night. It is not monotonous work, but it is certainly strenuous. The planters and business men of the island take me as a matter of course and treat me with kindly courtesy. Occasionally an Englishman will warn me against the "brown boys" of the island, little dreaming that I too am of the "brown people" of the earth.

When it begins to be whispered about the place that I am not all white, some of the "sporty" people seek my acquaintance. I am small and look much younger than my years. When, however, they discover that I am a very serious and sober-minded spinster indeed, they retire quite gracefully, leaving me a few amusing reflections.

One evening a card is brought to my room. It bears the name of some naval officer. I go down to my visitor, thinking he is probably some one who, having been told that I am a reporter for the local paper, has brought me an item of news. I find him lounging in an easy chair on the veranda of the hotel—a big, blond, handsome fellow, several years younger than I.

"You are Lieutenant ———?" I inquire.

He bows and laughs a little. The laugh doesn't suit him somehow—and it doesn't suit me, either.

"If you have anything to tell me, please tell it quickly, because I'm very busy."

"Oh, you don't really mean that," he answers, with another silly and offensive laugh. "There's always plenty of time for good times. That's what I am here for. I saw you at the races the other day and twice at King's House. My ship will be here for ——— weeks."

"Do you wish that noted?" I ask.

"Oh, no! Why—I came just because I had an idea that you might like to know me. I would like to know you. You look such a nice little body. Say, wouldn't you like to go for a sail this lovely night? I will tell you all about the sweet little Chinese girls I met when we were at Hong Kong. They're not so shy!"

• • •

I leave Eastern Canada for the Far West, so reduced by another attack of rheumatic fever that I only weigh eighty-four pounds. I travel on an advertising contract. It is presumed by the railway company that in some way or other I will give them full value for their transportation across the continent. I have been ordered beyond the Rockies by the doctor, who declares that I will never regain my strength in the East. Nevertheless, I am but two days in San Francisco when I start out in search of work. It is the first time that I have sought work as a stranger in a strange town. Both of the other positions away from home were secured for me by home influence. I am quite surprised to find that there is no demand for my services in San

Francisco and that no one is particularly interested in me. The best I can do is to accept an offer from a railway agency to typewrite their correspondence for $5 a month. I stipulate, however, that I shall have the privilege of taking in outside work and that my hours shall be light. I am hopeful that the sale of a story or newspaper article may add to my income, and I console myself with the reflection that, considering that I still limp and bear traces of sickness, I am fortunate to secure any work at all.

The proprietor of one of the San Francisco papers, to whom I have a letter of introduction, suggests that I obtain some subscriptions from the people of China town, that district of the city having never been canvassed. This suggestion I carry out with enthusiasm, tho I find that the Chinese merchants and people generally are inclined to regard me with suspicion. They have been imposed upon so many times by unscrupulous white people. Another drawback—save for a few phrase, I am unacquainted with my mother tongue. How, then, can I expect these people to accept me as their own countrywoman? The Americanized Chinamen actually laugh in my face when I tell them that I am of their race. However, they are not all "doubting Thomases." Some little women discover that I have Chinese hair, color of eyes and complexion, also that I love rice and tea. This settles the matter for them—and for their husbands.

My Chinese instincts develop. I am no longer the little girl who shrunk against my brother at the first sight of a Chinaman. Many and many a time, when alone in a strange place, has the appearance of even a humble laundryman given me a sense of protection and made me feel quite at home. This fact of itself proves to me that prejudice can be eradicated by association.

I meet a half Chinese, half white girl. Her face is plastered with a thick white coat of paint and her eyelids and eyebrows are blackened so that the shape of her eyes and the whole expression of her face is changed. She was born in the East, and at the age of eighteen came West in answer to an advertisement. Living for many years among the working class, she had heard little but abuse of the Chinese. It is not difficult, in a land like California, for a half Chinese, half white girl to pass as one of Spanish or Mexican origin. This poor child does, tho she lives in nervous dread of being "discovered." She becomes engaged to a young man, but fears to tell him what she is, and only does so when compelled by a fearless American girl friend. This girl, who knows her origin, realizing that the truth sooner or later must be told, and better soon than late, advises the Eurasian to confide in the young man, assuring her that he loves her well enough not to allow her nationality to stand, a bar sinister, between them. But the Eurasian prefers to keep her secret, and only reveals it to the man who is to be her husband when driven to bay by the American girl, who declares that if the halfbreed will not tell the truth she will. When the young man hears that the girl he is engaged to has Chinese blood in her veins, he exclaims: "Oh, what will my folks say?" But that is all. Love is stronger than prejudice with him, and neither he nor she deems it necessary to inform his "folks."

The Americans, having for many years manifested a much higher regard for the Japanese than for the Chinese, several half Chinese young men and women, thinking to advance themselves, both in a social and business sense, pass as Japanese. They continue to be known as Eurasians; but a Japanese Eurasian does not appear in the same light as a Chinese Eurasian. The unfortunate Chinese Eurasians! Are not those who compel them to thus cringe more to be blamed than they?

People, however, are not all alike. I meet white men, and women, too, who are proud to mate with those who have Chinese blood in their veins, and think it a great honor to be distinguished by the friendship of such. There are also Eurasians and Eurasians. I know of one who allowed herself to become engaged to a white man after refusing him nine times. She had discouraged him in every way possible, had warned him that she was half Chinese; that her people were poor, that every week or month she sent home a certain amount of her earnings, and that the man she married would have to do as much, if not more; also, most uncompromising truth of all, that she did not love him and never would. But the resolute and undaunted lover swore that it was a matter of indifference to him whether she was a Chinese or a Hottentot, that it would be his pleasure and privilege to allow her relations double what it was in her power to bestow, and as to not loving him—that did not matter at all. He loved her. So, because the young woman had a married mother and married sisters, who were always picking at her and gossiping over her independent manner of living, she finally consented to marry him, recording the agreement in her diary thus:

"I have promised to become the wife of ——— ——— on ———
———, 189—, because the world is so cruel and sneering to a single
woman—and for no other reason."

Everything went smoothly until one day. The young man was
driving a pair of beautiful horses and she was seated by his side, trying
very hard to imagine herself in love with him, when a Chinese
vegetable gardener's cart came rumbling along. The Chinaman was a
jolly-looking individual in blue cotton blouse and pantaloons, his
rakish looking hat being kept in place by a long queue which was
pulled upward from his neck and wound around it. The young
woman was suddenly possest with the spirit of mischief. "Look!" she
cried, indicating the Chinaman, "there's my brother. Why don't you
salute him?"

The man's face fell a little. He sank into a pensive mood. The wicked
one by his side read him like an open book.

"When we are married," said she, "I intend to give a Chinese party
every month."

No answer.

"As there are very few aristocratic Chinese in this city, I shall fill up
with the laundrymen and vegetable farmers. I don't believe in being
exclusive in democratic America, do you?"

He hadn't a grain of humor in his composition, but a sickly smile
contorted his features as he replied:

"You shall do just as you please, my darling. But—but—consider a
moment. Wouldn't it be just a little pleasanter for us if, after we are
married, we allowed it to be presumed that you were—er—Japanese?
So many of my friends have inquired of me if that is not your
nationality. They would be so charmed to meet a little Japanese
lady."

"Hadn't you better oblige them by finding one?"

"Why—er—what do you mean?"

"Nothing much in particular. Only—I am getting a little tired of
this," taking off his ring.

"You don't mean what you say! Oh, put it back, dearest! You know
I would not hurt your feelings for the world!"

"You haven't. I'm more than pleased. But I do mean what I say."

That evening the "ungrateful" Chinese Eurasian diaried, among
other things, the following:

"Joy, oh, joy! I'm free once more. Never again shall I be untrue to my own heart. Never again will I allow any one to 'hound' or 'sneer' me into matrimony."

I secure transportation to many California points. I meet some literary people, chief among whom is the editor of the magazine who took my first Chinese stories. He and his wife give me a warm welcome to their ranch. They are broadminded people, whose interest in me is sincere and intelligent, not affected and vulgar. I also meet some funny people who advise me to "trade" upon my nationality. They tell me that if I wish to succeed in literature in America I should dress in Chinese costume, carry a fan in my hand, wear a pair of scarlet beaded slippers, live in New York, and come of high birth. Instead of making myself familiar with the Chinese Americans around me, I should discourse on my spirit acquaintance with Chinese ancestors and quote in between the "Good mornings" and "How d'ye dos" of editors.

"Confucius, Confucius, how great is Confucius, Before Confucius, there never was Confucius. After Confucius, there never came Confucius," etc., etc., etc.,

or something like that, both illuminating and obscuring, don't you know. They forget, or perhaps they are not aware that the old Chinese sage taught "The way of sincerity is the way of heaven."

My experiences as an Eurasian never cease; but people are not now as prejudiced as they have been. In the West, too, my friends are more advanced in all lines of thought than those whom I knew in Eastern Canada—more genuine, more sincere, with less of the form of religion, but more of its spirit.

So I roam backward and forward across the continent. When I am East, my heart is West. When I am West, my heart is East. Before long I hope to be in China. As my life began in my father's country it may end in my mother's.

After all I have no nationality and am not anxious to claim any. Individuality is more than nationality. "You are you and I am I," says Confucius. I give my right hand to the Occidentals and my left to the Orientals, hoping that between them they will not utterly destroy the insignificant "connecting link." And that's all.

Independent, 21 January 1909

Chinese Workmen in America

In these days one reads and hears much about Chinese diplomats, Chinese persons of high rank, Chinese visitors of prominence, and others, who by reason of wealth and social standing are interesting to the American people. But of those Chinese who come to live in this land, to make their homes in America, if only for a while, we hear practically nothing at all. Yet these Chinese, Chinese-Amricans, I call them, are not unworthy of a little notice, particularly as they sustain thruout the period of their residence here a faithful and constant correspondence with relations and friends in the old country, and what they think and what they write about Americans will surely influence, and is influencing to a great extent, the conduct of their countrymen toward the people of the United States, and I can name many a one-time Chinese workingman, who after several years of laundry or other labor in this country, took a college course, was graduated and remained among his own people. A former Seattle laundryman is now president of the only railway in China owned by the Chinese. A one-time Canadian laundryman has been elected to represent his countrymen in Canada in China's new Legislature. A Canadian Chinese merchant's son is now Chief Magistrate in one of the Chinese provinces. Many of the American Chinese laundrymen have become missionaries to their people. It is the Chinese who have lived and worked in America who are establishing factories in their cities and towns and building schools and churches, in which undertakings they are substantially helped by their working countrymen in America. Furthermore, there is scarcely a Chinese mission school in America which is not contributing toward the support of some good civilizing work in China. The annual report of one small mission in Boston, the superintendent of which is a Chinese laundryman, contains the following account of moneys contributed and raised by the members: $160 for a loan to the Government of Canton, China; $185 for help to the Government of China; $60 for church at Nu Ben Sun Ning, China; $60 for Presbyterian Church at Ching Law Sun Ning; $72 for Canton College, Canton, China; $79.50 for Famine Relief Fund at Wu Nun and On Fee; $17 toward the expenses of Goon Tun Ying at a missionary school in Canton; $22 for the Rev. Ko Choo, of San Francisco; and so on thru a long list.

Many of the Chinese laundrymen I know are not laundrymen only, but artists and poets, often the sons of good families. There are, to be sure, men of the Chinese lower class among them; but these are not in the majority. The majority are stalwart, self-respecting countrymen from the district around Canton city and province, or are American-born descendants of the pioneer Chinese who came to this coast long before our transcontinental railways were built, and helped the American to mind his ore, build his railways and cause the Pacific coast to blossom as the rose.

The democracy of the Chinese in America is pleasant to witness. On New Year's Day I have met among the callers at the homes of western Chinese friends merchants, diplomats, business men, professional men, students, laborers and laundrymen, and have noted that the workingmen entered into the general conversation with as much freedom and authority and were listened to with as serious respect as was accorded the visiting consul. But this anomaly can be partly explained by the fact that many of the Chinese who come to this country to work as laborers are oftentimes cousins of government students, and, in several cases which came under my notice, brothers of students, it being a custom among the Chinese to educate but one boy of a family if domestic economy necessitates that course.

There are hundreds of Chinese children in America. Most of them are born here, and as their environment is more American than Chinese, it is safe to say that the next generation will see many Americans whose ancestors were Chinese. I noticed in one of the Sunday schools I visited in San Francisco that half of the little girls were dressed like American children, while the other half wore the dress of the Chinese woman, which is almost as old in style as the setting sun. I was told that in some cases, the ancient dress was obliged to be worn as a punishment, the modern permitted as a reward. Chinese mothers in Boston tell me that their children do not care to talk Chinese, and even when addressed by their parents in their mother tongue, reply in English. In the eastern states the Chinese public school children wear only the American dress.

Independent, 3 July 1913

The Chinese in America

Intimate Study of Chinese Life in America.
Told in a Series of Short Sketches—An Interpretation
of Chinese Life and Character.

In these days when the future of China is being discussed by all thinking people, one reads much in the papers and magazines about Chinese diplomats, Chinese persons of high rank, Chinese students, both boys and girls, Chinese visitors of prominence, scholars and others, who by reason of wealth and social standing, are interesting to the American people, but of those Chinese who come to live in this land, to make their homes in America, some permanently, others for many years, we hear practically nothing at all. Yet these Chinese, Chinese-Americans I call them, are not unworthy of a little notice, particularly as they sustain throughout the period of their residence here, a faithful and constant correspondence with relations and friends in the old country, and what they think and what they write about Americans, will surely influence, to a great extent, the conduct of their countrymen towards the people of the United States. For the Chinese on the Pacific Coast are numbered by the thousands. There is scarcely a city that does not have its local Chinatown or a number of Chinese residents. Many of these men are possessed of fine business ability, some are scholars; those of them who are laborers are stalwart, self-respecting countrymen from the district around Canton city and province, or are American-born descendants of the pioneer Chinamen who came to this Coast long before our transcontinental railways were built, and helped the American to mine his ore, build his railways and cause the Pacific Coast to blossom like the rose. In the romantic past of this western country, the figure of the Chinaman stands forth conspicuously, and every true Westerner will admit that the enlarged life in which he is participating today could not have been possible without the Chinese.

Their reasons for exile, apart from the "fortune" question, are individually interesting; the observations of the most intelligent on American life and manners are pertinent and instructive. If the Chinese can learn much from the Americans, the former can also teach a few lessons to the latter. No one, who, without prejudice, goes amongst the Chinese people in America and converses with them in friendly fashion but will find food for thought.

My father, who lived in China for many years, who married a Chinese lady, and who was a personal friend of Li Soon, Li Hung Chang's secretary, is of the opinion that one has a much better opportunity to study Chinese character in this country than in China, for here the Chinese are naturally more communicative than when in their own land. As for me, my interest in them has been keen and perpetual since the day I learned that I was of their race. And I have found them wherever I have wandered. In New York are some of my best Chinese friends; nearly every mail brings me news from Chinese Canadians, both east and west. Down in the West Indies I met a Chinese whose intelligence and active heroism in a moment of danger and distress will cause him and his compatriots to be ever remembered with gratitude and a warm feeling of kinship. In Los Angeles, San Francisco and the Puget Sound cities I know Chinese, both men and women, whose lives, if written, would read like romances, and whose qualities of mind and heart cannot help but win the interest and respect of all who know them understandingly.

It is true that they—these Chinese people—like other nationalities, have their own peculiar customs, manners and characteristics; but in a broad sense they are one with the other peoples of the earth. They think and act just as the white man does, according to the impulses which control them. They love those who love them; they hate those who hate; are kind, affectionate, cruel or selfish, as the case may be. I have not found them to be slow of intellect and alien to all other races in that "they are placed and unfeeling, and so custom-bound that even their tears are mere waters of ceremony and flow forth at stated times and periods." Thus a European traveler some centuries ago described the Chinese people, and travelers ever since, both men and women, have echoed his words and sentiments, while fiction writers seem to be so imbued with the same ideas that you scarcely ever read about a Chinese person who is not a wooden peg. There are a few exceptions, but the majority of writers on things Chinese echo those who enter before, which is a very foolish thing to do in these revolutionary days. The Chinese may be custom-bound—no doubt they are—but they are human beings, nevertheless. In this country they are slow to push their individual claims, and when with strangers, hide the passions of their hearts under quiet and peaceful demeanors; but because a man is indisposed to show his feelings is no proof that he has none. Under a quiet surface the Chinaman conceals a rapid comprehension and an almost morbid sensitiveness; he also possesses considerable inventive power and is more of an initiative spirit than an imitative one, whatever may be said to the contrary by those who know him but superficially. The pleasures of life he takes quietly; there is a melancholy trait in the characters of most Chinamen, as in all people of old civilizations. His mysticism and childlike faith in the marvelous is also an inheritance from his ancestors. Yet we are not without the Chinaman, merry and glad and full of exuberant animal spirits. Indeed, there is no type of white person who cannot find his or her counterpart in some Chinese. Therefore the following sketches of Chinese in America:

The Story of Wah

Wah was a leading member of the Chinese Reform party, whom I met in this city some years ago. He was an alert-minded young fellow, full of enthusiasm for the Reform cause and ambitious to learn the ways of the western people. His father, as he informed me, was a school teacher. "Then," I said, "you, being but a merchant, are not as much in the eyes of your people as your father was." Wah smiled. "We do not think in China as we did in the old days," said he. In Canton we have as much esteem for the clever man of business as we have for the scholar. When my father was a boy it was different." And he went on to compare his father's China with the China of his own remembrance, demonstrating in a surprisingly clear and convincing manner the progress that had been made.

"Why did you come to this country?" I inquired. "To make money and to learn western ways quicker than I could at home," he answered. Picking up an English paper lying on the table and pointing to a picture of an antique book which was advertised for sale, he inquired why it was marked at such a high price as $500. A lady explained that its age made it valuable. He thought for a moment, then said, "Why, then, is the Bible so cheap? It is very old book."

After a while he remarked that it might be a good plan to send to China for some old things for his store. "They will not be so expensive as newly manufactured goods," said he, "and if I can sell them at a higher price, I shall certainly make my fortune in a very little while."

Wah was a practical man of business, but his principles would have done honor to the noblest philanthropist. He had opportunities of making a great deal of money through the smuggling of opium from Canada into the United States. A safe and secret way was open to him through one of his own cousins. But Wah refused to have anything to do with the business. "No," he answered. "I wish for my countrymen to rise, not to fall, and when I speak at the Reform Club I advise that the pipe should be cast out. How, then, can I place it in their hand? Would that not be inconsistent?"

A Chinese Book on Americans

"I think," said Go Ek Ju, "that when I return to China I will write a book about the American people."

"What put such an idea into your head?" I asked.

"The number of books about the Chinese by Americans," answered Go Ek Ju. "I see them in the library; they are very amusing."

"See, then, that when you write your book, it is likewise amusing."

"No," said Go Ek Ju. "My aim, when I write a book about Americans will be to make it not amusing, but interesting and instructive. The poor Americans have to content themselves with writing for amusement only because they have no means of obtaining any true knowledge of the Chinese when in China; but we Chinese in America have fine facilities for learning all about the Americans. *We go into the American houses as servants; we enter the American schools and colleges as students;* we ask questions and we think about what we hear and see. Where is there the American who will go to China and enter into the service of a Chinese family as a domestic? We have yet to hear about a band of American youths, both male and female, being admitted as students into a Chinese university."

Scholar or Cook?

"You seem to enjoy your work," I remarked to Wang Liang, who was making cake in the hotel kitchen, meanwhile crooning a low song.

"It is very pleasant work," was his reply.

"What did you do when you were in China?" I inquired.

"I was a scholar."

"A scholar?"

Wang Liang went on making his cakes.

"Why," I mused aloud, "I thought a scholar in China was not supposed to know anything about work."

"True," answered Wang Liang; "a scholar must be helpless in all ways in spite of his learning. But my mother was ill and needed ginseng and chicken broth, and my father was getting old, and we were poor. All the time my heart was sad, for my parents had always been very good and kind to me and I loved them much. Then one day I read in my Classics, 'Those who labor support those who govern,' and I reasoned that if those who labored supported those who governed, then the laborer must in no wise be inferior to him who governs. So I decided to work with my hands, and in order that my parents might not be made to feel ashamed, I came to America. Since I have come here, with my labor I have supported myself, paid back my passage money to the agent who loaned it to me, kept my father and mother in comfort at home and have placed some part of every month's wages in a bank. When I have enough to live on for the rest of my life I will return to China and again take up my studies and do honor to my parents as a scholar."

Wang Liang rubbed his hands together and laughed softly and gleefully.

Westerner, May 1909

The Chinese in America, Part II

Intimate Study of Chinese Life in America.
Told in a Series of Short Sketches—An Interpretation
of Chinese Life and Character.

The New and the Old

The following story of youthful business enterprise is told by Lu Seek, a prosperous Chinese merchant and the owner of many shares in a Mexican railway.

"I came to this country at an early age. I first worked for my Uncle who gave me food, lodging and clothing in return for my services. I attended Mission schools of all denominations, Presbyterian, Episcopal, Baptist, Methodist and Roman Catholic. I learned the English language with little difficulty. From the American youth I also learned that a young person's time in America is quite as valuable as any elderly person's, and that eighteen years of age was a far superior age to forty-eight. Imbued with this knowledge I began to assume airs of dignity. When my Uncle bade me do this or that I would answer negligently—sometimes with hauteur. Whereupon my Uncle was one morning led to try the gentle persuasion of a stick. I objected. I said to him, 'Honorable Uncle, you do not respect me as you should nor do you consider that we are living in America, where a man instead of looking backward and admiring one's parents and uncles, fixes his mind on himself, thinks for himself and so acts that his parents and uncles, instead of wishing and requiring him to admire them wonder at and admire him.'

" 'Admire you,' exclaimed my Uncle, with an expression of furious contempt and another well aimed blow at my head, which, however, I successfully dodged.

" 'That is what they believe in the west,' I persisted, 'and that is why they of the west progress and those of the east stand still.'

"My Uncle's reply conveyed the impression that there was a difference of opinion between us, and as a difference of opinion is a very sad thing to have between those who live under the same roof, I suggested to my Uncle that he hand over to me the sum of money which he held in trust for me from my father, and I would walk my way which was evidently not his way.

"My Uncle considered for fifteen minutes, then he went to his till, took therefrom fifty silver dollars, the amount of my inheritance, and threw them down on the counter. I quickly pocketed them, and with what few personal belongings I possessed rolled up under my arm, started out in the world to seek my fortune.

"I had not gone very far when I met some of my white acquaintances. I informed them that I had been putting into practice the principles they had inculcated, and they cheered me on and told me that I would not take very long for me to become a real American of free and independent spirit. I showed them my fifty dollars and invited them to lunch with me. This invitation they accepted. The fifty dollars soon became ten. Half of that I spent in buying a present for my Sunday school teacher.

"I then tried to earn my own living as a cook or laundryman, but was not successful. I had no experience in the kitchen, neither was I learned in the lore of the laundry, and though I have known many of my countrymen, who as inexperienced as I, have yet made many successes of these callings, it was plain to be seen that as my American friends observed, I had a soul above domestic service. One day, my Sunday school teacher, who was unaware that I had left my Uncle's store, asked me if I knew of a good Chinese boy who could act as a general servant. I mentioned the names of several and she thanked me, remarking that I was better than an Employment Bureau. That put an idea into my head. I would start such an office and provide help for the American ladies. Though I could not secure employment myself I might obtain it for others. I was acquainted with many Mission and Sunday school ladies, whom I knew would bring their friends to me when they needed servants, and for all my estrangement from my Uncle, I was quite popular with the youth of Chinatown.

"But to start a business a little capital is necessary, and that I lacked. I was musing on this fact and a hungry stomach, when I met a second cousin of mine who did business as a fortune teller near the corner of Dupont and Kearney streets. 'Have you eaten your rice?' he exclaimed. That is a simple Chinese greeting but I took it literally and humbled myself to explain that I had no money with which to buy rice. He stroked his chin reflectively, and remarked that it was a pity that my forefathers had not bequeathed to me the spirit of divination; for if such had been the case, he himself would have been glad to adopt me as an assistant in the expounding of mythical lore.

"As we talked together, he in his long silken robes, I in my exceedingly shabby American store clothes, I envied him his prosperity, his calm and affable manners, his pleasing reposeful face. I knew that his elegantly furnished office was quite a resort for the perplexed of Chinatown's four hundred, and moreover, that many unsettled white people also surreptitiously visited him in the hope of having light thrown on certain difficult questions. I knew that through the fortunate reading of her father's horoscope, he had won as wife the prettiest American born Chinese girl in the City of the Golden Gate. Yet, curious fact—for all my envy of his accomplishments and attainments, I had not the slightest desire to be as he—reader of the stars. It was too ancient a business, and though my cousin had found it practical enough for all his purposes, it did not appeal to me in any sense as a business. I wanted a business which would call for a telephone and electric lights; not candles, incense, tortoise shells and diagrams.

"My cousin was both good hearted and good natured. After dining me, he himself proposed that he set me up in a small Chinese drug store. The herbs with which Chinese doctors' prescriptions are usually filled would not cost much; and the dried nuts, lily bulbs, fish eggs, and other stock necessary, could also be obtained without much outlay. In particular, he advised this business, as a Chinese fortune teller often acts as physician, and it would be in his power to occasionally send me customers.

"But I had in mind the Employment Bureau and nothing else would do for me. I said to my cousin: 'Since you are so kind as to propose to set me up in a business to your liking, perhaps you will be a little kinder still and help me to start a business to my liking.' And I told him of my dreams of the Employment Bureau. For a time my cousin scoffed. For one who was unable to find work for himself to seek to make a living by obtaining it for others seemed too absurd. It would be a case of the blind leading the blind.

"Thus he argued. My arguments are unnecessary to relate. Suffice it to say, however, that they won, and when I left my cousin I was furnished with the necessary funds to launch myself on the business career I had chosen.

"I set up my office near the Plaza. From my doorway I could see the drinking fountain which is put up as a memorial to your great writer, Robert Louis Stevenson. Well, to my great satisfaction, it was not long before I found myself standing under an electric light with a green shade answering a call from a society lady on Nob Hill. She was desiring a boy accomplished in the art of cooking. After that the calls came frequently—and I had dozens of Chinese boys ready to answer. Sometimes my customers would interview me several times before deciding on a boy. From their conversations I derived much benefit.

"That was the beginning of my good fortunes. I found that by maintaining a pleasant demeanor and an affable tongue I could manage to get along very well in the finding of employment for my countrymen in America. Because I was reminded of your great writer by the fountain in the Square or Plaza I bought all of his works from a book agent on the installment plan and read them between the hours of business. I admired much his 'Treasure Island,' and the reading thereof furnished me with good conversation whenever the ladies came to my office. Of course I used my discretion. There were some ladies who did not read Robert Louis Stevenson, you understand. There were other ladies who did. I am of opinion that taken all around Robert Louis Stevenson improved much my business.

"When I had made a few thousand dollars I decided to go to live in New York and sell out my business to my third cousin, Lu Wing. He was the adopted brother of the Fortune Teller cousin who had loaned me the money with which to start business and whose debt I had repaid with interest out of what I made my first year. Just before leaving for the big city I called upon my Uncle, and after making a most humble and contrite apology for my past conduct and the improper speeches connected therewith, persuaded him to pay me a visit at my office. There I smoked with him the pipe of peace, and there the old man, after speaking through the phone with some friend in San Jose, acknowledged that it was true—the days were over for young people to wonder at and admire their parents and the time had come for the old people to wonder at and admire them.

" 'That is progress,' I replied.

" 'When it is not carried to extremes.' supplemented my wife, an American Chinese girl."

Westerner, June 1909

The Chinese in America, Part III

Intimate Study of Chinese Life in America.
Told in a Series of Short Sketches—An Interpretation
of Chinese Life and Character.

Like the American

When Tin-a came over the sea to be wife to Sik Ping, there were great rejoicings in Chinatown, for Sik Ping was very popular. Many dinner parties were given, some very brilliant affairs indeed. The one that I attended was on the top floor of a Chinatown building. The dining room was elegantly furnished with black teak wood tables and carved chairs inlaid with mother of pearl; screens adorned the partitions between rooms, and there were couches along the wall where after dining one could lie at ease and smoke; the place was brilliantly illuminated with electric lights and red Chinese candles, and a large incense burner suspended from the ceiling in the middle of the room, filled the air with a truly Oriental fragrance.

Though it is not the custom for Chinese women to sit at meat with men, Sik Ping was Americanized enough to seat his wife by his side. The wife of Go Ek Ju, his friend, gave face to Tin-a as the Chinese say.

The tables were loaded with dishes of chicken, bamboo shoots and confections of all kinds known to the Chinese. Both men and women were attired in gorgeous silk robes, the latter wearing flowers in their hair and in front of their tunics. Each and every one of the Chinese guests presented Sik Ping with a sum of money, as is the custom amongst the Chinese on such occasions.

There was a strange scene at the close of the evening. The little bride, who throughout dinner had sat with downcast eyes, scarcely touching a morsel of food, upon leaving the table was seen to be weeping. Mrs. Go Ek Ju sought to discover the source of her tears, and after a murmured conversation with Tin-a reluctantly informed Sik Ping that his bride had confessed to being afraid that he would be angry with her.

"Afraid that I be angry with her!" exclaimed poor Sik Ping bewilderedly. "Ah No!"

Whereupon Amoy hung her head and shed more tears.

It came out at last that Ping's bride was not the girl whom a cousin had married for him by proxy and for whom he had sent the passage money from China to America. That girl had formed an attachment for her proxy husband, who reciprocated the feeling, they having reaped in the rice fields together. She accordingly prevailed upon Tin-a, her friend, who was an orphan of adventurous spirit, and whose name was the same as her own, to undertake the long ocean journey from which she shrunk and become in reality wife to Sik Ping.

But Tin-a no sooner beheld Ping's kind face when she became conscience stricken, and that feeling so overwhelmed her when he had placed her beside him at the dinner table that she had been unable to restrain her tears.

"Ah!" she cried, falling on the ground at his feet. "You are so good and kind and I so deceitful and evil." But Ping, who had never seen the girl to whom he was married by proxy and who had conceived an affection for the little Tin-a, instead of upbraiding her with hard words, comforted her with loving ones, and the day following bought a marriage license and was married over again by the Chinese missionary.

"I do as the Americans do," said Ping proudly. "I marry the woman I love."

The Story of Forty-niner

"Why did you come to America?" I asked a Chinaman who was beating a gold ring into shape. He was a manufacturing jeweler.

"Why did I come? Oh, it is so long ago since I came that I am not sure that I can remember the reasons."

And Hom Hing, being a good-natured fellow, began:

"My father had two boys, myself and my brother. I was the eldest, so my father chose me to be the scholar. Therefore, while I was clothed in the best style which the family circumstances would allow, my little queue tied neatly with a string, an embroidered cap on my head, and the whitest of white-soled shoes on my feet, fed on the best which the house afforded and kept in idleness save for study, my brother roamed about the village, bare-footed, bare-headed, and almost bare-bodied. He gathered the wood for fuel, hoed the ground, reaped in the rice fields and grew healthy and handsome. My mother and sisters treated me with respectful politeness, but to my brother they were always careless in manner. As I did nothing but study, naturally my body was weak and I suffered from the slightest exertion or exposure to heat or cold. I was kept at my books from morning till night while I was at home and attended the village school, and when I was old enough to be sent to the university I studied even harder. I was imbued with ambition to become a great scholar and do honor to my parents, but for all that I unconsciously envied my brother, whose lusty arms could fell an ox. When my sisters were given as wives for sons of other families, it became necessary that my brother and myself should marry in order that my mother should have a girl to help her in the house. I was accordingly married by proxy while still in the university. My brother also married, and when I returned home, there was a little son of his crawling about the floor. Our family had become impoverished during my university years, my father was old and unable to do much; almost the whole burden of supporting the family, including myself, fell upon my brother's shoulders.

That year agents of certain Chinese Companies came around our village bribing men to go to America. They offered my father quite a large sum for my brother, Hom Ling, and my father, after talking the matter over with my mother, decided to accept the money and send my brother, Hom Ling, to work in the country across the sea. My parents had no doubt, from what was told them, that Hom Ling's labor would soon repay those who advanced his passage money to America and then he would be free to send his wages home.

"Now, my brother, Hom Ling, loved his wife and child, and the thought of being separated from them filled his heart with sorrow. He spoke to me about it with many sighs, for, though the course of our lives ran in such different channels, we were brothers in affection as well as in blood. While he was lamenting his fate, an inspiration came to me. He was to leave the village at night in company with some other youths. In the darkness it would be impossible to distinguish one lad from another, and though I was weak and he strong, we were of the same build. The cause of this inspiration was the fact that, despite the respect that was paid me, I found home life unbearable. After having lived away from home for several years, my mother, my wife and my sister-in-law's tongues sounded discordantly in my ears. My sedentary life had made me nervous and irritable. Moreover, the wife that had been chosen for me was most repulsive to my taste.

"Why not, then," I suggested to my brother, "that I be the one to go and you be the one to remain?"

"But my parents have placed all their hopes on you," demurred my brother, albeit with brightening eyes.

"Fiddlesticks!" I answered in Chinese, "I shall be doing better by my parents by leaving them you than by remaining with them myself. It will be years before I can earn even my own living as a school teacher and you can help them straight along."

"So I came to America. On this side the change of brothers was never discovered. As for me, the new life brought with renewed health and strength. In the old California days the Chinese lived and worked in the open air, and the work of a laborer in America is easy compared to that of a laborer in China. I had better food and more than I had ever had in my life, and the sunshine and freshness of this western country transformed me both physically and mentally. It is living, not studying that makes a man. Adventures and hairbreadth escapes from death were frequent; hard times, too, but I managed to pull through after fifteen years of it with a nice little bag of gold with which I returned to China. My parents were still living and my brother was surrounded by a large family; my first wife had died. I married a pretty tea picker whom I met while rambling among the hills. She was a slave girl, but I paid her price, and in spite of my parents' opposition, brought her back with me to America. This business I learned after my mining days were over. I have two sons and one daughter, all married and living in this country."

The Story of Tai Yuen and Ku Yum

Tai Yuen was Ku Yum's lover; but whereas Tai Yuen was a See Yup, Ku Yum's father was a Sam Yup. A See Yup is a man from the fourth district of the Province of Kwangtung, a Sam Yup a man from the Third district. Some time before the tale of Tai Yuen and Ku Yum was told, a Sam Yup murdered a See Yup. This was in Southern California. All the See Yups knew that one of their number had been killed by a Sam Yup; but though they thirsted for revenge they could not discover the murderer. It therefore became a case, not of man against man, but of district against district, and as a result a Sam Yup soon went the way of the murdered See Yup. The Sam Yups, however, proved better detectives than their enemies, and traced the crime so that the actual murderer, a man belonging to one of the See Yup's Secret Societies, was convicted and punished by the law of the land. At this the See Yups became so bitterly incensed that notice to boycott all Sam Yups was sent by their chiefs to the See Yups all over the continent. The boycott spread and became a serious matter, for the See Yups are much more numerous than the Sam Yups, the See Yups being chiefly laundrymen and laboring men, and the Sam Yups merchants who depend for the success of their business upon the trade of the See Yups.

Now Tai Yuen was an Americanized Chinaman, having come to this coast at a very early age, and Ku Yum was American born. So when Tai Yuen and Ku Yum met, they fell in love with one another, just as any American boy and girl might have done, and after some more meetings became engaged in true American fashion. It was shortly after they became engaged that the boycott between the Sam Yups and the See Yups became established.

"Do not venture to see me any more," bade poor Ku Yum, fearful for her lover's safety.

But Tai Yuen, being imbued with the American spirit, heeded not her warning, and one night when on his way to see his sweet heart, trusted emissaries of the See Yups' secret society dogged his footsteps. And Ku Yum still looks for her lover.

Wah Lee on Family Life

Wah Lee had left his home when a youth of fifteen with a company of strolling actors who had pitched camp in his home village for a week. From what I learned from a clansman of his, his father's family was a very large one, and home had been full of strife and contention. One day I asked him if he did not wish to return to China. His face sobered at once.

"I love my parents," he answered. "I send to them some part of what I make every month; but when I am at home I am unhappy. Too many tongues in the house interfere with peace." His brothers and sisters numbered fourteen.

"Quite a Rooseveltian family," I observed.

"I think President Roosevelt likes a joke," was his quick reply. "He declares to his people that the best thing for a country is big families, and then he commands them to teach our people to be like them."

Lee had lived for some years in Eastern Canada, and as he had worked in families both there and in the United States, being smuggled backwards and forwards across the line whenever the fancy pleased him, his observations on family life and some of his comparisons were to me quite illuminating. "The French Canadians," he remarked, "are more like the Chinese at home than are the Americans. The parents boss and the children obey; but there is not as much affection of the heart between them as I see in some American families— some not at all. There is also much form of religion with the Canadians and the Chinese. In America it is different. I have been in some families where the religion is not seen at all; but it is felt. That is what makes the heart glad; and to see the father and mother the true friend of the son and daughter, not the boss. The poorer families in Canada have many children, just as in China.

"It makes me sad," said he, "to see a poor little niece of ten years old carrying in her slender arms her uncle or aunt of four or five months. Yet that is what I see very often in Eastern Canada. Some of the little girls never have time to play nor to go to school; there are so many babies to be carried. And if they are not carrying babies, then they must go to work, for the father has too big a family of younger children to support them. And the mother is so cross with so many, and hard words and cruel blows drive the children into the street to steal and do other things for which the priest and the Sunday school teacher scold them. And there is much noise and confusion all the time just like in the big families in China. I think it is better in America, where the family is not so large, but where the children have a happy time and are well brought up. When I was in Montreal I read that more babies die in that city than in any other city in the world. Yet, the men in the black dresses who do not have any children themselves go around to the poor man and advise him all the time, 'Have plenty children, Have plenty children!' The poor little children. I feel so sorry for them!"

The Bonze

I came across Ke Leang in a Joss house. He was a Bonze, or Chinese priest, and a remarkably handsome man. I used to enjoy wandering about the Joss houses, admiring the quaint carvings and images, pondering and wondering over the mysterious hieroglyphics, and now and then confiscating a piece of sandal wood. At that time I had a rage for sandal wood. One day, having possessed myself of a larger piece than usual, I was about to move quietly away from the green bowl or jar from which I had taken it, when a quiet voice just behind me said: "If you like the wood you can take some more." I started guiltily. It was the priest, Ke Leang. He had placed his hand on the bowl and was tipping it towards me. I had the grace to demur, but blunderingly, I said, "Oh, I don't like to take any more. It is sacred, isn't it?" "Not at all," he answered. Then, calmly, and I fancied sarcastically, "Is it so to you?"

I felt ashamed, and feeling ashamed, began to talk of other things. I told him that my mother was Chinese, but because my father was an Englishman and I had been born in England and brought up in Canada, and by choice, lived in America, I was unable to speak my mother tongue. He did not at first pay much attention to my chatter, but when I brought forth a letter of introduction from Chinese friends in my home city to Chinese in other parts of the world, he became more communicative, and I had quite a long chat with him about Chinese religion. He told me that it was error to think that the Chinese bow down in spirit to wood or stone or anything made of such materials. It is true the Chinamen prostrates himself bodily before his ancestral tablets, his images of male and female divinities, but he worships in spirit only the spirit that is supposed to dwell in the image, and not the image itself, which is nothing more to him that what it is—a piece of wood or stone. He declared emphatically that the Chinese worship spirits, not images. "We worship," said he, "in the same way that I have seen American people worshiping in Catholic churches. We kneel before Mother (Ahmah, a Chinese goddess) as the Catholics kneel to the Virgin Mary."

He shook his head gravely when I asked him, in my ignorance, if he were a Confucianist. He admitted, however, that Confucianism, pure and simple, was the religion of most of the learned men of China.

Before I left San Francisco an American friend of mine who occasionally told a true story told me this one of Ke Leang, the Chinese priest.

Ke Leang lived in the province of the Happy River. That was when he was young, happy and not a priest. There also lived Mai Gwi Far.

Their parents' houses were close together, the gardens being separated by high stone walls. There was a hole in the separating wall. Mai Gwi Far and Ke Leang looked through the hole. Moreover, they spoke—sighed—smiled. When Ke Lean went to the university in another province he carried within his sleeve one of Mai Gwi Far's little red shoes. Just before the examination for the second literary degree Ke Leang received a letter from Mai Gwi Far. She was in great distress. The leaves of her rose geranium were withering and the night before she had heard the cry of an owl, now near, now far away. These signs meant sorrow and trouble. She feared, she knew not what. Was Ke Leang forgetting her and laughing and jesting with the Sing Song girls—they who sung and danced and painted their faces? Would he be interested to know that her parents had betrothed her to the son of a friend, and that she was to prepare for marriage within five months? The engagement was short because she was beyond the age for betrothing, being seventeen. She was so troubled and sad. What should she do? She awaited his reply with a beating heart. On that same day Ke Leang also received word from his parents that they had betrothed him to the daughter of their neighbor, Mai Gwi Far, she who was called the Pearl of Honan. In the exuberance of his joy at this news Ke Leang lost wisdom and, seeing by Mai Gwi Far's letter that she was as yet in ignorance of the name of her future husband, the spirit of mischief prompted him to sit down and pen the following message to the girl: "Marry the one whom your parents have chosen." When his carrier dove reached Mai Gwi Far it was night. The little bird tapped at her pane as it was wont to do, and she arose and, bringing it in, untied from under its wing her lover's message.

In the morn her parents found her cold in death, the jesting note beside her. It had certainly been her death blow. That is the reason why Ke Leang was a priest in San Francisco's China town. All ambition to attain his literary degree perished with Mai Gwi Far. He entered a monastery and ten years later was ordered by his Abbott to cross the sea to minister to the Chinese people in San Francisco.

Westerner, July 1909

The Chinese in America, Part IV

Intimate Study of Chinese Life in America.
Told in a Series of Short Sketches—An Interpretation
of Chinese Life and Character.

Yip Ke Duck and the Americans

"I do not like the Americans," quote old Yip Kee Duck. "They do not speak the truth; they are hypocrites; they think only of money; they pretend to be your friends, to admire you, to like you; but for all their smiles and soft words, they mean to swindle you and do you harm. Behind your back they laugh and sneer; they make amusement for themselves out of all the Chinaman says and does. When they come to trade with him, they expect their goods for next to nothing. Around Christmas time, there are always plenty of Sunday School teachers ready to teach the Chinese. They know the Chinese boys never forget to give presents. Whenever a white man does a little business with or throws business into the way of a Chinese, he looks for a bonus bigger than any profits that the Chinaman may gain. I have been fooled by them too often. 'He that hath wine has many friends.' Now they can fool me no more. Moreover, I shall warn all the Chinese boys that believe in the American Sunday school and the American Sunday school teachers. I shall tell my people in China that Americans are not only devils when they call you names and throw stones at you; but they are worse devils still when they come to you and say, 'Oh, Mr. Yip Kee Duck, how quaint and curious and beautiful is your store. What wonderful people you Chinese are! I wish I were one!' and all that fool talk."

Poor old Yip Kee Duck! Like some others of his race in this country, the treatment accorded him by the Americans had made him very bitter and cynical. For, in spite of all the honest endeavors and good work of some of the Christian missionaries and church women there are those amongst them who are wolves in sheep's clothing, and who bring disrepute upon their cause.

It is almost unbelievable the shameless way in which some white people will act towards the Chinese. This was brought to my attention in many very pointed ways when I was in San Francisco. I was very hard up at that time, and in order to obtain bread and butter put in some time canvassing Chinatown for the San Francisco Bulletin. For every subscription that I secured the paper was to pay me thirty cents. When soliciting from the Chinese merchants I simply asked them to sign their name to the voucher setting forth that they agreed to take the paper. Many of these merchants in answer to my request that they subscribe for the paper, would offer me the amount of the subscription for my own use. "Never mind about sending the paper. Just keep the money yourself," said one. I had difficulty indeed in impressing upon them that I was collecting autographs, not money. One fellow, when reluctantly returning the cash asked, "Perhaps you take it next time you come."

It seems that women who would sooner jump into the fire than ask a white man for money or presents will boldly demand such things of a Chinaman, and I have myself seen American women enter a Chinese store, take up some trinket they fancy, and ask the Chinaman to give it to them. He can hardly refuse, and boldly she walks off with her prize. But she has made a mistake. If a woman sinks low in the eyes of a white man by acting that way, she sinks lower still in the eyes of a Chinaman. To retain the respect of the Chinese, both at home and abroad, one must be careful to keep themselves perfectly independent of them. The respect of the Chinese has been worth much more than mere cash or a few trinkets to me.

At the same time the Chinaman is naturally a very kind, generous and open-hearted fellow, slow to think evil, appreciative of goodness, and respectful to every woman who deserves respect. That is why it is such a pity that they do not always see and know the genuine American, the sincere Christian. They are anxious to learn the best that America can teach them, they are so quick to discern truth and goodness to admire it. Very few of them are Yip Kee Ducks. I have known Chinamen to lose faith in person after person, and yet retain his faith in the American people as a whole. Although the scholars and students who come to our shores are properly conservative when pressing themselves concerning things American, the simple yet intelligent Chinamen who are with us gladly acknowledge that many of the ways of the white man are better than the ways of the Chinese.

New Year as Kept by the Chinese in America

Have you ever noticed how very happy looking the American Chinese are from Christmas to the end of their New Year? They are happy because during this topsy turvy season they can indulge their heart's content in the pleasure of giving. Not indiscriminately, of course; but to those who during the year have won, sometimes designedly, sometimes unconsciously, their liking or their gratitude. The Chinese never think of telling you that "it is more blessed to give than to receive." Perhaps their minds have not yet been educated to grasp the meaning of the saying, but they prove its truth. Give a Chinaman a present and he will thank you gratefully, but very calmly. No emotion disturbs his countenance. There is no visible pleasure. But allow him to give you something and watch his face as you receive it from his hand. You will see expressed real, true solid happiness. Never refuse to accept a Christmas present from a Chinaman unless you wish to offend him. You need not feel that you are bound to return the compliment. A Chinaman gives for the sake of giving, not in the hope of receiving. A poor laundryman will sometimes spend a couple of months' hard earned wages and more in a Christmas present for some friend, say a Sunday school teacher. If he has two teachers, he may spend four months' wages, and so on. Such are known facts. But do not blame him for extravagance, do not pity him as a fool for so doing. He is not a fool; he is a wise man, for he receives more than his money's worth of pleasure in believing that he is giving pleasure.

The Chinese New Year is different from the English year; their months being lunar, that is, reckoned by the revolution of the moon around the earth, are consequently shorter. They have twelve, say, instead of January, February, etc., Regular Moon, Second Moon, Third Moon. Each third year is a leap year and has an extra month so as to make each of the lunar years equal to a solar year. Accordingly, the time of their New Year varies between January and February. The week or ten days during which they keep it is a season of relaxation and rest from the cares of business. There is a great deal of mutual giving and receiving and not even the poorest beggar goes hungry. Those of the American Chinamen who have children celebrate with more than ordinary glee. Little Fat One, Little Black One, Tiny Spring Fragrance and Gentle Peach Blossom are all very happy. Red Chinese candles and punk sticks are burning and the quaint little

Chinese people are having a good time, eating all manner of good things, dressing in all the colors of the rainbow, having their little hands and pockets filled with all sorts of trinkets, nuts, and sweets, and best of all, watching the fire-flowers. The fire-flowers are called fireworks by the Americans. The fathers and mothers, and all the grown up aunts, uncles and cousins of Little Fat One and Little Black One are also enjoying themselves. They are taking parts in religious ceremonies, listening to Chinese music, dressing, feasting, resting, laughing, enjoying everything. Red, the good luck color, is much in evidence. You see it all over in bright splashes of long narrow strips of paper pasted upon buildings with inscriptions in Chinese. The restaurants, with their deep balconies ornamented with carved woodwork, brightly colored or gilded, and set off with immense lanterns and big plants in china pots, are distinctively picturesque.

Ceremonies too numerous to be particularized are performed. The name of some of these ceremonies might cause a humorist to smile and the sober-minded to sigh. One is "Keeping company with the gods during the night," a ceremony which consists of making offerings and feasting before a collection of gods or images. The spirits of these gods are supposed to graciously receive the spirit of the food spread before them, while the devotees in order to be sociable with and agreeable to their august company of spirits, represented by the Gods, which, let it be understood, are not themselves worshiped, demolish the substance of the viands.

The Chinese are exceedingly fond of stories and story telling, their favorite themes being magic and enchantment. It is popular also to portray the blessings which fall to the lot of the filial son and the terrible fate of the undutiful. Some of their stories are very pretty. For instance, there is the story of the Storm Dragon, who began life as a snake, but having the misfortune to lose its tail, and, therefore, being unable to enter another world, retired to a mountain spring, whose clear never-failing fountain proved a safe hiding place. There he lived through several centuries, and was the cause of all the storms that came from the southwest. When he became very angry he was said to work fearful destruction through bringing about evil winds and tornadoes. His end, however, was peaceful. In the form of a silkworm's egg, he ventured one day to lie on a palm leaf waving on a tree above the spring. A little girl named Choy found him, and wrapping him in brown paper, placed him within her bosom, hoping by the warmth of her body to hatch him, a silkworm. In that pure and peaceful resting place, the dragon repented of his misdeeds, and when finally he became a silkworm, and from a silkworm to a butterfly, he soared far away on golden wings into the bright heavens, and throughout the region in which he had dwelt there were no more storms.

Another example is the story of the fairy fish. The fairy fish loved a fairy bird, but sacrificed itself for the sake of a poor old woman who had no grandchild to feed her. The fairy fish jumped into a frying pan full of boiling oil and allowed itself to be cooked and eaten by the old lady who was thereby much strengthened. The spirit of the fairy fish, however, entered into a little bird, which little bird became the mate of the fairy bird loved by the fairy fish.

Some Chinamen take advantage of the holiday season to patronize our theatres. I inquired of a well-informed Chinaman if the plays in Chinese theatres resembled those he saw acted on the American stage. He replied that the stories played in Chinese theatres are very much like the stories played here, but nearly all the actors are men, even the female parts being personated by men in the garb of women. He said that a Chinese audience showed its appreciation, not by clapping hands, but by calling out "Good, Good."

Gambling and opium smoking are somewhat indulged in by our black sheep Chinamen during New Year. In some of the gambling places may be found an image made of wood on which is painted a tiger with wings. This image is the God of Gamblers, and is called "The Grasping Cash Tiger." The gamblers light incense and candles before it and cast lots with bamboo sticks.

Chinese-American Sunday Schools

Chinese-American Sunday School festivals are very popular with the exiled Chinamen during the festive season. I was present one time at a gathering of thirteen Chinese Sunday schools, and the crowded room, decorated with Chinese flags and banners, beautifully wrought in various colors, Chinese lanterns, flowers and native plants, presented a very picturesque appearance. The festival was given, not by the teachers, but by the Chinese themselves, and was an expression of the gratitude which Chinamen feel towards those who try to benefit them, and as well, an evidence that these foreign laborers, practical working men for the most part, have buried deep in their hearts, a love and appreciation of the beautiful.

The American preacher who was Chairman said that it gave him great pleasure to see so many of his Chinese brothers, and only regretted that he could not speak to them in their own language and tell them how sorry he was that they had met with experiences which might perhaps cause them to think meanly of the Christian faith. He wished to say that he and all the friends there assembled would endeavor to give them a different impression of Christianity.

The Chinamen who helped in the entertainment betrayed very little embarrassment and acted their parts creditably. One spoke in a very bright direct manner, thanking the American friends for the interest in himself and his fellow countrymen. Another sang the hymn, "Precious Name," and a Chinese orchestra delighted the audience. There was the fiddler with his fiddle, the flutist with his flute, the banjo man with is banjo, and the kettledrummer with his kettledrum. A European gentleman present who could speak Chinese explained that one of the pieces of music was taken from a play in a Chinese theatre. The singer, a man with a falsetto voice, was supposed to be a maiden soliloquizing whilst her lover was in battle. The Chairman remarked with a humorous smile that a piece of such character was not usually chosen for a Sunday school entertainment; but they must "take the will for the deed" and enjoy it in spite of its impropriety. This speech, of course, added to the evening's enjoyment. A little spice is needed, even at Chinese Sunday school festivals.

Chinese Food

Speaking of feasting and festivities brings us to the question of Chinese food. I have partaken of many Chinese dishes, all of which were good and nutritious, many dainty and delectable.

There is, of course, a difference between European and Chinese cooking. For one thing, Chinese use neither milk nor butter in the preparation of food. In their soups they use mostly sundried comestibles and one may observe in their stews various kinds of dried nuts, fruit and vegetables. Their chief article of diet is, as is well known, rice, and the Chinaman cooks it so beautifully that if you will watch him as he manipulates his chopsticks, you will see that nearly every grain rolls separate.

There is nothing on a Chinaman's table to remind us of living animals or birds—no legs, heads, limbs, wings or loins—everything is cut into small pieces. The Chinaman comes to the table to eat, not to work—his carving is done in the kitchen.

At a Chinese banquet, to which I was invited, there were so many fragrant and appetizing dishes passed before me that I thought, even if I could not taste of all, I would take a list of the names. Here it is:

Sin Lip Ap Gang (Duck soup prepared with lotus seeds and flavored with ham)
Foo Yung Dan (Chinese omelette with herbs)
Ham Sun Goey (Sweet and sour fish)
Hung Yan Gaiding (Fried chicken with almonds, bamboo shoots, etc.)
Mo Kwo Bark Gop (Fried mushroom squab)
Jah Tau Goey (Fried fish in fancy)
Mo Kw Gai Tong (Spring chicken soup with mushrooms)
Gai Yong Goey Chee (Fried sharks' fins with chicken and egg)
Choong Taw Chee Yok (Pork with onion)
Foo Yong Har (Lobster omelette with herbs)
Ngow Yok Chop Suey (Chop Suey of beef)
Yin Wah Guy Ga (Chicken chopped with bird's nest)
Gai Yong Wong Ye Taw (Brain of yellow fish with minced chicken)
Hop Howe Gai Nip (Fried walnut and chicken)
Mut Geong (Ginger in syrup)
Mut Kim Ghet (Golden Lime)
Bor Lor (Preserved pineapple)
Mut Ching Moy (Green apricots)
Kwa Ying (Mixed sweet chow chow)
Know Mine Lie Chee Gon (Chinese nuts)
Far Sang Toy (Chinese peanut candy)
Hang Yen Soo (Almond cakes)
Lok Dow Go (Green bean cakes)
Long Sue tea.

A favorite dish is rice flour dumplings filled with mince meat. Another is shark fins boiled to the softest consistency and preserved ducks' tongues—something very gelatinous. Balls of crab and tripe boiled to a tenderness hard to express are also very tempting to the jaded appetite.

A peculiarity of the Chinese table to Europeans and Americans is that although furnished with sauces of every flavor and strength, salt itself is never in evidence.

As a diet for dyspeptics and men of sedentary habits Chinese food is recommended. It is mucilaginous and nutritious.

The Bible Teacher

A lady who had a Chinese pupil in her Bible class lectured him one day for not attending more regularly.

"I am sorry, Miss M——," he replied, "but I myself instruct at that hour two American young men."

"Instruct two American young men! Pray, Sir, in what do you instruct them?"

"In all that you have instructed me."

"From the Bible?"

"Do you mean to say that there are American young men who do not know the Bible?"

Liu Wenti smiled. "There certainly are," he answered. "One day, these two came to my store. I was busy reading a story in the Bible. I told them so. They laughed and asked me if it was a good one. I read it to them. They said they would come again to listen to further stories. They cannot read much themselves and wish me to illuminate them.

Americanizing Not Always Christianizing

It will be seen from the above sketches that some of the Chinamen in our midst are much more Americanized than others, and those who are Americanized are not always those who have been with us the longest. Americanizing does not always mean improving or even civilizing. It ought to, but it does not. Some Chinese are not nearly as fine men after coming in contact with Western civilization as they were before. The majority, however, it is safe to say, benefit by stepping into the Westerner's light, more particularly those who have met with genuine Christian people and have had the privilege of entering into and seeing something of the beauty of the truly Christian American home. I lay great stress on the word "genuine," because an insincere Christian or one to whom religion is but a form, does great harm to the cause of Christianity. This has been repeated over and over again, but there is still reason for its repetition.

The Reform Party

The Chinese of the Reform Party in America are acutely conscious, and have been for many years, of the necessity of a new way of living for the Chinese—and not only a new way of living—a new way of thinking. They are also keenly alive to what is taking place in their own country. Indeed, they may be said to be the only Chinese here who are so. In nearly every city of any importance in America, there are a number of these Reform men, and they are amongst the most influential and enterprising. Not a few of them are graduates from American colleges. Nearly all of the Chinese married to white women in America belong to the Reform party, and they may truly be said to be living revolutionized lives as compared with the lives of their ancestors. Yet their hope and belief in the future of their own country is vital, and nothing causes their eyes to glisten more than to know that China is encouraging educational and industrial reforms, while those of them who have become Christians look forward with bright faith to China's religious reformation.

Westerner, August 1909

The Sugar Cane Baby

Humming birds glistening like jewels in the sunlight darted from flower to flower; insects of all colors and shapes droned over the grass and vines; lizards, green, yellow, speckled, black-and-gold, glided close to earth or darted under the roots or up the trunks of trees. Coiled around a flat, smooth stone was a green spotted snake. In the midst of all sat the sugar-cane baby sucking a piece of green sugar cane and cooing softly to himself.

The mother of the sugar-cane baby was working in the cane field. All the morning she had carried him on her back; but in the afternoon he had become restless, so she had laid him under a clump of bamboo outside the plantation, and without misgiving had returned to her labor.

The baby sucked and cooed. He thought the world a most delightful place. And why not? High over his head, above the green bamboo, the sky was sapphire blue, and right in front of him, coiling and uncoiling for his delight and pleasure, the most beautiful snake in the world. At least so thought the sugar-cane baby. He watched it with wholehearted admiration and pleasure until he fell asleep. A brilliant butterfly poised upon his small nose. He stirred restlessly. The snake darted its head forward. The butterfly flew off to a scarlet and gold poinsettia bush. The sugar-cane baby slept peacefully.

Two serene-faced Sisters of Mercy came slowly down the road. They were enjoying, as they quietly paced, the loveliness of the landscape—miles of green meadows and fruitful plantations undulating toward the sea—and the sea beyond, so blue and misty that the eye could scarcely distinguish where it melted into the sky.

"It is a lovely land," said the younger Sister in a sweet, sighing voice, then gave a sudden start and clutched her companions arm.

"A snake!" she cried.

"A snake!" echoed her companion. She stopped and picked up a stone. "Where?"

"In the bamboo thicket. And, oh, Holy Saints protect it, there is a child!"

The elder Sister advanced to where the younger pointed, and threw a stone with certain aim at the coiling, shimmering reptile. Then she bent over the sleeping sugar-cane baby and peered into its face.

"It is unharmed," she announced, with a sigh of relief.

The baby opened its eyes and regarded the strange face above him very solemnly.

"Dear little thing!" murmured the younger Sister, as the elder raised him in her arms. "See, how pretty he is; his little features are almost perfect; his eyes as black as night; and his skin—his silky skin is the color of a dead leaf."

"A Hindu child!" observed the elder. Then almost passionately, "Oh, these mothers, these mothers! What love have they for their children when they can leave them like this?"

Followed by her companion she hurried along the road, the baby clasped close to her woman's bosom.

II

The sugar-cane baby lay in a little white crib in a long white room full of other little white cribs. Around him, some in cribs and some out, were a number of other babies, younger and older than himself. Most of them were pure pickaninnies, but not a few bore the mark of the white man in complexion and feature. The sugar-cane baby was distinguished as being the only little native of Asia.

The many windows of the ward were open, but were screened with green shutters through which the sunshine filtered, and a soft fragrant breeze.

The sugar-cane baby lay with eyes closed. His face did not wear the happy expression it had worn when the bamboo boughs waved above it.

A young woman came down the ward accompanied by the Sister in charge. The young woman paused before the crib wherein lay the sugar-cane baby.

"Oh, isn't he a darling!" she exclaimed.

The young woman was a reporter on a local paper, but originally from the United States of America.

"That Hindu baby is the least trouble of any child we have," informed the Sister. "He lies all day motionless and silent as you see him now. But he is wasting away for want of nourishment. We cannot get him to take even a drop of banana juice."

"Poor little thing!" murmured the young woman compassionately. "A foundling, eh?"

"Yes," returned the Sister, and she related the story of the finding of the sugar-cane baby.

The young journalist was very much interested. She patted the child's soft cheek. At her touch its eyelids flickered and it heaved a sigh—so soft and sad that the tears came to the young woman's eyes and she said to the Sister as she turned away, "I believe the baby is breaking its heart for its mother!"

The Sister's smile was very superior.

"A child of that age! Oh, no!" said she.

III

"How is the wee Hindu today?" asked the American girl.

"He is dying," answered the Sister. "Would you care to see him?"

Leila Carroll followed the Sister to where lay the sugar-cane baby. The little form was emaciated indeed. A pitiful heaving of the tiny chest alone betrayed that he was alive. Beside him, on the pillow, lay a short length of green sugar cane.

"There was a piece of cane in his hand when he was found," informed the Sister, "so we got that for him and have tried to persuade him to suck it. But all in vain. He turns from it as from everything else. Yet we cannot discover that he is suffering from any malady whatever."

"I must see the Mother Superior," said Leila.

She saw the Mother Superior.

"My dear Miss Carroll," said that wise woman, "even if you have found the baby's mother, it would not be right for us to deliver to her the child. Is a person who could leave her baby beside a snake on the high road fitted to care for him?"

"The snake was harmless," answered the young journalist. "As I have told you, it had been trained by the baby's father to guard the little one. But your question can best be answered by bringing the mother and child together."

"Where is the mother?" inquired the Mother Superior.

"In the lemon grove—waiting."

The Mother superior raised her hands, "Oh, you people from the North!" she exclaimed. "To speak of a thing is to do it with you, is it not?"

"I hope so," returned Leila. "Shall I call her?"

"Well!" slowly assented the reverend young woman who was head of the convent orphanage, "but the child is dying!"

• • •

They led the Hindu mother to where lay her baby. "Asof, my little son! Light of my eyes! Hope of my heart! Is it indeed thou?" she cried, clasping the tiny form in her arms. The child clung to her, so tight, so close, that they wondered at his strength. He snuggled his little head into his mother's neck and thrusting out his tongue began to lick her chin.

"He is starving!" she exclaimed. She picked up the sugar cane and held it to his lips. He sucked eagerly.

Leila looked at the Mother Superior. The Mother Superior returned her gaze through a mist of tears.

"You are right, Miss Carroll," said she. "Please, Sister Agnes, bring some milk for the little one and make the mother comfortable until she is ready to take her child away."

Good Housekeeping, May 1910

An Autumn Fan

For two weeks Ming Hoan was a guest in the house of Yen Chow, the father of Ah Leen, and because love grows very easily between a youth and a maid it came to pass that Ah Leen unconsciously yielded to Ming Hoan her heart and Ming Hoan as unconsciously yielded his to her. After the yielding they became conscious.

When their tale was told to Yen Chow he was much disturbed, and vowed that he would not disgrace his house by giving his daughter to a youth whose parents had betrothed him to another.

"How canst thou help it if thy daughter loves me and becomes my wife?" boldly answered Ming Hoan. "We are in America, and the fault, if fault there be, is not upon thy shoulders."

"True!" murmured the mother of Ah Leen, smiling upon her would-be-son-in-law.

"America!" Yen Chow shook his head. "Land where a man knows no law save his own — where even a son of China forgets his ancestors and follows his human heart."

"Sir!" returned Ming Hoan, "when the human heart is linked to the divine, ought we not to follow thereafter?"

There was much more said, but it all ended in the young people wedding — and parting. For that was Chow's stern decree. Ming Hoan must face his parents and clear away the clouds of misunderstanding before he could take Ah Leen.

And now Ming Hoan is gone and Ah Leen stands alone. Her mother enters the room. Ah Leen must have some tea. The wife of Yen

Chow leads her daughter into the wide hall, where refreshments are laid. The usual ceremonies attendant upon a wedding, and which in the case of Ah Leẹn's cousins, Ah Toy and Mai Gwi Far, had lasted over a week, were to be postponed until Ming Hoan's return from China.

Her mother congratulates her. Ming Hoan is good to behold, wise beyond his years and had seen the face of the world. His fortune is not large, but it will grow. Most comforting thought of all, there will be no mother-in-law to serve or obey. Ming Hoan's home for many years to come will be in the great City of New York.

See, there is Ah Chuen, the wife of the herb doctor, and Sien Tau, the mother of the president of the Water Lily Society. They are coming to wish her felicity. Mark the red paper they are scattering on the way. They are good-natured women, and even if their class is below that of the wife of Yen Chow, their gifts prove natural refinement. Thus Ah Leen's Mother.

"Mother," murmurs Ah Leen, "I beg that you will kindly excuse me to our friends."

She carried her tea to the veranda, and, seated in a bamboo rocker, muses on Ming Hoan. She is both happy and sad. Happy to be a bride, yet sad because alone.

It has been a strange ceremony—that wedding. It is not customary, even in America, for a Chinese bride to remain under her father's roof, and only because, in his bended arm, she had wept her tears away, could Ah Leen realize herself the wife of Ming Hoan.

How beautiful the day! Above her a deep blue dome, paling as it descends to the sea. Around her curving, sloping hills, covered with a tender green; here and there patches of glowing, dazzling color—California flowers. It is springtime—the springtime of the year.

A little carol of joy escapes Ah Leen's lips. It is good to love and be loved even if—

What is that Lee A-chuen is saying? "'Tis a pity that Yen Chow should have sent the bridegroom away. Youth is youth and soon forgets. The sister of my mother writes me that the choice of his parents is the loveliest of all the lovely girls in the Provinces of the Rippling Rivers."

The day has suddenly darkened for Ah Leen.

Five moons have gone by since Ming Hoan went over the sea, and no letter—no message—not even a word has come to his waiting bride. But it is whispered in all the Chinese merchants' families that Ming Hoan, disregarding his first marriage, which, being unconsented to by his parents, could scarcely be considered binding, had taken to himself as wife in his own land Fi Shui, the daughter of his father's friend.

The cousins of Ah Leen regard her with pitying looks whilst they whisper among themselves, "An autumn fan! An autumn fan!"

Ah Leen meets them with a serene countenance. Her American friend suggests that she should obtain a divorce; that that is the only course open for a deserted wife who wishes to retain her self-respect.

"A deserted wife!" echoes Ah Leen. "Ah, no; 'twas my father who compelled him to leave me. And what has he done that I should divorce him? Men cannot live upon memories, and it is perfectly right and proper, since he has decided to remain in China, that he should take to himself another wife."

At the time of the year when the heavens weep, as the Chinese say, there comes news of the birth of a son to Ming Hoan.

Again the American girl watches sympathetically the face of the first wife of the man to whom a son has been born by another woman. Sun Lin, wife of the Sam Yup Chief, brings the news to the house of Yen Chow. It is sundown and the American girl is sitting on the porch with Ah Leen.

"Joy!" cries Ah Leen. "My husband has a son!"

And she herself, on red note paper, sends news of the event to those of her friends who have not yet heard of it. These notes are proudly signed: "Ming Ah Leen, First Wife of Ming Hoan."

The year rolls on. There comes to the house of Yen Chow a Chinese merchant of wealth and influence. His eyes dwell often upon Ah Leen. He whispers to her father. Yen Chow puffs his pipe and muses: Assuredly a great slight has been put upon his family. A divorce would show proper pride. It was not the Chinese way, but was not the old order passing away and the new order taking its place? Aye, even in China, the old country that had seemed as if it would ever remain old.

He speaks to Ah Leen.

"Nay, father, nay," she returns. "Thou hadst the power to send my love away from me, but thou canst not compel me to hold out my arms to another."

"But," protests her mother, "thy lover hath forgotten thee. Another hath borne him a child."

A flame rushes over Ah Leen's face; then she becomes white as a water lily. She plucks a leaf of scented geranium, crushes it between her fingers and casts it away. The perfumes clings to the hands she lays on her mother's bosom.

"Thus," says she, "the fragrance of my crushed love will ever cling to Ming Hoan."

It is evening. The electric lights are shining through the vines. Out of the gloom beyond their radius comes a man. The American girl, seated in a quiet corner of the veranda, sees his face. It is eager and the eyes are full of love and fate. Then she sees Ah Leen. Tired of woman's gossip, the girl has come to gaze upon the moon, hanging in the sky above her like a pale yellow pearl.

There is a cry from the approaching man. It is echoed by the girl. In a moment she is leaning upon his breast.

"Ah!" she cries, rising her head and looking into his eyes. "I knew that though another had bound you by human ties to me you were linked by my love divine."

"Another! Human ties!" exclaims the young man. He exclaims without explaining—for the sins of parents must not be uncovered—why there has been silence between them for so long. Then he lifts her face to his and gently reproaches her. "Ah Leen, you have dwelt only upon your love for me. Did I not bid thee, 'Forget not to remember that *I* love thee!' "

The American girl steals away. The happy Ming Hoan is unaware that as she flits lightly by him and his bride she is repeating to herself his words, and hoping that it is not too late to send to someone a message of recall.

New England Magazine, August 1910

A Love Story from the Rice Fields of China

Chow Ming, the husband of Ah Sue was an Americanized Chinese, so when Christmas day came, he gave a big dinner, to which he invited both his American and Chinese friends, and also one friend who was both Chinese and American.

The large room in which he gave the dinner presented quite a striking appearance on the festive evening, being decorated with Chinese flags and banners, algebraic scrolls, incense burners and tropical plants; and the company sat down to a real feast. Chow Ming's cook had a reputation.

Ah Ming and Ah Oi, Chow Ming's little son and daughter, flitted around like young humming birds in their bright garments. Their arms and necks were hung with charms and amulets given to them by their father's friends and they kept up an incessant twittering between themselves. They were not allowed, however, to sit down with their elders and ate in an ante room of rice and broiled preserved chicken—a sweet dish, the morsels of chicken being prepared so as to resemble raisins.

Chinese do not indulge in conversation during meal time; but when dinner was over and a couple of Chinese violinists had made their debut, the host brought forward several of his compatriots whom he introduced as men whose imaginations and experiences enabled them to relate the achievements of heroes, the despair of lovers, the blessings which fall to the lot of the filial and the terrible fate of the undutiful. Themes were varied; but those which were most appreciated were stories which treated of magic and enchantment.

"Come away," said Ah Sue to me.—We two were the only women present.—"I want to tell you a story, a real true love story—Chinese."

"Really," I exclaimed delightedly.

"Really," echoed Ah Sue, "the love story of me."

When we were snugly ensconced in her own little room, Ah Sue began:

"My father," said she, "was a big rice farmer. He owned many, many rice fields, but he had no son—just me."

"Chow Han worked for my father. The first time I saw Chow Han was at the Harvest Moon festival. I wore a veil of strings of pearls over my forehead. But his eyes saw beneath the pearls and I was very much ashamed."

"Why were you ashamed? You must have looked very charming."

Ah Sue smiled. She was a pretty little woman.

"I was not ashamed of my veil," said she. "I was ashamed because I perceived that Chow Han knew that I glanced his way.

"The next day I and my mother sat on the hill under big parasols and watched the men, sickle in hand, wading through the rice fields, cutting down the grain. It is a pretty sight, the reaping of the rice.

"Chow Han drove the laden buffaloes. He was bigger and stronger than any of the other lads. My mother did not stay by me all the time. There were the maid's tasks to be set. Chow Han drove past when my mother was not beside me and threw at my feet a pretty shell. 'A pearl for a pearl,' he cried, and laughed saucily. I did not look at him, but when he had passed out of sight I slipped the shell up my sleeve.

"It was a long time before I again saw the lad. My mother fell sick and I accompanied her to the City of Canton to see an American doctor in an American hospital. We remained in Canton, in the house of my brother-in-law for many months. I saw much that was new to my eyes and the sister of the American doctor taught me to speak English—and some other things.

"By the spring of the year my mother was much improved in health, and we returned home to celebrate the Spring Festival. The Chinese people are very merry at the time of the springing of the rice. The fields are covered with green, and the rice flower peeps out at the side of the little green blade, so small, so white and so sweet. One afternoon I was following alone a stream in the woods behind my father's house, when I saw Chow Han coming toward me."

Ah Sue paused. For all her years in America she was a Chinese woman.

"And he welcomed you home," I suggested.

Ah Sue nodded her head.

"And like a Chinese girl you ran away from the wicked man."

Ah Sue's eyes glistened mischievously.

"You forget, Sui Sin Far," said she, "that I had been living in Canton and had much talk with an American woman. No, when Chow Han told me that he had much respectful love in his heart for me, I laughed a little laugh, I was so glad—too glad for words. Had not his face been ever before me since the day he tossed me the shell?

"But my father was rich and Chow Han was poor.

"When the little white flowers had once more withdrawn into the green blades and were transforming themselves into little white grains of rice, there came to the rice country a cousin of Chow Han's who had been living for some years in America. He talked much with Chow Han, and one day Chow Han came to me and said:

" 'I am bound for the land beyond the sea; but in a few years I will return with a fortune big enough to please your father. Wait for me!'

"I did not answer him; I could not."

" 'Promise that you will ever remember me,' said Chow Han.

" 'You need no promise,' I returned. Chow Han set down the pot of fragrant leafed geranium which he had brought with him as a parting gift.

" 'As for me,' said he, 'even if I should die, my spirit will fly to this plant and keep ever beside you.'

"So Chow Han went away to the land beyond the sea."

Ah Sue's eyes wandered to the distant water, which like a sheet of silver, reflected every light and color of the sky.

"Moons rose and waned. I know not how, but through some misfortune, my father lost his money and his rice farms passed into other hands. I loved my poor old father and would have done much to ease his mind; but there was one thing I would not do, and that was, marry the man to whom he had betrothed me. Had not the American woman told me that even if one cannot marry the man one loves, it is happier to be true to him than to wed another, and had not the American woman, because she followed her conscience, eyes full of sunshine?

"My father died and my mother and I went to live with my brother-in-law in the city of Canton. Two days before we left our old home, we learned that Chow Han had passed away in a railway accident in the United States of America.

"My mother's sister and brother-in-law urged my mother to marry me to some good man, but believing that Chow Han's spirit was ever now beside me, I determined to remain single as the American woman. Was she not brighter and happier than many of my married relations?

"Meanwhile the geranium flower throve in loveliness and fragrance, and in my saddest moments I turned to it for peace and comfort.

"One evening, my poor old mother fell asleep and never woke again. I was so sad. My mother's sister did not love me, and my brother-in-law told me he could no longer support me and that I must marry. There were three good men to be had and I must make up my mind which it should be.

"What would I do? What should I do? I bent over my geranium flower and whispered: 'Tell me, O dear spirit, shall I see the river?' And I seemed to hear this message: 'No, no, be brave as the American woman!'

"Ah, the American woman! She showed me a way to live. With her assistance I started a small florist shop. My mother had always loved flowers, and behind our house had kept a plot of ground, cram full of color, which I had tended for her ever since I was a child. So the care of flowers was no new task for me, and I made a good living, and if I were sad at times, yet, for the most part, my heart was serene.

"Many who came to me wished to buy the geranium plant, which was now very large and beautiful; but to none would I sell. What! barter the spirit of Chow Han!

"On New Year's day a stranger came into my shop. His hat partly concealed his face; but I could see that he was of our country, though he wore the dress of the foreigner and no queue.

" 'What is the price of the large geranium at your door?' he enquired, and he told me that its fragrance had stolen to him as he passed by.

" 'There is no price on that flower,' I replied, 'it is there to be seen, but not to be sold.'

" 'Not to be sold! But if I give you a high price?'

" 'Not for any price,' I answered.

"He sought to persuade me to tell him why, but all I would say was that he could not have the flower.

"At last he came close up to me and said:

" 'There is another flower that I desire, and you will not say me nay when I put forth my hand to take it.'

"I started back in alarm.

" 'You will not sell the geranium flower,' he told me, 'because you believe that the spirit of Chow Han resides within it. But 'tis not so. The spirit of Chow Han resides within Chow Han. Behold him!'

"He lifted his hat. It was Chow Han."

Ah Sue looked up as her husband entered the room bearing on his shoulder their little Han.

"And you name your boy after your old sweetheart," I observed.

"Yes," replied Ah Sue, "my old sweetheart. But know this, Sin Far,

the Chinese men change their name on the day they marry, and the
Chow Han, who gave me the scented leafed geranium, and after many
moons, found me through its fragrance, is also my husband, Chow
Ming."

New England Magazine, December 1911

Who's Game?

He came in the month of June, transformed a patch of wild land into
tame, and built himself a cedar cabin thereon. Back of him rose the
living forest. The river ran down between the hills and wound around
his clearing and beyond until it fell in with the county road, which it
followed for some distance. This county road, which traversed many
miles of timber covered country and a fertile valley, connected several
villages, the most important of which was Zora.

Now, the Lonely, as he was called, had been living in the vicinity of
Zora for at least three months, yet never had his face been seen nor his
voice heard, in any church building. What glory then was in store for
whoever could bring him into a fold! It mattered not whether Baptist,
Methodist or Presbyterian. All of the three churches were friendly
with each other, and when one gave an entertainment, the members of
the others attended in full force.

For a time, therefore, the number of would-be shepherds or
shepherdesses who were seeking him, was many; but long before the
end of summer, it had dwindled down to two, Mrs. William Bennett
and Mrs. Thomas Page; both prominent members of the Methodist
Church. These two ladies were untiring in their efforts to accomplish
his conversion; more particularly so, as on the occasion of their first
visit to him, they had found the occupant of the cedar log cabin
apparently quite amiably disposed and "very intelligent." Their report
to the minister was to the effect that though the Lonely appeared to be
an enlightened man, so far as worldly matters were concerned, his
ignorance in regard to spiritual was such that they could not obtain
from him any opinion, or even remark, concerning the higher life. As

to church, though he had not, in words, refused their invitation, yet he had certainly evaded giving any promise to attend.

The minister thanked them for their kind offices and remarked with a genial smile that it was up to them to bring the stray sheep within the church's influence. He also observed that a worker alone could sometimes effect better results than a plural number, and suggested that each lady should in future visit by herself.

It was October. The heads of all the streams and all the little brooks among the mountains were filled with humpbacked salmon pushing their way upward; the big brown bear, their only lover, save the Indian, fed thereon; the pretty deer lurked in the forest ready to give chase to the sportsman; the quail whistled sweetly, now near, now far away; the partridge had left the fir woods for the grain fields, and the cry of the wild geese was heard in the sky.

In the woods of Washington, there was scrambling and cracking. The sportsman, with his shot gun, his rifle and his dog, was providing much amusement for the denizens thereof. Wasn't it great fun to see him falling over logs, barking his shins, tumbling into ditches and jumping for dear life? Even on the county roads the smaller game were fooling him. What cared they for his sly lurking in corners of fences or behind clumps of bushes? If he did bring down one of their number, were there not hundreds that escaped? And, oh, the joy of escaping!

There was a twinkle in the Lonely's hazel eye as he caught sight of Mrs. Bennett turning from the county road and bending her footsteps towards his hermit dwelling. He laid down a letter he had been reading. It was a three sheet epistle written in a very pretty feminine hand. It began: "Dear old boy," and ended with, "Your girl forever."

The Lonely was not a very young man, neither did he appear to be very robust. His hair was grey and there were a few lines across his brow. But his form was straight and vigorous, and the smile that lurked around his eyes and mouth explained how he came to have a "girl forever."

"Well, Mrs. Bennett, how do you feel yourself to-day?" he enquired as he handed his visitor a chair.

"Mean as ever," she returned. Her quick eyes traveled around the room, taking in every detail; the low cot in the corner, the pile of books near the window, and the rough mantel-piece over which hung a rifle and accessories, also a pair of deer's horns.

"I have come," said she, "to try to interest you in the social we are to have next month and to give you an invitation."

"You are very kind."

"It is for the benefit of the incurably poor of the parish, and we intend to make it a success. All our local talent will be represented, and Miss Howland and Mrs. Jackson of Seattle, who are both well known musicians, are to give several selections."

"No doubt of it being a success," heartily responded the Lonely. "If you have any passports I will take some."

"That is very nice of you!"

Mrs. Bennett, much gratified, drew forth from her reticule some tickets and handed a couple to him.

"You might let me have a few more," said he. "I shall run up to Wellspring and Flashlight next week, and will probably see some folks who will be glad to spend a social evening with you. Meanwhile, here's the change for a dozen."

"You are too generous," approvingly rebuked Mrs. Bennett, "but you will come yourself, will you not?"

"I intend to. Oh, by the way, you will see me in church next Sunday."

Mrs. Bennett started and stared in disbelief of her senses. Only the evening before, she and Mrs. Page, had, after many long weeks of conscientious striving, confessed to each other that the conversion of this man might be dreamed of, but never realized. And now, here he was, actually offering of his own free will be to present at a church service.

"Oh, Mr. Talbot!" she exclaimed, when her scrutiny had convinced her that he really meant what he said, "How glad I am! We had about given up hope!"

"You underestimate a woman's influence."

Mrs. Bennett flushed with pleasure: "Mrs. Page has wonderful persuasive power; personal magnetism, one might call it," she observed.

"Far be it from me to depreciate Mrs. Page's talents," returned the Lonely, "but between you and me, Mrs. Bennett, it is someone else's personal magnetism that will draw me into the congregation of the faithful next Sunday."

"Oh, indeed!"

Mrs. Bennett's modesty prevented her from voicing her exultation; but she was happily aware that she and Mrs. Page were the only church workers that had operated on the seemingly obdurate heart of the Lonely for some time, and if it was not Mrs. Page who had been successful, why then—

After his visitor had left, the Lonely sat down to answer the three sheet epistle.

"My darling girl," he wrote, "got your letter and am mighty glad that I shall see your dear face before next Sunday. That will give us two happy weeks together before I return to work.

"I like the place and am having good sport. The deep blue clear cut mountains never lose their charm. As yet, no one, not even your father, knows who I am. I am leaving introductions for you.

"A couple of good ladies have been making strenuous exertions to turn my steps churchward, but up till to-day I've been a shy bird— almost as good sport to them as the deer to me. However, I have just informed one of the two that next Sabbath will see me in a pew, and she has retired, happy in the belief that her labors are about to be rewarded."

"Good day, neighbor Talbot."

It was the cheery voice of Mrs. Page. The Lonely rose to greet her. After a few preliminary remarks, the lady, like her predecessor, broached the subject of tickets, and a number of the pieces of cardboard were transferred from her hands to the Lonely's.

Her seven year old twins made themselves at home on his knees, and edged in questions between the intervals of conversation. Indeed, their thirst for information was at times rather disconcerting.

"Are you a naughty man?" finally asked the little girl.

"Very!" was the smiling answer.

"I know why," said the boy.

"So do I," rejoined Rosa.

"You never go to church," declared both together.

The Lonely laughed.

"Then you'll think I'm good if you see me there next Sunday?" he queried.

"Indeed they will; but that's too good to be true," said Mrs. Page.

"My dear lady, you're mistaken. I'll be there, sure."

The astonishment of the mother of the twins was even greater than Mrs. Bennett's had been.

"This, of course, is due to my friend's efforts," she said at last.

"Well," returned the Lonely, "Mrs. Bennett has certainly been very kind; but to confess the truth, there is another lady whose influence has been more potent."

"But who scarcely hoped for success," murmured Mrs. Page. She held out her hand to the converted, her face glowing, her eyes shining.

"Dear," wrote the Lonely, returning to his letter, "since writing the preceding paragraph, the news that Sunday will see me listening to your father's sermon, has caused another heart to rejoice. Each of the ladies mentioned above is now congratulating herself that she has accomplished my conversion, and I have not the heart to undeceive either—"

II

Only the hunter who brings down his fleet-footed deer after a long and weary chase can appreciate the joy and satisfaction of a conscientious church worker whose efforts to bring a contrary sheep into the fold are at last rewarded.

Both Mrs. Bennett and Mrs. Page beamed over their teacups that evening, and each to her husband told the story of her success with the Lonely, the children sitting around the respective tables listening with attentive ears and young hearts swelling with pride.

The next morning, little Rosa Page and Teddy Bennett, playing together in the Page's back yard, suddenly assumed belligerent voices and attitudes.

"Rosa," called Mrs. Page, who was looking out of the kitchen window. "Come right in."

"I don't want to come in," shrieked Rosa, dissolving into tears. "I haven't been a naughty girl. It was Teddy who was naughty."

Teddy was climbing the fence which separated his yard from Rosa's.

"But Rosa was naughty too," reproved the mother. "I saw her scream and stamp her foot at Teddy."

"Because—because he told a story about my mama."

"A story about mama, Rosa!"

Mrs. Page could hardly suppress a smile as she surveyed her indignant little daughter.

"He did, mama. He said it wasn't you who was getting Mr. Talbot to go to church next Sunday. He said it was *his* mother."

The smile faded from Mrs. Page's countenance.

"Said it was his mother," she echoed. "Oh, no, daughter, you are mistaken!"

"He did. He said his mother told his father so last night."

"Well, never mind, dear. Come into the house and I will give you a piece of cake."

Comforted with cake and the society of her twin, who had stubbed his toe so badly that morning that he was confined to a couch, Rosa soon forgot her troubles. It was not so, however, with her mother.

Meanwhile, Teddy lost no time in reporting his disagreement with little Rosa Page.

"Mother," cried he, "Rosa says that her mother has got Mr. Talbot to promise to go to church next Sunday."

"Deary me!" exclaimed Mrs. Bennett, quite taken by surprise.

"I said that I guessed she meant my mother and not hers. I knew, because I had heard you tell father about it last night."

"That is true, son," approved Mrs. Bennett.

"But Rosa said I was telling a story. She said she heard her mother say that Mr. Talbot was going to church because she had asked him."

"She! Who?"

"Rosa's mother."

Mrs. Bennett rose hastily. "Teddy," said she, "you and Ida just play in your own yard."

• • •

For many years Clara Bennett and Fanny Page had been neighbors and the best of friends. They took tea together at least twice a week, and never failed to sample one another's pies, cakes, bread, sausages, pickles, preserves and homemade wine. They cut their little girls' frocks from the same pattern and their little boys' pants from the same piece of cloth. They employed the same dressmaker, read the same books and papers, enjoyed the same recreations, and occasionally enlivened their companionship with an amiable disagreement. They were both esteemed in the community in which they lived as broad-minded women, being members of the Literary Club, sewing circle and several other uplifting or benevolent country societies, and by reason of their social standing, Mrs. Bennett's husband being the superintendent of the logging camp, and Mrs. Page's, the proprietor of the shingle mill, no social function was considered a success without their presence. The closest tie, however, which bound them together, was the church, and for that both had worked earnestly, eagerly and harmoniously—until their last visit to the Lonely.

But there was a "little rift within the lute," and the music of friendship was now mute.

For five whole days Mrs. Bennett and Mrs. Page avoided meeting one another, kept their children apart, and absented themselves from the sewing circle and the Thursday night service. Mrs. Bennett baked that week and Mrs. Page made preserves; but there were no sweet exchanges offered or accepted. Instead of which, the women went about with set faces, and when any neighbor ventured a remark concerning Mrs. Page to Mrs. Bennett or vice versa, it was received with chilling silence. Needless to say that this behavior on the part of the two most prominent women of the village created much comment.

III

Kate Lesley, the Minister's daughter, who had been visiting east of the mountains, returned to Zora on Friday, and was greatly distressed to hear of the estrangement between her two old friends, which was one of the first pieces of news that she was told.

"The worst of it is," said her aunt, "though everyone can see that they are suffering through the unnatural state of affairs, yet they have confided in none. I don't suppose they have even told their husbands."

"Of course not!" Kate threw a saucy glance at the Lonely, who had called upon her that afternoon and been introduced to her astonished father and aunt as her fiancée, Professor Will Talbot of the Ohio Wesleyan College.

"Who for over three months has been known or unknown to us as the Lonely," had remarked the Minister, half jestingly, half reprovingly.

Whereupon Kate had explained that Professor Talbot's physicians had ordered him to rest up in the western woods, and how utterly impossible such rest would have been had he made himself known as the fiancée of the minister's daughter.

After dinner, as Kate and the Professor strolled down the garden walk, she again reverted to the trouble between her friends.

"Only something very serious could have caused it," said she. "Ever since I was a little girl, they have been as sisters. It was a beautiful friendship, and even now, in their anger, I know they are loving one another."

" 'And to be wroth with one we love, Doth work like madness in the brain!' " quoted the professor. "Oh, Kate, my bonny, bonny Kate, cease talking and thinking about other people while I am here, or I shall be wrathy with you."

IV

The next morning, Kate Lesley, passing through the village, met a couple of the Bennett children. Half an hour afterwards, the little Page twins threw themselves into her arms. The result of these meetings was that Kate postponed her visit to the mothers of the children.

"You ought to be ashamed of yourself, sir," was the greeting that the Lonely received that evening.

"Why! Why?" he stammered.

"Yes, you ought. You, sir, are at the bottom of the whole mischief."

"The whole mischief!"

Kate thrust a letter before him, and pointing to a paragraph which read:

"Each of the ladies mentioned above is now congratulating herself that she has accomplished my conversion, and I have not the heart to undeceive either of them,"

cried:

"See there. Your own words condemn you."

The Lonely glanced at the writing and repressed a smile.

"I have sympathies," he remarked, "and I know it's hard luck to hunt a buck all over the woods and then see another fellow bring him down."

"But you knew they would have to know the truth sooner or later," replied Kate uncompromisingly.

"The truth, my dear. I told them no untruth."

"You are incorrigible!"

The Lonely's face became serious.

"Well, I'm sorry," said he contritely.

Kate's eyes softened.

"But I had no idea that they would boast of it," he added blunderingly.

"Boast of it!" exclaimed Kate. "Oh you—you man! Why, they were too considerate even to mention the matter to each other, though naturally enough they rejoiced over it with their husbands and the children overheard."

"It was the little pitchers then," observed the Lonely, his eyes twinkling again.

"Yes, and it was their chatter to-day that caused me to reflect upon your letter."

"And convict me."

"And convict you. You have made miserable two women who are of the salt of the earth."

"The salt in this case seems to be more like pepper!"

"The best of us are human. I love them all the more for feeling as they do."

The Lonely sighed.

"I suppose," said he, "I will have to go and explain."

"Explain!" cried Kate with fine score, "add insult to injury."

"Then what am I to do?" he cried helplessly. "Tell me. I am ready for any penance."

Kate stole a side glance at him from under her long eyelashes.

"How do I know," she asked, "that you have not the heart to undeceive *me?*"

He strode over to her side, imprisoned her hands in his, and said:

"Because there has not been, and is not now, and never will be any question as to the deer I want."

"This shall be your penance," said Kate, lifting a flushed face from her lover's shoulder, "to sit beside me in church to-morrow."

"What!"—in delighted tones—"you will not sing in the choir!"

"No, I shall neglect that duty for once."

"Darling little penance giver!"

"Oh, please don't imagine I am considering your pleasure or mine. I am simply seeking to explain by actions what cannot be explained in words."

"You are eighteen karat gold, sweetheart!"

V

Sunday morning dawned bright and beautiful, calm and quiet. It had been a long and weary week to both Mrs. Page and Mrs. Bennett. Everything had seemed to go wrong; the children had been unusually mischievous and perverse; the husbands more than ordinarily exacting.

It had hardly seemed worth while making preserves and cake when no competent critic over the garden fence satisfied one that they were about the best made, and the new fall suits that had been ordered from Seattle the week before did not please nearly so well upon their arrival as when two pairs of feminine eyes had scanned them together. It had certainly been trying to Mrs. Page's nerves when Tommy cried for Mrs. Bennett's toothache drops, and far from soothing when Mrs. Bennett's husband, in an absent minded manner, advised his wife, when she complained of being out of sorts, to run over to Fanny Page's—a little gossip might do her good.

When the woman who did the extra cleaning for both the Bennetts and Pages informed Mrs. Page that Mrs. Bennett was in bed with a severe headache, the former shut herself within her room and cried until her own had felt as if a ton-weight were resting upon it. She remembered how when she had typhoid fever Mrs. Bennett had nursed her night and day with the tenderest care. Likewise, Mrs. Bennett, sighing over troublesome Johnnie, recalled how many times her neighbor had gathered her restless children in with her own brood, and kept them under motherly wing until her own tired nerves had been well rested.

But all the little acts of neighborly love and kindness, the restful gossip over books, children, dress and village matters were now things of the past.

Sad and melancholy, separate and alone, Mrs. Bennett and Mrs. Page wended their way to church. Hitherto, they had always walked the road together. Their husbands attended service in the evening only; their children went to morning Sunday school.

Down the street came Miss Hepburn, the village gossip, her broad good-natured face aglow with the news within her. She was on her way to the Baptist Church at the north end of the village. The Methodist Church was situated south.

"Good morning, Mrs. Page."

"Good morning, Miss Hepburn. Fine day, is it not?"

"Just as pretty as can be. Have you heard the news?"

"Miss Kate is home."

"Not only that. D'ye remember her aunt talking of the Wesleyan College fellow to whom Miss Kate engaged herself last winter—a professor, if you please. Well, he's here too. Was up at your minister's house last night."

"You don't mean to say so. Well, that is news. But I must hurry. Good morning."

"Good morning, Mrs. Page! Wish I were a Methodist for to-day. Miss Kate will sing in the choir, of course; but he's sure to be there."

Mrs. Bennett, lingering behind, under pretence of scolding back the sheep dog that would persist in following her, received with quiet interest the same news that had been imparted to Mrs. Page, then followed closely in the hurrying footsteps of the latter.

In the distance rose the inspiring mountains, snow capped and majestic, the sky was that of April; blue, dappled with fleecy white clouds, the air was like wine. Though late in the season, the gardens were still bright with color, and by the orchard fences the lambs and ewes were feeding, the little ones leaping high in the joy of life.

But unheeding all that had hitherto made their churchyard walk so pleasant and refreshing after the week's routine, the two women proceeded, and at last, one, a few minutes after the other, entered the church and took their seats in pews across the aisle from one another.

Down the aisle, in her radiant youth and beauty, came the minister's daughter. Both Mrs. Page and Mrs. Bennett glanced up as she passed between them and felt the brighter for her passing. But who was that leading the way into the minister's pew, unnoticed until he stood beside it, waiting for the minister's daughter to precede him to her seat? Who was that who took his place beside Bonnie Kate Lesley, and with an air of lover-like authority assisted her to remove her wrap? Who? Who?

Mrs. Bennett's and Mrs. Page's gaze turned from the Lonely's back and met across the space between them. In one understanding moment they were friends again. Mrs. Bennett made a motion as if to pass her hymnal to Mrs. Page, but the latter slipped across to the other's pew, and standing side by side, with full eyes and full hearts, both women joined in the hymn, "Blest be the tie that binds."

New England Magazine, February 1912

Chan Hen Yen, Chinese Student

He was Han Yen of the family Chan, from the town of Choo-Chow, in the Province of Kiangsoo. His father was a schoolmaster, so also had been his grandfather, and his great grandfather before him. He was chosen out of three sons to be the scholar of the family, and during his boyhood studied diligently and with ambition. From school to college he passed, and at the age of twenty, took successfully the examinations which entitled him to a western education at government expense.

One of a band of Chinese youths he came to America and entered an American University. The new life and the new environment interested and exhilarated him. His most earnest desire was to absorb every good element of western education, so that he might be able to return to the Motherland well equipped to render her good service. He fully believed that he and his compatriot students were the destined future leaders of China, and his ambition to add lustre to the name of Chan, was almost holy.

The American widow with whom he boarded described him to her friends and neighbors as the best of all Chinese students. "And you know," she added with almost family pride, "the Chinese have the reputation of being the best students of all."

The widow, whose name was Mrs. Caroline Bray, had a daughter named Carrie. Carrie was a pretty girl of nineteen, with eyes and hair almost as dark as the eyes and hair of the little girl who had been adopted by Han Yen's parents to become his future wife. For seven months Carrie paid little attention to Han Yen. Her time was well occupied with housework, and in the evenings and Sundays, there was the Chinese Mission. Besides there were other students in the house.

It was one evening in early spring. The other Chinese students were dining a member of the Legation at a Chinese restaurant in the city, and Han Yen, who was unacquainted with the official, was alone with Mrs. Bray and her daughter. Mrs. Bray had been talking cheerily during the meal and Carrie had occasionally joined in. When Han Yen finally arose and was about to ascend the stairs to his room, the girl looked up with a smile and bade him not study too hard.

"What should I do with myself if I did not study?" asked Han Yen.

"Well," suggested Carrie brightly, "you might, for instance, come with me to the Chinese Mission sociable."

Han Yen had never before taken a walk with a young woman, but he had heard a paper read by a senior student, in which it had been stated that chatting with members of the fair sex, even though folly was their theme, should be part of the Chinese student's American curriculum. So politely expressing his pleasure at being permitted to accompany Miss Carrie, the boy put on his hat and solemnly walked down the street beside her.

Suddenly she began to laugh.

"What is amusing you?" he enquired.

"You walk too far away," she replied, "one would think you were afraid of me."

Han Yen, blushing and embarrassed, but desirous above all things of conforming to what was right and proper according to western ideas, lessened the distance between him and his companion.

The evening passed pleasantly if somewhat bewilderingly. On the way home the student learned from the youthful and self constituted missionary that through her instrumentality over one hundred Chinese boys had become acquainted with the English language and converted to Christianity.

"In behalf of my countrymen in America, accept my heartfelt gratitude," replied Han Yen.

The next afternoon, he repeated to his cousin, Chan Han Fong, what Miss Carrie had told him, adding: "I feel ashamed that a young female should be able to do so much more than I for the cause of humanity."

Though to Han Yen, Confucianist, the Missions certainly did not appeal as Temples of Ethnical Culture, he was well able to appreciate the fact that they were the only bright spots in the lives of his laboring compatriots, exiles from their own homes and families.

After that evening Han Yen was invited occasionally to sit in the parlor of the widow Bray, where he listened to Carrie talking, playing, singing and otherwise entertaining her Chinese company. She was neither a clever nor well educated girl; but she was bright and attractive, and such as she was, dazzled the young student, to whom everything western, including women, was wonderful and worshipful.

One evening Carrie and Han Yen were alone. The girl was playing some sentimental melodies. The boy felt very happy. He always did feel happy when he was alone with Carrie. It was different when the other students were present, and Carrie smiled, first at this one, and then at that. Han Yen had not analyzed the painful sensations which took possession of him whenever Carrie smiled or spoke in friendly or familiar fashion to another student. On one occasion, however, these feelings had so overpowered him that he had risen abruptly from his seat and left the room. "Where are you going, Mr. Chan?" Carrie had called after him, and with innocent rudeness, he had replied: "To where you are not."

Carrie had returned to the room, demure and smiling. She understood Chinese students much better than they understood her, learned though they were and simple though she was.

This evening, for instance, she was fairly conscious of Han Yen's state of mind, and as she was a good natured little thing, continued playing for him for some time. Finally, she arose from the piano stool, and going over to the table on which stood a jar of hothouse flowers, took therefrom a piece of heliotrope.

"It was awfully sweet of you, Mr. Chan," said she, sniffing at the spray, "to bring me such beautiful flowers, and heliotrope is my favorite."

"It is very fragrant," murmured Han Yen.

"I had my fortune told yesterday," said Carrie, standing before the old fashioned mirror and fastening the flower to her hair.

"Was it a good one?" enquired the boy. Ordinarily he had no faith and little interest in mystical lore.

"I don't know," replied the girl, "it was rather funny, though. I don't think, Mr. Chan, that I shall tell you."

"I wish you would," urged Han Yen earnestly.

"Well, then, it was this: that my future husband would be a foreigner, and that he would bring me to-day a bouquet of flowers in which there would be one that was neither pink, yellow, green, blue nor red."

II

When Chan Han Fong learned that his cousin loved a woman of the white race, and was resolved to do as the American men do when they fall in love, his face became pallid.

"What!" he cried, "you will relinquish your sacred ambition to work for China, dishonor your ancestors, disregard your parents' wishes, and set at naught your betrothal to the daughter of Tien Wang—all for sake of a woman of alien blood?"

"Yes," declared Han Yen, his face shining, "love is more than all."

"You have gone mad," cried Chan Han Fong, "think of the sorrow and disgrace which you will bring upon all to whom you are bound by the ties of relationship, gratitude and affection. Is a feeling which obliterates and destroys every virtuous thought and sentiment, worth cherishing?"

"The feeling which possesses me," replied Han Yen, "is divine."

Chan Han Fong stepped to his desk and took therefrom a paper: "Listen," said he, "six months ago you wrote:

> Oh, China, misguided country!
> What would I not sacrifice,
> To see thee uphold thyself,
> Among the nations,
> For bitterer than death, 'tis to know,
> That thou that wert more glorious than all,
> Now lieth as low as the lowest,
> Whilst the feet of those whom thou didst despise,
> Rest insolently upon thy limbs,
> The Middle Kingdom wert thou called,
> The country that Heaven loves,
> Thou wert the birthplace of the arts, the sciences,
> And all mankind blessing inventions,
> Thy princes rested in benevolence,
> Thy wise men were revered,
> Thy people happy.
> But now, the empire which is the oldest under the
>   heavens is falling,
> And lesser nations stand ready to smite,
> The nation that first smote itself,
> Truly Mencius has said:
> 'The loss of the empire comes through losing the
>   hearts of the people.'
> The hearts of the people being lost,
> Who shall restore the Empire?"

Silence followed this declamation. Chan Han Yen's face fell, bowed upon his hands.

"Alas for China!" exclaimed Chan Han Fong, his own young eyes glowing with fateful fire. "When those who know how she can and must be saved — the very ones who could and should be her saviours — turn traitor to her."

The bowed head was lifted.

"Oh, Fong," plead Han Yen, "I can no more be as I have been. The aim and purpose of my existence has changed. And what is one student to China?"

"Why are you here?" sternly demanded Chan Han Fong. Then, because his young cousin was dear to him, he went over to where the boy leaned, and laying his arm around his shoulder, pleaded with him thus:

"See, my cousin! The flowers of the fields and of the woods and dales! Those of a kind come up together. The sister violet companions her brother. Only through some mistake in the seeding is it otherwise. And the hybrid flower, though beautiful, is the saddest flower of all."

Han Yen trembled.

At that moment a girl's voice floated through the window.

"Yen, Yen," it called, "I want you to go into town with me."

Han Yen shook off his cousin's detaining hand.

"Pardon me," said he, "but I must go."

"Ah!" soliloquized Chan Han Fong, gazing sadly after him. "A low caste American girl has disordered his mind."

The year before Han Yen had come to the University, Han Fong had been invited, with several other Chinese students, to spend an afternoon at the home of a wealthy and cultured maiden lady who lived on the other side of the river. This lady, who was white haired, soft voiced and comprehending, had entertained the Chinese youths in what to them, was a most delightful fashion. Han Fong had never forgotten that afternoon, nor one who had been a part of and in harmony with it — a young girl, almost a child in years, tall and slender, with thoughtful eyes and quiet ways. That young girl had not belittled the foreign students by flirting with and plying them with numerous personal questions; but Han Fong had taken note that she had listened with interest while their hostess charmed them to talk of their work and aspirations, and that the few remarks which she had made, were intelligent, and proved, that young though she was, she understood the purpose of their lives and sympathised with it.

Because of that young girl, seen and heard but one, Chan Han Fong, called Carrie Bray, "low caste."

III

Carrie had returned home tired out with a day's watching by the bedside of a sick Chinese woman.

"Why are you so good to everybody but yourself?" enquired Han Yen, meeting the girl as she entered the house in the dusk of the evening and following her into the sitting room.

"I *am* good to myself," answered Carrie cheerfully. "I'm accustomed to helping the poor Chinese. Indeed, I don't know what I shall do with myself after I give them up for you, Yen."

"I shall not require you to give them up altogether," replied the boy tenderly. "It is a work for humanity which you are doing and I hope to be able to help you with it."

"Why, dearie, what are you talking about?" exclaimed Carrie.

"About—when we shall be happy."

"You mean—when we go to China."

"No—here. I cannot go back to China for many years—perhaps never."

"Why?"

Carrie's voice sounded sharp.

"Because I must work for my living—and for yours," answered the boy, "and if I were to return to China I would have to work for the government until I had repaid what I owed for my education here."

"Oh! Then you are not rich!"

"Rich!" echoed Han Yen. "My father had to sell his land to enable me to complete my studies. Otherwise I would not have been able to compete at the Pekin examinations."

"You always used to say that you were going back to China."

"Yes," said Han Yen. "It was my great ambition to return to China and work for her—and alone I could have done so. But now, I shall not be alone—and I have a higher and loftier ambition than to work for China—it is to work for humanity—with you."

"I do not understand you," gasped Carried.

"But you will," said Han Yen. "Listen. I have yet to tell you how much I love you, and how all my heart is weeping and laughing for you. I am giving up all for you, to be with you, to work for you. I am not returning to my native land, because all my thought is you—and everything else is naught."

The girl shrank before the rising emotion in the boy's face and voice.

"Good night, Yen, dear," said she, her hand upon the door knob. "I am so tired that I can't sit up one moment longer. See you to-morrow."

And then she stole away to the kitchen and said to her mother:

"What do you think? Yen's people are poor and after we are married, he will have to stay in America and live and work here just like a common Chinaman."

"Lands sakes!" ejaculated Mrs. Bray. "Ain't that awful! And I've been telling all around that you was to marry a Chinese gentleman and was to go to China and live in great style!"

"And he isn't a Christian either," murmured Carrie.

IV

"Dear Friend:

Mother and I have been talking over things, and we have both decided that it would not be right for me to marry a man who is not a Christian. I am very sorry. I am going into town for a few days.

Your affectionate friend,

Carrie Bray."

Chan Han Yen read the little note over many times. Finally he folded it, put it back into its envelope and slipped it under the rubber band which bound together a neat bundle of letters lying on his desk.

Then he went out into the night. He did not know where he was going. All he knew was that the girl who had altered his life and driven everything else out of it, had cast him aside, because, oh, *not* because of the reason she had given. Chan Han Yen, Chinese student, was wiser than Carrie Bray in that respect.

His rage and mortification, his distress was indescribable. As he walked along, he clenched his hands so that his nails sunk into his soft palms and the blood trickled down. He was only twenty-one.

Thus till morning dawned. The birds had begun to twitter when a turn in the road revealed a little hamlet lying in the semi-darkness of a valley. It was a peaceful scene and brought before the boy's mind his own home so far away—the home that he had been willing to cut himself away from forever. It seemed to him that he could see his father and his mother, his brothers, and the sweet little adopted daughter of the family. Yes, all the dear people who had been so proud of him, and who, one and all, had made so many sacrifices that he, the scholar, the talented one, might travel far and bring back to the east the wisdom of the west. To him they had trusted and were trusting, to reflect honor and glory upon them and their country.

And he! Chan Han Yen threw himself down upon the soft turf. All anger and passion were spent; but in their place, what shame and abasement of spirit! The air was sweet with the scent of the earth; the leaves hung silently on the bushes near by. Chan Han Yen fell asleep.

When he awoke the sun was well up. He turned his face to its brightness.

"Good morning, benign friend," said he, "the Lesson of the Woman is over."

New England Magazine, June 1912

Sui Sin Far, the Half Chinese Writer, Tells of Her Career

The Interesting Author's Book, "The Dream of a Lifetime," Which Will Appear This Spring, Tells of Her Vocations

As the Globe thinks that my experience in life has been unusual, and that a personal sketch will be interesting to its readers, I will try my best to furnish one. Certainly my life has been quite unlike that of any literary worker of whom I have read. I have never met any to know—save editors.

I have resided in Boston now for about two years.

I came here with the intention of publishing a book and planting a few Eurasian thoughts in Western literature. My collection of Chinese-American stories will be brought out very soon, under the title "Mrs. Spring Fragrance." I have also written another book which will appear next year, if Providence is kind.

In the beginning I opened my eyes in a country place in the County of Cheshire, England. My ancestors on my grandfather's side had been known to the county for some generations back. My ancestors on my grandmother's side were unknown to local history. She was a pretty Irish lass from Dublin when she first won my grandfather's affections.

My father, who was educated in England and studied art in France, was established in business by his father at the age of 22, at the Port of Shanghai, China. There he met my mother, a Chinese young girl, who had been educated in England, and who was in training for a missionary. They were married by the British Consul, and the year following their marriage returned to England.

As I swing the door of my mental gallery I find radiant pictures in the opening, and through all the scene of that period there walks one figure—the figure of my brother Edward, a noble little fellow, whose heart and intelligence during the brief years of early childhood led and directed mine. I mention this brother because I have recently lost him through an accident, and his death has affected me more than I can say.

At the age of 4 years I started to go to school. I can remember being very much interested in English history. I remember also that my mother was a fascinating story teller and that I was greatly enamored of a French version of "Little Bo-Peep," which my father tried to teach me.

Arrival in America

When I was 6 years old my father brought us to America. Besides my first brother, who was only 10 months older than myself, I had now three sisters and another brother. We settled in Montreal, Can, and hard times befell, upon which I shall not dwell.

I attended school again and must have been about 8 years old when I conceived the ambition to write a book about the half Chinese. This ambition arose from my sensitiveness to the remarks, criticisms and observations on the half Chinese which continually assailed my ears, also from an impulse, born with me, to describe, to impart to others that I felt all that I saw, all that I was. I was not sensitive without reason. Some Eurasians may affect that no slur is cast upon them because of their nationality; but I dislike cant and desire to be sincere. Wealth, of course, ameliorates certain conditions. We children, however, had no wealth.

I think as well my mind was stimulated by the readings of my

teacher who sought to impress upon her scholars that the true fathers
and mothers of the world were those who battled through great trials
and hardships to leave to future generations noble and inspiring truths.

I left school at the age of 10, but shortly thereafter attracted the
attention of a lovely old lady, Mrs. William Darling of Hochelaga,
who induced my mother to send me to her for a few hours each day.
This old lady taught me music and French. I remember her telling her
husband that I had a marvelous memory and quoting "Our finest hope
is finest memory," which greatly encouraged me, as compared with
my brother and sister, who had both splendid heads for figures, I
ranked very low intellectually. It was Mrs. Darling who first, aside
from my mother, interested me in my mother's people, and impressed
upon me that I should be proud that I had sprung from such a race.
She also inspired me with the belief that the spirit is more than the
body, a belief which helped me through many hours of childish
despondency, for my sisters were all much heavier and more muscular
than I.

When my parents found that family circumstances made it necessary
to withdraw me from Mrs. Darling, my old friend's mind seemed to
become wrought with me, and she tried to persuade them to permit
her to send me to a boarding school. My father, however, was an
Englishman and the idea of having any of his children brought up on
charity, hurt his pride.

I, now in my 11th year, entered into two lives, one devoted entirely
to family concerns; the other, a withdrawn life of thought and musing.
This withdrawn life of thought probably took the place of ordinary
education with me. I had six keys to it; one, a great capacity for
feeling; another, the key of imagination; third, the key of physical
pain; fourth, the key of sympathy; fifth, the sense of being differentiated from the ordinary by the fact that I was an Eurasian; sixth, the
impulse to create.

Little Lace Girl

The impulse to create was so strong within me that failing all other
open avenues of development (I wrote a good deal of secret doggerel
verse around this period) I began making Irish crochet lace patterns,
which I sold to a clique of ladies to whom I was known as "The Little

Lace Girl." I remember that when a Dominion exhibition was held in Montreal a lace pattern which I sent to the art department won first prize—a great surprise to all my people as I was the only little girl competing. My mother was very proud of my work. I remember that when the church asked her to donate something she got me to crochet her a set of my mats as a gift.

At the age of 14 I succumbed to a sickness which affected both head and heart and retarded development both mentally and physically. Which is the chief reason, no doubt, why an ambition conceived in childhood is achieved only as I near the close of half a century. But for all this retardation and the fact that I suffered from recurrent attacks of the terrible fever, I never lost spirit and always maintained my position as the advisory head of the household. We had a large family of children and my father was an artist.

The wiseacres tell us that if we are good we will be big, healthy and contented. I must have been dreadfully wicked. The only thing big about me were my feelings; the only thing healthy, my color; the only content I experienced was when I peeped into the future and saw all the family grown and settled down and myself, far away from all noise and confusion, with nothing to do but write a book.

To earn my living I now began to sell my father's pictures. I enjoyed this, and no doubt, it was beneficial, as it took me out into the open air and brought me into contact with a number of interesting persons. To be sure, there was a certain sense of degradation and humiliation in approaching a haughty and contemptuous customer, and also periods of melancholy when disappointed in a sale I had hoped to effect or payment for a picture was not made when promised. But the hours of hope and elation were worth all the dark ones. I remember starting out one morning with two pictures in my hand and coming home in the evening with $20. How happy was everybody!

This avocation I followed for some years. Besides offering me opportunities to study human nature, it also enabled me to gratify my love for landscape beauty—a love which was and is almost a passion.

My 18th birthday saw me in the composing room of the Montreal Star, where for some months I picked and set type. While there I taught myself shorthand.

Became Stenographer

As last I took a position as stenographer in a lawyer's office. I do not think a person of artistic temperament is fitted for mechanical work and it is impossible for such to make a success of it. Stenography, in particular, is torturing to one whose mind must create its own images. Unconsciously I was stultified by the work I had undertaken. But it had its advantages in this respect, that it brought me into contact and communion with men of judgment and mental ability. I know that I always took an interest in my employers and their interests, and, therefore, if I did not merit, at least received their commendation.

I recall that the senior member of the firm, now Judge Archibald of Montreal, occasionally chatted with me about books and writers, read my little stories and verse as they appeared, and usually commented upon them with amused interest. I used to tell him that I was ambitious to write a book. I remember him saying that it would be necessary for me to acquire some experience of life and some knowledge of charac-ter before I began the work and I assuring him seriously that I intended to form all my characters upon the model of myself. "They will be very funny people then," he answered with a wise smile.

While in this office I wrote some humorous articles which were accepted by Peck's Sun, Texas Liftings, and Detroit Free Press. I am not consciously a humorous person; but now and then unconsciously I write things which seem to strike editors as funny.

One day a clergyman suggested to my mother that she should call upon a young Chinese woman who had recently arrived from China as the bride of one of the local Chinese merchants. With the exception of my mother there was but one other Chinese woman in the city besides the bride. My mother complied with the clergyman's wishes and I accompanied her.

From that time I began to go among my mother's people, and it did me a world of good to discover how akin I was to them.

Passing by a few years I found myself in Jamaica, W. I., working as a reporter on a local paper. It was interesting work until the novelty wore off, when it became absolute drudgery. However, it was a step forward in development. I had reached my 27th year.

Sir Henry Blake was the Governor of the island while I was there, and I found the Legislative Council reporting both instructive and amusing. How noble and high principled seemed each honorable member while on the floor! How small and mean while compelled to writhe under the scorn and denunciation of some opposing brother! I used to look down from the press gallery upon the heads of the honorable members and think a great many things which I refrained from putting into my report.

I got very weary and homesick tramping the hot dusty streets of Kingston; and contracted malarial fever, the only cure for which, in my case, was a trip up North.

I remained in Montreal about a year, during which period I worked, first, as a stenographer for Mr. Hugh Graham (now Sir Hugh) of the Star, and then in the same capacity for Mr. G. T. Bell of the Grand Trunk Railway. Both of these positions I was compelled to resign because of attacks of inflammatory rheumatism.

At last my physicians declared that I would never gain strength in Montreal, and one afternoon in June what was left of me—84 pounds—set its face westward. I went to San Francisco where I had a sister, a bright girl, who was working as a spotter in one of the photograph galleries. I fell in love with the City of the Golden Gate, and I wish I had space in which to write more of the place in which all the old ache in my bones fell away from them, never to return again.

As soon as I could I found some work. That is, I located myself in a railway agency, the agent of which promised me $5 a month and as well an opportunity to secure outside work. But despite this agency's fascinating situation at the corner of a shopping highway I made slight progress financially, and had it not been for my nature and my office window might have experienced a season of melancholy. As it was, I looked out of my window, watched a continuously flowing stream of humanity, listened to the passing bands, inhaled the perfume of the curb stone flower sellers' wares and was very much interested.

To eke out a living I started to canvas Chinatown for subscribers for the San Francisco Bulletin. During my pilgrimages thereto I met a Chinese whom I had known in Montreal. He inquired if I were still writing Chinese stories. Mr. Charles Lummis made the same inquiry. Latent ambition aroused itself. I recommended writing Chinese stories. Youth's Companion accepted one.

But I suffered many disappointments and rejections, and the urgent need for money pressing upon me, I bethought me of Seattle. Perhaps there Fortune would smile a little kinder. This suggestion had come some months before from Lyman E. Knapp, ex-Governor of Alaska, who had dropped into my office one day to get some deeds typewritten. Observing that I understood legal work, he advised me to try "the old Siwash town," where, he added, he was sure I would do better than in San Francisco.

To Seattle I sailed, and the blithe greenness of the shores of Puget Sound seemed to give me the blithest of welcomes. I was in my 29th year, and my sole fortune was $8. Before 5 o'clock of the first day here I had arranged for desk room in a lawyer's office and secured promise of patronage from several attorneys, a loan and mortgage company and a lumber and shingle merchant. I remember that evening I wrote my mother a letter, telling her that I had struck gold, silver, oil, copper and everything else that luck could strike, in proof of which I grandiloquently shoved into her envelope a part of my remaining wealth.

As always, on account of my inaccuracy as a stenographer and my inability to typewrite continuously, my earning capacity was small; but I managed to hold up my head, and worked intermittently and happily at my Chinese stories.

Chinese Mission Teacher

Occasionally I taught in a Chinese mission school, as I do here in Boston, but learned far more from my scholars than ever I could impart to them.

I also formed friendships with women who braced and enlightened me, women to whom the things of the mind and the heart appealed; who were individuals, not merely the daughters of their parents, the wives of their husbands; women who taught me that nationality was no bar to friendship with those whose friendship was worthwhile.

Ever and again, during the 14 years in which I lived in Seattle, whenever I had a little money put by, some inward impulse would compel me to use it for a passage home. The same impulse would drive me to work my way across the Continent, writing advertisements for the different lines. Once when I saved up $85 toward a rest in which to write the book of my dreams news from home caused me to banish ambition for a while longer; and I sent my little savings to pay a passage out West for one of my younger sisters. This sister remained with me for several months, during which time I got her to learn shorthand and typewriting, so that upon her return to Montreal she would be enabled to earn her living. Thus did the ties of relationship belate me; but at the same time strengthen.

A year later, a shock of sudden grief so unfitted me for mechanical work that I determined to emancipate myself from the torture of writing other people's thoughts and words with a heart full of my own, and throwing up my position, worked my way down South as far as the city of Los Angeles. Arrived there, I gave way to my running passion—the passion to write all the emotions of my heart away. But it was hard work—artistic expression, if I may so call it. I had been so long accustomed to dictation that when I sat down to compose, although my mind teemed with ideas tumultuously clamoring for release, I hesitated as if I were waiting for a voice behind me to express them. I had to free myself from that spell. My writings might be imperfect, but they had got to bear the impress of thoughts begotten in my own mind and clothed in my own words.

I struggled for many months. The Century Magazine took a story from me; but I remained discontented with my work. I was not discontented with life, however. If there was nothing but bread to eat and water to drink, absorbed in my work I was immune to material things—for a while. You have to come back to them in the end.

Located in Boston

As I have already said, two years ago I came East with the intention of publishing a book of Chinese-American stories. While I was in Montreal my father obtained for me a letter of introduction from a Chinese merchant of that city to his brother in Boston, Mr. Lew Han Son. Through Mr. Lew Han Son I became acquainted with some Americans of the name of Austin who live in Dorchester and who have been my good friends ever since. I am also acquainted with a lady in Charlestown, Mrs. Henderson, who is a sister of one of my Western friends. Save, however, some visiting among Chinese friends, I do not mingle much in any kind of society. I am not rich and I have my work to do.

I have contributed to many of the leading magazines.

During the past year I have been engaged in writing my first book, and completed it a couple of months ago. In this undertaking I was encouraged by the managing editor of the Independent. Truth to tell, if I had not received some such encouragement I could not have carried the work to a successful completion, as I am one of those persons who have very little staying power.

To accomplish this work, or to enable me to have the leisure in which to accomplish it, I was obliged to obtain some financial assistance, for one cannot live upon air and water alone, even if one is half-Chinese. Two of my lawyer friends in Montreal kindly contributed toward this end. I hope soon to be in a position to repay them.

My people in Montreal, my mother in particular, my Chinese friends in Boston and also American friends are looking forward to the advent of "Mrs. Spring Fragrance" with, I believe, some enthusiasm. I am myself quite excited over the prospect. Would not any one be who had worked as hard as I have—and waited as long as I have—for a book!

Boston Globe, 5 May 1912